The Ladies of Lyndon

MARGARET KENNEDY

The
Ladies of Lyndon

With a new introduction by
Nicola Beauman

The Dial Press
New York

Published by
The Dial Press
1 Dag Hammarskjold Plaza
New York, New York 10017

First published 1923.
Introduction copyright © 1981 by Nicola Beauman
All rights reserved.
Manufactured in the United States of America
First Printing

Library of Congress Cataloging in Publication Data

Kennedy, Margaret, 1896–1967.
The Ladies of Lyndon.

(A Virago modern classic)
Originally published: London: Heinemann, 1923.
I. Title.   II. Series.
PR6021.E65L3   1982   823'.912   82-1443
ISBN 0-385-27227-8   AACR2

TO
MY MOTHER

CONTENTS

		PAGE
INTRODUCTION		ix

CHAPTER I
THE VIRTUOUS STEPMOTHER 9

CHAPTER II
THE FLORENTINE 63

CHAPTER III
THE KIND COMPANIONS 113

CHAPTER IV
THE BRAXHALL FRESCOES 162

CHAPTER V
THE FOOLS' PROGRESS 248

INTRODUCTION

Margaret Kennedy's name is inextricably linked with the title of her bestselling novel *The Constant Nymph*. Published in 1924 when she was twenty-eight, it soon, after six weeks of sluggish sales, caught the public imagination so forcibly that over the next five years a million copies were sold. The reviews, apart from a couple by two septuagenarian 'men of letters', were not particularly favourable and publicity as we know it did not exist; yet it touched a chord in the same way as did, for example, *The Four Feathers, Lost Horizon, The Citadel* or *Rebecca*.

To the eternal dismay of publishers, bestsellers are almost always chance creations and there is no obvious reason why *The Constant Nymph* was so hugely successful. Two things helped: the unforgettable Sanger family, and the intense passion with which the novel is imbued. Not the passion of sexuality, despair or longing but the passion for life (what used to be called spirit) and each individual manifestation of it. The underlying message of the book is that spirit and integrity are the only values worth holding out for, and the Sanger family are shown doing just that.

This same theme had already been explored by Margaret Kennedy in her first novel, written a year previously, called *The Ladies of Lyndon*. Considered as a novel, as a work of art, it is undoubtedly superior. And yet it too received lukewarm reviews, sank without trace during the winter of 1923-4 and only sold a magnificent 10,000 copies a year or two later, after the success of the second novel. Even then many readers concurred with the writer in *The New York Times* who observed that 'many persons who joined in praising *The Constant Nymph* will buy *The Ladies of Lyndon* and feel themselves to have been woefully sold'.

Modern readers will find the first novel far richer, more moving and certainly less sentimental. Margaret Kennedy herself always had an especial fondness for it in the way that people tend to for their first creations, whether works of art or children. She once told a reporter that 'the memory of its appearance is sweeter even than the success of *The Constant Nymph*'. And this was not merely because she had fulfilled a twenty-year-long ambition to write (and publish) a novel; it was surely because in her heart she knew that the first novel had fewer of the qualities that appeal to the mass reading public but more to recommend it as a carefully crafted work of fiction. The lightness of her touch, her shrewd social comment and clear, often ironic insight into human nature are here displayed to perfection. *The Ladies of Lyndon* also has its own special interest for us as a period piece, as an early statement of the clash between the Edwardian and the post-war age.

Margaret Kennedy had always wanted to write, even from childhood. Born in 1896 and brought up in comfortable upper middle-class circumstances in Kent (her father was a barrister) she went to Cheltenham Ladies' College, as did May Sinclair before her. She is alleged to have been unhappy there and looking at the perhaps solitary, sometimes aloof figure that she became later on it is hardly surprising that the gregarious life of a boarding school did not suit her. In the autumn of 1914 she went up to Somerville: among her Oxford contemporaries were Dorothy Sayers, Winifred Holtby and Vera

Brittain. It is mere speculation whether she was entirely preoccupied with reading history or whether she suffered as did Winifred Holtby from that 'fear of immunity from danger when our friends are suffering . . . Oxford in 1917-18 . . . seemed intolerable'.

Only the exceptions abandoned Oxford in order to endure the rigours of nursing or other war work. What does seem mysterious to us today is that the war did not, as one might have thought, bring everyone very close together, for after all the agony of mind described in *Testament of Youth* was common to all the female undergraduates (Margaret Kennedy indeed lost her brother). But no: Vera Brittain wrote:

> Occasionally at lectures I met a girl who was then in her last term (this was the spring of 1919) waiting to take her History Finals; I never spoke to her, but I carried away a definite impression of a green scarf, and dark felt hat negligently shading a narrow, brooding face with arrogant nose and stormily reserved blue eyes; it was Margaret Kennedy.

Obviously the two girls did not know they would be contemporary novelists with 'so much in common'—but that they never spoke, although at the same college and reading the same subject, does seem odd. However, in later life, they developed a mutual respect and mild liking for each other.

After the war Margaret Kennedy's parents had moved to Cornwall, to a house in St Ives and here she went to live when she left Oxford in the summer of 1919. Armed with a glowing recommendation from the Master of Balliol she obtained a commission to write a book for a projected Methuen history series. In fact, although *A Century of Revolution* was published in 1922, very few copies were printed because the 'series' was rapidly stillborn and the publisher wanted to avoid producing any at all. But Margaret Kennedy, determined after two years hard work to establish a reputation, insisted on the letter of her contract and the book was published.

As soon as she had finished this, her first and only historical work, she began *The Ladies of Lyndon*. For a first novel, written by someone in her mid-twenties, it is extraordinarily rich in theme and subtle in overtone; in some ways Margaret Kennedy never did anything quite so accomplished again. The novel is one of social comedy rather than plot. The central 'lady' is Agatha Clewer, née Cocks, who married in haste and repents at leisure, a repentance that is activated partly by her own dawning self-knowledge and partly by her newly recognised love for her cousin. The other main character is James, her brother-in-law, who is a budding painter of genius treated by his family as not only beyond the pale socially but also as a near half-wit.

Reviewers at the time treated the Agatha theme as most important, but in Margaret Kennedy's mind James mattered most. *Queen* magazine reported:

> The idea for *The Ladies of Lyndon* arose from a children's party where Miss Kennedy met a little boy who was considered mentally deficient. He was having a sad time with the other children, so she took him into another room and played the gramophone to him and found that he could hum perfectly all the tunes she played, though he was not more than three years old. That made her consider the possibility of a child quite different from others, perhaps with genius in his strangeness, who might be treated kindly, but in quite the wrong way, by those in charge of him. Not his mother, but possibly a stepmother. And so James in *The Ladies of Lyndon* came to literary life. 'I meant to make James the central character of the book,' said Miss Kennedy, 'But I did not have the courage of my convictions and he was swallowed up by Agatha and the others. If I were to re-write it, it would be different.'

As the novel turned out, Agatha was definitely the central character. Having married promptly and well she has, by 1914, transformed herself into the young Lady Clewer dispensing tea under the cedar tree to young men in white flannels, effortlessly radiating charm, sympathy and beauty. At first only her cousin Gerald with whom she had once had a brief but happy flirtation wonders whether 'she might be wasting a very exceptional brain in this futile life of hers'. Slowly she begins to realise that her 'soul was gone, dead and buried beneath the gorgeousness of Lyndon', that she and the other 'ladies' had become 'perfect monuments of conspicuous waste'.

James plays an important part in her 'sentimental journey'. He realised on her wedding-day that the eighteen-year-old bride had been bred to look upon marriage as 'after all, a duty to one's neighbour and not a personal affair'. ' "Here! What are you frightened of?" Turning to rebuff his foolishness, she was silenced by his expression. In that ugly countenance she perceived so much gravity, indignation and concern that she was mute.' But she shrugs him off and only gradually comes to accept him as the most sensible person she knows, the only one to have retained his sanity and individuality. The climax of the book is when she defends his engagement to Dolly the housemaid: 'This was an open defection and was felt as such by the company.' Ironically, Dolly turns out to be far more of a lady than any of her relations-by-marriage.

Agatha begins to see herself as potentially something other than a beautiful but marble monument, dependent on the deference of others for her own self-esteem, her spirit dead to art, feelings, moral values and tenderness. During the war she has the 'volcanic notion' of trying to work in a canteen and, confusedly, assumes that true love is sufficiently expressed in financial sacrifice. In trying to ignore her expensive upbringing she is also trying to run away from the world of Lyndon where people never

speak directly to one another but, inevitably, plunge into
the accustomed 'abyss of irritation, suspicion, veiled
criticism, secret conclaves, tactful hints and plain speaking'.

For Lyndon is the villain of the book. It is all external
trappery, obsessed with appearance and display, luxurious
rather than beautiful. Just as, in Paris, James discovered
that 'the ones who drew worst talked most' so at Lyndon
the lusher the exterior the shallower the reality. As, for
example, the library: 'seldom used by the household',
crammed with books, yet none of them straightforward
enough to provide the simple facts for a lecture on Dante
at the Village Institute.

And it is Lyndon which is the symbol of the change
which creeps over both Agatha and the world: after the
war it represents the sloughed-off skin of England's past.
It can no longer be the greedy, devouring 'shrine of ease'
it had once been. It can either distintegrate, adjust to the
'sensible' values of post-war life or become a Braxhall.
This is the house built by Sir Thomas Bragge in 1919
which 'marked monumentally, the excessive prosperity of
Sir Thomas during the war with Germany'. He is a 'new
gentleman' and, to Agatha's distress, 'proclaimed blatantly
an ideal of life which, in her own household, was discreetly and beautifully intimated'.

As a character, the Profiteer, he is drawn with crude
strokes and there is a rather distressing hint of anti-
semitism in the tone used by Margaret Kennedy to describe him. But there is nothing crude in the handling of
the most richly comic scene in the book, the unveiling of
the frescoes which he has commissioned from James. And
he and Cynthia, with their quite unashamed worship of
luxury, provide a wonderful foil to Agatha's painfully
awakening spirit.

The war is shown to have wrought enormous, totally
unexpected changes. Lyndon has to change, Agatha

changes, the Sir Thomas Bragges of this world are in the
ascendant, John contracts his eventually fatal strained
heart as a result of gas poisoning. Even James is 'taken
up'. As Lois remarks: ' "James has improved a lot lately
... Besides, all the canons of artistic taste have changed so
much lately. It's the war, you know".' James resists
attempts to turn him into the 'tame family genius' and
baffles his family by living domestically in Hampstead
rather than in romantic squalor in a one-room studio—
which course of action would have been considered more
conventional.

Agatha too tries to adapt herself, to bridge the gap
between the two worlds she sees to each side of her. But
the conflict between the artists and the moneyed, the
sensitive and the insensitive, the cultured and the
philistine is well-nigh inevitable. It is a conflict which has
often been described in fiction, the most obvious paral-
lels (because they too use a large house as hero/villain)
being *Mansfield Park* and *Howards End*. The former
explores the opposing pull of principles and worldliness,
the latter, which was published when Margaret Kennedy
was in her early teens, describes the struggle, either futile
or dependent on compromise, to connect the world of
'telegrams and anger' with the world which holds personal
relations paramount. Virginia Woolf too was ever
conscious of the apartness of the two worlds believing
that 'the gulf we crossed between Kensington and
Bloomsbury was the gulf between respectable mummified
humbug & life crude & impertinent perhaps, but living'.

It was this theme, as well as that of the 'genius' in
society, which was re-explored with even more obvious
point and such public success in *The Constant Nymph*. In
this novel, the father of the family, a musical genius, dies
early on and his children are left to wade in the murky
waters of the real, orderly, civilised world, a world which
had hitherto been hidden from them in their unfettered

life on an Austrian alp. There the constraints of civilisa-
tion had been completely ignored in deference to the
sacred worship of music. But in South Kensington music
was granted its appropriate place in the scheme of things,
it was 'only part of the supreme art, the business of living
beautifully'.

The core of *The Constant Nymph* is the contrast between
Tessa (the nymph) who brings her direct and innocent
view of the world to bear on Kensington values and
Florence, who is trying to subdue the whole Sanger
family with those values. Both women love Lewis Dodd,
the musical genius who adopts Sanger's mantle and who,
misguidedly, marries Florence without recognising that it
is really the adolescent Tessa who is his destiny. And
both women are crushed by him in the end, his wife
because she is turned from a naïve Cambridge girl into
an embittered woman trying to subdue Lewis's spirit
with the values of 'decency and humanity and civilisa-
tion' and Tessa because she is physically crushed by the
onslaught of the real world on 'the wild, imaginative
solitude of her spirit'.

Time after time Margaret Kennedy describes women
who lack the inner strength to forge their own destinies,
who are at the mercy of their circumstances, domestic
responsibilities or inner natures. Agatha has been
stifled by her mother and her life is subtly sabotaged by
her mother-in-law's interference. There is the memorable
scene at Braxhall where the two older women parry
verbal blows and finally 'Marian, having eased her bosom
of some of her furniture, departed'. The theme of
sabotaging mothers is also central to the later novel
Together and Apart (1936), where again home truths
administered for people's own good render a death blow
to something precious and living—a happy marriage.

Another theme throughout Margaret Kennedy's early
novels is the weariness of the married woman who wishes

that she could escape from the myriad of people, objects and chores which depend on her for their life's blood, who feels that somehow life has passed her by yet has no clear idea of what she wants out of it. A character in *Return I Dare Not* (1931) thinks dejectedly:

> She must go to Mrs Duckett's Registry again on Monday. She must make a list of all the things to be done on Monday... laundry... teeth... shoes... Ada... it was damned unfair! For nearly half her life she had been smothered under teeth and laundries, when really she was not that sort of person at all. She had married too young. She had never lived her life. They (some hidden influences, not specified) ought not to have allowed her to marry so young.

And Agatha too felt the same ensnared feelings, though hers were more of the soul since the everyday harmony of her family's material world was not her responsibility.

But it seems that Margaret Kennedy, although preoccupied with the imprisoned woman, did not have those feelings herself—she always put her work first and there is an element of contempt, certainly not of sympathy, in her descriptions of subjugated women. It is the rebels, the Sangers and James's of this world, who have her sympathy—they, as she, took their art deeply seriously. When, with *The Ladies of Lyndon,* she 'felt for the first time that I had written something which need not be burned', she sent it to an agent and on the same day began *The Constant Nymph.* By the New Year of 1925 she was a celebrity, at work with Basil Dean on a dramatisation of the book. The play opened in September 1926 with Noel Coward as Lewis Dodd; by this time Margaret Kennedy was married, to a barrister (like her father) called David Davies and they had set up married life in Kensington.

In her thirties she had three children, but all the time she continued to write fiction as well as the occasional play. The children were brought up in true upper-middle class fashion, looked after in the nursery by nanny and 'produced' at bedtime or on stipulated occasions. But their parents were devoted to them, enjoying their company as much as that of their large circle of friends.

Margaret Kennedy presumably shared the determination of another novelist Enid Bagnold in whose household 'housemaids used to give me their notice as I tried to climb the stairs to my writing room, but I would shake them off'. For writing was the most important occupation to the extent that she refused to accept any social engagements when in the throes of a book and it is clear that she would never have had children if she had had to put them to bed herself.

During the late 1920s Margaret Kennedy was taken seriously as a writer. 'Everyone' read *The Constant Nymph* and there were several articles about it, for example one by H. E. Wortham in *Nineteenth Century Magazine* which also discussed other 'musical' novels such as *Maurice Guest* by Henry Handel Richardson, *Martin Schüler* by Romer Wilson and *Christine* by Alice Cholmondeley (a pseudonym for Elizabeth von Arnim). She also tried to continue the Sanger family saga in *The Fool of the Family* (1930); yet the special magic was gone and the novel, though written with style and confidence, is dead at the centre. Irritating it may have been when people continued to ask her until the end of her life – she died in 1967 – 'and have you written anything since the wonderful *Constant Nymph*?' But there was some truth in their questioning.

Although the fourteen novels after the first two all sold respectably, and some were Book Society choices, in a way she never did anything as good again. *A Long Time Ago* (1932), *Together and Apart* (1936) and *The Midas Touch* (1938) are in the next rank, all three novels having many outstanding qualities. She continued to publish good fiction until 1964, but somehow, whether it was chance or the effect of success or the responsibilities of marriage, something disappeared from her writing. Not the wit, not the eye for social comedy, and not the range; but the Forsterish ironic understatement, the suggestions of profundity and the tragic overtones were never recaptured in quite the same way. And perhaps the intelligence of the writing and the deftness of form displayed in *The Ladies of Lyndon* will bring it a new popularity; to set it, after nearly sixty years, against Huxley's famous *Antic Hay* published in the same month is an instructive experience, for there is little doubt which has greater staying power. The comedy, the insight and the sombre conclusion make this novel memorable, on its own terms a work of fiction of a high order.

Nicola Beauman, London 1981

The Ladies of Lyndon

CHAPTER I

THE VIRTUOUS STEPMOTHER

I.

IN the first decades of the twentieth century, London contained quite a number of distinguished, grey-headed bachelors who owed their celibacy to Mrs. Varden Cocks. In her youth she had refused offers of marriage from most of them and they found themselves unable to choose again when she tardily but finally dashed their several ambitions by selecting Varden. Indeed they almost gloried in their shackles, for this lady had reached, at forty-seven, the very zenith of her attractions. She was excessively handsome in the liberal style of the First Empire, and endowed with a wit in keeping with her appearance. She talked a great deal, in a rich, temperamental contralto,, and had fine eyes which spoke for her in her rare silences. Her photographs were seldom successful since few of her friends were acquainted with her face in repose.

The fatigued erudition of her husband set off her animation with an especial piquancy. He had been a distinguished scholar when she married him and was, subsequently, never heard to speak. At intervals she would discuss with her friends the advantages of a political career for him, but his views on the subject were not known. He was, fortunately, very tolerably well off.

They had one child, a beautiful but silent daughter, who accompanied them to most places of entertainment and whose wardrobe was a perpetual testimony to a mother's taste. It was generally believed that Agatha Cocks was a very nice girl and everyone was pleased when she became engaged, a few months after her introduction, to an entirely suitable young man, a baronet, wealthy, and devotedly attached. Mrs. Cocks, who believed in early marriages for young women, was overjoyed. The bridegroom had an additional advantage; he possessed a most exceptional stepmother. Mrs. Cocks was accustomed to point out that a stepmother-in-law, of the right kind, is so much easier for a young bride to get on with than the usual mother-in-law. She is less likely to interfere; she has fewer claims. The dowager Lady Clewer was this kind of stepmother. She was a perfect monument of tact. " I had thought," Mrs. Cocks would say in her rapid, vibrant voice, " I had thought it to be impossible for a widow and a widower, each with children, to marry and produce a third family without a certain amount of storm and stress. But the Clewers have undoubtedly done it ! There they all are, his sons and her daughter, and their child (I forget its sex), living together in perfect peace and amity. But then of course she is unique . . . and he died pretty soon. . . ." One evening, about ten days before the wedding, this paragon gave a dinner party to which Mrs. Cocks took her family. None of the trio anticipated a very pleasant evening, but only Mrs. Cocks said so, since she alone could talk audibly and without discomfort while driving through London traffic. Her gloomy forebodings enlivened the entire journey from South Kensington to Eaton Square. This sort of party, she said, was apt to be trying. " It isn't as if you didn't know all your in-laws already," she

complained. " You've met them all by now, haven't you ?
Except the mentally deficient one. To go on meeting in
this way is quite unnecessary. I don't gather that anyone
will be there in the least congenial to me. Or to your
father. Only Clewer relations, I expect. I shouldn't
wonder if there aren't enough men to go round. That's
what people generally mean when they call a dinner ' quite
informal.' I hate a superfluity of women. Even dull men
are better than none."

Agatha sighed. She was disturbed by the tinge of
petulance in these remarks. She had never supposed that
the vogue of John's stepmother would last for ever, since
Mrs. Cocks was very variable in her friendships and, before
the engagement, had been accustomed to remember that
Lady Clewer's first husband had been some kind of successful
Northern manufacturer, that the upholstered prosperity
which her money had brought to Lyndon gave it a very
odd look, and that Lois Martin, the manufacturer's
daughter, was rather a second-rate little person. All this
she had, for the moment, comfortably forgotten, but
Agatha had little doubt but that the Martin vulgarity
must be, eventually, disinterred. Only she had hoped for
fair weather until after the wedding, and she sighed because
she feared that a dull dinner at this point would be most
inopportune.

It was, unfortunately, very dull indeed. Besides Varden
there were but two men present—Sir John Clewer, the host
and bridegroom, and a sadly stolid Major Talbot, his uncle.
These failed to inspire the ladies with any sort of liveliness.
Depression, like a murky fog, hung over the tasteful
brilliance of Lady Clewer's table and barely lifted with
the appearance of dessert, when the company rallied a
little, sustained by the prospect of release. Mrs. Cocks,
with some show of animation, embarked upon the conquest
of Major Talbot and was soon discoursing fluently to him

about the government of India. At the other end of the table old Mrs. Gordon Clewer, John's great-aunt, was making her neighbours laugh. Her butt was probably the rising generation, a topic upon which she was in the habit of being funny in the epigrammatic style of the early 'nineties. The sulky face of little Lois Martin suggested that some shaft had gone home. Lois did not know what to make of Mrs. Gordon Clewer. Against old ladies who were not thus entirely surrendered to age she had the weapons of youth and personal attraction. But this small, terrifying woman, with her sharp tongue, her arrogant dowdiness and her quaint curled fringe, was invulnerable. She was securely entrenched in the past and made Lois feel disconcertingly raw : mere prettiness went for nothing with her, she had seen so much of it in her time. Her high incisive tones rang out in a sudden pause while Mrs. Cocks was eating a *marron glacé* :

". . . a whole roomful, I assure you, all dancing in this concentrated, painstaking way ; all with this stupefied air. No conversation, you understand ; almost like convicts taking exercise. ' Good heavens, my dear ! ' I said to Lady Peel. ' What has happened to them all ? Surely the ventilation is insufficient ? The children appear to me positively *abrutis !* And why do they never change their partners ? ' ' Oh,' she said, ' it isn't the ventilation. They always look like that now somehow. And they can't change their partners. You know it's this new American dance, the . . . the Tango, and it's very difficult. . . .' "

Lois decided that Youth must speak ; an attack like this could not be endured in silence. She leant across the table and inquired rather aggressively, in a voice loud enough to be generally heard :

" I say, Agatha, don't you think those old Victorian times, when they danced nothing but stupid old waltzes, must have been perfectly beastly ? "

"Perfectly beastly!" murmured Mrs. Gordon Clewer joyfully, as though committing the phrase to memory for some future narrative.

It was an unhappy expression: everyone was acutely aware of its stark unsuitability. Poor Lady Clewer, crimson with mortification, was but too sure of the manner in which Mrs. Gordon Clewer would tell the tale:

". . . That Martin child, Marian Clewer's daughter by her first marriage. A really horrid memorial of poor Marian's remoter past. One wonders so what the father was like. Of course, one always thinks, looking at the girl, that Martin isn't a Jewish name. Marian is so clever with her—dressing her rather inconspicuously in pale pink, don't you know? But what was it she said? Oh, yes! . . . Perfectly beastly!"

The unhappy mother plunged into a general discourse upon dancing in a vain attempt to cover her daughter's lapse. Was it true that the Queen disapproved of these new American dances? But Mrs. Gordon Clewer was too much pleased with the situation to destroy it.

"Well, child?" she demanded sharply of Agatha. "What do you think? Do you consider the customs of your elders . . . er . . . perfectly beastly?"

The entire table waited to hear the young bride's opinion.

Agatha hesitated, not liking her position. Under her mother's quelling eye she dared not agree with Lois. But to disagree would be a sorry course and hardly sincere in a person of her years. With all the courtesy due to John's great-aunt she must make a stand for her own generation. So she smiled very prettily at Mrs. Gordon Clewer and said:

"You know, I can never quite make out what the customs of my elders were exactly. There are such discrepancies in the accounts one gets. This matter of partners, for instance! I've been told that nice girls never danced more than three times with the same man. But . . . I find it very difficult to believe. Because once I was tidying an old bureau for my mother, and I came upon some of her dance programmes. . . ."

" Never tell me I danced the whole evening with one man ! " broke in Mrs. Cocks.

" No, Mother ! With two."

They laughed, and she felt that she had not done badly. She had been a little impertinent, but they apparently forgave her for it. Catching the sparkle of approval in her lover's eye, she felt her heart leap with pleasure.

" No good, Mrs. Cocks," Major Talbot was saying to her protesting mother, " you should have burnt 'em, y'know."

Lady Clewer, however, did not look pleased. Scarcely recovered from the irritation of her daughter's exposure, she found nothing soothing in the spectacle of Agatha's discretion. Ill-temper was written clearly upon her smooth, fresh face, furrowing her still youthful brow, and emphasizing the massiveness of her jaw. She had the air of rehearsing to herself all the caustic reproofs which Lois should hear when the company departed. She glanced round the room, preparatory to rising, and her little blue eyes were ominous— hard as pebbles. The five women left the dining-room in an atmosphere of heavy displeasure.

Upstairs they found Cynthia, the youngest of the Clewers. This was the solitary child of Marian's second marriage. At fourteen she did not dine downstairs but came into the drawing-room for a short time after her schoolroom supper. She was an exquisite creature, slim but well grown, with a mane of shining hair the colour of honey. She had her mother's flawless skin, but her sharp eyes were dark and set rather close together in the creamy oval of her face. She advanced and made her civilities to the guests with cool self-possession. Lady Clewer immediately demanded, with unconcealed impatience, where James might be. Cynthia

replied that he would not come, though Miss Barrington
had said that he ought. Lady Clewer's jaw became grim
and she was preparing to send for James on the instant
when Cynthia demurely added that he had gone to bed.
He had further threatened to come down in his pyjamas if
anyone bothered him. Lady Clewer sharply bade her
daughter to have done, and Cynthia was silent, her keen
eyes flitting from face to face. She secretly enjoyed these
trying situations invariably created by James; they gave
variety to a monotonous life.

The guests were embarrassed at this exposure of the
family skeleton. James, the younger brother of John, was
supposed to be a little queer in the head. This was due to
nothing " in the family," as his stepmother had carefully
explained to Mrs. Cocks when the engagement was pending.
She believed that she had traced it to an injury to the brain
received by James at the age of seven months. The first
Lady Clewer had died at his birth and he had not acquired
a stepmother until he was almost six years old; it must
have been during the period when he lacked a mother's
care that the harm was done. The servants, who had
tended him, could at first remember no accident and
indignantly denied Marian's accusations of neglect. But
under her astute cross-examination they contradicted themselves and each other, and it became established that there
had been a fall. Marian, who had thought the child
alarmingly backward, discovered that her worst fears were
confirmed. She consulted a specialist immediately; he
looked grave but would say nothing save that the child was
abnormal. This abnormality became more marked as
James grew older. Nothing, it seemed, could be done. At
twenty-one he could not be depended upon sufficiently, in
the matter of table manners, to dine with the family. He
shared Cynthia's schoolroom meals, and his stepmother,
always anxious to make the best of him, had decreed that

he should be in the drawing-room every evening after dinner.

He had but recently come up to town with Cynthia and the governess, and Agatha had hitherto escaped the introduction. She dreaded it, fearing that she would find him very disagreeable. His future was, she knew, uncertain. Hitherto the whole family had lived at Lyndon, John's property in Oxfordshire. But, upon his marriage, the dowager intended to settle with her daughters in the Eaton Square house which had been left to her by her second husband. She had offered to warehouse James for a time until the young couple, comfortably settled at Lyndon, could make up their minds what to do with him. Agatha had a secret fear that they might have to invite him to live with them.

She had never seen Lyndon, but she understood it to be an imposing mid-Georgian affair, well stocked with the proper sort of furniture and portraits. Sometimes she wondered whether Marian had been able to impose as much of her essential mediocrity there as in Eaton Square. She had such a faculty for making nice things look insignificant, to all her possessions she seemed able to impart a hard, shining newness. Old things looked quite modern when she got hold of them. And her rooms were always so very full of chesterfields ; they had struck Agatha's attention when calling in Eaton Square for the first time, and were all she could remember of the drawing-room when she was not in it, save perhaps a portrait of the mother of James and John which hung over the fireplace.

This picture had interested her. The sheen of the green velvet gown, cut in the æsthetic style of the 'eighties, toned well with the green Sèvres on the chimneypiece and was painted with unquestionable ability. The brooding peevishness of the face, however, gave food for reflection. It was a discordant note in a complacent room, suggesting

a hidden, bygone rebellion, beyond the power of time to
cancel. Glancing towards it, Agatha perceived with
surprise that it was gone. A large looking-glass hung in its
place. Lady Clewer, observing the direction of her eyes,
became extremely benevolent and important :

" Ah, the portrait ! Yes, it's gone. I've sent it down to
Lyndon. Oh, yes, it's always hung here. . . . But I
thought . . . John's mother . . . he ought to have
it. . . ."

Everyone felt how right this was and Mrs. Cocks warmly
said so. Marian, beaming, said that it must hang in John's
study. Agatha murmured something pretty, but she
privately believed that John would not want it in his study.
She happened to know that he hated it. He had a photograph, which he much preferred, in which his mother was
wearing the clothes he best remembered, a little sailor hat,
a blouse with full sleeves and a broad, tight belt. She was
sitting on the south terrace at Lyndon between two dogs.
The portrait was certainly less cheerful.

Mrs. Gordon Clewer, who had been clucking to herself,
now startled Agatha by observing :

" If John takes after his father he won't want it. My
poor nephew couldn't do with it at all. That's why he
wouldn't have it at Lyndon. It was a great deal too good.
And that gown was symbolical of so much in poor Mary
that he couldn't abide. She got the greeny-yallery craze
very badly and would go about looking like an invertebrate
Burne-Jones. That's a little trying, you know, for a man
who likes his wife to be well corseted. Smart women in
those days had waists. Nowadays we condemn waists as
artificial ; but a man like John appreciates a certain amount
of artificiality in a woman as a tribute to civilization, you
understand. And, if I'm not mistaken, his son takes after
him."

She shot a glance at Agatha.

"The portrait has always been considered a very good one," said Marian in an offended tone.

"Oh, very clever! Undeniably clever!" agreed Mrs. Gordon Clewer. "It was a very clever young man who painted it. A protégé of one of Mary's peculiar artistic friends. Rather *du peuple*, you know, but that was really what gave him distinction. The other artists of the period were mostly gentlemen, or, at any rate, cultured. He came down to Lyndon to paint her, I remember, and if you met him about the house you were apt to mistake him for some tubercular under-gardener or something, come in to water the plants. It's a pity he died so young. He would have distinguished himself. As it was, John would never believe that he really had talent. He used to ask Mary why she must bring such people into the house and why she couldn't get the thing done by somebody really good. Poor Mary! How furious she used to be!"

"Cynthia! Isn't it your bedtime?" inquired Marian with meaning.

It was not, and she knew it, but Mrs. Gordon Clewer must really be reminded that poor John was Cynthia's father. She was going a little too far, even for an old lady. Perhaps she felt so herself, for, after a few seconds, she added sweetly:

"Of course it's wonderful of you to have given it up, my dear Marian. And so like you! You have a positive *flair* for this sort of thing."

Lady Clewer was not quite sure in her own mind what a *flair* was, but she took the remark as a compliment, as it was undoubtedly meant.

2.

Lois at the piano did much to relieve the languors of the evening. It was an employment in which she always appeared to advantage, having good hands and arms. Her mother, fully sensible of this, encouraged her music. She had a little talent and a great deal of temperament—qualities which urged her towards musical composition. She had written several " Tone Cycles," which sounded very effective when she sang them. To-night, however, she larded these more intellectual items in her repertoire with a few simple love songs out of compliment to John and Agatha, who were sitting together on a distant sofa looking at photographs of Lyndon. Cynthia, who never relaxed a sidelong surveillance, was forced to decide that they were dull lovers. They were, indeed, far too well bred to betray themselves by any form of public endearment ; their very conversation, though pitched too low to reach the others, was pointedly impersonal.

John appreciated immensely this discreet semi-privacy ; it was symbolical of his entire courtship. He had chosen his bride for her gravity and for the sedate composure of her manner, enchanted to find so much reserve and dignity in anything so young. He did not generally care for girls, disliking their vivacity and finding no recondite charms in inexperience. He had always looked forward to marriage as a duty, inevitable, but infinitely boring and to be postponed if possible.

He had not danced above two or three times with the silent Miss Cocks, however, before he began to be aware that duty can be agreeably reinforced by inclination. Here at last was a girl, beautiful and innocent, yet possessed of a delicate and deliberate assurance ; she sampled life discriminately, never losing her poise and never permitting herself to be engulfed. He was vastly pleased to find that he could be so completely in love.

The brevity of their courtship had given them few opportunities for intimate conversation, but he had seen all that he wanted. He suspected that she might be naturally cold in temperament, but this, in a wife, did not displease him. He had no great opinion of fond women, for he had encountered too many of them. Agatha was like none of her predecessors. He could almost enjoy the barriers put upon their intercourse. These decorous weeks, with their wealth of social functions, were like a prologue to the bridal day when, veiled and mysterious, she should be given entirely into his possession. The prolonged privacy of the honeymoon would give him leisure enough in which to contemplate and examine his prize. He was content meanwhile just to watch her as she bent over his photographs and to mark, with a recurrent shock of pleasure, the still pose of her little head. Though she seldom raised her eyes, he was quite sure that she knew all about the admiration in his regard. She had, in such matters, an intuition which she had probably inherited from her mother.

For that mother he had the warmest admiration, since to her training and experience he ascribed many of his bride's perfections. His good opinion was amply returned. Mrs. Cocks could not praise him enough to Mrs. Gordon Clewer; he was an ideal son-in-law. The two ladies sat on an enormous chesterfield in the middle of the room, conversing in undertones because of the music. Mrs. Gordon Clewer nodded and chuckled. She, too, had a good opinion of John. He was her favourite great-nephew. The boy had taste. She had always prophesied that he would choose well.

"And your girl, too," she added, "I remember saying at the beginning of the Season that you wouldn't have her on your hands for long."

"I'm very glad she's marrying so promptly," said Mrs. Cocks. "I do believe in girls marrying young. Of course, she's very young; only just eighteen. But it's so much easier and wiser for them to marry before they form their tastes too much, don't you think?"

"Dear me, yes! They get such decided opinions once they are past twenty, that there's no doing anything with them."

The old lady took a good look at the unformed Agatha through a small quizzing glass, adding :

" She's being so pretty behaved over those photographs, it's quite a pleasure to watch them. I've known you long enough, haven't I, to say without impertinence that her manners are quite charming ? "

" And even if she is young," pursued the mother, looking gratified, " he is twelve years older. Old enough to look after her properly."

" A sensible age," said the old lady tranquilly. " Just the age for settling down. And quite time, too ! In fact Marian was getting rather anxious. Poor Marian ! Always so conscientious ! So determined that we are never to forget that John is the head of the family. She couldn't have taken his position more seriously if he'd been her own son. Her feudal instincts are really amazing. And for some months she's been greatly put about because she thought he wasn't going to do his duty and take a wife ; so this engagement is an immense relief to her. She has such a sense of responsibility, you know ; I really believe she had persuaded herself that she was in some way to blame because he was evidently enjoying his bachelor-hood. And lately I fancy she caught wind of an establishment which . . . but I expect I'm being in-discreet. . . ."

She paused for a moment, to discover, perhaps, whether her reference had been news to her companion. It apparently was not, for Mrs. Cocks made a little sound of assent. Mrs. Gordon Clewer continued :

" Ah, well ! I daresay you've heard as much about that coil as I have. Marian was very funny about it. She won't see when things are really best ignored."

There was a short silence, and then Mrs. Cocks said gravely : " I think John is very sensible, don't you ? I mean, I think he'll make a sensible husband."

" Of course he will, my dear. Men of his type generally
do. They marry late, very often, but then they choose
well and carefully."

" I'm so glad you think so," exclaimed Mrs. Cocks. " Not
everyone upholds me on that point."

And she glanced across the room at her husband who,
seated beside Lady Clewer, was sleeping with painful
obviousness. His faint objections to the match had been,
for a day or two, an inconvenience to her. Mercifully they
had soon wilted before her own overpowering common
sense. She listened complacently to Lois, who was singing :
" Glad did I live and gladly die ! " to an accompaniment of
consecutive fifths. Mrs. Cocks was not musical, but she
had been to enough concerts to mistake the piece for Grieg.
Lois was perfectly scarlet with pleasure as she set her right.

" It seems that she composed the thing herself," observed
the lady to her family on the way home. " She's my friend
for life."

Varden woke up for a few minutes in order to make some
strong remarks about the music they had been hearing. He
spoke at unusual length and with extraordinary venom.
Mrs. Cocks defended Lois, maintaining that the evening
would have been very much worse without her.

" And you can't have heard much, Varden," she added,
" for you slept the whole evening."

" Not nearly as well as I could have wished."

" She looks nice playing," observed Agatha.

" Yes. It's a pity she has her mother's little blue eyes.
They don't go well with that rather Jewish colouring. And
that clumsy mouth ! But she's not bad looking. Personally
I'm rather sorry for her. I expect she's catching it now.
At dinner I felt Lady Clewer was just saving it up until
we'd gone. Didn't she look fierce ? For all the world like
a wax doll in a tantrum."

" She was rather tempersome about James, too, I thought."

"Oh," cried Mrs. Cocks, "weren't you disappointed not to see James? I was. I'm dying to see how he has grown up. I remember him as a little boy, of course; about nine, I should think. When we stayed at Lyndon once. He was queer then, wasn't he, Varden?"

"I don't recollect him, my dear."

"Well, we didn't see much of him. But he came into the drawing-room one evening with the little girls. Cynthia was quite a baby; it was very soon before Sir John died. Lois was very nicely behaved—came and shook hands with us quite as she should. But nothing would induce James to look at us. He crawled away and hid himself under a sofa. Such an ugly little boy, too, with this enormous head and very gappy teeth. Children like that are always very slow getting their second teeth, I believe. It's a great sign. She was so good with him, not apologizing particularly, you know, but just saying: 'Oh, James is rather shy to-day, I'm afraid.' She really has been wonderful with him."

It occurred to Agatha that the wisest course would have been to put James under some special training. But she did not say this, as she had no wish to criticize Lady Clewer if she could help it. Varden, however, said it for her.

"Well, she thought it over," explained Mrs. Cocks, "and felt that it would really be very cruel to send him away to school. He is so shy and sensitive, and at home they understand him and don't tease him. She felt that his own mother would not turn him out. And, of course, after his father's death she had all the responsibility for him."

"But surely there are specially trained governesses. . . ."

"Oh, but Miss Barrington has been so splendid! So patient! Lady Clewer was telling me about her the other day. She is really Cynthia's governess, you know, but she has taken the greatest pains with James. She taught him to read after a fearful struggle. He would not fix his attention. And Lady Clewer hasn't neglected the question of special training, I can assure you. She's gone into all this manual training, which is so important where deficients are concerned. Getting him very good drawing lessons. She says he has quite a turn that way."

Varden gave it up. His wife was evidently determined to see no flaws in Lady Clewer's stepmotherhood. He went to sleep again and they finished their journey in an unaccustomed silence. It occurred to the bride, with a slight shock, that this was one of the last of their little family expeditions. Very soon she would travel back from parties alone with her husband. This was an odd idea, for she was hardly ever permitted to drive alone with John. It had only happened three times—each of them a most glowing adventure. She was sure she would never get used to the notion of being alone with him as a matter of course. She did not know that she wanted to get used to it. In a way, being engaged was probably nicer than being married. It was more exciting. She ascribed her faint reluctance to regret at parting with her parents. She was convinced that she would miss her mother dreadfully, but she could not manage to feel very strongly over the loss of her father. He never seemed quite like a real person, somehow, though he had given her pearls for a wedding present.

Struck by an unusual contrition, she kissed him good-night very kindly in the hall before going up to bed. Varden looked a little surprised but had the presence of mind to pat her shoulder with a creditable appearance of tenderness.

"Well, well, well!" she heard him mutter. "That's a very handsome young sprig you've got hold of. Very handsome! I shouldn't wonder if it turned out quite a success."

And he shuffled off to dream over books that smelt of dust, crouching all night beside his green-shaded lamp. He looked very withered and old, with his bent shoulders and sharp, yellow face. He was fumbling with the handle

of his library door as she climbed the stairs ; a strange, dim
figure, centuries removed from her own vital youthfulness.
She thought that years alone had flung this gulf between
them ; she could not guess that he was already sundered
from his kind by the recognized shadow of approaching
death. He knew that his days were short and looked at the
rest of humanity as across the unbridgable abyss of the
grave. There was not very much time, now, for this father
and daughter to know each other better.

Arrived in the seclusion of her bedroom she sat down
before a looking-glass and studied herself carefully for a
few minutes. She decided happily that fatigue was not
unbecoming to her ; it merely invested her with an interesting pallor. To these meditations she was impelled by no
personal vanity, but by a conscientious and painstaking
sense of duty. It was with some difficulty that she had
learnt to be concerned over her appearance ; for she was
naturally indifferent to it. Since her engagement, however,
she had made real efforts, aware of the power of her loveli-
ness over John.

Her cousin, Gerald Blair, who had loved her first, was
different. He took very little account of her beauty ;
indeed she had reason to suppose that he scarcely regarded
it at all. But then she had not seen him for two years ;
not since that undignified episode at Canverley Fair.

She felt herself beginning to blush and saw that the pale
person in the glass had got quite pink. The memory of
that afternoon was a constant humiliation to her, for she
knew that she had been very vulgar. She had conducted
herself as no lady should, and a most unladylike retribution
had overtaken her. Instigated and abetted by her graceless
cousin she had done a lot of low things ; she rode in swing-
boats, and sucked Dorchester Rock in long pink sticks, and,
finally, insisted upon having a look at the Fat Lady. This
sight, so unexpectedly horrid, had hastened her doom.

She had felt a little sick, she remembered, as she entered the Fat Lady's stuffy booth; its occupant had been a *coup de grâce*. Gerald, who was at that time a medical student, supported her manfully to a fairly private spot behind some caravans. To her gasping apologies he replied that he was used to much worse things in hospital.

Mrs. Cocks took a stormy view of the event and was unappeased when the totally ineligible Gerald announced, with some show of penitence, that he and Agatha were engaged. He was promptly eliminated from the horizon and Agatha was sent to school in Paris, where she soon learnt to be ashamed of herself. But, in a mood of self-discipline, she had preserved a memento of her escapade, a wonderful photograph of the pair of them, taken, developed and framed, all in five minutes, by a machine on the fair ground. The proprietor merely had to pull a handle and the photograph came out in " Brooch, Locket or Tie Pin, As Suits Lady Or Gent, Price One Shilling." They had purchased one apiece upon entering the fair, which, as the shameless Gerald remarked, was a good thing, for they were in no condition to be photographed when they departed.

She thought of him now a little shyly. He was away in America, working with a friend in some very new kind of hospital. She wondered if he had forgotten all this; it would be most convenient if he had. Anyhow, when she met him again she would be married and very dignified. As the Lady of Lyndon she could surely manage to live down the past. Gerald would come to stay with them, and she would be extremely nice to him, but matronly. These speculations were interrupted by her mother who, entering briskly, demanded why she was not in bed.

" I brought you home early especially in order that you might get your proper night's rest. I don't want you to be over-tired and in bad looks next week. Hurry up, dear ! "

Agatha obediently began to hurry and her mother sat on the bed as if for conversation.

" Not a bad man, Major Talbot, when you come to talk to him. But uncommonly little to say for himself. What is that mark on your shoulder, child ? Is it a little spot ? Come into the light and let me look! Oh, it's only where a hook has rubbed you. Tell Andrews to sew it down. What was I saying ? Oh, yes ! About Mrs. Gordon Clewer."

" You began about Major Talbot."

" Did I ? Oh, well, I'd finished about him. Mrs. Gordon Clewer said such nice things about you, my dear. I was so pleased. I felt I must tell you. For she's not a person who likes people easily.   She thinks your manners are so nice."

Agatha shook herself free from the clinging softness of her clothes and strolled away to the wash-hand stand. At intervals, while she splashed the warm water into her face and over her ears, she heard fragments of her mother's dissertation on good manners : ". . . the longer one lives the more one sees the importance . . . especially in marriage . . . at the bottom of all these horrid scandals and divorces . . . ill breeding, pure and simple, is nine-tenths of the trouble . . . among decent people such things really don't occur. . . ."

Mrs. Cocks broke off suddenly to descant upon trousseau lingerie as Agatha slipped into a nightdress. She had, after all, countermanded those sets in embroidered lawn that Agatha had wanted. Silk was so much more serviceable: Agatha, reflecting that, once married, she could have as many lawn nightdresses as she pleased, assented and jumped into bed. Mrs. Cocks continued gravely :

" I expect you think all my remarks about manners and marriage are beside the point. Perhaps they are, now. You are in love for the time being and I daresay it's all very nice. Of course, while that lasts it's all plain sailing. And, my darling, I don't see why it shouldn't last, in your case. For a very long time, at all events. It's such a suitable marriage. But, in case of accidents, a really well-mannered husband is a great stand-by. You'll know what I mean someday, if you don't now."

She kissed her daughter and departed. Agatha was not at all disturbed by all this talk of love lasting or not lasting. It was unthinkable that John should cease to desire her while she remained beautiful. And, at eighteen, she could expect to be that for years and years. Thirty years at least, since she took after her mother. She would possess all the aids to beauty which wealth can supply. There would be no hardships to dim her fairness or slacken her hold on him. Nothing else could shatter love's illusion save the dallying years. She could very tolerably endure the idea that at sixty his ardour might begin to cool a little. She herself would be forty-eight, and everyone has to get old sometime.

Then, as her mother had said, there would always be beautiful manners. These would perpetually adorn his passionate demands and her own guarded compliance. They would dignify the late season of love's decay. This sentiment reminded her of something she had lately read. She turned to the shelf by her bed, where the carefully chosen books of her girlhood stood in well-dusted rows. Pulling out *Mansfield Park*, she sought through it for a passage dimly remembered. It was something, surely, said by Mary Crawford when she was congratulating her brother on his attachment to Fanny Price :

" I know that a wife you loved would be the happiest of women ; and that even when you ceased to love she would yet find in you the liberality and good breeding of a gentleman ! "

3.

Three days later Agatha met James Clewer, the strange brother-in-law of whom she had heard so much. Her first impression was not pleasing, but she was very tired, having spent the afternoon with her mother at a dressmaker's. There they encountered Lady Clewer and Lois, who was trying on a bridesmaid's frock and looking very sulky. Agatha perceived that she did not like the dress at all, and seized a moment when the matrons were discussing shoes to whisper anxiously:

"Do you like it?"

"Quite," said Lois, without enthusiasm.

"But you don't! Please say! Is there anything you'd like altered?"

"Not unless you altered the entire dress," burst out Lois. "It's so . . . dull!"

"Plain white is always rather nice, don't you think?"

"No, I don't. It suits you, that style. But it makes me look like a mincing missie. And it's so smug. Almost like a confirmation dress!"

"We did think of orange sashes shot with gold and bouquets of orange-lilies to match. Do you think that would improve it?"

"Why, yes! That would be original. If you'll excuse me, I think pale pink carnations are frightfully ordinary for a bouquet. Why did you give up the idea?"

"My mother . . . your . . . our mothers . . . decided, I think, that it would be unsuitable for the younger bridesmaids."

"Our mothers! It's not their wedding!"

"Isn't it?" Agatha's eyes danced. "I'm not so sure. But . . . I'll see what I can do."

When she could gain her mother's ear she asked politely:

"We've quite decided, then, against the orange scarves and flowers?"

"Yes, quite," said Mrs. Cocks. "As Lady Clewer says, they will be much too conspicuous."

"It's a pity you didn't decide before your gown was ordered, Mother. You're bound to have an orange-tawny bouquet with it and it will clash so with the pink and white bridesmaids."

"Oh, do you think it will?" Mrs. Cocks looked distressed. "How tiresome! In that case the bridesmaids must have orange bouquets."

"A little pointless without the sashes, don't you think?"

"The sash could always be taken off afterwards if Mam'selle wanted to wear plain white," put in the dressmaker, who was all for the more striking effect.

Lady Clewer's face cleared and she conceded:

"That is so. We can take it off after."

"Not if I know it," was the outspoken comment of the two young women.

They exchanged triumphant glances but said nothing until they were left together in the car while their mothers paid a short call, later in the afternoon. Lois dropped the slightly hostile manner which she had formerly adopted towards Agatha and said with confidential friendliness:

"You managed that very well. Do you always get your own way like that?"

"Very seldom. It's too much trouble."

"I do hate my clothes. They are so disgustingly *jeune fille*. I wonder if I shall ever be allowed to choose my own things! It's the limit! I've been out two years, and I'm less free than I was in the schoolroom. I'm chaperoned all over the place, and have to read Italian with Miss Barrington, and can't buy so much as a pair of stockings for myself. Other girls aren't treated like this; not so badly! You are two years younger than me and after next week you'll be absolutely free and allowed to buy what clothes you please, just because you're married. It's simply silly."

" You must hurry up and get married too, Lois."

" How am I to get married I should like to know ? There is literally no one. All the boys Mother makes me dance with are so stupid. I couldn't marry anybody but a clever man that I had something in common with. And I'd never be allowed to, because clever men are nearly always poor. Anyhow, I've only met one man I could ever marry, and "—with a stifled giggle—" I'm afraid he's quite impossible. I don't know what Mother would say if she knew I was in love with him."

Agatha looked very much embarrassed.

" Were you ever in love before you met John ? "

" No."

There was a distinct chilliness in Agatha's voice. She had been brought up to regard this sort of conversation as extremely ill-bred. Her courteous priggishness infuriated Lois, who would have given the world not to have giggled. After an uncomfortable pause Agatha made an attempt at conciliation. She said :

" You'll be allowed to come and stay with us at Lyndon, won't you ? I'll invite entire house parties of clever men to meet you. I'll have all the intellect of Oxford to tea every afternoon."

Before so glorious a prospect Lois softened.

" Oh, Agatha, that will be fun ! Will you really ? You may laugh, but you don't know how much the idea of any sort of escape appeals to me. My mother is so much worse than yours, if you'll excuse me saying so. She treats me sometimes as if I had no more sense than James."

" Do you know, I haven't met James yet."

" Haven't you ? Well, you have got a treat coming ! It's a good thing you didn't see him before you accepted John. It might have scared you off."

" You alarm me."

" I'm only preparing you. You know, Mother doesn't
see that she only makes him worse, the way she goes on."

" But how, Lois ? "

" Oh, well . . . though he's so quiet he's really very
sensitive. And he minds frightfully when she treats him
like a baby. He understands quite enough to feel the
indignity. It's that, more than anything, which makes him
so shy. He's got perfectly awful now. He won't go anywhere. And he's always worse if she's there."

" But he was always shy, wasn't he ? "

" Oh, yes. He never would go to parties or anything,
even when he was a little boy. And when other children
came to play with us he always hid. Sometimes he came
with us to tea at the rectory, but that was the most he
would do."

" Shyness grows on people so."

" Yes, I know. And he's just terrified of meeting you.
He's been lectured so tremendously about being civil and
saying the right thing. If you come back to tea with us
to-day, you will see him."

" Am I to come back with you ? "

" John said we were to bring you because he will be
in. Then he can take you home if your mother can't
come."

" A drive with John ! A drive with John ! " sang Agatha's
heart.

Lois was saying :

" If you do come, please be nice to James and help him
out if he puts his foot in it. You know, I sort of understand
him, as far as anyone can. We used to back each other up
a good bit in the schoolroom days. And I know how much
he minds things. She shouldn't speak to him, in front of
people, as if he wasn't all there."

" But . . . frankly . . . is he ? "

"I suppose not, if it comes to the point. But he's got more sense than she thinks."

"She" here reappeared, having obtained leave to bring Agatha back to Eaton Square for tea. On the way there Agatha found the prospect of meeting James was quite unnerving her. She told herself that he could be no shyer than she was.

As they climbed the stairs a strange figure bolted suddenly from the drawing-room and made for the upper floor. Lady Clewer raised her voice to an unusually raucous pitch and bawled after the fugitive :

"James ! James ! Where are you going ? Come down and be introduced to your new sister ! "

James hesitated, lurking in the obscurity beyond the turn of the stairs. Then he came down and followed them into the drawing-room.

Agatha had been prepared to find him strange looking, but he was a greater shock than she had expected. She immediately thought him the most hideous creature she had ever encountered. But, on a second glance, it struck her that there was not quite the vacuity she had feared to see. Those sad eyes were too observant, the lines of the young face too severe to suggest imbecility. His build was massive, though short, and very uncouth by reason of his stooping shoulders and the immense length of his arms. His head was rather too big and his large, pale face, with its prominent cheekbones, was unrelieved by the faintest suggestion of eyebrow. This was the more noticeable since his brow was spacious and heavily constructed, especially in the region immediately above his light, sorrowful eyes. Sparse sandy hair grew far back upon his splendid, thoughtful forehead. His expression was one of discomfort and terror.

He advanced, smiling nervously, and shook with enthusiasm the hand which she gave him. She was most anxious to be nice to him, but she could think of nothing to say. What sort of thing did he talk about? What remark on her part would penetrate that amazing skull and convey to him her cordial intentions? An awful little pause ensued. She was aware that the whole Clewer family were trembling with anxiety to see how she took him. At last she bethought herself to say that he must have disliked leaving the country at so lovely a time of year.

"Lyndon is beautiful in June, isn't it?" she asked.

He took no notice of the question. He was plainly labouring with some form of utterance. From Lady Clewer's prompting glances it was obvious that he had been coached beforehand in the civilities of the occasion.

"I must congratulate you," he pronounced at length, "upon our approaching relationship."

This, it seemed, was not quite right. He thought it over and then tried again:

"It is a great pleasure to meet you." Then with a sudden glibness: "John is a very lucky man. Indeed, we are all very lucky to have you in the family. We are quite pleased, I can assure you."

This was obviously very nearly what he had been told to say. She thanked him gravely. But he did not appear to think that he had done his full duty, though he was visibly perspiring with the effort. He babbled on:

"I wish you both every happiness. I . . . er . . . hope. . . ." He stuck for a moment and then got it triumphantly: "I hope the marriage will be blest. . . ."

"That will do, James!" exclaimed Lady Clewer.

She spoke with a luckless promptitude which could emphasize the unfortunate phrase but never obliterate it. He took her words, however, as a literal intimation that his task had been performed to her satisfaction, and relapsed into smiling silence. Agatha, glancing from Lois' crimson blush to John's bland vacancy, had much ado not to laugh.

It occured to her that James was going to be very much more of a trial if the Clewers would insist upon taking him seriously. They were all ridiculously put out, and began discomposedly to hand plates of bread and butter and teacups to each other. Lady Clewer became vehement upon the beauties of a silver rose-bowl which the Lyndon tenants had presented to John. It would be so nice for large white roses ; she did hope Agatha would use it constantly.

"You like flowers, dear ? Ah, you'll enjoy the Lyndon roses. I am a great gardener myself."

Marian had not always been a great gardener. She had acquired the taste, with others, upon her second marriage. As mistress of the well laid out Martin " pleasure grounds," she had never thought of admitting to a close acquaintance with her garden. That was the affair of the hirelings who tended it. At Lyndon, however, she realized that every lady in the country is a great gardener. The country dames who now called on her inquired tenderly after her herbaceous borders. They made nothing of asking each other for a root of this or that, which was apparently by way of being a compliment, though Marian thought it a very odd habit. She was a woman who could conform rapidly to any type, so she promptly provided herself with a large straw hat, leather gloves, and a pair of scissors. She took to spending her afternoons among the roses and learnt to talk of daphne cneorum, romneya, hepatica, arenaria, gaultheria and berberis darwiniæ. She flung a few of these exotic names about the drawing-room now, and Agatha, duly impressed, wondered whether she, too, would be transmuted into a great gardener when she was established at Lyndon.

"But I don't like weeding," she confessed. "When I used to stay with my godmother in the country she used to make me weed. It was so hot and stoopy."

"Oh, weeding ! " Lady Clewer was amused. "I don't do that, naturally."

John began to laugh at the idea of his frail bride wrestling with docks and thistles. Cynthia looked a trifle disdainful. "We have some sort of an old woman to do that," she said.

"Griselda Pyewacket," said James unexpectedly.

"What?"

Everyone was startled.

"Griselda Pyewacket. That's her name."

"Really? I didn't know," said Lady Clewer looking repressively at James. "I thought it was a little boy."

"It's rather a nice name," said Agatha thoughtfully.

"Isn't it?" agreed James. "Her husband was called Pyramus Pyewacket. There was a little boy. He was her grandson. But he couldn't weed because he got a whitlow on his thumb."

"Indeed! Just hand me Agatha's cup, please, James!"

He rose with anxious alacrity, became entangled with the cake-stand and scattered several platefuls of macaroons and cress sandwiches over the floor. Agatha was very sorry for his discomfiture; she longed to laugh and help him to pick up the fragments. But under Lady Clewer's uneasy glances she dared not. A bell was rung and they sat uncomfortably ignoring the food at their feet until menials had come and removed it.

The meal wore on and Agatha was glad to escape early. The strain of the afternoon, following upon the fatigues of the dressmaker, had almost overpowered her. As she took her leave she was aware of John's hardly repressed impatience. She knew that he had joined them at tea merely in order to earn the brief bliss of escorting her home. It was a prospect which had sustained them both. Knowing this she became more punctiliously deliberate in her parting civilities, a reaction which her lover perfectly understood and which moved him to a restive approval.

"Are you sure," said he, when they were at last in their

taxi, " are you sure that this fellow isn't taking the corners too quickly? You are looking quite pale! Let me tell him to go slower."

" No, thank you! " she said, in some surprise. " I don't call this fast. There is no traffic."

" Personally I don't like this pace at all," he said gravely.

He seized the speaking tube and gave an order, whereupon the fellow not only crawled but adopted a strangely circuitous route.

" Well, and what do you make of old James? " he asked.

" Oh, I was so sorry for him. It's always difficult to congratulate a bride-elect, even for a person who isn't shy."

" I know. One's tendency is to be too much surprised, which isn't really complimentary. And he always has had a knack of saying exactly the wrong thing, don't you know."

He slid a glance at her where she sat, withdrawn and tranquil in her corner of the car. She met his eyes with candid gravity and asked:

" Do you think he will live at Lyndon in the future? "

" Not unless you want him, darling. But as a matter of fact I don't know at all what's to be done with him unless he does. I should think he'll always have to be with people who will keep an eye on him. But enough of James! He's no topic for a *tête à tête*, do you think, Agatha? "

The fond pair passed to points of greater interest to them, conversing always with sufficient decorum but never without a disturbing suggestion, on his part, of ardour temporarily restrained. As they crept into Agatha's street, however, she reverted to James:

" He seems to be very good-tempered," she said.

" Oh, yes, quite. In a way. He's perfectly harmless. I don't think he'll give us any real trouble. I take it he'll fall in with any plans we make for him. He's got no particular views of his own, you see."

4.

John was mistaken. In after life it seemed to Agatha that the whole of her wedding day had been filled with commotions about James and his inconvenient, unexpected views. It was entirely typical of him that he should have seized such a moment to launch them on his family. Wind of the trouble came to South Kensington the night before the wedding, when a note from Lois was brought in to Agatha :

"My mother forgot to say to yours that a large slice of wedding cake and a photograph of you and John ought to be sent to :

> Mrs. Job Kell,
> Old Forge Cottage,
> Little Baverstock,
> Tiverton.

She's a superannuated housekeeper or something, who ran Lyndon in the interval between John's mother and mine, and J. is the apple of her eye. Incidentally, I may add that James is even more of an apple, she having ' reared him from a babby', when even his own nurse had given him up. Indeed, she will never admit that there is anything the matter with him ! Fact ! ! !

Apropos of James, we are all in such a way about him. Nothing very unusual in that, you'll say ; but wait till you hear ! This is something quite new and too appallingly funny and unexpected. He has got the most extraordinary idea in the world into his head. I, for one, sympathize with him entirely. But, then, you know I often do. No time to tell you now, but I will to-morrow if I get the chance. . . .

> (Almost) your affectionate sister,
> Lois."

Agatha showed this letter to her mother, who was interested and perplexed.

" I do hope he hasn't had any kind of a fit," she said. " But anyway, it's better to-day than to-morrow."

" Lois says an extraordinary idea. That doesn't sound like an illness of any kind."

" Oh, dear ! " complained Mrs. Cocks. " They have James on the brain. You mustn't catch the habit when you are one of the family."

" He's rather dreadful, but I think he's much nicer when he isn't trying to conform to their ideals of good manners. When he is on his best behaviour he is so painfully nervous and makes such dreadful faces that it's almost unendurable. When he's left to himself he isn't at all bad. He has a wonderful smile, when he's really smiling and not grinning. I must say I don't think Lady Clewer does very well with him."

" You are the first person I've met who thought so. I remember when Sir John died everyone used to say : ' Poor Lady Clewer ! So good and kind, and so nice to that peculiar little stepson ! She's quite broken-hearted.' It was almost a catchword."

" But he isn't little any more," argued Agatha. " That is where she is mistaken. I should like very much to know what Gerald would make of him."

She said this with a splendid detachment. If she could not mention Gerald on the eve of her marriage with John, when could she ? Mrs. Cocks, not to be outdone, took this once dangerous name with the utmost calm. She replied easily :

" I thought Gerald was studying nerves rather than mental cases. Hasn't he gone to America especially to study nerves ? "

" Yes. But Aunt Hilda says that his next move will be to Paris to work in a clinic for mentally deficient children."

"Of course," said Mrs. Cocks, "all this special study must be very interesting, and will get him a better position in the end, I suppose. But he seems to be taking a very long time about it. I never knew a young man so slow in getting started. It's a pity, in a way, that he has independent means. What he has isn't enough to be any good, though it's enough for him just to live on. He might have done better if he'd had to support himself."

Agatha, who knew that having "enough to be any good" was a periphrasis for matrimonial eligibility, was moved to protest:

"But specialists are badly needed. And it's seldom possible for a man to specialize who hasn't got private means."

"I know, dear. But I feel he might have done better for himself in another career. But perhaps America may do him good. He may acquire a more commercial spirit."

Agatha tried to think of Gerald with a more commercial spirit. She was unable. Instead she stumbled dismayingly upon a vivid recollection of his old self—of the friend whose love she had once accepted. She thought of his quick, clever hands, the nervous composure of his gestures, and remembered how eagerly and brilliantly he had talked. She saw afresh his incongruities, his storms and indecisions, and recalled the tenderness which they had awakened in her.

And, remembering this, she was invaded by a tide of devastating, insupportable sorrow. To ease herself she rose and moved about the room, tormented by an anguish so sharp, so sudden, that she almost groaned aloud. Mrs. Cocks, placid and handsome upon the sofa, continued her friendly conversation:

"You don't realize your luck, child, living in an age when girls are sensibly brought up."

"Don't I?" asked Agatha inattentively.

" Oh, my dear ! If you only knew what one used to have to put up with. I remember the night before I was married I had a most gruesome interview with my old step-aunt, my mother being dead. She came into my room, just when I was getting sleepy, and said the most upsetting things. It was done in her day. Fortunately she said nothing which I did not expect. Girls weren't such fools as they were supposed to be, even in those days. And I wasn't so very young, either. But it was all most disagreeable and you can't think how I resented it. What's the matter ? Have you got toothache ? "

" No."

Agatha had almost subdued her trouble and sat down by her mother, saying :

" I can quite imagine how you resented it. You'd find me very chilly, Mother dear, if you tried any treatment of the kind on me."

" But you have got toothache ! You are perfectly green ! "

" I had just one sharp stab, but it's gone now."

It had. But she was feeling strangely exhausted.

" You'd better go to bed. If you look like this to-morrow I shall go distracted. As stony as a gorgon ! "

" The gorgons weren't stony. It was the other people . . . "

" They were very plain, and so are you at the moment But, *apropos* of what I was saying of my step-aunt, there is nothing I ought to say to you, is there ? "

" Nothing, thank you ! " replied Agatha hastily. " You've given me solid good advice for the last six weeks. I couldn't absorb any more."

" That is so," agreed Mrs. Cocks placidly. " But I wouldn't like to feel I hadn't done my duty by you."

To the bride the future yawned like a precipice almost at her feet. Light cast by her mother's experience upon the abyss could but disincline her for the inevitable plunge. She clung rather to the reflection that, by every standard known in her world, she was marrying a man whom she loved. The plunge ought not, in these circumstances, to turn out so very bad.

Mrs. Cocks kissed her tenderly and bade her good-night. " I shall let you sleep late to-morrow," she said, " and you shall have your breakfast before you get up. Come to me if you have any return of that toothache in the night, and I'll give you something for it."

Then, with a recollection of the sentiment due to such a moment :

" Have you said good-night to your father ? "

Agatha shook her head.

" I don't think I'd better. I never do. And it might disturb him."

" Perhaps it would look rather silly."

" After dinner I played that Scarlatti he likes. I thought it would be rather touching on my last night at home. But he went away in the middle."

" Did he ? Oh, well. . . ."

The underground trains, passing the end of the garden, punctuated the night with their intermittent rumbling. Agatha lay awake listening to them and awaiting repose. Her feverish fatigue held sleep away from her and she was still frightened and shaken by that violent, intolerable pang which had rent her when she thought of Gerald Blair.

It was terrible, to know that her heart still concealed such weapons, for she was almost certain, now, that she had never loved her cousin. His wooing, though it had moved her at the time, had been a boyish, inexperienced affair. It was John who had roused her to the possibilities of emotion ; from him she had learnt the subtleties of guarded speech, the contagious fire which can lie hidden in a glance. For him her heart beat quicker.

She had never known any of these things before. Gerald had been no more than a friend; but a friend in whose company she had found, inexplicably, perfect happiness. It was not for him but for the memory of this contentment that regret assailed her. She believed that she yearned after a mental completeness, once captured and then lost for ever. There had been an intensity of sensation, a full current of life transcending the sorry measure of normal existence. For a little time she had perceived creation as a unity. It had been this abounding of the spirit, this marvellous clarity of mood, this apprehension of profound significance in everything, which had driven her to her career of folly at Canverley Fair. She had escaped, for a moment, from the isolation which binds us; she was no longer a detached figure upon an unfocussed background, but part of a gay and simple pattern.

This exaltation had vanished soon enough, but the memory could still hurt her when she thought of it, or when she thought of Gerald who had shared it with her. She knew that she could never hope to find it again in the conscious, deliberate life upon which she was embarking.

For her consolation, in this endless oppressive night, she turned to the image of her lover. But he evaded her; he was blurred by the mists of romance. She wanted to see him sharply and clearly, as she had seen her cousin, but she could only recall, vaguely, the brief ecstasy of her interviews with him. She began, in despair, to catalogue his qualities; he was dark, he was prosperous, he was experienced and determined. Everything, in fact, that poor Gerald was not.

At last, when London sparrows chirped to the dawn in the plane trees and milk carts rattled in the street below, she fell asleep, to dream neither of John nor of Gerald, but of the frightening, mysterious James. He pursued her through countless, shifting scenes, led her to the altar, and climbed snowy mountains with her. They were lost in the endless glare of blinding glaciers. And when, still in her dream, she rose and leant from her window for air, his large face grinned up at her from a menacing street, all empty and heavy with a strange grey dawn. The vision so terrified her that she could not shake off the horror of it when she woke. The day took on the vague, poignant qualities of a nightmare in which nothing seemed real save the sense of impending doom. She did what she was told, listened to her mother's rapid, authoritative voice, ate an intolerable number of small meals brought to her on trays, and submitted to an excited toilet. The silence in which she drove with her father to church was lovely and comforting.

John, handsome and competent as ever, waited for her at the chancel steps, and at the sight of his cheerful self-possession she became more collected. While the clergyman was haranguing them about those carnal lusts of which the bride is supposed to know nothing, she reflected composedly that John ought really to be married as often as possible, he did it so well. He was obviously enjoying himself. She was aware that he had deliberately removed his thoughts from her in order to be able to concentrate on his part. This was the right way to do it ; being married was, after all, a duty to one's neighbour and not a personal affair. Fired by his high standard of social exertion she threw herself into the business with energy and gave a very pleasing and stately performance. By the unusual stillness of the church behind them she divined that they were getting it across. As she returned down the aisle Mendelssohn's triumph seemed to epitomize her own satisfaction in her beautiful behaviour. She had quitted the maiden state becomingly.

They were no sooner bestowed in the car than John burst out : " Have you heard about James ? "

" Not in any detail. Lois said there was trouble in a note last night. But she didn't say what it was."

" It's the most extraordinary affair. Desperately annoying, just when we are going away. They'll have to settle it without us, that's all. We can't be bothered."

" But what's the matter with him ? "

" It's unheard of ! The fellow wants to go to Paris. Says he is going, in fact."

" Paris ! Paris ! "

" Yes. Paris, my child ! "

" But . . . oh . . . why ? "

" Heaven knows ! To work at his painting, he says. He has quite an obsession for that kind of thing, you know. He always had, even when he was a kid."

" But does he want to be an artist ? "

" God knows what he wants ! He seems to have got the idea from someone who's been teaching him drawing. It would be funny if it wasn't so idiotic. James going to Paris ! Good lord ! "

" But does he draw well ? How well does he draw ? "

" Not so badly. He caricatures rather well." There was an irritable reminiscence in John's tone. " Mamma got him jolly good lessons, when she saw he was keen on it. I believe it's not uncommon for that sort of chap to have a purely mechanical turn of the kind, don't you know. But it's not as if anyone was stopping him from doing it here. He can do it all day for all we care. We don't interfere with him."

" Poor James ! "

" Poor James, does she say ? Poor James be . . . well, perhaps I'd better not say it till I've been married a little longer. It would be rather shocking on one's wedding journey. But, do you know, Agatha, we can't really stop him going if he wants to. It sounds incredible, but there it is. He's of age, and he has a small independent income, inherited from our mother. Of course, we've always taken it for granted that he'll be guided by us. But now . . ."

" Surely you can do something ? "

" Oh, if the worse comes to the worst, we could, I imagine, get a doctor's certificate or something. But it would be very awkward. We ought to have done it before. You see he can behave so sensibly when he likes ; and if, just to spite us, he showed up at his best with the doctor, we might have quite a job to get him certified. Still, he can't be allowed to go."

" Would it really be impossible if he wants to very much ? "

" Why just think of it ! James in Paris ! A place like Paris ! "

" It isn't so different from any other place."

" No, but he is different from any other person. There's no knowing what mischief he mightn't get up to. It all comes from taking this scrubbing and daubing too seriously. I was against it from the first. But Mamma had all these ideas about manual education. However ! I've told him I won't sanction it. As head of the family I've put my foot down. And he needn't think I'll help him if he gets into difficulties."

" What did he say to that ? "

" Nothing. He's as obstinate as a mule. . . . Hullo ! Here we are ! "

They had drawn up before the Cocks's door, triumphant with its gala awning and crimson carpet. It was flung wide by beaming maidservants and John handed Agatha and her lilies, her pearls, her satin train and lace veil, out of the car. In the hall the bride dispensed a little of her mild sweetness to her father's servants. She was already rather tired of hearing her new name. She had been called Lady Clewer a hundred times in the vestry while she signed herself, for the last time, as Agatha Cocks. But she submitted smilingly and had pleased, happy glances for everyone.

John began to grow impatient. He liked watching his wife do the right thing, but he was unwilling that she should waste too much time among sooty cook-maids. She knew that he was fidgeting on the stairs behind her, and turned to join him. They had scarcely reached the drawing-room before other taxis were heard outside and there were voices in the hall. John twitched her train into becoming folds round her feet and assumed the posture of happy groom at her side. She felt that she quite hated James for spoiling the romance of her wedding drive. It was the first expedition she had ever made with John that had no flavour of adventure. They had been all absorbed in domestic discussion. It was very disappointing, for they could never be married again. This unique occasion was gone—lost !

" I've not crushed your flowers," he murmured in her ear as a bevy of bridesmaids flocked into the room. " Isn't that exemplary in a bridegroom ? "

This interesting point was immediately marked by the youngest of the Clewers. There was only one quality which Cynthia found admirable in her sister-in-law, and that was her exquisite neatness. Mrs. Cocks also recorded with pleasure the immaculate freshness of Agatha's lilies, and added another mark to John's credit. She might have known he would take care ; there never was a man who knew better what was expected of him in a public position.

The outer world poured in, flooding the house of Cocks with a jubilant tide. Agatha gave herself to the embraces of countless women and heard them congratulating her mother upon getting rid of her. In the midst of all this clamour the sight of the troublesome James advancing to greet her had a calming effect. She decided that his new ambitions became him, however impossible they might be in themselves. He wore a look of sulky obstinacy which was a great improvement upon his earlier manner. His very walk was more purposeful. He shook hands with her and scowled at John. Cynthia, however, who had followed him, was determined to exhibit him a little.

"Why don't you kiss her, James?" she drawled. "You ought to. She's your sister now, you know."

He remained cool.

"I'd better not," he said to Agatha. "You wouldn't like it and I shouldn't like it."

"Oh, what a gentleman!" mocked Cynthia. "You'll have to learn better manners before you go to France. Did you know James was going to France, Agatha?"

"I had heard something of it."

"Did John tell you about it in the car coming back from church?" demanded James with interest.

"Er . . . yes."

"There, then!" He nodded at Cynthia, and explained: "She wondered what you would talk about. I said it would be me."

"You do think a lot of yourself, don't you?" retorted she. "He'll have to hurry up and learn French, won't he?"

"I know French," he asserted.

This was true, for he had shared several French governesses with Lois and Cynthia and had become quite as articulate in the tongue of these poor ladies as in his own.

"It doesn't make much difference," said Cynthia, tired of baiting him. "John says you aren't to go, so you won't be allowed to."

They all looked at John, who was ably defending himself against the congratulations of an hysterical old lady.

"I don't mind what John says."

"He'll have to mind, won't he, Agatha?"

"I really don't know what will be settled," replied Agatha coldly.

She disliked Cynthia.

James turned away to one of the windows where he spent the remainder of the reception absorbed in the constant arrival and departure of taxis in the street below. Agatha noticed that the other window was occupied by another solitary watcher—her father. He was looking extremely small and shrunken and was making no attempt to fulfil his duties as a host. The isolated bleakness of these two figures, withdrawn amidst the babble, struck her strangely. They brooded in the background like skeletons at the feast.

An hour later, when she came downstairs erect and slim in her blue travelling suit, she glanced into the drawing-room to see if they were still there. Varden Cocks was gone, but James was at his post. Sunlight and emptiness filled the room, and a great clamour of conversation, an enormous rattling of spoons and forks in the dining-room below proclaimed the whereabouts of the wedding guests. Anew she felt most anxious to be nice to poor James; to bring balm to that lonely, mutilated mind. She felt indignant with the Clewers for scorning him. It was as if they were all determined to deny to him that dignity and self-respect which is the birthright of the lowest. His sorrowful eyes turned upon her were an accusation.

She advanced into the room.

" They are all downstairs eating ices," he told her.

" I know. Aren't you coming ? "

" No ! I don't like them."

" Well, James, it's good-bye for the present, then. You'll come and pay us a long visit, won't you, when we get back from Norway."

" I shall be in Paris then," he stated.

Without conscious readjustment she began to accept his point of view. Of course he would be in Paris. How stupid they all were !

" We may be stopping in Paris before the end of our

honeymoon," she said. " If you are there, we must meet and go about to things."

" What things ? "

" Oh . . . theatres and things."

" But I'm going to paint," he objected.

" But you don't want to paint all the time, surely ? You'll go round and see the sights, I suppose ? "

He thought it over and then said conclusively :

" I don't here."

She felt baffled and wondered what else she could say. There were fresh sounds of a car in the street and he looked out of the window.

" It's yours," he said. " They are putting your luggage on to it."

Agatha yawned.

" What are you yawning for ? " he asked sympathetically.

" I don't know. I keep on doing it. It's silly. I can't help it."

" I know," he averred.

There were cries for her downstairs, and she thought she heard John's voice. She stood still, gaping. James, surprised at her rigidity, looked into her face exclaiming :

" Here ! What are you frightened of ? "

Turning to rebuff his foolishness, she was silenced by his expression. In that ugly countenance she perceived so much gravity, indignation and concern that she was mute.

" Look . . . You woman . . . Agatha . . ." he said urgently, " . . . don't go if you don't want to ! "

" Agatha ! Are you ready ? Agatha ! "

People were coming upstairs.

" Don't listen to them," muttered James, catching her arm. " I don't. They are very silly, you know. You shouldn't let them . . ."

A shrill laugh wrenched itself out of her throat. She shook off his hand and admonished him :

" Don't talk like that ! It's you who are silly, James ! "
For a moment he stood as if barring her way. Then the
horrified penetration died out of his eyes and he let her go,
indifferently. She ran down to her husband.

5.

Marian Clewer prided herself upon the regularity with
which she conducted her household. There was no varia-
tion in her iron laws. Immediately after the wedding,
therefore, she flogged her family back into the routine of
everyday life, sternly checking any attempt to prolong the
feast. Upon the return of the Clewers to Eaton Square
she demanded whether Lois had read Italian with Miss
Barrington. Lois, who resented her Italian lessons more
deeply than any of her other shackles, replied sulkily that
she had not. She had supposed that John's wedding
would be a holiday.

" That has nothing to do with it," replied Lady Clewer
coldly. " Go and take off your frock and give it to Peters
to put away for you. Put on your green dress and go into
the schoolroom for your reading. You can have your tea
there to-day as I want to talk business with Major Talbot
and Mrs. Cocks."

The schoolroom was a nice sunny place at the top of the
house, well equipped with all the paraphernalia of modern
education. Miss Barrington, the notable woman who had
succeeded in teaching James to read, was sitting comfortably in a rocking-chair by the window. She also had hoped
for a holiday and was engaged upon one of those endless
letters to her cousins at Cape Town which occupied her
infrequent leisure hours. But when she saw Lois she sprang
to her feet with an eager display of activity such as Marian
liked to see in her subordinates. She was a sensible, apple-
cheeked young woman, with high academic qualifications, a

morbid conscience, and great personal humility : an ideal
governess for the Clewer household. She belonged to that
type of energetic worker for which Marian had a positive
cult.   There were squads of them down at Lyndon ;
secretaries, lady gardeners, dairy-women and the like. Lady
Clewer was uniformly generous to them, bullied them,
nursed them when they were ill, paid for their false teeth,
kept them continually on the run in her employ, and, in
short, scarcely allowed them to call their souls their own.
All that she required in return was loyalty.

Miss Barrington was very loyal. She even thought it
necessary to display enthusiasm over the mild pages of
I Promessi Sposi, which book it was her duty to read with
Miss Martin. She said sometimes that she thought it an
interesting story. She looked very unhappy when Lois
exclaimed :

" I suppose it's because Mother can't even speak her own
language properly that she thinks I ought to know four ! "

" She has a very high ideal of education," said the
governess.

" Most people idealize what they haven't got."

" Lois ! "

" Well ? I was only generalizing. Where's the wretched
book ? Let's get it over ! "

" Lois ! You know quite well that you oughtn't to talk
like that."

" I can't help it. It's too irritating. Here's Agatha, two
years younger than me, allowed to go to Norway with a
strange man she hardly knows. . . ."

" Let me see ! Where did we leave off ? " said Miss
Barrington hastily.

" I don't want to be married, goodness knows," stormed
Lois. " Except to get a little peace and freedom and
quietness. But I never shall, anyway. I never get the
chance. I never see any man to speak to."

"You go to balls and things. You've been presented,"
put in Cynthia from the sofa.

"What earthly good does being presented do? I'm not
going to marry the Prince of Wales. And as for dances,
Mother scares away any man who attempts to be at all
friendly. I never get the chances other girls do."

"Lois! I've found the place!"

"Well, why didn't you marry John?" asked Cynthia.
"I should have, in your position. You could, you know.
You aren't really related. And you've had plenty of oppor-
tunities."

Lois, to whom this was a new idea, gasped. So did Miss
Barrington.

"Well, but . . . John didn't want to marry me. . . ."

"That's your fault. You could have made him. . . .
I think you missed an excellent chance. Just think what
fun it would have been taking Lyndon out of Mother's
hands!"

"Cynthia! I can't have you talking like that. It isn't
very nice," exclaimed the agonized Miss Barrington.

The two girls laughed.

"How do you mean, I could have made him . . .?"
pursued Lois.

"Oh, well! If you don't know that much!"

"You don't know what you're talking about. You
couldn't, at your age. Why, you've not even been confirmed!"

"I don't see what that has to do with it."

"It shows what a baby you are."

Cynthia needed occasional repression, but it seldom had
any effect on her. She smiled mysteriously and examined
the ends of her finger-nails.

"Well, all things considered," she said, "I think I'll get
married before I come out."

"Nonsense! You won't be allowed to. Nobody does."

"Well, I expect I shall. You see! As for you. . . .
There's still James. You'd better take him."

James, seated at the table, was drawing in a small sketch-
book. He was, as usual, absorbed in his work, and did not
look up when his name was mentioned. Lois could not
avoid an expressive grimace at the idea of marrying him.

"Lois and Cynthia! You really mustn't talk in this way.
Not in the schoolroom. Cynthia, get something to do!
Your mother thinks you are too indolent. It's nonsense to
lie on the sofa doing nothing in the middle of the afternoon."

"I'm not doing nothing. I'm polishing my nails."

"Lois! Hadn't you better get on with your Italian?"

The two girls took no notice and calmly continued their
argument. Under the eye of their mother they were civil to
their governess, but not otherwise. They had, naturally, no
idea of obligatory courtesy towards dependents. Marian's
own demeanour to her subordinates, for all her benevolence
and generosity, was not calculated to instil such a principle
into their budding minds. Lois, who prided herself upon
her interest in James's work, leant over his shoulder to inspect
the drawing. It was, she perceived, a pencil study of the
Cocks family, presented with the unpleasing bleakness of
outline peculiar to James. Mrs. Cocks, seated in a magnificent amplitude, more than suggested Mrs. Siddons as the
Tragic Muse. Behind her chair hovered two shadowy
creatures, types of death and despair. Executed by anyone
else, the intention of the piece must have been deliberately
malicious. But Lois, from long experience, had come to
believe that James was incapable of malice. He had too
little grasp of situation; too little comprehension of human
character. Sketches which looked like caricatures were, for
him, a simple exposition of the subject as he saw it.

"I like the way you've put Mr. Cocks and Agatha in the
background," she commented. "But you've made them

too tragic. Agatha does look a little *triste* sometimes, but in quite a placid way. She never has that crucified sort of look. And Mr. Cocks may be ill, but he isn't dying."

" Isn't he ? " asked James.

" Not that I know of." Lois began to wonder why she had been so sure about it. " It may be because his wife looks so lively," she concluded. " What a splendid creature she is ! And just like Mrs. Siddons. I love it when she piles up all her hair on that coronet comb. You've done it justice, James ! "

" You'd better show it to her," advised Cynthia. " It may make her speak for you this afternoon."

" What's that ? " exclaimed Lois.

" Well, she's having tea in the drawing-room this minute with Major Talbot and Aunt Edith. That's why you aren't allowed there. They are settling what's to be done with James."

" But how do you know ? "

" She listened at the door," James asserted.

Miss Barrington exclaimed, but Cynthia only laughed. Lois became impassioned :

" Oh, isn't it too bad ? They've no right to do it. No right at all. When you aren't there ! As if you were a child ! "

" It makes no difference," said James calmly.

" But suppose they say you aren't to go ? "

" Well, they can. I shall go all the same."

" It's doing it behind your back which is so disgusting. They ought to let you speak for yourself."

" James isn't much of a speaker," observed Cynthia. " Why don't you do it for him ? "

" I've a good mind to. Shall I, James ? "

" You can if you like," agreed James absently, as he returned to his drawing.

Lois bounced out of the room and burst like a whirlwind upon the astonished party in the drawing-room.

"It's very unfair of you to decide about James without consulting him," she stormed. "Why should you insult him like that? If you don't take care he'll go just to spite you."

Lady Clewer became crimson.

"I never heard such a thing in my life!" she cried. "Considering that for sixteen years I've done nothing but study his welfare. . . ."

"You don't study his feelings. . . ."

"Will you hold your tongue, Lois?"

"You've no right to discuss him when he can't speak for himself!"

"How did you know we were discussing him, my dear?"

The high drawl of Mrs. Gordon Clewer cut into the dispute with deadly power. The shrill, angry tones of the mother and daughter subsided. Marian had been so furious that she had overlooked this obvious retort. She now proceeded to make use of it, in her own thorough way, speaking about an octave lower.

"Yes! You young people think yourselves so important, don't you? You can't imagine that we ever have anything else to discuss, can you? But, my dear Lois, when we do discuss James we shan't ask your advice. We may summon him, but we won't need to consult you. Have you finished your Italian reading?"

"No."

"Well, then, pray go and do so."

"All the same," exploded Major Talbot, when Lois had retired in disorder, "something's got to be done about the lad, I suppose."

He spoke so seldom that the three ladies jumped.

"We'd better settle it, one way or the other," he went on. "How, exactly, do you stand, Lady Clewer? I mean, how much legal control have you over his movements?"

"That's the difficulty. He's of age: twenty-one three

weeks ago. He seems to have had this extraordinary plan for two years. But he kept it to himself because he had got it into his head that he could do as he liked as soon as he was twenty-one. I don't know who can have told him that."

" Then this isn't a new idea, this Paris scheme ? "

" It's the first we've heard of it. But he says that he always meant to go when he was twenty-one. It's been very deceitful of him. And then he has this money of your sister's. About £400 a year, doesn't it come to ? "

" But have you . . . er . . . no medical certificate ? "

" No. Nothing that really quite justifies . . ."

" When did he last see a doctor ? "

" When he was about fifteen, I think," said Marian, after reflection. " They all had measles and I suppose he saw one then."

" He hasn't been having special medical treatment ? " asked Mrs. Cocks in surprise.

" There was no call for it. Physically he was always very strong and healthy. I took him to a specialist when he was very little, of course. He said that the child was very abnormal."

" Quite ! " said Major Talbot judicially. " And I suppose from time to time some qualified doctor has had a look at him ? "

" N-no. Where was the use ? " said Lady Clewer in distress. " So little can be done for that sort of thing when once you've accepted it."

" D'ye mean to say you've never definitely established what's wrong with the boy ? " cried Major Talbot.

" Really ! " Marian became flustered. " I should have thought it was obvious to anyone looking at him. It always has been. Directly, the first time I saw him, I guessed that there was something very wrong. But, of course, I never foresaw that he would get these foolish ideas into his head, or I would have been more careful to get the whole thing cut and dried before he came of age. Only I shrank from it. Having these things in the family is so awkward. It's so painful! I'm not accustomed to it."

"Poor Marian!" murmured Mrs. Gordon Clewer.

"Of course, if you think I've been mistaken, I've no more to say. I acted for the best, as I thought. It hasn't been easy; I don't expect you can realize what a difficulty it's been. He didn't even learn to read properly till he was past sixteen. It's been impossible to teach him civil manners. We couldn't send him to an ordinary school, or even let him be very much with other children."

"Oh, quite! Quite! Quite!" soothed Major Talbot, who was overwhelmed by this flow of rhetoric.

"I kept him at home with my girls. It's often been a little trying for them. But I thought he would be happier. If you think he should have been sent to some institution, I've nothing more to . . ."

"Oh, no, indeed!" protested Major Talbot. "I'm sure you did all that was best. It's only the question of preventing him from making a fool of himself now. This idea of going to Paris! What's to be done about it?"

"Of course," suggested Mrs. Cocks, "I suppose it would be better for him to have something to do? Something that really interests him, and gives him an object in life."

"Oh, yes! That's why I have done everything in my power to encourage his drawing. But why Paris? Why not here?"

"Well," said Mrs. Gordon Clewer, "I think it might have been very much worse. It's quite respectable to want to draw in Paris. He might have wanted to draw battle-ships and sections of salmon in crayon on the pavement."

"But Paris is such an impossible place."

"He'll have to be looked after wherever he goes, won't he?" asked Mrs. Cocks. "If you gave in on the essential

point, and let him go, perhaps you could induce him to
stay with people who would look after him a certain
amount."

"Exactly, Mrs. Cocks," exclaimed Major Talbot.
"Exactly! I quite agree with you. It would be much
easier to let him go, under proper supervision, than
to get a medical certificate to prevent it. Doctors are
uncommonly careful who they certify, you know, especially
when there's any money in the case."

"Then you all think I should let him go?" asked Lady
Clewer dubiously.

The general opinion seemed to be that James should go
if a suitable establishment could be found for him. Presently an idea occurred to Lady Clewer.

"Somebody now . . . who was it? . . . Somebody told
me the other day of a family who takes paying guests.
Young girls, generally, and there is a certain amount of
chaperonage. An old lady and her daughters I think it was.
I wonder if they would take a young man! And they
were strict Protestants."

"French Protestants are always strict," said Mrs. Gordon
Clewer. "But it's a point. We don't want our James
going over to Rome. If he did, he would undoubtedly
want to become a Trappist monk, and I don't know but
what the vocation wouldn't suit him."

"It was Mrs. Temple told me," recollected Lady Clewer.
"I was wondering if a little time in Paris wouldn't be nice
for Cynthia. But I rather gathered that these people were
a little—" *bourgeois* had been the word used by Mrs. Temple,
but Marian shied at it and substituted: 'middle-class.'
"So I did not think it would quite do."

"It would be a pity for Cynthia's tone to be con-
taminated," said Mrs. Gordon Clewer sententiously.

"Yes," agreed Cynthia's mother. "She's at such an
impressionable age. I wouldn't like to send her among

second-rate people. But it would be different for James.
Mrs. Temple says they often have girls who are studying
music or art, and they will take them about to their lessons.
I daresay they would take James every day to the studio,
or wherever it is he will work."

" But would that quite do, in this case ? " protested
Mrs. Cocks. " I mean, a young man can't be escorted quite
like a girl can. It puts him in such a ridiculous position."

Mrs. Gordon Clewer shot an amused look at Major
Talbot, but he had evidently failed to find anything ludicrous
in the prospect of James under daily escort to the Latin
Quarter. Concealing her joy, she innocently remarked :

" But in France, you know, Mrs. Cocks, things are very
different. You see quite big boys taken to school by *bonnes*
in white aprons."

Marian took this in perfectly good faith. She rejoined
tranquilly :

" Yes. France is quite different."

" But you can't ! " Mrs. Cocks was beginning to think
that Agatha had been right. " The thing's impossible !
Can't you see ? You can't treat the poor boy like that !
It's cruel ! Think how he will be laughed at, taken about
by a nursery maid ! "

" But," urged Marian, " he must have somebody to
look after him."

" Well, then, don't let him go at all. But don't expose
him to the universal derision of every boy of his own
age ! "

" Don't you see, Mrs. Cocks," said Major Talbot, " it's
a rash step letting him go at all ? It doesn't alter the fact
that he can't look after himself. He must go under peculiar
conditions."

" He can choose," said Marian. " He can go if he will
accept the arrangements we make for him. If he doesn't
like them, he needn't go. Of course," she conceded, " it

needn't be a nursery maid. No! That would look foolish. But there must be someone."

Mrs. Gordon Clewer rose, preparing to depart. She kissed Marian on both cheeks with the utmost affection.

"Good-bye, my dear," she said. "I'm glad you've come to so satisfactory a conclusion. You are inimitable; you never disappoint me. But I'm very much afraid you are only at the beginning of your troubles. You'll never find that he really settles down. Never! It's heredity, my dear; environment is so much overrated. You've done what you can, I'm sure, but you'll never alter his heredity. With those parents he is bound to give trouble. . . ."

"I never met his mother," said Marian in some surprise. "But from what I know of his parents, I should have thought . . ."

"You knew neither of them, my dear," said the old lady unexpectedly.

Everyone felt that she must have forgotten that Marian had been married to James's father for two years. Old age was beginning to tell upon Mrs. Gordon Clewer. She sometimes said these odd, disconcerting things. She nodded thrice, very emphatically, clucked at them and ambled away under the attentive escort of Major Talbot.

Mrs. Cocks took her leave, hoping that the unfortunate James would have the sense to give up the Paris idea. She underrated his tenacity. James never wasted energy over non-essentials. Provided that he might go to Paris and paint he agreed calmly to any arrangements his stepmother might like to make. Lois, however, felt for him all the indignation that was proper.

It was a fine evening, and Mrs. Cocks walked most of the way to South Kensington. As she turned into her own street she saw a taxi drawn up before the awning and crimson carpet which still decorated her door. Upon the steps was a young man, talking to the parlourmaid. Before she could make out who he was, he ran down again, jumped into the taxi and drove off.

"Who was that, Meadowes ? " she asked.

"It was Mr. Blair, Madam."

"Oh ! I didn't know he was in England. Did he want to see me ? "

"No, Madam. He asked for Miss Agatha. Lady Clewer, I mean. He said he'd only got back from America this morning. He didn't seem to know that she had been married to-day."

"Oh. Did he say he'd come again ? "

Mrs. Cocks had no objection, now, to seeing her young kinsman about the house.

"No, Madam. When he heard Miss Agatha was gone out of town on her honeymoon, he said he wouldn't wait. He said he was just going to France."

"Oh ! Oh, yes ! "

"If you please, Madam, Mr. Cocks has gone to bed and sent for the doctor. I thought I'd better tell you at once."

"Gone to bed? I'd better go up. Thank you, Meadowes."

As she climbed the stairs, Mrs. Cocks reflected that her husband's collapse was not very surprising. He had been looking ill all day, and she had meant to take him in hand as soon as the wedding was over.

This visit of Gerald's was very odd, and just like him. An invitation to the wedding had been sent to him in America, in case he should return to England in time for it. But it must have missed him. On the whole, she was not sorry that it had. Agatha was now safe.

Mrs. Cocks smiled a little grimly, remembering his hasty departure from her house along the crimson carpet spread for his successful rival.

CHAPTER II

THE FLORENTINE

I.

MR. HUBERT ERVINE accomplished the five miles from Oxford to Lyndon in a disordered frame of mind. Elation and misgiving possessed him alternately. It seemed to him, as his car spun over the long flat road, that he was arriving too quickly. He would be at Lyndon, confronted with his fate, before he should be ready for it.

He strove to become a deliberate and composed individual, summoning to his aid his entire stock of self-esteem, which was not small. His mission was certainly delicate. He hoped to find Miss Martin at Lyndon, and he intended to propose marriage to her in the course of his fortnight there. Nor did he expect her to deny him. They had met many times in London during the winter and she had always been kind. He rather thought that she would have him, if her relations did not dissuade her.

It was these Clewers, with their strange, complicated family ties, who made him uneasy. He was afraid they might not like him. They might not provide him with the field in which he could most happily display himself before the admiring eyes of his lady. He liked opportunities for being clever. No piece of cultural gymnastic could frighten him. He could discuss Chaucer before breakfast, and improvise operatic charades in the afternoon, and hold his own in that kind of brilliant conversation which is apt to spring up about midnight. He could write witty parodies, imitate most literary styles, and was personally acquainted with a sufficient number of live artists to pass in most places as a critic of their works.

All this, however, might not impress the Clewers. He did not suppose that they were very intellectual. His few encounters with them had only led him to reflect upon the strangeness of discovering the so different Lois in such a gallery. The promise of her intelligence was admirable, but he was blest if he knew where it came from. Lyndon, though so near to Oxford, was not an academic centre. It was known that a man stood or fell there according to his power to divert and entertain the lady of the house, and the most learned dons had to leave their erudition behind them if they wanted to be invited a second time.

Hubert admired young Lady Clewer immensely, of course, but he was decidedly afraid of her. He knew that he must go warily in any attempt to display himself. She would listen readily enough to interesting conversation and could discuss anything with anybody provided that she was amused. She was very far from being a fool. But she was known to have a positive horror of persons who tended to become instructive. Moreover, she never saw him at his best. Like most men, he was a little in love with her, and that upset him.

He was seized with a tremor of panic as his car turned off the high road, with its flanking hedges and telegraph poles, through lodge gates into Lyndon Park. It was the first time in his life that he had ever felt shy and he did not like it at all. He tried to key himself into the temper of a bold and daring raider snatching a bride from a hostile stronghold. This descent upon Lyndon ought to have a sort of " Young Lochinvar " swoop in it. But the illusion was destroyed by his slow and spasmodic progress down the park. The swoop was barred by innumerable gates, for

Sir John, who bred pedigree cattle, had divided the park into
a series of fields. At each gate the car stopped and Hubert
began to grow impatient. Eager now to have arrived, he
sat well forward as the car slid along as though his urgent
attitude might increase their pace. The road lay slightly
downhill, for Lyndon, like many houses of its period, was
built in a hole. The park was really a long, tree-studded
slope, ending in water meadows.

In the last field he perceived the approach of two young
women, and identified one of them with a start of pleasure.
It was not too much to believe that she had come to meet
him. As for her companion, a slender person in white, she
was probably his hostess. He was only a little in love with
Lady Clewer. As the car drew nearer he set up a delighted
grin while he was yet some way off, but, realizing how
foolish this must appear by the time he reached them, he
banished it from his features and only allowed it to light up
again when the car stopped beside them. Out he bounded
in a torrent of polite greetings and shook their self-possessed
hands. The car, with his luggage, slipped off again towards
the cluster of trees which hid Lyndon, and he was left in
the midst of solitary pastures with his two companions.

The insignificant other was not Lady Clewer, he discovered, but one Cynthia, a half-sister. He knew her by
sight, having admired her beauty from a barge at the
" Eights," but he had never been formally introduced. She
was, apparently, not out, since her hair still hung down her
back. She greeted him with a demureness suitable to her
situation, flashed one disturbing look out of her dark eyes
and immediately veiled them with the longest lashes he had
ever seen. In a becoming silence she walked home upon his
left hand.

All his attention was given to Lois, who was looking
brilliant and happy in her yellow dress. She was obviously
delighted to see him ; friendliness beamed in her little blue

eyes and bade him welcome. Walking in that green field he thought her like some sturdy, shining spring flower—a marsh marigold perhaps.

"Nobody else is staying with us," she said, "except a cousin of Mother's, Sir Thomas Bragge. He's come to advise her about some investments or something. He's rather an awful old gentleman, but quite harmless really. He has made a lot of money, I forget how, and is going to build a house. He'll tell you about it. Then a cousin of Agatha's, a brilliant young doctor, is expected shortly on a rest cure from overwork."

Hubert, who was on the look out for possible rivals, felt a little apprehensive. His spirits, which had soared when he heard Sir Thomas called an awful old gentleman, came to the ground at the mention of the brilliant young doctor. But he reflected that the fellow might possibly be married. Doctors often marry young and married men often overwork.

"Then," said Lois, "there is John's brother, James. Have you met him?"

"I don't think so. He wasn't with you in town, was he?"

"No. He was in Paris. He's just come back. He's been there for three years. He's an artist, you know."

"No. No, I didn't know. An artist?"

Hubert had some difficulty in digesting the idea of an artist among the Clewers.

"Yes. And I'm anxious to know what you think of his work. I rather like some of it. But of course," she added modestly, "I'm no judge."

His gallantry did not prompt him to contradict her. As a disciple she was exquisite, but as a judge . . . no! Later on, perhaps, when she should be a little more matured, he might temper this decision. But at present her enthusiasms were too indiscriminate, though she evinced a tendency to draw back and modify her opinions in deference to his experience which pleased and touched him.

They passed through the last gate and proceeded up the avenue of elms leading to the house. Lyndon, architectural and complacent, gleamed whitely amid the sombre green of ilex and cedar. Its classical façade stretched in ample wings to East and West. The grounds, originally laid out by the famous " Capability Brown," and improved upon by successive generations of landscape gardeners, were admirably in keeping with the dwelling-house they guarded. They maintained its note of assured artificiality : they belonged to an age when gentlemen of property owned the earth and could do what they liked with it—an age which had not read Wordsworth and which took for granted that Nature could be improved upon. The measured, decorative mind of man was everywhere apparent. Upon the knolls in the shrubberies were to be found pensive little temples to Friendship and Solitude. A long stone terrace ran the whole length of the south side of the house. This bordered on a vast lawn leading to sloping rose gardens which descended to the Holmbrook, a tributary of the Isis.

Lois led Hubert round to the lawn where the party was gathered for tea. They walked slowly, conversing volubly as was their habit. Already he was beginning to draw comparisons between the candid loquacity of Miss Martin and the provocative silence of Miss Clewer. This Cynthia was a piece of goods ! Despite his preoccupation with her sister he had been made aware of it. He could not quite make out how she had done it, for she had said nothing during the whole of her short walk with them. He rather wanted to hear her speak. It would perhaps be polite to address a remark to her.

" Do you know, when I first saw you, I thought you were Lady Clewer."

He had not meant to say this. But there was something about the girl that provoked one to personalities.

" Oh, Agatha ? She would never walk as far as this. She never goes anywhere except in a car, you know."

There was an undercurrent of contempt in her voice and he surmised that she disliked her sister-in-law. Nor could he be surprised when he caught sight of his hostess in the distance and felt anew all the shock of her beauty. She sat under an enormous cedar tree in the middle of the lawn, presiding over her guests with unhurried grace, and as he approached he knew that she must be a galling chaperon for Cynthia. Lois suffered less. She had vitality, the charm of eager interests and a lively mind. Even at Lady Clewer's side she must have her appeal. She could never be completely overlooked. Hubert, for instance, preferred her infinitely. But the unfortunate Cynthia was doomed to a perpetual eclipse, since she was of the same type as her senior and not nearly so effective. Both were sirens—lovely, indolent and exotic ; both had achieved that air of expensive fragility which is beauty's most precious setting. But Lady Clewer with her cool, witty assurance, her youthful maturity, possessed unfair advantages. As a married woman she could wear richer clothing. She, too, was clad in white this afternoon, but of some clear, silky-soft material, matching her pearls and bestowed about her with a sort of subtle amplitude, while Cynthia had to put up with the harsh, maidenly lines of starched *piqué*.

The guests under the tree were mostly very young men who had come out from Oxford for tennis, and games were still in progress on the raised courts at either side of the lawn. Also there was Sir Thomas Bragge, an important and rubicund-looking person. Lois had called him old but he really was not : it was his grossness which had created the illusion of age in her fastidious mind. Certainly he was awful. He sat sunk deeply in a deck chair at Lady Clewer's right hand, his portly stomach bulging gently upward and heaving with his occasional rumbling guffaws. Never for a moment did he remove from his hostess a gaze of unqualified admiration, devouring her with small, unabashed eyes.

Behind her chair, dominating the background, hovered the master of the house. He was pleasant and attentive, more silent than most of the throng, but obviously the host.

Lois and Hubert crossed the brilliant turf a little nervously and advanced into the middle of the group. The guest was greeted with a cordiality which cheered him. Lady Clewer gave him an unmistakably kind glance; it told him that she was his ally and his heart warmed to her. Sympathy, he instantly decided, was the secret of her charm. Her beauty was but the symbol of a generous temper and she deserved all the homage she got. With new courage he turned to greet the formidable dowager who was approaching briskly from the house with the air of having concluded competently some very important business. She ran her sharp eyes critically over the company, and he found himself beginning to wilt again under her appraising looks. He doubted whether she would ever think him good enough for Lois and began feverishly to rehearse to himself a statement of his income. This reassured him, for he really had quite a lot of money. He was able to control his surprise when the dowager said, in her heavy, uncoloured voice:

" I have a favour to ask of you, Mr. Ervine."

He almost bounded from his chair in his eagerness to serve her, but he was a little dashed when he heard what the favour was. It appeared that Lyndon possessed a Village Reading Union, patronized by the aristocracy; an institution whereby culture was administered in small doses to deserving rustics and contingents of the Lyndon housemaids.

" We meet on Friday evenings," said the lady, fixing him with an uncompromising regard. " And, whenever we can, we get kind people to read us papers on literary subjects. Now I'm sure you . . ."

" Oh, well," he murmured, " literature isn't my . . ."

" It's Modern Art, your subject, isn't it ? " said she wisely.

All the young men in white flannels left off eating their tea to look at the fellow whose subject was Modern Art. Or so it seemed to him. In desperation he threw an appealing glance at James, the artist, who should surely have helped him out. But no assistance was coming from that quarter. James was not going to talk. Seated on the edge of the group, as it were, he was eating up his tea with a quick despatch and paying no attention to the conversation. Hubert was disgusted and decided that James was probably a cubist. Anyhow, he was a very ugly brute.

" I'm afraid," said his tormentor, " that Modern Art wouldn't be quite suitable . . . just a little beyond us at present. It's only simple village folk, Mr. Ervine. No! But I was wondering if you could manage to give us a paper on Dante. That would be a splendid subject ! "

" Dante ! But, my dear lady, I know nothing about him."

" Oh, I'm sure you do ! All people interested in art must. Such a subject for great pictures. . . . Burne-Jones, you know . . . and all those. And you've lived in Italy so much. I'm sure you could tell us a great deal which we do not know."

Hubert wondered if he looked as ill as he felt. In a sickish voice he protested. He said he knew nothing about Italy before the Renaissance. He offered to lecture upon modern Italian novels if she liked. But Lady Clewer, who was a little suspicious of all continental novels, stuck to Dante. She would have nothing else. She bore him down and he dropped the subject until he could argue it out in a less public place. He was deeply disturbed and felt that she must have done it on purpose. She could have hit upon no surer means of making a fool of him and his intellect, which was very hard when he could be clever in so many ways. He wondered miserably whether he could entreat Lois not to come and listen to him, supposing he was forced to read this wretched paper. He looked at her and caught a glance of amused sympathy. Directing her regard to her mother, she assumed for an instant an expression of despair. This confidential by-play relieved him and he began to hope that he might carry the thing off creditably.

The meal drew to an end and some of the players returned to the courts. James, the artist, having finished his substantial tea, brought his cup and plate and placed them on the tray in front of his sister-in-law. She greeted this ceremony with a smile and a murmur of thanks.

"Are you going to work, this lovely evening?" she asked with some commiseration.

He nodded and shambled off towards the house.

"He works too hard," she said, turning to Hubert. "I've never seen anyone work so. He uses an attic with a large north window and he simply lives up there. He should take more exercise. But Lady Clewer," with a nod at the dowager, "finds a good many energetic little things for him to do."

"What's his line?" asked Hubert. "In Paris, wasn't he? Who did he work with?"

Lady Clewer considered for a moment and then recollected a name which galvanized Hubert slightly.

"Oh! . . . He can draw then . . ." he stated thoughtfully.

"Can he?"

Lady Clewer looked amused.

"Who? James?" cried the dowager, who had been busy telling Sir Thomas that he must lecture on Blake at her Reading Union. "Oh, yes! James can draw. He could draw when he was quite little, couldn't you, James?

Where is he? Has he gone? How tiresome! I wanted
him to take a note down to the village for me. And now
he will be up all those stairs. Miss Barrington, kindly run
up to his studio and tell him to come and speak to me,
please. In my sitting-room."

She hastened into the house, driving her secretary before
her. Sir Thomas turned to his hostess with renewed gusto.
Hubert felt a faint distaste at seeing them side by side.
So fair a nymph and so foul a satyr were too striking an
essay in contrast. These blatant tributes of admiration
should have sickened her, but they obviously did not. She
looked at Sir Thomas with palpable amusement, as though
she perceived in his regard something to which she was but
too well accustomed, and which, in him, diverted her by
its obviousness. The same amusement was reflected upon
the face of her husband as he strolled away towards the
house a moment later. Hubert surmised that the possessor
of such a wife must get used to a good deal.

"All the same," he said to himself, "I'd put my foot
down if any man looked at my wife like that. But I suppose
Clewer knows his own business."

A short sojourn in that household proved to him that
Clewer knew his own business perfectly well. That very
evening he routed Sir Thomas completely in the matter of
a canoe. The night was exceptionally warm and after
dinner it was agreed that a turn on the river would be
pleasant. Lady Clewer and Sir Thomas led the way to the
lowest terrace of the rose garden, where a small landing-
stage had been put up. A punt and a canoe strained gently
at their moorings and Sir Thomas, with crackling shirt-front
and many stertorous breathings, stooped at once to the
latter and began to pile it with gay cushions. The proceed-
ing took some time since the current continually carried
the frail craft beyond his reach. Lady Clewer, on the
landing-stage, watched in brooding silence the last streaks

of sunset smouldering on the edge of the water meadow. At length her cavalier, having prepared a resting-place for her, straightened himself for the delicate, delicious business of placing her in the canoe. There was no lady. Her husband, joining them, had with silent determination handed her into the punt, upon the deck of which he now stood, arrogantly wielding a pole. Sir Thomas made a chagrined attempt to plant himself upon the cushions at her side but was frustrated by the dowager.

Marian was not intending to accompany them, as she had important letters to write. But she had pursued them thus far expressly, so Hubert believed, to wreck his chances of an interview with Lois. She drove Sir Thomas back to the canoe and gave him Cynthia by way of consolation. Lois and Hubert were put into the punt and the party pushed off into midstream, leaving the matron upon the rose terrace. Her voice boomed down the dusky reaches after them, warning them not to stay out if the dew was heavy.

They slipped between green banks, sniffing the new-mown hay in wide, silent fields. Far ahead the canoe, with its ill-assorted freight, disappeared into the gloaming beneath some tall trees which overhung the stream. Wild roses, close to the water's edge, splashed the darkness like little moons, their faint sweetness lost in the rich savour of Sir John's cigar. Lady Clewer talked to Hubert in a voice pitched low to match the space and leisure of the night.

" Do you know," she said, " we have something rather terrible to break to you. I'm afraid it will be a shock. You will have to lecture on Dante at the Village Room next Friday, for it has been already billed."

" What ! Since tea ? "

" No ! The bills were up before you came."

" It's a little way she has," observed Lois. " I expect she'll make Mr. Blair give a lecture."

" If she'll let him lecture on neurosis I'm sure he won't mind, for he can talk of nothing else."

" Oh . . . is he a nerve specialist ? " asked Hubert.

" More or less; though he seems to dabble in diseases of the brain. I can never remember quite what his official line is. It's all so modern."

" Quite young, isn't he ? "

" Oh, yes. Young as they go, I suppose."

" Very young to have got so far as he has, Agatha," put in Sir John.

" Married ? " asked Hubert carelessly.

The lady started slightly and paused a second before saying : " No. Not married."

They fell silent, pushing through a reedy backwater, while far off, across the flat, mysterious fields, the bells of Oxford rang down the evening. When at last they returned to the landing-stage, they found the dowager wandering impatiently in the gathering night.

" I came to call Cynthia," she cried. " There's a heavy dew and she has only that thin muslin. Where is she ? What ? Somewhere in the canoe with Sir Thomas ? How tiresome of them to be so late ! "

" Poor Cynthia," whispered Lois to Hubert, as they walked up through the garden. " How awful to spend this heavenly evening alone in a canoe with Sir Thomas ! "

2.

Hubert's execution on the pianoforte was energetic and skilful. He could go on playing, rapidly and accurately, for a long time. Lois, as she listened to him, was glad that he had not heard her Sussex Cycle. She knew now that he would see through it. He would be very polite and tell her that her work was effective, and adjective which, three weeks ago, she would have accepted as a compliment. But

she had learnt a good deal lately. Beholding her composi-
tions with new eyes she blushed for them. She had become
aware that the few really great works of art in the world
are all relentlessly professional, and the others are scarcely
worth mention.

In the past week she had begun to grasp in detail her
new friend's attitude towards the arts. She thought it
austere yet fascinating. Despite her mother's vigilance
they had enjoyed several long and enchanting conversations
and she found herself adopting many of his views. He was
so delightfully arrogant in the laws he laid down; she
longed to be able to speak with that assurance, that air of
initiation. He had confessed to her the history of his own
inner life, and how, in his fear of producing work which
might be second-rate, he had decided that it would be
better to do none at all. Rather than betray himself as
the gifted amateur, he preferred to remain the mere critic,
the friend of great men. His attitude struck her as very
noble. Also it possessed undoubted compensations.

Beyond the window she could hear fragments of a
prolonged conversation. Agatha was sitting on the terrace
with that disagreeable cousin of hers. Lois and Hubert
did not like Mr. Blair. They thought him a dreary fellow,
and his reputed brilliance in medicine did not excuse his
lack of humour. He trod heavily on their witty conversation;
indeed, he could scarcely open his mouth without saying
something which contravened the taste of the house. He
was serious, to the point of ill-temper, when they jested,
and then he was unjustifiably flippant. His ill-judged
sarcasms looked very shabby beside the agreeable audacities
which flowed so easily from Hubert. Nobody had any
patience with him but Agatha who was, after all, his cousin.
And it had been her mother who had sent him there.

Mrs. Cocks, now a widow, was enjoying a popularity as
conspicuous as ever. Her activities were innumerable

and so were her friends. These she was in the habit of
sending to Lyndon whenever they were recovering from
an illness. The place, she said, was as good as a hydro;
John and Agatha were so lazy themselves that they required
almost nothing from their guests. The cooking was perfect
and nobody need come down before lunch-time. Meeting
Gerald one day in town she had been shocked at his look
of fatigue. Under cross-examination he had admitted to
sleeplessness and overwork. Forthwith she had proffered
an invitation to Oxfordshire on her daughter's behalf.
Despite his earnest protests she had insisted upon his going,
and, once planted at Lyndon, he seemed too much exhausted
to go away, though he liked little that he found there.
Hubert was especially uncongenial to him, and all the while,
as he talked to Agatha, he was frowning irritably because
of the din in the drawing-room. At last he broke off to
exclaim :

"Isn't that fellow playing much too fast ? "

"He always does," replied Agatha. "He belongs to
that generation. Mrs. Gordon Clewer, John's great-aunt,
explained it to me once. Have you met her ? "

"No. But I've heard her quoted."

"One does, doesn't one ? Well, she says that about
twenty years ago there was a great reaction against young
ladies' drawing-room music. It was felt to be amateurish
and inefficient. All the clever young men took to playing
very fast, just to show that they could do it. Nowadays
there is no particular merit in pace, as people don't usually
play at all unless they can do it well. So the most modern
performers try to go more or less by what the composers
obviously intended. But there is still a school which
believes that there is something intrinsically a little vicious
in Largos and Andantes."

She laughed as Hubert galloped with evident embarrassment through the pathos of a slow movement and crashed

joyfully into a finale conveniently marked Presto. But
her cousin did not laugh : his scowl of annoyance deepened.
He was sitting well forward in his deck chair, ignoring the
cushions which stretched away untenanted behind him.
His attitude irritated her ; she thought that no one else
at Lyndon would so use a chair meant for relaxation.
John and Hubert could lounge very effectively, giving an
attractive picture of muscularity in repose. Sir Thomas
would sag heavily, straining to their utmost the frail canvas
and tintacks. But Gerald did not seem to know how to
take his ease and had sometimes a very lofty air towards
the comfort of other people. She had once asked him,
teasingly, if he never leant back in his chair ; he had laughed
and adopted an easier posture, but, a moment later, she
was aware that he surveyed her own graceful lassitude
with a detached severity.

This detachment was beginning to alarm her. She had
observed it on the rare occasions when they met in town,
but she had never thought that it meant very much. At
Lyndon, however, it became uncomfortably obvious that
he belonged to another world, and it did not please her
that he made no attempt to adjust himself. She was
disappointed in him. He looked unkempt and he said the
wrong things. Four years had changed him unbelievably.
He had lost his vitality and wit. He was becoming intolerant
and dogmatic. She missed the personable, audacious companion of her childish escapades. And she was sure that
he criticized her.

She knew that his hateful, mysterious work, the career
to which he had prematurely sacrificed his youth, had done
all this to him. She had asked him about it, anxious to
discover something of the grim world which had absorbed
him and made him a stranger. And he began to tell her,
with a growing eagerness, of his work in a Parisian clinic.
She thought it all rather horrible, shivering at the images

he conjured up—the whitewashed walls, the smell of antiseptics, the bleak exposure of human agony, the alien standards of relentless toil. Yet these things were his life, just as Lyndon was hers, so she must listen.

Hubert ran down at last and the piano in the drawing-room was silent. Lyndon was hushed save for the perpetual humming of mowing machines on distant lawns. The musician and his lady came out on to the terrace. They both seemed to be very pleased with themselves and Hubert was humming :

> " Non mi dir
> Bell' idol mio
> Che son io
> Crudel con te."

Lois hoped, with a faint suggestion of superiority, that the music had not disturbed anyone.

" Not at all," rejoined Agatha sweetly. " We liked listening. But we were wondering why Mr. Ervine always plays so fast."

" Do I play fast ? " parried Hubert, looking pleased.

" It seemed to us that we had never heard that Beethoven played so fast before."

" Most people play it too slowly," he stated.

" Yes ? I wonder why that is ? "

" Of course, it's a matter of taste," Lois told them.

" Why yes, I thought it might be that," considered Agatha.

Hubert looked unhappy and she instantly said something which restored his equanimity, for it gave him an opportunity of displaying his knowledge of the moderns. He took her lead and they began a discussion which made Lois a little jealous. It was unfair that Agatha should be able to talk so well about things of which she really knew nothing at all. It was not as if she even pretended to knowledge

or to any settled standards of taste. Her levity was shocking ;
she admitted to ignorances which would have covered Lois
with mortification, and dismissed an acknowledged master-
piece airily as being too long and apt to bore her. Yet
Hubert did not crush her, or lay down the law, he merely
exerted himself to be amusing. It was strange how beauty
could make a man forget himself. But perhaps he was
secretly so contemptuous that he did not think her worth
snubbing. Lois, remembering how didactic he could be
in other company, trusted that this was so.

Gerald also was puzzled. He perceived that his cousin
was talking with unexpected ability and it occurred to him
that she might be wasting a very exceptional brain in this
futile life of hers. Ervine was evidently the sort of man
she liked, since she was so ready to use her wits when she
talked to him. She was looking animated and amused.
She did not see what a mountebank the fellow really was.
Strange creature !

Agatha thought that the silent pair must be brought
back into the conversation and turned to Lois, saying :

" Has Mr. Ervine heard you sing that religious song
you have ? You know ! The one about the procession."

Lois was alarmed, wondering which of the songs she
would rather not sing to Hubert was about to be disinterred.
Agatha, however, recollected the name and it was quite a
safe one. Hubert leapt at it delightedly and began to hum :

" La foule autour d'un chêne antique
    S'incline, en adorant."

" Wonderful, that octave descent ! " he told them.
" Have you ever heard Mass in a Breton church ? Have
you seen the wave that goes over the people when the Host
is raised ? Like the wind over a sea of corn. . . . It's
thrilling. He's got it exactly. That's devotional, if ever
music was."

" Not a bit of it," put in Gerald, seizing his opportunity.
" I don't agree with you at all. When first I heard that
thing it struck me as being absolutely false. Music can't
be devotional unless it's written devotionally. That fellow
isn't on his knees himself. He's outside the thing, thinking
how effective it all is. It may be a magnificent song, but
it's too self-conscious to be devotional. It doesn't in the
least remind me of Mass in a Breton church ; at least, I'm
sure it wouldn't if I'd ever heard Mass in a Breton church.
But it does convey an excellent impression of you, Ervine,
being thrilled at the simple faith of the peasant."

" It's always interesting," said Hubert in a nasty voice,
" to entrap the scientific mind into an opinion on the arts.
You especially, Blair, are generally so cautious. You stray
so rarely beyond the fields of medical science and social
economics. It's a treat to hear you give yourself away."

" I expect he includes music in social economics," said
Agatha, who was entertained by the antagonism between
the men. " They are so amazingly elastic, you know.
They can be made to include almost anything."

" Not music," Hubert assured her. " Dear lady, music
at least has nothing economic about it. We may thank
Heaven for that ! "

Agatha frowned, not at Hubert's piety, but because
she did not like people who said " dear lady." She was
quite pleased with Gerald for replying contentiously :

" Yes it has. All art is founded upon economics."

Hubert groaned.

" But it is," persisted Gerald. " Every opinion you
express betrays your social status. Your tastes are all
acquired tastes ; and acquired tastes are the mark of the
man of leisure."

" Well, there's something in that," agreed Hubert.

" And what's an acquired taste but a piece of conspicuous
waste ? Waste of time. Proof that the acquirer has time

to waste. Proof that he needn't work. Why do Chinese grandees let their finger-nails grow? Why do they crush their wives' feet? Same reason."

Hubert remained contemptuously silent, but Lois contributed a remark. She thought it was time she spoke, so she hazarded:

"Taste isn't always confined to the leisured classes, surely. What about . . . er . . . Robert Burns, for instance?"

"Do you think his taste was always very good?" asked Gerald.

"Well, then . . . genius . . ." she amended.

"Not at all the same thing," Hubert told her.

She saw that it was not, but was uncertain whether genius or taste were the nicer quality to possess. Gerald continued to dogmatize about the leisured classes:

"Taste is merely a laborious form of auto-suggestion, upon which only an idle man can embark. But, like a public school education, it gives you a certain *cachet* by reason of its very uselessness. Look at it like this. The leisured class was originally released from the necessity of earning its own bread in order that it might preserve the State in safety. As things become more civilized this work gets handed over to paid officials and then the mere possession of leisure comes to be the mark of the aristocrat. People invent all these ways of showing they are leisured . . . sport and culture and so on. Complete bureaucracy and the golden age of art generally arrive together. A really useful aristocracy doesn't have time for culture. It's too busy doing its job; governing the herd and fighting the foe, and all that sort of thing. Its pleasures are simple and it shares them with the masses. The Norman knight, even the hunting squire in the eighteenth century, was not so far removed in culture from the hind at the plough as Clewer is from one of his farm labourers."

John put his head out of the window behind them and said : " I don't agree."

He had been sitting in the smoking-room with Sir Thomas, but, catching the drift of Gerald's remarks, he now came and balanced on the low window-sill, explaining :

" I'm not an aristocrat who has left off being really useful. I spent most of to-day in a stuffy court-house fining people for riding their bicycles on the pavement, don't you know. And what do I get for it ? Somebody has to do it. But why should I ? "

" Now, Clewer ! Do you really think that bullying people two days a week can be called a life work ? "

" That's not all," said John modestly. " Agatha's mother says I'm going into Parliament some day. Of course," he added with British haste, " I don't pretend to artistic tastes and so on. But I know what I like, and I don't deny that having decent things about the place," he glanced over his perfect lawns and then at his wife, . . . " pictures and things, you know . . . it does make a difference to me. And my point is that these chaps owe it to us for all we do for them."

Agatha laughed, as she always did when her husband referred to the proletariat as " these chaps." But she grew grave when she heard Gerald say :

" Well, I admit that you are more useful than Ervine here, and consequently you make fewer claims to culture. It only bears out what I say. That's why the women of the leisured class go in for art more, on the whole, than the men do."

" Oh, the women," she murmured. " We are perfect monuments of conspicuous waste, I suppose."

" Of course you are. The ideal of beauty set up before the women of a leisured class is almost always incompatible with usefulness. They must look incapable of hard work ;

their dress must hamper them; their health is often injured; their duties as mothers are set aside. They are to be decorative luxuries, unfitted for any uses save one, and they must look it. Simply because that's a standard of appearance which can't be attained by the working classes. Women like . . ."

His eye wandered round the company and he looked a little disconcerted for a moment. Then he boldly continued:

"Such women . . . women of the odalisque type, are symbols of an assured, unearned income. A piece of blatant waste, like a scratch handicap. . . ."

He broke off and met the glance of his cousin. She sat there, looking so like and yet so unlike his lost love that he was silenced. He could scarcely believe that this was not she but the husk of her, the beautiful tomb, the unhappy, corruptible flesh which had once clothed an ardent spirit. He had to remind himself that the soul was gone, dead and buried beneath the gorgeousness of Lyndon.

She had listened to his strictures upon her and her kind without modifying her languorous pose. With a gentle mockery she looked him over and then gave him that quick, soft smile which was her last weapon. Her husband marked it and grinned.

"I know that in theory beauty and utility should go together," she said mildly. "But practically I have never found that they do. Do you really find most idle women plain, Gerald?"

Very few men could have continued to say that they did, but he was obdurate. He considered the question, staring at his boots, and then said:

"I see a good many in a professional way. They are not beautiful. They are generally appalling."

"But," she took him up with more energy, "you don't see anything to admire in these wretched, squalid women one sees in slums and places, surely? You don't call them beautiful?"

"An overworked woman is a shocking sight," he agreed. "Though not as bad as one who does no work at all. Our society is made up of extremes. We have lost all standards of how a woman should look."

"A beautiful woman," observed Hubert, "is a work of art in herself. But then we have learnt that Blair has no use for works of art."

"I never said that," exclaimed Gerald. "Works of art are all right. So are artists. But I don't include them in the leisured class. The man of leisure is an amateur. When he leaves off being that, he leaves off being a man of leisure. His art isn't an exploit, it's a profession."

"Quite," said Hubert. "I agree. But the cultured amateur forms the cream of the artist's public."

"I doubt it. He's a drone, and inclined to demand work which only drones can appreciate. Work which is an acquired taste . . ."

The sight of James Clewer wandering round the corner of the house reminded them that at Lyndon they were not all drones. They had an artist with them. Agatha called to him and he joined them with an expression of vague dissatisfaction.

"What were you looking for, James?"

"Oh . . . for Dolly. . . ."

"Dolly? What Dolly?"

"Dolly Kell."

"Kell! Kell, the housemaid? What did you want?"

"Some bits of rag to clean my brushes."

"I'll tell her to bring some up to you. Listen! Do our standards of taste make any difference to the pictures you paint?"

"What?"

James looked terribly startled.

"We are discussing taste. You know; saying one picture is second-rate and another decorative, and so on. You must have heard it done. Do you see any point in it?"

"I know what you mean. In Paris they used to talk a lot about those things. The ones who drew worst talked most. I didn't listen."

"Then it makes no difference to you what we think of art?"

"No! Why should it?"

"We are the cream of your public."

James looked horrified. He cast a scared glance round the group and withdrew hastily. John, who was afraid they would begin discussing art again, looked at his watch and mentioned that the first gong had gone some time ago. They dispersed, leaving the issue undecided. Twenty minutes later John opened the door between his room and Agatha's, and finding that her maid had gone, he left it ajar so that he could talk to her while he finished dressing.

"Not a bad sort, Ervine," he called through. "I quite like him, in spite of his parlour tricks. Hope he and Lois make a match of it."

"They seem to be very well suited," replied Agatha. "Do you know at all what Lady Clewer thinks of it? It struck me that she is taking pains to keep them apart."

"Oh, that's nothing. It doesn't mean disapproval. She thinks it puts a girl's price up to keep her well chaperoned. I think I agree."

"You would."

"And in any case, I happen to know that Mamma was getting rather worried about Lois and James. Thought they saw too much of each other. Rather late in the day, what?"

"It's perfect nonsense."

"'Course it is. James is more presentable than he was,

and that's all you can say for him. Lois wouldn't look at him and I can't say I see much sign of his looking at Lois. But Mamma's anxious. It's natural in a mother to get worried, I suppose. They all do."

Agatha said nothing. She had never, consciously, been a mother. Her child, though born alive, had not survived long enough to engage her attention. By the time she had recovered from the anæsthetic sufficiently to ask for it her brief maternity was already over.

John continued, after a pause :

" No, what really does annoy me about James is the impossible way he goes chasing round after that housemaid. You never saw that scene the other day. She was polishing the floor in the library when we all went up to find some book or other. The poor girl was trying to melt away quietly, as she certainly should have done ; but not a bit of it ! James rushes up to her, greets her effusively as his dear Dolly, and inquires after her aunt's bronchitis. 'Pon my word, I thought he meant to kiss her ! "

" Well, but isn't she a very old friend of his ? I'm sure Lady Clewer told me that her aunt was housekeeper here and ran the place when your mother died."

" Old Mrs. Kell, do you mean ? "

" Yes. She's Kell's aunt by marriage, and she's practically brought her up. I believe the child had a mother, but couldn't live at home because of a very unsatisfactory step-father who ultimately went off his head or something. I know Lady Clewer told me some very tragic story when first I engaged the girl. She seems to have stayed here a good deal with her aunt, when she was little. You must have been away at school, so you don't remember. But, being much of an age with James, she used to play with him. So he really has some reason for asking after her aunt's bronchitis."

" It's not that I object to, it's his manner of doing it. She didn't like it at all, poor girl. She's well trained enough, and she hadn't an idea what to make of him. She was very stiff and ' Thank you, sir, I'm sure ' with him. And then he gapes at her as if she'd slapped his face and asks if anything is the matter. And it isn't as if these scenes only took place in the bosom of the family. Blair and Bragge were there, and what they made of it I don't know. I don't take to Blair, by the way, Agatha. Talks too much, doesn't he? I was expecting you to shut him up. You don't generally tolerate people who preach."

" He doesn't generally talk as much as that. I egged him on to-day."

" I didn't think much of his views either. Practically Socialism, don't you know. Bad taste to force it on people."

" His general turn of mind is affected a good deal by living in France so much, I think."

" What ? The way he talks about women do you mean ? "

" No, I didn't," she said with some irritation. " I'm sure I don't know where he got his views from, and I don't agree with them. I mean that his manner, the way he discusses things, puts us out. It mayn't be French particularly ; he may have picked it up in America. Only he takes exactly the same tone about everything, even when he's serious. English people put on a special manner to show when they are serious ; they either become solemn or excessively flippant. And anyhow they don't like discussing really important things. They seem to think that there is something belittling in conversation. They don't regard it as continentals do."

" Awful beasts, the French," asserted John cheerfully. " They made me sick. Agatha ! If you can't fix these studs, I shall have to ring for Peters."

She strolled in, cool and elegant, and arranged his difficulties for him. As she did so he heard her murmur .

" Passionate . . . discursive . . . and unsentimental. . . ."

" What's that ? "

With an arm behind her shoulders he detained her.

" I was trying to sum up in my own mind the character-
istics of the best of the French nation. But they are rather
fox, goose, and cabbage qualities to the Anglo-Saxon mind.
Really, John, take care, or you'll have powder coming off on
your sleeve."

" You can put on some more in a minute when I've
finished. Tell me, is that chap . . . Blair . . . what is it
. . . passionate, discursive . . ."

" And unsentimental. He might be. I don't know him
as well as I used."

John reflected upon the first of these qualifications and
said :

" Well, now, I should have called him rather a St. Thin-
gummy. You know, the fellow who threw the inkpot at
the lady. What are you laughing at ? He is. I saw a
beautiful woman smile at him this afternoon and he didn't
so much as blink."

" He didn't see," she said quickly.

" Oh, didn't he ? I'm inclined to think that he did. But
I expect he thinks it's an insult to argue with a woman as if
she was one. He's that sort."

" What ! You think it was on purpose ? "

" Of course it was. The man's not an absolute fool."

" He thought it would be rather degrading to lower the
conversation to the level of gallantry."

" He's that sort, I tell you. A cold-blooded fish."

" But it would have been, wouldn't it ? "

" What ? "

" Rather degrading ? "

" I don't know." He released her as the gong rang. " The
whole discussion bored me personally. Does my sleeve
really need brushing ? "

3.

Upon the following morning, John and Sir Thomas departed with some ceremony for the Cheltenham races. The car which was to take them was a large one, but when they had packed themselves into it, with their greatcoats, and their road maps and their glasses, they filled it completely. The other guests, gathered on the steps, called injunctions as to the money they wished these emissaries to make for them. John replied briefly that he would put nothing on for anybody but himself; Sir Thomas, however, agreed with leering alacrity to make a little for Cynthia.

As the chauffeur was climbing into his place, the lady of the house appeared among the group upon the steps and informed the world that it was going to be a wet day. It had been bright too early, said she. Everyone was surprised to see her, for she seldom rose before lunch-time and her statement that it had been bright too early was greeted with some mockery upon this account.

The car hummed up the avenue and several large raindrops spotted the whiteness of the steps in answer to her prophecy. A sudden wind blew all the leaves silver against a leaden sky, and the party fled into the hall for shelter. Agatha then explained the reason of her early appearance. She was due to lunch with her mother on the other side of Oxfordshire and would be starting immediately.

" I don't suppose I'll get away until terribly late," she said. " My mother will have a hundred things to talk about. I'm rather afraid," turning to Hubert, " that I may be a little late for your lecture. It's at six, isn't it ? But you'll forgive me ? I'll get away as soon as ever I can. I'll come home through the village and run straight in to the Institute. Then I can hear as much as possible."

Hubert, who had been looking very miserable since breakfast, assured her with perfect sincerity that he would not mind in the least if she missed his lecture altogether. Looking round cautiously to see that the dowager was not in hearing, he said :

" I'm afraid I'm no democrat. I have no desire to lift the masses."

" A genuine democrat hasn't," rejoined Gerald instantly. " He thinks they are all right as they are."

With an imploring look, Hubert drew Agatha aside :

" Can you tell me," he asked nervously, " if there are any books on Dante in this house ? "

" Oh, there must be. Let's go and look in the library."

She took him upstairs. The library was a long, beautiful room with six windows looking out over the park. It was seldom used by the household. Miss Barrington worked there occasionally, and Kell, the third housemaid, expended much labour upon the polished floor.

The chill severity of the place abashed Hubert. Its classic simplicity made him feel slightly uncomfortable. Its long array of solid, calf-bound books seemed to cheapen his " two-pence coloured " culture and put him out of humour with the showy little lecture which he was composing. It was as if the presiding spirits of the place, the scholars and the polished stylists of the eighteenth century, were frowning on him from the lofty cases where their busts ruled the solitude. He moved his eye quickly from Voltaire to Johnson, and from Johnson to Swift, and turned to examine the view from one of the windows. Even Agatha shivered a little at the frigid atmosphere of the place with its composite smell of erudite vellum and furniture polish.

" I'll have a fire lighted," she said. " It's quite cold. Then you can write your lecture up here in peace and quietness. But first we will find Miss Barrington and ask her about books on Dante."

She rang the bell.

" This is an admirable room, isn't it ? " said Hubert.

" Yes, but I'm a little afraid of it. The sight of so much learning makes me feel that my own knowledge is very meretricious. Don't you agree that it ought to be rather void of furniture, like this ? When I first came here it was quite full of chesterfields ; Lady Clewer is very fond of them and in a room of this size she was really able to have as many as she wanted. But I insisted on moving them out. Oh, Kell ! Will you light the fire, please ? And will you ask Miss Barrington if she will be so good as to come here for a moment ? "

Miss Barrington, when she came, was most helpful. There was a very fine edition of Dante, she said. Hubert's face fell, and she hastened to add that there were several translations, including Carlyle. There were also Boccaccio's Commentaries, *Il Duca di Sermoneta*, and several other heavy-looking tomes. The lecturer regarded them dubiously.

" Let me see," he said. " My lecture is at six this evening. I haven't got very long. And to tell you the truth, I've written absolutely nothing yet. I know nothing about the fellow, you see. Really nothing ! You haven't by any chance some quite small handbook which epitomizes the whole thing ? "

Agatha had seated herself in a tall, straight-backed chair. She looked at him with severity.

" Oh, no," she protested.

" I'm afraid it will have to be."

" But not from you ! "

" The second-rate at second-hand ? Dear lady, what else am I to do in the time ? I put it to you ! I didn't ask to give this lecture, did I ? The whole thing is abhorrent to me."

" I have a little book," suggested Miss Barrington doubtfully. "An Oxford Extension book. It's called *The Florentine and His Age*. It's about two hundred pages. Would that be any use?"

"The very thing," cried Hubert in relief. "Will you lend it to me, Miss Barrington?"

"I lent it to Kell, one of the housemaids, who is going to the lecture. She told me she knew nothing about Dante. Kell! Have you finished that book I lent you?"

Kell was on her knees lighting the fire. She now rose to her feet and approached them. She was a pretty girl with a round freckled face, apricot-coloured hair and tawny eyes. Her neck was as white as milk. She surveyed Miss Barrington with sedate respect.

"I beg your pardon, ma'am?"

"Have you finished that book on Dante?"

"Not quite, ma'am."

"Will you bring it here? Mr. Ervine wants to look at it."

If this demand surprised Kell she did not show it. She departed and Miss Barrington explained:

"You see, Mr. Ervine, all the Lyndon servants belong to the Reading Union. Lady Clewer likes it."

This was a new aspect of Agatha and Hubert gaped. But she laughed and set him right:

"Not me. John's stepmother. She is down here so much that she supervises parish work and all that sort of thing. She really likes it and it's a great relief to me, for I would hate it."

"Of course," said Miss Barrington, "all the maids cannot go to all the meetings. They take it in turns. This time it happened to be Kell who is going, so I lent her the book. She is a very intelligent girl."

"She is the friend of James's youth that he was looking for yesterday," added Agatha. "I'd like to know what she thinks of Dante."

Kell returned with the book, which she had neatly wrapped in a cover of brown paper. The fire was lighted and Hubert was left to himself.

The hall was full of Marian superintending the disposition of some flowers in pots. She was rather annoyed with a gardener, and was so occupied in scolding him that Agatha was able to carry on a significant conversation almost at her elbow.

" Lois ! Will you tie my veil for me ? "

Lois, who had been reading the *Tatler* with a very disconsolate expression, came sulkily to her side and helped to dispose of the masses of grey tulle which were to protect her head in the landaulette.

" I can't think, Agatha, what you want to wear a veil in a closed car for."

Agatha's voice grew softer.

" Poor Mr. Ervine is in the library. I'm afraid he's rather stuck in his lecture. He might like help . . . books and things. I wish you would look in some time this morning and see if he has all he wants."

Lois bloomed once more. She had begun to think that he must have gone for a walk.

" Oh, all right. I certainly will if you want me to."

On these occasions one remembered with pleasure that Agatha was really the mistress of Lyndon.

Hubert listened to the departing landaulette with a hopeless heart. He had not written a word. He sat with his head buried in his hands while the rain beat a tattoo upon the window-pane. Presently Lois put her head timidly round the door.

" How are you getting on ? "

" Not at all."

" Oh, dear ! I am sorry ! " She came nearer. " Have you got all the books you want ? "

" Far too many. That's the trouble."

He pointed to the pile of library books on the table and waved the little atrocity in his hand.

"If Miss Barrington hadn't taken it upon herself to prime my audience with this little handbook, I could have copied out a chunk of it and given it as my lecture. But the third housemaid has heard it all already. She'd spot it if I tried."

"Would it be any easier if you dictated to me?"

Hubert thought that it would. He might manage to sparkle a little for her; her admiration for everything he said was rather stimulating. She seized a pad and a pen, expectantly. After a moment's creative abstraction he began:

"The advent of a great poet. . . ."

He caught the eye of Voltaire.

"Come away," it said. "You and your great poets!"

Hubert coughed and tried again in another vein.

"'The man who has seen Hell!' That is what they called him, those thirteenth-century citizens of wherever it was (leave a blank space, we can look it up in a minute), as they watched that sinister figure shouldering its way through their crowded market-places. 'The man who has seen Hell!' Not, mark you, the man who has seen Heaven, although the Divine Comedy includes a book called the *Paradiso*. Why is this? Why is it that in both contemporary and subsequent opinion the *Inferno* is incomparably the greatest book of the three? For us in these latter days it has, of course, lost something of its piquancy. We have forgotten what a *Chronique Scandaleuse* it was. But if a man of genius were to arise in our midst to-day and versify, say the eternal tortures of Manning and Gladstone, were he to limn for us a picture of Parnell and Mrs. O'Shea, a second Paolo and Francesca, blown upon the gales of Hell, we might recapture the old thrill. . . ."

He paused to draw breath and Lois diffidently protested:

" I don't know if this is quite what Mother wants. It's for
poor people, you know. I don't think she wants anything
amusing."

" Oh, all right. Tear it up."

" You don't mind my saying so, do you ? "

" Oh, no. Indeed not. I'm most anxious to please your
mother. You can have no idea how anxious."

Lois flushed and fidgeted with the ring at the end of
her pencil. Hubert began again :

" *Lasciate ogni speranza. . . .*"

" They won't understand Italian. You must translate
it."

" Abandon hope all ye who enter here," said the lecturer
peevishly, adding, a moment later, " no, don't put it. I
don't think I will begin that way. I was going to say that
this was the artist's comment on the condition of the mind
prior to creation. But I forget why."

" Really nobody very clever is coming," she assured him.
" It's a much simpler affair than you think. Why can't
you just say where he was born, and all that ; and then say
what he wrote. That is the sort of thing Mother wants."

" Dante," dictated Hubert. . . . " No . . . put Dante
Alighieri . . . was born in . . . in . . . I say . . . was he
born in Florence, or did he go there after he was born ?
Would you mind looking it up in that little book ? "

Lois studied *The Florentine and His Age.*

" It doesn't put," she said at last.

" Oh, Lord ! What's a book like that for, if it doesn't
give you the facts ? "

" That's the gong for lunch."

Hubert jumped up with alacrity.

" Shall we go on after lunch ? " he said. " I may feel
brighter after food."

" Of course we will," said the obliging Lois, " if you feel
it's any use to you."

Marian's face was greatly troubled when she joined them at lunch.

"This rain is terrible," she complained. "It's so awkward, Mr. Ervine. They've just sent in to say that the big station car is out of order and can't possibly be put right before Monday. It's most tiresome. Because, of course, we all meant to drive to your lecture in it. The Village Room is quite two miles off, across the park, and if this rain goes on it will be much too wet to walk."

"It's extraordinary how these things are always happening," said Lois. "We have four cars, and yet I do believe that we are more often held up for want of transport than many people who have only a motor bicycle and a side-car."

"Well, you see, John and Thomas have the limousine, and Agatha the landaulette. There is the little two-seater, of course, which will take you down to the village, Mr. Ervine. But I'm very much afraid that the rest of us will be deprived of hearing your lecture unless it clears up. I'm so sorry! But it's really too wet to walk. I catch cold so easily, and so do the girls."

"Perhaps, as it's such a bad day, I might postpone it," suggested Hubert hopefully.

"Oh, no! Please don't do that! All the folk from the village will be there, Mr. Ervine. And they would be so disappointed; some of them have to walk several miles. Poor things! Their lives are so dull and it is such a treat for them! No, don't put it off. Only it's so disappointing for us. But perhaps you will read it to us later."

"Oh, no! I couldn't inflict it on anybody twice."

"James will go, of course. Won't you, James? He doesn't mind the rain a scrap. And Miss Barrington. You mustn't think that everyone from Lyndon is deserting you. And then Agatha will be dropping in on her way home."

"But will Miss Barrington walk?" asked Hubert doubtfully. "Let me walk with you, Clewer, and Miss Barrington can go in the two-seater."

"Oh, but that's quite unnecessary," protested Miss Barrington, casting a nervous glance at her employer. "I don't mind the rain. I like a little turn in the fresh air."

"Yes, she likes it," asserted Marian, but was interrupted by a very tactless explosion of sneezing on the part of her secretary.

She waited in heavy patience until Miss Barrington had done.

"I say! You have got a cold!" observed Gerald.

"Oh, no! Not at all. It's nearly gone now."

"Do go in the car and let me walk!" urged Hubert.

"I think fresh air does a cold good," observed Marian judicially. "I always go out for a cold myself. And I have a few notes to be left in the village. I think Miss Barrington had better walk. Mr. Blair, will you care to go? Lady Clewer would have room for you in the landaulette on the way home, I'm sure, so there would only be the walk one way."

"Yes, I'd like to come," agreed Gerald.

"There, you see, Mr. Ervine! Three people are going from Lyndon in spite of the rain. You mustn't think we have all deserted you."

"Dolly Kell is going, so it's four really," observed James.

"Hush, James!" remarked his stepmother mechanically.

A silence fell upon the lunchers while they devoured roast beef and Yorkshire pudding. Hubert eyed Gerald.

"You'd really better not come, Blair," he said. "You'll be bored stiff, you know."

"But I want to come. I know nothing at all about Dante. I'll hold an umbrella over Miss Barrington."

Hubert sighed and wished the affair well over. But he

could not quarrel with an occasion which was to secure him an afternoon alone with Lois. When they emerged from the library at tea-time the lecture was written and neatly fastened together with a paper clip.

4.

" Sooner you than me," said Clara, the scullery-maid, as she peered out into the rain. " It's a good thing your boots is thick."

" I'm glad to get the chance of a walk," said Dolly Kell. " I'm not afraid of a bit of rain."

" This isn't a bit of rain; it's a flood. It's terrible. There won't be many there, I shouldn't think. I wouldn't go, not if I was you, Dolly."

" Oh, I got to. Old Lady Clewer would see if I wasn't there. She's so sharp. Everyone from the house is going."

" Yes. I seen Mr. James waiting by the yard gate." Clara popped her head out of the scullery window for a moment. " He's there still. I wonder who he's waiting for, don't you ? "

" Not knowing, can't say." Dolly was not deceived by Clara's innocent curiosity. " I've got something better to wonder at. I'd get on with my vegetables if I was you."

She buttoned up the last button of her mackintosh and moved down the passage.

" Oh ! Ain't you going out through the yard ? "

" Never you mind what way I'm going out."

A little side door at the end of the old schoolroom passage led into the shrubbery. Through this Dolly slipped, holding her skirts well away from the splashings of soaked bushes. As she picked her way into the avenue she was glad of the prudence which had prompted her to spend her last quarter's wages on new boots and an umbrella instead of a summer costume. The drive was deep in puddles and the rain pattered everywhere. It fell in great splashes from the trees and dimpled the flowing gutters.

She thought with compunction of poor Mr. James waiting in the downpour by the yard gate. Her evasion seemed to be a little heartless. It would have been kinder, after all, to have gone out by the yard. But then she must have rebuffed his offers of escort under the inquisitive eye of Clara, who would have seen it all from the scullery window. She had not the courage.

This affair of Mr. James was very worrying to Dolly. It was worse than any of the "social puzzles" in *Home Words*. She did not know how she ought to act. They had been, of course, playmates and equals, but that was a long time ago. On her return to Lyndon as third housemaid she knew that things ought to be very different. He was a young gentleman now, and it was her business to remind him of the fact should he show signs of forgetting it.

She had grown up in the creed that Mr. James was "put upon." Her aunt, Mrs. Job Kell, had never liked the second Lady Clewer and her interfering ways. The dislike was mutual, for Marian had been quick to divine the element of contempt which lay behind the old housekeeper's civility. She had pensioned her off at the first opportunity, feeling that old retainers are sometimes better at a distance.

Their hottest battles had been fought over James. Mrs. Kell, who had mothered him from birth, was enraged by Marian's unfavourable comments on his person and intelligence.

"Soft-headed," she would say to Dolly. "She's soft-headed herself. You mark my words, if anything ails that boy it's too much brains, not too little. Didn't I rear him from a babby? I ought to know. He was always as sharp as they're made. A regular old-fashioned child if ever there was one; ever so knowing. You remember him yourself. The funny little dear!"

Dolly remembered a sturdy, ugly child some months older than herself. A lonely, secretive boy he had been, but excellent company when he had got over his shyness. They had played endless, mysterious games in the gardens at Lyndon. They had kept house in the old brick potting shed, cooking elaborate meals in Dolly's little saucepans and rearing a large family of dolls. With these, James, as a father, was allowed very little say though he sometimes took the stick to them when they got beyond petticoat government. The household reflected Clewer luxuries and the artless simplicity of the four-room cottage. Dolly, having despatched the children to school, would scrub out the " liberry " and announce :

" Now I'll have a good cup of tea and a lay down."

These memories made her feel very kindly towards him. She was a good-natured girl, in spite of her sharp tongue, and hated giving real pain. She soon perceived that she was wounding him deeply ; he would stare at her, when she snubbed him, with a startled grief in his eyes. As she grew to know the household better, and saw the scorn and derision in which he was held, she became very sorry for him and longed to unbend to his wistful advances. But this would have been to carry on with a gentleman of the house, a lapse unpardonable. Of course, he was quite different from any other gentleman she had ever met ; he always had been. She had once said as much to her aunt, whereupon Mrs. Kell had become very mysterious and refused to discuss the subject. She said she didn't know but what it mightn't be accounted for.

The road across the park led through an iron gate into the wet village street. The postman, one of Dolly's admirers, was clearing the box at the corner.

" Hullo, Dolly ! " he greeted her cheerfully. " Rain-water's good for the complexion, so they say."

She passed him with her round chin in the air.

" You'll catch plenty of it in your mouth that way, if you're thirsty," he called after her.

She stalked on, her head held so high that she failed to perceive the approach of the grocer's young man and almost collided with him. The postman guffawed rudely in the distance, but young Mr. Hopkins, nothing daunted, fell into step beside her.

" Good afternoon, Miss Kell," he ventured. " It's a wet day."

" It is," she agreed.

" You going a walk ? "

" No."

" Well, it's a wet day for a walk, isn't it ? '

" Yes."

" Perhaps you'll be going a walk after chapel, Sunday ? "

" I may and I mayn't. What of it ? "

" I was wondering," he said diffidently, " if you've not fixed up with any other chap, that is . . ."

" Oh, I haven't fixed up with anybody, thanks. And I'm not going to. I'd sooner walk by myself."

" Really now. . . ."

" I would. Till I can find a man that can talk sense, thank you, Mr. Hopkins. I haven't seen one yet."

" If you'd only let me come along I wouldn't talk at all. Would that please you ? "

" It wouldn't. I said a man that could talk sense, not anybody dumb ! "

He looked a little dashed, but toiled by her side until they reached the Village Institute. Dolly turned in at the gate.

" You going in there ? " he said, gaping.

" Oh, no, of course not," snapped Dolly. " I'm only going to climb trees in the garden."

" You're very clever, aren't you ? "

He was beginning to get riled.

" Well, what do you want to ask such a silly question
for ? Was I going in. Couldn't you see I was ? "

" What's taking you in, anyway ? "

" Haven't you eyes ? It's wrote large enough."

She pointed to a bill on the paling executed in Miss
Barrington's best poster writing. It said :

CLEWER VILLAGE INSTITUTE

June Session, 1914.
On Friday next, at 6 p.m.

Mr. HUBERT ERVINE will lecture on :

" DANTE, THE GREAT ITALIAN POET."

Free to all.   Come early.

" Dant the Eyetalian Poit ! " read Mr. Hopkins. " Who's
he when he's at home ? "

" Well, you are a Mr. Ignorance and no mistake. You
didn't ought to say Dant. Dunty ! That's the proper
way to say it."

Thus Dolly, who had heard all about Dunty from Miss
Barrington.

" Well, but what d'you want to bother your head about
him for ? That's what I want to know."

" Curiosity killed the cat. Good-bye, Mr. Hopkins."

Too much incensed to answer, he strode on and left her.

The Clewer Village Institute was a dreary place. A
lending library of an instructive nature, carefully chosen
by Marian, lined the walls. All the books were uniformly
clad in drab holland covers. The baize table near the stove
was littered with old newspapers of a strictly Tory nature
and some pamphlets issued by the Primrose League. Two
Union Jacks, draped between the windows, testified to
the patriotism of the village of Lyndon.

As Dolly shook out her mackintosh she wondered

anxiously how long James would wait in the rain. She
trusted that he would soon give her up. It was so very wet
and he had not got on his Burberry. She wished she could
have made him put it on without sacrificing any of her
hard-won aloofness. The room was empty, but this did
not surprise her, for she knew she was early. With the
patience of a well-disciplined nature she settled herself to
tranquil inactivity on a bench at the very back of the room.
Divested of her mackintosh she was revealed, supple and
sturdy, in a navy coat and skirt of indifferent fit. Her best
black hat, abob with cherries, hid the apricot meshes of
her hair.

She was flushed with the routing of Mr. Hopkins, though
the suppression of followers was an art in which she was
much practised. She had many, but she detested them all
and was determined never to marry. Her young intelligence
had been dreadfully haunted by the shadow of that maniac
stepfather who had made life so frightful for her mother.
It was a memory which still terrified her and distorted her
ideas ; the risks of marriage, its possible disasters, seemed
to her insurmountable. Nor was it likely that she would
meet a man who could inspire her to face these difficulties ;
strength and weakness alike antagonized her, since the one
stirred her to revolt against possible domination and the
other roused her ridicule. An affectionate, intuitive
creature, built for womanly ends, she was likely to remain
single.

The rain drummed on the roof and the large clock over
the door ticked loudly. She began to grow nervous,
wishing that somebody else would turn up. Suddenly she
had a perfect horrible apprehension. Suppose that she
were all the audience ! It might well be. She would never
have come herself, on such a nasty evening, if she had not
been obliged. But it would be awkward if she were the only
one. Of course there would be the party from " the

house." But Dolly knew that it was for herself and her likes that this lecture was given. It was meant to elevate her. She did not mind being elevated along with other proletarians, but she barred the notion of enduring it quite by herself. If nobody from the village put in an appearance she would have to sit marooned on the benches designed for the commonalty. A semicircle of her betters, installed in arm-chairs behind the lecturer's back, would confront her for at least an hour. Every time she looked up she would face a battery of aristocratic eyes. She was a brave girl, but she quailed at the idea. She would have withdrawn had she dared; but, with old Lady Clewer coming, flight was impossible. Old Lady Clewer saw everything, except perhaps the way Miss Cynthia was carrying on with that Sir Thomas. But then Miss Cynthia was very deep.

She strained her ears to catch the approach of the station car which would bring the family. It was surely time they arrived. The clatter of boots and a great scraping in the porch relieved her. She was, it seemed, to have at least one companion.

But her heart sank again when James appeared.

"Hello, Dolly!" he exclaimed. "I thought you couldn't be coming. I waited by the back gate for you."

Dolly grew pink.

"I went out by the shrubberies, sir," she observed.

"Well, why didn't you tell me?" he persisted. "I wanted to walk with you."

"I'm sure I'm very sorry, sir."

"But why didn't you? Are you angry about anything? What is the matter with you? Why are you so different? Because if you are angry I wish you'd tell me why," he complained.

After all there was no great need to be shy of him, for she had known him all her life. Now that they were alone together she had much better speak plainly to him.

" I'm not angry. It's only this. Now we are grown up it's quite different to being little. We can't be friends like we used to be. Our stations in life is so different."

" I don't mind about our stations in life."

" Ah, but I do. A girl like me can't be friends with a gentleman without people thinking things."

" They always do," he argued. " It's no use to worry about what people think. I never do. I used to. But when I saw that they'd really rather think wrong than right I gave it up."

" Yes. You can. But I can't. I got my living to earn." He digested this and grew grave.

" It's very hard, that is," he said at last.

" It can't be helped," quoth Dolly. " We didn't make the world. If we had, it would have been different, I daresay."

" It would," agreed James feelingly.

Dolly remembered with dismay that she had not called him " sir " for at least two minutes. This was always happening to her. Also she was inclined to relapse, insensibly, from the refined grammar and diction with which she usually addressed her employers. It seemed more natural, somehow, to converse with him in the rough and ready speech of her own caste.

" This sort of thing is maddening," he declared. " I like you better than anyone I know. I always have. I don't suppose I shall ever find anyone I like better. It isn't only the people here . . . I used to think that it would be different if I got away and went to Paris. But it wasn't. Paris was all right for working in. I learnt a lot. But I felt just as out of it there as here. I never knew what to say to them. And they all laughed at me, like they do here. Even the ones who liked my work did."

" Well, you know, sir, you act a bit queer sometimes."

" I can't help it. Do you see anything very serious the matter with me, Dolly ? "

" I don't see there's much wrong with you, I don't. And Auntie doesn't neither."

" But you are the only ones. And isn't it hard . . . ? "

" Everyone has their troubles," interrupted Dolly.

" I know. But why ? I don't want my station in life. Who gave it to me, anyway ? "

" Almighty God," she told him austerely.

" Well, I suppose so," he assented.

She was overjoyed to hear at least two people in the porch, but wished that he would move from his pleading posture at her side. The newcomers turned out to be Mr. Blair and Jimmy Pyewacket, the boy who weeded the graden. She was distressed to think that Mr. Blair was a visitor at the house, but consoled herself with the reflection that he was a born gentleman and wouldn't get thinking things, even if James's attitude did look a little odd. This was a great compliment to Mr. Blair, for Dolly's standards were cruelly high, and very few of the Lyndon guests were allowed by her to be born gentlemen.

James, with the air of a man of the world, immediately effected an introduction.

" Miss Kell, Mr. Blair. But you ought to know her, for she brings your shaving water in the morning, doesn't she ? "

His triumphant glance told Dolly that he believed himself to have done exactly the right thing upon this occasion. Let her retract her statement that he acted a bit queer !

Mr. Blair was looking a little puzzled and she set them right.

" Not me, sir. Mr. Peters waits on gentlemen staying in the house."

" That explains it," said Mr. Blair. " I thought you must have changed very much since this morning. Are we all the audience ? "

Dolly looked round for Jimmy Pyewacket and saw him

edging away towards the door. She made a dash at him and detained him.

"Now then, young Jimmy! You don't! Do stay, there's a little love! I don't want to have to sit on these benches all by myself."

"These gents 'll sit with you," said Jimmy, poised for flight.

"No they won't. They have to sit on the platform with the family."

"Shall we?" exclaimed the gents, and Mr. Blair added: "We won't. We'd much rather sit on the benches. What's the point of sitting behind the lecturer's back?"

"There won't be any family," observed James. "We are all that's coming. So we can sit where we like, I should think."

"Nobody coming!" cried Dolly. "Not Lady Clewer nor Miss Lois?"

"Not they. It's raining and their car is out of order."

Dolly cursed her fate. If she had only known this she would have absconded herself.

"You mustn't go, you know," went on Mr. Blair, attacking Jimmy in his turn. "Think of the wretched lecturer! Four are better than three."

"It's so cold," objected Jimmy, shivering at the damp odour of the place. "The stove ought to of been lighted."

"It's laid," said James, inspecting it. "Shall I light it?"

"Will you stay if we do?" pleaded Mr. Blair of Jimmy, who nodded graciously.

"I don't see why we shouldn't," Dolly encouraged them.

So they lit the stove and the four students of Dante gathered round the crackling sticks. Dolly could not digest the idea that no one else was coming from the house.

"But isn't Miss Barrington coming?" she asked. "She always does."

" He," James indicated Mr. Blair, " wouldn't let her.
She has a very sneezy cold. And when we were all in the
hall after tea he told her to go to bed. You should have
heard him, Dolly ! It was like Mamma and God and a
magistrate all at once. She went rather quickly ! "

" My most effective professional manner," murmured
Mr. Blair. " She wasn't fit to be up at all."

There was a great snorting and tooting outside as a little
car bustled up to the gate. The lecturer, nervously grasping
a roll of MS., sidled into the room. He glanced around,
prepared for the beefy stare of innumerable rustics, all the
simple village folk who would be so disappointed if he did
not brighten their lives. He beheld empty benches. The
group round the stove rose to receive him in sympathetic
solemnity.

" I'm afraid most of your audience has been frightened by
the weather," observed Gerald Blair.

Jimmy Pyewacket said hopefully :

" The rain's stopping. P'raps some more will come."

Hubert clutched at this.

" Yes, they might," he said. " Shall we wait a bit in case
they do ? "

There was a pause and Dolly said encouragingly :

" Just as you like, sir."

So they all sat down again and the warming stove drew
clouds of steam from their wet boots. A few minutes of
uneasy silence passed. At last Hubert thought fit to ask
Dolly if she liked poetry.

" Some poetry I like," she said. " There was one piece I
read. I saw it on the pictures first and it was beautiful.
So I read the book. ' Evangeline ' it was called. All about
the olden times."

" Ah . . . Longfellow ! "

" That's right."

" You like his works, then ? "

" Yes, sir. I think it's beautiful."

" And what," asked Hubert, " do you think of Dante ? "

Dolly was nonplussed and said she didn't know much about him.

" But you read that little book . . . er . . . *The Florentine and His Age ?* "

" Pat and his Ape ! " muttered James, with such concentration of scorn that Dolly stifled a giggle.

" I read a bit of it, sir," she replied.

" And what did you make of it ? "

" It was a very nice book I'm sure," she said politely.

She had no wish to hear more of Dante. What she had read in *The Florentine and His Age* had been quite enough. The fellow was, apparently, a foreigner, an idolatrous Roman Catholic, a blasphemer and a bad husband. A shiftless creature, moreover, incapable of supporting himself and very rude about the steep stairs of the kind gentleman who patronized him. His picture in the frontispiece had not been pretty. And his poem, all about Hell, revolted her. Her stepfather, whose mania had a religious turn in it, had talked a good deal about Hell, with all the gusto of a cruel and perverted imagination. She thought the Florentine must have been a little like him.

A few minutes elapsed and nobody could think of anything further to say. At length another car was heard to arrive. Agatha, sumptuous in furs and veils, slipped noiselessly through the door as though desirous not to disturb a lecture which she imagined to be in full swing. She also looked at the empty benches with a surprised air and then at the people round the stove. Taking them in she became mirthful.

" Now, Mr. Ervine," she commanded, when she had heard the facts. " Tell the truth ! You'd much rather not read that lecture at all, wouldn't you ? "

" Much rather," said Hubert earnestly.

"Well?" she looked round her with a question in her eye. "What about it? Shall we let him off?"

Everyone fidgeted. At length someone mentioned the dowager.

"We won't tell," laughed the mistress of Lyndon. "Burn it, and we'll all vow it was the best lecture we ever heard."

With jubilant thankfulness Hubert thrust his lecture into the stove. He sent a benediction with it, however, for it had secured him an afternoon with his love. Agatha sat down in one of the most comfortable of the arm-chairs and stretched a silken ankle towards the blazing manuscript.

"We must wait here for a bit," she said, "to give him time to deliver his lecture. What shall we do? I wish we could roast chestnuts."

"I got pea-nuts," volunteered Jimmy, producing a dirty paper bag.

"What are pea-nuts?" asked Lady Clewer, peering. "Can one roast them? Are they nice?"

Jimmy said that they were very nice and was commanded to superintend the roasting. Agatha looked round the room.

"This is fun," she said. "It's the first time I've enjoyed myself in this place. What shall we play at? Consequences? No!" She glanced at Hubert. "It's a risky game. Too risky. Shall we tell ghost stories?"

"Ah! Ghost stories!" said Hubert at once. "That reminds me of something I heard in Morocco. . . ."

If ghost stories were to be told, he had better demonstrate how it should be done. He had a horror of the amateur narrator. As a matter of fact he was really rather good at it and enthralled them for half an hour with one startling anecdote after another. Jimmy's eyes opened wider and wider and he edged closer to Dolly's protecting skirts. And she, as the rainy dusk drew in, thought nervously of the lonely walk through the park. It would be very difficult to refuse James's company.

At last Agatha decided that enough time had elapsed and they might return in safety. Jimmy scooted off into the twilight as though all the demons of Morocco were at his heels. The others paused uncertainly in the porch until Agatha declared that nobody must walk home in this rain. The little two-seater was nowhere in sight but she insisted that they could all pack somehow into the landaulette. Hubert was put in front with the chauffeur and the four others climbed in behind. The roof was too low for anyone to stand in comfort and the only way for them all to get in was for the men to sit with the ladies perched on their knees. Dolly would have preferred Mr. Blair's knee, but she was given to James. She vaguely understood why Mr. Ervine had been put in front; he would not have supported this intimacy at all well. As it was, she felt that the barriers raised against James were sensibly weakened by this enforced proximity. The car, turning into the drive, swayed them all backwards and forwards so that she nearly fell off his knee. He put an arm about her to keep her steady. She looked at his hand as it lay in her lap. It was a broad, muscular hand, not over clean,˙ and stained with paint; a working hand, like her own. Behind her shoulder, through the thin cloth of her coat, she could feel the strong beating of his heart. Consciously she checked an impulse of tenderness and comprehension. She tried to sit on his knee in a distant and respectful manner. Lady Clewer might think it very forward in her to allow him to put his arm round her waist. She glanced nervously at the others.

She need not have disturbed herself. Lady Clewer was secure in the arm of her cousin. She also was staring pensively at the hand of the man who held her. Dolly was struck for the first time by her employer's youthfulness; not more than twenty-one, so they said. You'd never think it, she had such a stately way with her. But it wasn't really very stately for a married lady to sit in the lap of a strange gentleman, cousin or no cousin. And she was looking as if she enjoyed it too.

Arrived at Lyndon, Dolly ran round to the back door and upstairs to change her dress. Later in the evening she was sent with a tray of invalid delicacies to Miss Barrington, whose cold was very much worse. In the sick-room she encountered the dowager, who was determined that her secretary should be competently nursed.

"Well, Kell," said she, "and how did you enjoy the lecture?"

"Very much indeed, thank you, my lady," replied Dolly, mindful of instructions.

"And was Mr. Ervine very interesting?"

"Oh, very, my lady. We all got so scared."

"Scared?" said Marian. "Scared?"

Dolly recollected herself and became very much confused.

"The Idferdo!" croaked Miss Barrington from the bed. "D'you bead that the descriptiod of the dabbed alarbed you, Kell?"

"Yes, ma'am," said Dolly, when she had identified the "dabbed."

Being a truthful girl she blushed as she said it.

CHAPTER III

THE KIND COMPANIONS

I.

AGATHA would have called Hubert's proposal of marriage a thoroughly British affair. Discarding all superficial eloquence, he told his tale of love in the baldest, most colloquial terms. Lois was profoundly impressed. This lapse from fluency was exactly calculated to convince her of his earnestness. The emotion must be strong indeed before which Hubert could be dumb. She searched about in her memory for the speech which she had prepared for the occasion.

" I think," she said, " that my feelings towards you are all that you could wish."

Her candour charmed him. He caught her to his heart with but a passing fear that she would find him deficient in originality. Then, invaded for a few moments by a genuine emotion of self-forgetfulness, he kissed her a second time with no misgivings at all. They were truly happy.

A strange noise, a pervading, humming throb, at length shook them out of their preoccupation. The whole air seemed full of it.

Lois exclaimed :

" What can that be ? Is it a threshing machine ? "

They were in the library, a room which they habitually frequented since the epoch of the Dante paper. Moving to one of the windows they looked down into the avenue. John and the head gardener stood together gazing upward.

Other gardeners were seen running in the distance ; they also stared at the sky. Lois and Hubert threw up the sash and leaned far out of the window just in time to see the tail of an airship disappear over the house. It was the first Lois had seen and she nearly fell out of the window in her excitement. Hubert, after a second's consideration, decided that he must be excited too. Earlier in his courtship it would have been more impressive to remain calm, but just now he had better fall in with his lady's mood.

"We can see it from the terrace," she cried, and flew down to the south side of the house.

Gerald and Agatha were discovered there, gaping intelligently, while Cynthia and Sir Thomas were seen advancing from the rose garden at a pace which, in any other couple, might have been a run. Lady Clewer and Miss Barrington hung out of a window on the first floor, and everyone enjoined everyone else to look at the airship. The elusive machine turned suddenly north, however, and disappeared behind some trees. A short discussion was held as to the best vantage point from which to see it again. Lois suggested James's studio, which had a window looking that way. She ran indoors again, up the main staircase, down a long gallery, through a baize door into the kitchen wing, up more stairs, noisy and uncarpeted, through a corridor and up a narrow garret ladder into a spacious loft running the whole length of the wing. The company panted at her heels.

The loft was not entirely given over to James. The darker end of it was used as a box room, and old luggage, gay with the labels of continental hotels, was piled there. Here also was Cynthia's bassinette, a high nursery-chair, bed-tables and other less sightly appliances for nursing the sick. Everything in fact which the household did not normally require. At the further end of the room, by the large window, many canvases were stacked, and a small table was covered with rags and brushes. There was an easel and a

moulting arm-chair, condemned in the Lyndon nurseries.
Here sat James, looking more peculiar than usual, in a strange
chintz pinafore which his stepmother had forced him to
assume while painting. He spoilt his clothes so. He was
peacefully smoking a pipe, and at their incursion he rose and
retreated as far as possible, eyeing them suspiciously.

"May we come in, James ? " asked Lois, tapping the door
after she had entered the room. "We want to see the
airship."

He looked in alarm at the furniture by the door and asked :
"What airship ? "

"We don't accuse you of having one here," said Cynthia,
pushing her way in. "It happens to be outside in the sky.
I don't suppose you noticed it."

"No, I didn't," he agreed, glancing out of the window.

"My dear James," remonstrated Marian, as she toiled up
the last of the garret stairs, "how unobservant you are !
It's making a tremendous noise."

James paid no attention to this, but moved to the door
and looked anxiously down the stairs demanding :
"How many more people are going to come up ? "

Agatha, who never hurried, was achieving the taxing
ascent under the escort of Hubert, John, Gerald and Sir
Thomas Bragge. Their voices floated up beyond the well
of the narrow stairs. Sir Thomas could be heard remarking
sententiously :

"The future of the world lies in the air, Lady Clewer."

"Yes, but . . ." panted Agatha, "I don't see how it can
ever be really safe . . ."

"From the military point of view, Agatha, safety isn't
always the first consideration. In the next big war . . ."

"Oh, come, Blair ! Isn't that rather an exploded idea ?
Just consider ! It would be almost impossible to use the
things without endangering the lives and property of non-
combatants. . . ."

Agatha appeared in the doorway, a little flushed with so much unusual exertion, and began at once to apologise to James for their intrusion.

" I do hope you weren't working very hard and that we are not interrupting you," she said. " But there is this airship outside, which we want to see. Come and look at it."

She caught his arm and drew him to the window where the others were already gathered. They stood watching the marvel until it disappeared behind the low, wooded hills on the horizon. Whereupon, without more ado, the majority of the group prepared to depart. But Agatha was determined that for once a modicum of civility should be paid to James. She asked him, with her most engaging smile, if he would not show them some of his pictures. She assured him that it would give them all great pleasure, ignoring tranquilly the furtive signals whereby Marian sought to prevent such a catastrophe. James looked surprised but not ill pleased. He took a canvas from the pile and set it on the easel in a good light.

The party viewed it in silent embarrassment and nobody ventured upon comment until Sir Thomas rushed into the breach.

" Well, Mr. Clewer, and what is this supposed to be ? " he inquired with uneasy geniality.

Cynthia tittered and James explained that it was a bit of country beyond Boar's Hill.

" I didn't know you painted landscapes," said Agatha. " I . . . I rather like all those telegraph posts going up and down."

" Oh, but James," exclaimed the stepmother, " you have done nicer ones than that. Do show us one of your portraits."

" I will in a minute," said James. " You can't have finished looking at this yet."

They stared for a little longer at the mustard fields and

ploughed furrows beyond Boar's Hill. Lois glanced at
Hubert in extreme anxiety. She had staked much upon his
first view of James's work, for she had hinted more than once
that she thought it might have merit. Hubert's face was
perfectly expressionless, and her heart sank. At last they
were permitted to see something else. James put up a
picture of a man driving a traction engine, explaining :

"That's old Jellybelly."

"Old what ? " demanded Gerald, who was looking
happier than he had done since he came to Lyndon.

"He used to drive the traction engine when they were
making the new road across the park," explained the artist.
"His real name was Jellifew, but the men in his gang called
him Jellybelly because of the shape of his stomach."

John gave a shout of laughter.

"Lord, yes, I remember him ! This is uncommonly
good, James ! Best thing you ever did in your life."

"Do you think so ? " said James seriously. "Now I don't
think it is, myself. But it's one of the best I've done."

"But you ought to have seen this old man," said Agatha
to the others. "He was like somebody out of a Russian
novel. And with this head like Samuel Johnson. I'd
forgotten how impressive he was."

"I don't remember him," said Marian coldly.

"A most striking portrait," murmured Gerald. "What
do you make of it, Ervine ? You know about these things,
and I don't."

"It's . . . well observed . . ." said Hubert after a
pause.

"The composition is rather unusual, don't you think ? "
queried Lois hopefully.

"Possibly," rejoined Hubert, bland and enigmatic.

Marian, who found the whole subject of Jellybelly a
little coarse, now determined that they must not disturb
James any longer and swept them all from the room. She

was more than annoyed with Agatha for exhibiting him in
this way; it had been perfectly unnecessary and very
embarrassing for everyone. James took himself much too
seriously already, without any encouragement from his
sister-in-law. She pursued Agatha and Gerald out on to the
terrace in order to tell them so.

"If you don't mind my saying so," she began, "I really
do think it's a pity to take too much notice of James's
pictures. You must know, with all your experience, Mr.
Blair, how difficult these cases are. They are so liable to get
a tremendous opinion of themselves."

"What cases?" asked Gerald in surprise. "Is there
anything the matter with him?"

Marian raised her eyebrows as though she had expected
more perception from a London specialist.

"Well . . . he's queer," she said, pursing her lips.

"How do you mean? Neurotic? He doesn't look it."

"Not neurotic. Not that. No!" Marian shook her
head sadly. "But we've always had a great deal of trouble
with poor James. Mentally, you know, he has never been
quite like other people."

"Really? Well, that mightn't be altogether a disadvantage. I don't think I should expect the man who
painted those pictures to have a mind quite like other
people. But hasn't he been off, studying in Paris, like any
other lad?"

"Oh, yes. He was in Paris. But not alone. He was very
carefully looked after, poor boy. It was necessary. He
can't really look after himself. He made no friends of his
own age, for instance, as any other young man would have
done."

"He had very little chance," said Agatha.

"My dear Agatha! He could have made friends perfectly well if he had wished. What was there to stop him?"

"Everything, I should have thought. His peculiar

position. The supervision under which he lived. His own eccentric manner. . . ."

"There you are," said Marian triumphantly. "That's what I said. It was his own fault that he did not make friends. His queer ways put them off, and no wonder."

"He looks extraordinary," observed Gerald thoughtfully. "But that doesn't prove him to be without ability at his own job. Many men of very exceptional powers have been rather strange looking."

"I'm afraid," sighed Marian, "that long experience has taught me not to hope too much. It isn't exceptional ability that ails poor James."

She hastened off to dictate letters to Miss Barrington.

"Who says that fellow is mentally deficient?" inquired Gerald testily.

"Oh, nobody of any consequence," replied his cousin. "No doctor has, of that I am convinced. It was an established family legend when I first met him, and it probably has as much truth as most family legends. He certainly was very much more peculiar when he was younger. What do you think of him, Gerald?"

"I like him. Really very much. There's no sort of temperamental humbug about him, is there?"

"There isn't, certainly."

"A little direct at times, perhaps. But it's a good fault. You like him, don't you?"

"I do," she confessed. "I find him a very restful companion. But I cannot understand how he comes to be John's brother."

Gerald said nothing to this, an issue which disappointed her. Irritably aware of his unspoken disapproval she was always seeking to entrap him into some criticism of her house or her husband which could be challenged and resented. But he would not give her an opening. Only from his silences did she guess his hostility to Lyndon and its proprietor. She had in consequence no chance of telling him that he was impertinent, a thing which she was longing to do.

Their estrangement had grieved her sharply and she was truly anxious to punish him for all the disquiet he was causing her. She had never supposed that four years could bring no changes. She was steeled against the shock of hearing that he loved another, although she would hardly have been surprised to discover that he still loved herself. But for this mute, melancholy condemnation she had not been prepared. At one moment he would treat her with all the old friendliness ; on the next he would harden and draw away. She was most desirous of an open dispute in which she could tax him with intolerance. Such an encounter would relieve them both. She would demand whether he expected her to remain seventeen all her life. She would force him to blame John, to blame Lyndon, for the changes which he thus condemned. Then she would hurl at him all the dignified wrath of a loyal wife. She began to compose some very scathing sentences as they paced side by side towards the Dutch garden.

Sheltered amid its clipped hedges another pair of kind companions wandered in close conversation.

" A queer chap, your younger brother, what ? " quoth Sir Thomas. " I understand from your mother that he's a little. . . . "

He tapped his forehead and Cynthia laughed. She made no attempt to deny the inference.

" Well, now," he continued. " Those pictures, y'know ! A bit thick ! What ? "

" Lois admires them like anything."

" Does she now ? Really ! Well ! "

" But then she's clever, you know. I'm afraid I'm not clever like that."

The golden eyelashes flickered over the dark eyes. It was quite obvious that Cynthia had no particular wish to be clever.

" Quite right too," approved Sir Thomas. " Personally
I've no use for clever women. Bluestockings! No reflection
intended upon little Miss Lois, though. But what's a
woman want brains for ? "

" They don't need them like men do."

" That's right. They don't. What I always say is, let the
women leave the brain work to the men. What, after all, are
brains for ? To make money, ain't they ? Well, and that's a
man's job. What's a woman's job, you'll say ? Why, to
spend it ! No need of brains to do that, eh, Miss Cynthia ? "

" Rather not," agreed the maiden earnestly.

" That's what a man needs," continued Sir Thomas with
unction. " A wife who can enjoy spending what he's made.
It gives him something to work for. It's a lonely game, you
know. Piling up cash and no one to spend it on. Yes!
Very lonely ! A little girl like you would never guess how
lonely an old chap like me can feel."

He looked almost pathetic as he said this, for he was really
coming to believe that business successes are an empty
triumph for a single man.

" It's very harrowing," said Cynthia thoughtfully.

If her dark eyes held a hint of derision, he could not know
it, for she kept them modestly upon the ground.

" If I had a wife now, that's what I'd want," said he. " A
girl who could turn herself out properly. Who'd make every
other woman look green. But a lady, mind you ! A girl
who could hold her own in any society. I'd be proud to foot
her bills, I tell you. But then, I don't suppose any nice
girl would look at me. Not an old chap like me."

" Are you old ? "

This was evidently a surprise to Cynthia and Sir Thomas
beamed.

" Well, not so very old when you come to think of it. But
old, I daresay, compared to the young fellows you're
accustomed to."

"I'm not out," said Cynthia primly. "I don't know any young men except James and John."

"Really? Now is that so? I could hardly have believed it."

Sir Thomas was thinking how very accomplished she was if this were true. He could have sworn that hers was no prentice hand in the tender game.

"Of course I'm not out. My hair isn't up."

She shook the shining, honey-coloured mane upon her white neck. They paused in their walk and Sir Thomas delicately picked up a silky tress between a stubby red thumb and forefinger.

"I see that," he said. "No, I knew you weren't out. But don't tell me you haven't got a fancy boy for all that."

"Oh, no. Think of Mother!"

He thought of Marian. She was indeed an indefatigable duenna. It might really be that this damsel was as flawless as she seemed. Her complacence was all the more gratifying to him on account of a recent rebuff which he had received from another quarter. This wound seemed to smart less as he fingered Cynthia's yellow hair.

"Well," he suggested, "I suppose you'll soon come out? Be presented and all that? You're just longing for it, eh?"

"I'm not quite sure," said Cynthia doubtfully. "I don't want to come out if it means going about with Mother. Lois has been out four years and I don't think she gets much fun. She has no freedom."

"A girl gets a better time once she's married," he observed.

"Yes. I suppose so."

"Little girl . . ." he began, and paused, at a loss.

He had slipped an arm round her shoulders and she permitted the embrace with an indifference admirably calculated to encourage him. He was on the point of further demonstrations when Agatha and Gerald came round the corner of the hedge. Sir Thomas removed his

arm. As he met the cool, speculative gaze of Lady Clewer
the slow purple mounted to his bald brow. The two
couples passed each other with brief civilities. Sir Thomas,
once out of sight and hearing, hinted that Blair and his
cousin seemed to be very fond of each other's company.
Cynthia assented, and he was about to say that he wouldn't
be in Sir John's shoes. But he desisted. It wouldn't do for
his companion to think that he sympathized with jealous
husbands. A very little might still be sufficient to scare her.

Agatha laughed at the encounter.

" These yew walks are dangerous," she said.

" He's an old horror," said Gerald. " How can you
allow it ? "

" I'm not responsible for Cynthia. She isn't my
daughter."

" No. But this is your house."

" And you feel that our escutcheon is blotted ? "

Gerald said nothing.

" You mustn't worry about Cynthia," she urged. " She's
perfectly able to look after herself."

" I've no doubt of it."

" You used not to be so censorious."

" You used not to be so . . ."

" So what ? " she demanded quickly.

" So tolerant."

" Well ? Do you object to my being tolerant ? "

" Oh, no ! " he said politely, " I wouldn't dream of
questioning your right to be anything you like."

" I should hope not ! But for all that you are growing
rather critical, don't you think ? You're always making me
feel it."

He did not deny it, but said :

" We've got into different galleys, my dear. We've
drifted apart, as the sentimental songs say."

" I know. But I'm sorry. I don't like it."

There was an accent of genuine distress in her voice which touched him. He had not supposed that she could be hurt by anything he said or did.

"I was very sorry myself when first I realized it," he told her. "But I saw that it was inevitable, so I resigned myself."

"I don't resign myself to things so easily," she said sombrely.

"Oh, you'd better!"

He stopped and looked at her in consternation. All his peace of mind was based upon a belief that she was happy, and in harmony with the life she had chosen. He was frightened by the restiveness of her tone.

"You'd better," he repeated.

"Oh, Gerald!"

He wished that she would not look at him so sorrowfully. Too intolerably reminiscent, she was, of the woman he had lost. He must either fly from her or challenge her. If he held his ground an instant longer he must attempt some master word which would bring this ghost to life.

"Agatha! Do you remember Canverley Fair?"

Rooks, cawing loudly in the elm trees behind the house, seemed to echo his own dismay at what he had said. She was reflecting and he jogged her memory in spite of himself.

"We went on swing-boats . . . and we saw a fat lady . . . and you were . . ."

"Sick! Oh, yes, Gerald! I do remember. Oh, of course! How funny that was! What funny little things we were!"

"We managed to enjoy ourselves."

"Did we? I suppose so. Fancy my forgetting! But do you know, I believe I made myself forget about it deliberately. I think I used to be very ashamed of it. And now it seems just funny! It's strange how one outgrow one's follies! One does at least leave off blushing for them."

" Thank heaven ! "

" But that was a very pretty fair," she exclaimed, delving further into the past.

" Was it ? "

" Well, wasn't it ? I seem to remember it as very pretty. All the colours were nice. Bright colours . . ."

She stood looking at him : looking beyond him into that resplendent memory. And it seemed to him that she could never have changed at all. Her eyes, innocent and candid, were the eyes of his early love. She had been restored to him, and he knew that his hard-won peace was gone for ever.

They walked on again. He followed her towards the house, confused and sad. His dislike of her surroundings, their luxury, materialism, and sensuality, deepened to a sharp horror. He was so certain now that she would one day see them with his eyes. It seemed to him that endless suffering was in store for her.

Lois, observing their lugubrious approach, remarked to Hubert that Agatha and Mr. Blair seemed to spend their time in walking about the garden in silence. Considering how old was their friendship, she said, they had uncommonly little to say to each other.

" Not like us," exulted Hubert.

This was very true. Lois and Hubert had an eternity of things to say to each other. It was as if the whole of their united future, now spread so gloriously before them, could scarcely suffice for all the wagging their tongues would have to do. But first of all she wanted to know what he thought of James's pictures. He was unwilling to tell her, for he believed her to be fond of James.

" Of course, the ones he showed us weren't his best," she said wistfully.

" One would hope not."

" Oh, Hubert ! Were they so very bad ? "

" Oh, no ! The boy can paint all right. But they weren't

the kind of thing that appeals to me. My taste isn't infallible, you know. Now, Lois. What am I to say to your mother ? And when and where ? "

Lois considered and then decided :

" You will have to be careful. She will think, you see, that you should have spoken to her first. Not that she objects to you. I don't see how she can do that. But she will pretend to at first, just to show how careful she is. And you must get her leave to speak to me, and then allow her to arrange an opportunity for you. She won't do that for a day or two, but eventually she will. Then, when we've been shut up in the drawing-room, or sent out in the punt, or whatever it is, for a suitable length of time, we will emerge and say we are engaged. She will think about it for a week and then put it in the *Morning Post*. It honestly will save trouble for her to think she has managed it all. I used to fight over things, but it isn't worth while, really. Now I use guile, as Agatha does, or did, with her mother, and life is much calmer."

" Well, it all seems rather complicated to me, but you know her best. I'll follow any plan you recommend. Shall I go now ? "

" Yes, you'd better. She'll be with Miss Barrington in her sitting-room. You know where it is ? Opening out of the long gallery. Ask to see her alone for a moment. Rather mysteriously. She loves being asked to see people alone."

" Right, my angel."

Hubert went, and she decided that she could not spend the palpitating interval better than in scolding James. It would relieve her spirits, and he needed it. Mounting again to the loft she discovered the artist plunged in contemplation before the portrait of Jellybelly.

" James, I'm furious with you," she began.

" Why ? " he asked mildly.

" Why on earth did you show those pictures to Hu—

to Mr. Ervine ?   Why couldn't you have shown him the
portrait you did of me, or that thing you got the prize for
in Brussels ? "

" These are better."

" You think so ?   Nobody else does.   I was so ashamed,
seeing you make such a fool of yourself in front of Mr.
Ervine.   Anyone could see what he thought.   I'll never
praise your work again."

" No.   I expect you'd better not."

" I was never so humiliated in my life."

" Yes.   I expect you felt a pretty good fool," said James in
an interested voice.

" I don't believe you are one bit sorry."

" Not a bit.   Why should I be ? "

" When I've always backed you up, I really do think . . .
however, you suffer for it.   I don't."

He thought this over and then asked :

" Where does it hit me ? "

" Only that everyone laughs at you.   You could have
impressed him if you'd tried.   As it is, it's easy to see that he
thinks your work isn't worth his attention."

" Well ? "

" Well, that's your loss.   You really are very dense, James.
He is a thoroughly artistic person.   He could be a lot of use
to you."

" How ? "

" Let me tell you that you are getting altogether too
conceited.   Since you came back from Paris you seem to
think you know everything.   Other people have been to Paris.
Mr. Ervine has.   He's a more experienced man than you are.
He's been everywhere and knows everyone.   You might
profit considerably by his advice."

" I don't want his advice.   I've no doubt he talks.   You
all do.   Like a lot of rooks cawing."   He stared at the elm
trees beyond the stable roof.   " Worse than any rooks.   I'd

sooner hear rooks any day. What's he done? Show me
that. These talking people make me sick."

"It wouldn't do you any harm to listen to us occasionally.
You only make us all laugh at you, giving yourself such airs.
I can assure you that your pictures were not admired this
morning."

James turned round suddenly and, angry as she was, she
quailed before the whiteness of his face. She recognized the
onset of one of those rare but terrific rages which had been
a legendary terror in the Lyndon nurseries. It had always
been accepted that, when James did lose his temper, he might
do anything.

"Get out!" he muttered, advancing towards her. "Get
out! Or I'll throw you out of the window."

"Nonsense, James," she scolded. "Don't dare to talk like
that."

But her voice shook a little and she took a step back.

"I will," he said, coming quite close to her. "And I'll
throw out the next of you that comes up here without being
asked."

He picked her up and carried her towards the window.
She screamed loudly and tugged at his hair, but the grip of
his long arms never slackened. She experienced, for the only
time in her life, all the humiliations of weakness before
violence. Her sharp heels drummed against his shins. She
told Hubert afterwards that it was like being carried off by a
gorilla. He steadied himself with one knee against the low
sash, held her out over the void, and spoke:

"Will you keep out of here after this?"

"Yes, James. Oh, you are a brute!"

"You'd better be careful. Will you leave off telling me
whose advice I'm to take?"

"Yes."

"Will you keep your opinions to yourself? And your
friends' opinions, too, if you can?"

"Yes. Do you call yourself a gentleman?"

"No. But if you'll promise you may come in again."

He spoke too late. Before he could lift her back into safety she had slipped from his arms. She fell six feet on to a sloping roof and slithered down the slates. A leaden gutter-pipe at the extreme end of the roof checked her descent. She lay still on the slope, too frightened to move, while below her there was a clear drop of three stories into the paved kitchen yard. James, his passion evaporated, leant out of the studio window and looked at her. His eyes were popping out of his head with horror.

"Are you hurt?" he called.

"No. But I shall fall if I move. Oh, you shall pay for this, James!"

"Could you get along a little that way and jump into that tree, do you think?"

"No, I couldn't. I shall fall if I move, I tell you."

"I'll get a ladder. I won't be long."

He ran down and met Marian and Hubert emerging into the long gallery from Marian's sitting-room.

"Lois is on the roof," he announced. "She can't get down."

"On the roof," cried Marian. "How did she get there?"

"From my studio window. I dropped her out. She is on the sloping bit. She says she will fall if she moves."

"Good heavens!" Marian turned pale. "But how dangerous!"

Hubert bounded up to the studio and looked out of the window at his love on the slates below. She lay there sobbing to herself.

"Lois!" he called. "Are you all right?"

"How can I be all right?" she replied with some irritation. "Look at me!"

"Don't look downwards whatever you do. You might get giddy."

" I won't."

" They are getting a ladder. I can see them bringing it through the kitchen garden."

" I do hope, after this, you'll have James shut up in a lunatic asylum."

" Is it his fault ? "

" Of course it is. He put me here."

" But not on purpose ? "

" Oh, yes. He simply picked me up and threw me out."

" Good God! The brute! It's incredible. He must be mad."

" He is."

" But what did he do it for ? "

" Oh, . . . he was annoyed."

" What about ? "

" Well, it was something I said."

" But what did you say ? "

Lois felt suddenly very reluctant to tell Hubert what she had said. It did not lend itself to repetition in cold blood.

" What were you quarrelling about ? " he asked again.

" Well, . . . you, for one thing."

" Me ? "

" Yes. I'll tell you after."

A crowd had now collected in the kitchen yard. Marian and Miss Barrington, Agatha and Gerald, Cynthia and Sir Thomas, James and John, all the gardeners and most of the servants stood gazing up at Lois on the roof much as they had gazed at the airship earlier in the morning. Ladders were collected and tied together but still fell short of the required height. Hubert, at the window, swore at the general stupidity and encouraged Lois in such endearing terms as should have left no doubt, in the mind of a less preoccupied audience, as so the relations between them.

" They are sending into Oxford for the man who cleans the gutters," he told her. " His ladder is longer."

Lois burst into fresh sobs.

" I can't possibly wait here till then," she wailed. " I shall move, and then I shall fall off."

James, John, and Gerald consulted together in the yard; they shouted to the gardeners for a strong rope and ran into the house. Joining Hubert in the studio, shortly afterwards, they explained that James was going down after her.

" It's his idea," explained John. " He thinks he can take the rope with him and tie it round her waist. Then we can pull her up. When we've got her safe we can send it down again for him."

" Doesn't look too safe," said Hubert frowning.

" It isn't. But that gutter isn't strong and I'm uncommonly afraid of it breaking under her. That's why I don't want to wait for this man from Oxford. I don't think the thing will hold ; you can see it bulging from the yard, and if it broke she would shoot straight off the roof."

" Look ! Let me go ! " said the gallant Hubert, a little uncertainly.

" No. James must go. He's the lightest of us. And I don't want to put any extra strain on that gutter. You're too heavy."

" Clewer thinks he can manage it ? " asked Hubert sourly.

" He's got a good head for heights. Are you ready, James ? "

James dropped over the edge of the window, fell heavily on to the slates, and slipped down to Lois's side. Leaning upon one elbow he knotted the rope round her waist. As they writhed distressfully together upon the sloping roof they reminded the distracted Hubert of the figures on the Medici tomb. James gave the signal to the men above to pull, and the gutter cracked.

" Hurry up ! " commanded John. " The thing's going."

Lois was hoisted into safety as the gutter broke and fell into the yard below. James saved himself by wriggling along

the roof to where a drain-pipe gave him a little extra
purchase. But he was now out of reach of the window and
the rope. Beneath him a large chestnut tree shaded the
kitchen court. He eyed it meditatively for a second or two,
balanced himself, sprang, and landed in the branches.

"He really is like a monkey," cried Lois, struck by the
resemblance for the second time in half an hour.

But his agility failed him at the critical moment. He
crashed through the leaves and fell to the ground with a
heavy thud. John and Gerald silently hastened from the
studio.

"The branches broke his fall," said Hubert reassuringly,
as the group in the yard closed round the motionless figure
at the foot of the tree.

He and Lois stood alone together at the window. Both
were rather pale.

"I hope he isn't much hurt," she whispered. "I'm sorry
I was so angry with him."

"But what was it all about?"

She reflected how best she could narrate to him this
rather discreditable affair.

"Poor James," she began, " . . . you know we used to be
great friends. And it's naturally rather a shock to him now
to find that I think more of your opinion than his."

Hubert remembered a hint that Marian had just given
him and saw light.

"You mean he doesn't like being cut out?"

Lois had not quite meant that, but she left it uncontra-
dicted. It was, on the whole, a nicer explanation than the
real one. And it might have some truth, when she came to
think of it. Such fury does not arise from ordinary pique,
but a disappointed lover will do anything. A roar of pain, as
Gerald stooped to examine James, caused the pair at the
window to exclaim in relief:

"Then he isn't dead!"

Hubert began to be indignant again.

"All the same, you know, it's no excuse for throwing you out of the window."

"No, I know. With anyone else it wouldn't be. But he, you know . . . well, he can't be judged quite like other people."

"I suppose not, poor chap. Anyhow, he took some risk getting you up again."

"Don't tell anyone. I think we'll say it was an accident."

"Oh! All right! Perhaps it would be best."

Gerald put both his hands to his mouth and shouted up to them :

"A broken collar-bone ! "

"But that isn't at all serious ! " said Lois in some disappointment.

2.

Immediately after breakfast it was generally a cardinal object with Gerald and Hubert to escape from Sir Thomas Bragge. At this time of day he was most dangerous, for the ladies were seldom on the scene so early. But the young men considered that it was John's duty to entertain him since John had, presumably, invited him. They did not like hearing about his successful business career, and the constant recital of the glories of the house he meant to build disgusted them both, though on different grounds. Gerald thought it stank of money. Hubert, who did not on principle object to dividends, jibbed at the implied scheme of decoration. They shared a hearty sympathy for the unfortunate architect, who was regarded by Sir Thomas as a kind of stone-mason and bullied abominably.

Gerald thought the garden a safer place than the house and fled to a concealed walk, under a rose-covered pergola, in which to smoke a morning pipe. From this shelter he observed with immense satisfaction the buttonholing of

Hubert. Sir Thomas got his victim on the terrace and began to tell him funny stories. Up and down they walked and Hubert seemed to get sadder and sadder. Gerald could not help being a little compassionate, for Sir Thomas's stories, though almost always improper, were so long and punctuated by so many guffaws that people generally forgot the beginning before he reached the end. It was not quite as bad for Hubert, however, as it would have been for Gerald, since he was studying Sir Thomas and needed to collect more copy. He had already " Bragged " a little for Lois's entertainment.

Gerald, in delicious security, took his ease under the roses. In a very few days he was hoping to be out of this demoralizing place and back at his work. Lyndon was altogether too full of ladies for his liking. He had shut women out of his life on the day that he learnt of Agatha's desertion. He took no interest in them, and, except in his consulting room, saw as little of them as a religious in a monastery. His friends were men and he worked with men.

This newly awakened preoccupation with his cousin was, therefore, wholly undesirable and must be shaken off. But he did not believe that it would trouble him long when once he had got away from her. His broken heart had been mended very quickly before ; sooner indeed than he quite liked. His profession had absorbed him and he was able to see how disastrous marriage might have been. His particular field was, as yet, almost uncharted. He was one of the pioneers in a new branch of medical science. He possessed enough means to support himself if he did not marry, and he intended to devote his life to experimental research ; to use to the full his peculiar opportunities.

He had scarcely thought of Agatha since the first despairing weeks. They had not met until she had been married some two and a half years, for she lay ill at Lyndon when he returned from his sojourn in Paris. He had heard of the

death of her baby with detached compassion. Soon afterwards he went to Austria and thence to Italy. Now he was
returned to London, was working sixteen hours a day, and
accomplishing a third as much as he could wish.

He should not have allowed himself to be entrapped into
this visit. But his relatives pestered him and he resented
their intimations that he avoided Lyndon for a particular
reason. All that was over and done with ; he was immune.
If a spark of the old feeling had been left he could never
have criticized her so coolly. A man must be genuinely out
of love who can condemn as he condemned. But he should
have distrusted this inclination to protest too much. He
now suffered for his over-confidence. He had discovered
that she could still command his unreasoned pity. Criticism,
as strong as ever, could not kill it. And his conviction that
she was destined to pain was the more agonizing to him since
he could not leave off condemning her.

For his own sake he must immediately put an end to this
state of things. He told himself that it would never do.
That it was no concern of his whether she were happy or
not . That hers was no isolated case and not to be compared
with the pain and sorrow which he encountered daily among
his patients. He must get the thought of her out of his
head. And he smiled as he thought how he would lecture a
patient who had thus lost his sense of proportion. But few
physicians can heal themselves.

The path where he walked ended in a low brick wall
enclosing part of the kitchen garden. Upon the other side
of this wall he heard a voice which startled him into instant
attention. A rather peculiar duologue was going on.

" Really, Kell . . . you can't manage it alone. I oughtn't
to let you."

" Oh, that's all right, my lady. It's not heavy really.
Only a bit awkward."

" It would be much better if I were to take the other end.

Just wait a minute. . . . Oh, I'm sorry! Did it catch your elbow ? "

" Not at all, my lady."

" It's just till I get used to the weight. . . ."

Staggering steps ensued, and then :

" Surely it's much too large ! Couldn't you find a smaller one ? "

" This was the one Mr. Higgins gave me, my lady."

" He should have brought it himself. It's too heavy for a woman. Wait till I call one of the men. Two men. . . ."

Gerald brushed aside the larkspurs in the border, stepped up to the wall, and looked over it. He saw Agatha and the pretty housemaid who had attended the Dante lecture ; they were struggling with a large step-ladder. Both were very pink.

" Where do you want it taken ? " he called.

Agatha pointed to a brick building at the end of the enclosure. Swinging himself over the wall he picked up the ladder for them and set off between the raspberry canes and onion beds. Agatha, following, explained in a distressed voice :

" It's so silly. It's to get some cherries for James. It seems that he has a passion for those little dark morello cherries against the potting-shed wall. They are rather hard to get, they grew so high, and are not very good when you've got them. At least, most people don't care for them. But James likes them better than anything else. Of course, I ordered fruit and flowers to be sent up to him while he was in bed, but Kell tells me it hasn't been done. She has asked twice for the cherries, but Higgins wouldn't take the trouble. So to-day she went and got a ladder, intending to get them herself. I saw her dragging this heavy ladder along. You really shouldn't, you know, Kell."

Kell smiled respectfully and helped Gerald to place the ladder against the potting-shed wall. She then produced a little basket which hung from her arm and looked doubt-

fully from it to the top of the ladder. She was evidently
wondering which of the three should climb up and fill it.

" We will get the cherries and take them up to Mr. James,"
said Agatha. " You must be very busy at this time of the
morning. It was most kind of you to take all this trouble."

The housemaid murmured a word of thanks and departed,
walking sedately up the box-edged path.

Gerald climbed the ladder and began to fill the basket,
glancing down from time to time at his cousin as she sat
in the sun upon an upturned rhubarb pot. He picked the
cherries very slowly, prolonging as far as possible this
moment of satisfaction and contentment. He had become
aware that it was better to suffer in her company than to
be tranquil in her absence. She appeared to him perfect.
Nothing she said or did could make the slightest difference
to his feeling for her. He could find no fault, and her
words and thoughts were beyond reproof simply because
they were hers. He had been overtaken unawares by that
overpowering need of one individual for another which
defies reason and shapes our ends. This final stage of his
subjugation had been so sudden and so surprising that he
almost fell off the ladder.

At last the basket was full and he descended to her side.
Together they strolled away through the vegetables. She
was pensive, reflecting upon the strangeness of a lover.
She knew him to be that and was just a little triumphant
at having won him again. But she could not tell what she
had done to bring him back. She asked him to come with
her on a charitable visit to James, and they mounted to
the sick-room.

James's bedroom gave no clue to his tastes. The furniture
was that which Marian had provided when he had been
promoted from the night nursery to a room of his own.
Only the bed had been changed in deference to his added
inches. There were no memorials of the past, no photo-

graphs of school groups, no relics of obsolete, boyish collections, nothing that could throw light on the essential James. His hair-brushes and a couple of ties lay forlornly upon the dressing-table, while on the mantelpiece was a china money-box in the shape of a bathing machine which had been there since his eighth birthday. Pictures had formed part of Marian's scheme : *The Boyhood of Raleigh*, *Nelson in the Cockpit of the " Victory*," and *When did you last see your Father ?* had hung on the walls for seventeen years. To remove them now would have revealed large, brilliant squares on the trellised paper. The whole room was suggestive of a little boy recently deported to a preparatory school with all his more intimate possessions. James, sitting upright in bed and badly needing a shave, did not seem to belong to it at all.

Gerald, used as he was to the study of abnormal mentalities, was struck anew by the baffling qualities of this one. He divined a degree of contra-suggestibility beyond any he had previously encountered. It was impossible to make any impression upon James. He lived in a strange world of his own, developing character, as it were, in spite of his surroundings. Agatha put the basket of cherries on his bed and asked him how he did.

" I had thought," he said very seriously, " that I must be extremely ill. But Dr. Crosbie tells me that this kind of injury, though always painful, is seldom serious."

" I sent up flowers," she said, glancing round the room with dissatisfaction. " Didn't they come ? "

" Dolly took them. We don't think flowers are healthy in a bedroom."

" Not healthy ? How funny of you, James ! What makes you think so ? "

" Well, Dolly has a married friend at Brixton who was a trained nurse. And she told Dolly that flowers in bedrooms give people cancer."

" Kell seems to look after you very nicely," said Agatha,
trying to hide her amusement. " Did she give you these
to read ? "

There was a pile of literature on James's bed, including
several numbers of *Home Chat* and a Sunday School prize
called *Leonard's Temptation*. James nodded but explained
that the Bible was, in Dolly's opinion, the best reading for
an invalid. She had lent him hers, which had pictures in it,
and a large number of pressed flowers and memorial cards
of which he apparently knew the several histories.

It was always difficult to talk to James, even if he was, as
now, in an expansive mood. His visitors were glad when
Lois and Hubert appeared, inspired also to visit the sick.
Under the pretext that the room must be crowded the
cousins made off.

Agatha said, outside the door :

" Everyone seems to visit James in couples. I wonder
if Cynthia and Sir Thomas have been yet."

" That girl . . . Kell . . . is very good to him."

" Isn't she ? I don't know what he would do without
her. Of course, she isn't cut out for a housemaid really.
She oughtn't to be in service. She's too rough and countri-
fied ever to soar beyond being an under-servant ; she
doesn't adapt herself like most of them do. She has too
much in her. She ought to be a farmer's wife or something
like that. She'd run things splendidly if she were in a
position of responsibility."

Lois and Hubert found that conversation flagged. They
were oppressed by the memory of the studio window. The
accident which had led to James's illness was always with
them and it tied their tongues. Lois had by now quite
convinced herself that it was disappointed love which had
caused him to throw her out of the window, and she was inclined to be very forgiving in consequence. But Hubert was
not softened ; he regarded the fellow as a homicidal lunatic.

James was taciturn and made no attempt to help them out. At last they abandoned the effort of talking to him and diverted themselves by laughing at the pictures in Dolly's Bible. It is to be hoped that they did not know it was hers, for they continued their merriment when she brought in James's lunch.

" Who is this party contemplating a sort of astral butcher's shop ? " demanded Hubert.

" Oh, that's Peter on Cornelius's roof. It's in Acts."

" I never read Acts. It's got shipwrecks and all sorts of excitements in it, hasn't it ? "

The luncheon tray reminded them of their own need for food and they departed. Dolly, her cheeks deeply flushed, gathered up the markers and pressed flowers, which had been scattered over the bed, and replaced them in the despised Book. James regarded her with sorrow and comprehension.

" Dolly," he said gently, " I'm ever so sorry they laughed at your things. I couldn't stop them."

" Miss Lois ought to know better," said Dolly. " She's had enough education, I should think, to know it's wrong to make a mock of sacred things."

" He did it first."

" More shame to him ! " she cried hotly. " And then he comes and sets himself up to teach us ! Education ! If education makes people talk like ignorant heathen, I'm glad I haven't got any."

" Don't think about them," he urged.

" People like that call themselves ladies and gentlemen ! I wonder they have the face ! When they talk so bad that poor people are ashamed to hear them. Don't you never want to teach them manners, James ? I do."

She bit her lip, realizing that she had called him by his name.

" They get taught sometimes," said James, grinning

reminiscently.   " Do you know how Lois fell out of the window ? "

" No. How ? "

" I put her out."

" You never didn't ! What for ? "

" Bad manners."

" My stars ! " Dolly gasped. " You shouldn't ought."

" I know. I was very much frightened. I thought I'd killed her. But it's done her no harm."

" It hasn't done her no good neither, seemingly."

" I'm afraid not."

" But you was really very wrong to do it. You have got a nerve ! Whatever will you do next ? "

" How should I know ? "

He grew morose again.

" What do you live here for ? " she asked suddenly. " I wouldn't. Not when they treat you like they do. Haven't you got any money of your own ? "

" Yes. I've got about four hundred pounds a year."

" What ? As much as that ? Why, it's nearly eight pounds a week ! "

" Do you think that much or little ? "

" Depends on how you look at it. At my home we think a man gets good wages if he gets three pounds a week. Why ! Lots of men marry on two pounds."

" Marry ? " said James. " Marry ? "

" Have you finished your soup ? "

She bent over him to take the bowl but with his free arm he caught her and forced her to sit on the bed beside him.

" Marry ! " he exclaimed again. " I was a fool not to think of it ! Look here, Dolly ! I can marry you, can't I ? "

" Don't talk silly. . . ."

" It's not silly. Couldn't we be married and have a house of our own ? Would you like it ? "

" What ? "

"Why shouldn't we? Don't you think we'd be very happy?"

She perceived the gravity of his intention and began to reflect.

"I used to think I'd never marry anyone," she said at last, indecisively. "But you're different somehow. I don't believe you'd annoy me the way other men would."

"Of course I wouldn't. I don't annoy you now, do I? Well, why should I then?"

"That's right. That's where it is. And then I believe you'd let me have my way about the house and everything. I like managing things."

"Oh, yes, you can do what you like in the house as long as you don't get telling me how to paint."

"Tell you how to paint! Me? Not much! I can't even draw. But listen while I explain. Will you come to chapel with me Sundays? That's my trouble. I never felt I could marry a religious man, because my stepfather was religious. And the way he went on . . . well, it made you hate the name of God sometimes, if you know what I mean. But then, I couldn't marry an unbeliever, because I'm religious myself, somehow, in spite of my stepfather. Divine worship I like; it's only religious people I can't bear. If you'll come to chapel Sundays and hold your tongue about it other times, and not always be asking blessings, it will just suit me."

"Me too," said James. "I know what you mean."

"I never thought I could fancy a husband," she observed. "But there's something about you, James . . . well . . . I don't know! So gentle as you are generally and then throwing anybody out of the window!" She laughed. "It seems like I've got to keep you out of mischief."

"We'll be married at once," he said, revolving the great idea in his mind.

"We might as well," she agreed.

There was a pause while the betrothed pair stared at each other. Dolly began to wonder whether she would have to prompt him, so slow was he in arriving at a clear conception of his own needs. But at last he drew her towards him and began to kiss her fresh cheek, tentatively, and with an embarrassment which seemed to her pitiful. She realized that these were probably the first caresses ever offered by him to any human being since the departure of her aunt from Lyndon. This was not the diffidence of an inept lover but a symbol of the complete isolation in which he had lived.

The knowledge filled her with a passionate tenderness, and, half sobbing, she flung a protecting arm round him as though to shield him from a world which had been too unkind.

3.

" I can't quite understand what is going on in the shrubbery," said Agatha, sitting up and shading her eyes. " First of all I saw Lady Clewer and Mr. Ervine walking up and down on the terrace. Then, with a determined air, they went into the shrubbery, just as if they had lost something and were going to look for it. Then she came out without him and went into the house. Then she reappeared with Lois and marched her into the shrubbery. Now I see her coming out again alone. She has presumably left them inside together."

" Rather unusual on her part, isn't it ? " said Gerald.

" Very. That's why I'm puzzled. What can be the meaning of it ? "

" Well, she's coming to tell us."

Marian was advancing across the lawn towards the cedar tree, her face aglow with smiles. Though she was at least a hundred yards from the shrubbery she had the air of one who walks on tip-toe. She joined them.

"I hope you won't mind my giving you a hint," she began, "but I wouldn't go into the shrubbery just now if I were you."

"Not if you'd rather we didn't," said Agatha, feeling that no power on earth should induce her to ask why not.

"Of course, I don't know," pursued the joyful mother, "if anything will come of it. But Mr. Ervine is having a little talk with Lois. A very important little talk."

"So we saw."

"Oh, did you guess? How quick of you, dear! Between ourselves I have a very shrewd suspicion of what her feelings are. And nothing could please me more. He is such a nice fellow! And he has been so straightforward about it all, speaking to me before he ever said a word to her. I just had to give him the opportunity."

"I see Sir Thomas going into the shrubbery from the terrace," exclaimed Agatha.

"Oh, dear!" cried Marian, looking much distressed. "I can never reach him in time. Can we shout? How can we stop him?"

"I'll run," said Gerald.

He ran and Marian sank exhausted into his chair.

"Dear me!" she said. "How all this takes me back to your engagement, Agatha. I never shall forget that dance at the Calthorpes', and how your mother and I stood at the door of the little conservatory, blocking up the entrance, so that you and John should have time to settle things before anyone came in."

"Did you?" asked Agatha curiously.

"Yes. And your poor mother was so afraid that you would refuse him. I was a little nervous myself. You were so young. And you hadn't seen Lyndon."

Agatha glanced at the house which should have prompted her to so immediate an acceptance of John. It was indeed a magnificent possession. There was no end to its beauty.

But she was quite sure that she had never thought of it once during that half-hour in the conservatory. As far as she could remember she had not thought about anything at all. If she had entertained any intelligent ideas they had made no impression. She could recall the heavy scent of the conservatory, and the flame of orchids, the cadences of a distant waltz, John's hand on her heart and the urgency of his voice. These things had brought her to Lyndon.

"I was very young," she said. "I hardly knew what I was doing."

Gerald was now on the terrace talking to Sir Thomas. She looked at him resentfully. He was unfair and she often wished that she could tell him so. He did her an injustice in supposing that she had not married for love, according to her lights. Everyone, her mother even, had encouraged her to believe that her attachment to John was of an enduring nature. If she had learnt the impermanence of such passion, it was irrevocable experience which had taught her. She could not be expected to know then.

Not that she feared for Lois. This manipulated proposal, so typical of Marian and her kind, did not go for much. Lois and Hubert were really suited to each other ; they had a community of tastes which augured well for the future. They would probably make a better thing of it than she and John had done. They would rise to a level of intimacy and companionship impossible to her. And yet, it might not have been impossible if . . . Here, woman-like, she was able to skip a few thoughts and safeguard her conscience.

Gerald was returning with Sir Thomas and two more chairs. They all sat down under the tree in silence, bending an expectant regard upon the entrance to the shrubbery. At last Gerald asked Marian how long she supposed her young couple would be. Marian looked rather scandalized and said she really didn't know.

"They would have to come out by now, surely, if she

had refused him," suggested Agatha. "But do you think it's quite nice of us to sit here waiting ? "

"I must know when they have finished their little talk," urged Marian. "I shall have to speak to Lois."

"But the rest of us ? I think it would be more tactful if we removed ourselves."

Agatha began to prepare for departure, while Gerald unkindly suggested that the interesting pair might have left the shrubbery by the gate into the park. This idea horrified Marian, and she was about to pursue them when they were all given pause by the hasty approach of Cynthia. They were instantly aware that she had news of interest to communicate to them. So seldom did she move with animation that only the deepest excitement could cause her to hurry as she was now doing. She surveyed them triumphantly for a moment and then drawled :

"James has torn it this time."

"Oh, James ! " said Marian with bored irritation. "What has he been doing now ? "

"He wants to marry Kell."

"Kell ! "

"Kell, the housemaid ? "

Everybody gaped, and Agatha immediately wondered why she had not foreseen it. It was so patently obvious.

"The third housemaid," said Cynthia with relish.

"Good heavens ! But why . . .? " began Marian.

"How should I know ? " replied Cynthia, who believed that she did.

"Who told you ? " demanded Agatha.

"John. He and James are hard at it in the study. James got up this morning, you know. The doctor said he might as long as he keeps his arm all tied up. And he went straight off, as soon as he was up, and found John and made this announcement. They want you, please, Mother."

"Oh, dear," cried Marian, with a glance at the shrubbery.

" I can't possibly come yet. I must stay here for a minute or two."

" But isn't it like James ? " exclaimed Agatha.

" She seems a nice girl," contributed Gerald.

" An uncommonly pretty girl," pronounced Sir Thomas. " What does she say to it ? Will she have him ? "

" You bet she will if she can," Cynthia assured them. " You'll have to sack her now, I suppose, Agatha ? "

" Yes, indeed ! My dear, it will be most disagreeable for you," said Marian sympathetically. " Having a thing like this happen in one's own house ! Would you like me to see her for you ? "

" No, thank you," replied Agatha a little coldly.

" I don't see how you can possibly blame yourself, though," continued Marian. " Nobody could have foreseen this. I suppose it's all the result of our letting him go to Paris. However . . ."

Her glance suggested that they could not really discuss this delicate matter in the presence of gentlemen. Agatha was thinking swiftly. She remembered Kell tugging at the heavy ladder to get cherries for James. She thought of Kell's Bible on his bed. Kell was really a very nice creature. It was monstrous that anyone should regard the affair in the light of a scandal. Marian's suggestive hints were not to be endured. Neither James nor Kell should be insulted while Agatha was the lady of Lyndon.

" I shall be very sorry to lose her," she announced. " She is such an exceptionally nice girl. But I don't suppose she will want to stay on as housemaid after she is married."

This was an open defection and was felt as such by the company. Marian looked dumbfounded. Cynthia and Sir Thomas had much ado not to laugh. The affair, to them, could have but one significance. Gerald Blair became extremely joyful.

" I think James has shown the most astounding good

sense," stated the amazing Agatha. "I think he will be very lucky if he can succeed in marrying such an admirable creature. I am sure she will make him happy, which no one else has ever tried to do."

"My dear Agatha . . ." began Marian, but the rebel, quite exhausted by her own violence, had turned away towards the house.

Gerald recognized the frightened pallor which had succeeded her flush of excitement. He had seen it before on an occasion, the only occasion in her life, when she had defied her mother. That was five years ago, and her defiance, if he remembered rightly, had been shortlived. This time her rash impetuosity must be encouraged, upheld. He hastened after her and found her, still palpitating, in the flowery spaciousness of her drawing-room. They looked at each other and Gerald ejaculated :

"Cleared it ! "

"Well, but don't you agree with me ? Don't you ? If she cares for him, don't you think it's the best thing that could happen to him ? And I honestly don't think she'd have accepted him if she didn't."

"Of course it is. Any man would be in luck to get a girl like that. She's splendid. Well balanced, healthy, sane . . . a good stock. I watched her at that Dante lecture and thought what a fine woman she was."

"Oh, don't talk like that. I don't mean that. They love each other really and properly, as only one couple in a thousand manage to do. Stop talking like a eugenics text-book."

"It's my job."

"Yes. But you know better than that ! Gerald ! Stop looking out of the window ! You know better than that."

"I know . . ." he began, and pulled up, appalled at the indiscretion of the remark he had been about to make.

The contagious properties of love are proverbial and it is

always dangerous for a couple divorced by fate to reflect in unison upon the happier romances of other people. These ill-starred cousins were unlucky in that they had been thrown together at a time when the whole of Lyndon was mating. A moment after Gerald's too significant pause, they had the prudence to withdraw, somewhat hastily, from an interview which was leading them beyond the bounds of decorum. Agatha ran upstairs and Gerald bolted into the billiard-room.

4.

He left Lyndon next day before she had finished making her leisurely breakfast in bed. She heard the throbbing of his car at the door and the change of gear as it hummed away up the slope. Silence fell upon Lyndon when he was gone, scarcely broken by the peaceful, everlasting sound of mowing and the shouting of cuckoos far off across the water meadows.

She lay drowsily, watching the tempered sunlight which streamed through the half-shaded windows. It fell in great rainbow splashes upon the crystal and silver of her dressing-table. Her breakfast steamed on a tray beside her bed and her morning's letters were strewed upon the counterpane. At last she roused herself sufficiently to pour out another cup of coffee and examine her mail. There were several pages from her mother, and she frowned a little as she perused them. One passage in particular made her flush and sigh :

" By the way, I've had such a funny letter from Marian. (How I wish we had not got on to these Christian name terms of intimacy ! They tie one so !) I must show it to you. It's most veiled, of course, but it seems she really is getting worried upon the family question. Has she been dropping tactful hints to you ? If not, I think you may expect them. Personally, I consider it's exceedingly impertinent of her, in spite of my own views on the matter, of which you are already aware. *Of course* it's important that the place shouldn't go to the Causfield Clewers, and I really think that the sooner that contingency is provided against, the better. Still, you've heard all this before, and I expect you think you know your own business.

Have you talked to J. about standing for Parliament in the next election? I met Tim Fenwick at Lady Peel's yesterday, and he seemed to take it for granted that the Government would come to grief over this Ulster question. If this is really so, John has no time to lose. He, T. F. I mean, has been nursing his constituency for months. Do get J. to stir himself. I think it would be such an excellent thing for you both; you can do so much for him, canvassing and so on, and people without a family need something of the kind, some common interest to bring them together. And I think a serious object in life would be good for him. If you will persist in what I cannot but regard as a very rash obstinacy, I think the safest course will be to get John into Parliament if possible. . . ."

Agatha, angry as she was, could not help laughing a little at these tactful suggestions. It was so like her mother to think that politics would provide John with a good substitute for paternity.

Since the death of her first-born, the luckless heir of Lyndon, she had steadily refused to bear children or had, rather, postponed the bearing of them to a more convenient epoch. She could not bring herself to face again the trials of that first year of wifehood. It had taught her, with an enduring shock, the nature of her hold upon her husband. She had felt him slipping from her at a moment when she stood in the most need of his supporting tenderness.

It had been his obvious pity for her condition which had alarmed her. He had been much too considerate for her peace of mind. Never for a moment had he forgotten that her eclipsed beauty had made her an object of compassion. This attitude struck her as an insult ; a piece of brutality thinly veiled by sentiment. She knew that she had lost all her real power over him and that he was behaving to her in accordance with his ideas of civility. His renewed ardour at her recovery of health and good looks had made her sure of this. And at that time she cared a great deal for his devotion. She did still. On his subjugation depended most of her own self-esteem.

She had decided to wait some years before taking such a risk again, and he, happy in the recovery of his beautiful wife, had acquiesced. There was plenty of time before them, for Agatha was, in those days, barely nineteen. But the subject was a sore one with Mrs. Cocks, who continually urged her daughter to " get it over." As for Marian, she looked upon such a refusal of responsibility as flighty and a little ill-bred. It is to be doubted whether anyone in the world guessed what tears had been shed by the mother in secret over the child she had never even seen. Now, as she lay at ease in her magnificent bed, a small and very bitter drop splashed on to Mrs. Cock's letter and blurred the large handwriting. For Agatha had a morbid and unconfessed conviction that no child born to herself and John would meet with a better fate than the first.

His step in the gallery recalled her to herself. Instantly she put her hands to her hair beneath the falling silk and lace of her cap. Searching under her pillow she found a small handkerchief and carefully removed the traces of her tears. When he greeted her she was smiling.

" Blair has gone," he informed her. " I expect you heard him go."

" Yes."

"Hope being here has done him good. He assures me that he is sleeping better. But I can't say I see much improvement. He came looking haggard and he's gone away looking haggard."

"I don't think visits to relations are very good rest cures."

"You're right. He should have gone a sea voyage or something."

He was wandering round the room picking up photographs and putting them down again and fidgeting among the things on her dressing-table."

"Lois and Ervine are settled," he said. "Mamma is going to send the notice to the papers to-day. Hello! What's this?"

He held up a small, common-looking object. It was that pocket photograph of Gerald and Agatha which had been taken so long ago at Canverley Fair. She had on the previous night removed it from the cabinet where it had lain forgotten and stared at it for a little time, thinking strange thoughts. She remembered now that she had not put it away.

"This is Blair, isn't it?" continued John. "But who's the kid?"

"Don't you recognize her?"

"Not . . .? You never wore your hair dragged back like that, did you?"

"When I was sixteen I did. I was sixteen when that was taken."

"But how on earth could your mother allow it?"

"She didn't know. We got photographed without her leave at a country fair."

"I didn't mean that. I mean how could she allow you to do your hair like that?"

"Oh, she liked it like that. It's unbecoming, isn't it? But I wasn't out, you see.".

"It's hideous. I didn't think you could look like that."

He put it in his pocket and said :

" I can't have this thrown away. It's a family curio."

" It wasn't going to be thrown away. Please give it back, John ! "

" Oh, no. I'm going to keep it. I'll put it among the miniatures."

" No, John ! I want it ! "

" You won't get it. Though I don't wonder that you don't want to let it out of your hands. It's a very compromising piece of evidence, you know."

" What of ? " she asked, tremendously startled.

" That you were ever plain. No one would believe it without positive proof. It gives me unlimited power over you. Cynthia would give her eyes for a squint at it. By the way, now that Mamma has disposed of Lois, I think she will wake up a bit about Cynthia and Bragge."

" What do you think about that ? " asked Agatha sitting up.

" Oh, well . . . he's rather a bounder, but if she will have him it's a good match from the financial point of view."

" But he's so much older. . . ."

" Yes, it's a drawback. But if she doesn't mind, why should we ? "

" I can't see how she can contemplate such a thing."

" I expect she wants her freedom."

" But I can't believe it will turn out happily."

" There won't be any scandals in the family, if that's what you mean. Cynthia's got her head screwed on too well for that. And that's all we need worry about."

" I hate his ideas. So vulgar . . . so mercenary. . . ."

" What about hers ? "

Agatha was silent.

" You may take it," he said, " that they will be well matched. She knows her own business. So does he. And a pretty penny she'll cost him."

"At her age," argued Agatha, "a girl ought to have ideals. . . ."

"Ought she? Had you?"

He had seated himself beside her on the bed. Silhouetted against the shaded window she could study his massive profile and the slight thickening of his neck over the back of his collar—the first indications of approaching corpulence. Though not really fat, he had too much flesh for thirty-four. But all the Clewer men were large; James would be fat in ten years' time, fat and pale, whereas John would be fat and red. He was toying with her hand, pressing each white finger slowly back, and she conquered an impulse to snatch it from him.

"I think I had ideals at seventeen," she said thoughtfully.

"You'd got rid of them by the time I met you. That was one of the first things that struck me about you, Agatha; your sense of proportion! Don't start losing it now!"

"If only Sir Thomas wasn't so . . ." She paused and met his eye. "Well, you know quite well, don't you, that . . .?"

"She got him on the rebound after a break?" He laughed. "How far did he go before you turned him down?"

"Oh, a good way, horrid old thing."

"Old blackguard!" He laughed again. "I thought as much. In fact it was pretty obvious. But he can't be blamed so very much. He has a certain amount of excuse, you know, my dear."

"But he was your guest."

"Well . . . er . . . yes. He is a bounder, isn't he? But Cynthia probably knows all about it, don't you think?"

"Are you never jealous, John?" she asked curiously.

"Not of that! Consider, my love, what a stormy life we would lead if I began. No. But just occasionally, when you get these soul qualms, you alarm me. I have a suspicion that if you ever deceive me it will be with a bishop or somebody like that."

After a pause he continued :

" Oh, I remember now what I really came to talk to you about. It's this affair of James. . Something's got to be done about it. And my only hope is the girl. I want you to talk to her and see if you can't scare her off. You know she's played her cards uncommonly well. She must be a clever girl. I've been talking to James and I gather she's succeeded in hooking him without giving any tricks away. There's been absolutely nothing in their relations which puts her at a disadvantage. She isn't forced to have him, you understand ? "

" Perfectly."

" I must confess I was surprised."

" I'm not. I don't think you understand either of them."

" I don't understand James, certainly, and you are more likely to understand the workings of another woman's mind than I am. My own opinion is, however, that she'll chuck him when she finds that four hundred pounds is all she'll get with him. She must have thought he had more. When she finds that he hasn't, she'll probably change her mind, don't you think ? "

" I don't know. It isn't a bad match for a girl in her class."

" Not if the fellow were presentable. But really, you know, the girl's a fine girl. She must expect some compensation for putting up with James."

" Really and truly I think you are mistaking the nature of her attachment to him."

" Well, that's what I want you to find out. You talk to her, quite sympathetically if you like, but just hint what a bad bargain he will be."

" But do you think it's altogether a thing to be discouraged? She is, after all, a nice, respectable girl and he is not quite like other people. He's a misfit here. Nobody regards him and he's not happy, obviously. With a wife and a home of his own he might do much better. And he's very fond of her."

"It wouldn't do at all," said John decidedly. "Don't you see that they would probably be in continual financial difficulties? Always dragging us down and coming to us for help. Besides," he added, with some constraint, "I think it would be rather a misfortune for James ever to marry anyone. We don't want a heap of his brats swarming all over the place."

"But they won't live here, surely?"

"No, but they would eventually, if James came into the place."

"It's early days to think of that."

"I can't help thinking of it. Hang it all, I do care for the place."

"It isn't any worse than the Causfield Clewers getting it. You've always said you wouldn't mind so very much if that happened."

"Nor would I. They are a very decent set, I believe. This would be quite a different thing."

"Well," she said, "I'll see Kell and I'll put the financial question before her. But I can't promise not to back her up if she sticks to him. I shall think too well of her."

"No, don't. I don't want a quarrel. James is so persistent that he may carry this through, just as he did us all over the Paris business. I shouldn't be a bit surprised. And in that case I don't want an open breach. It will only make things worse. That's why I don't want Mamma to get her finger into this pie; she's so uncompromising. Be nice to Kell, but tell her firmly that, if they insist upon marriage, we won't help them in any way. That should scare her."

" All right. I'll see her now."

" Need you worry so early ? " He looked grateful.
" Wait until after lunch. Any time will do. You've nothing
doing to-day, have you ? "

" Nothing. But I'll see her at once and then get up,"
said Agatha briskly.

He kissed her and departed, leaving her to arrange her
thoughts for the encounter. Kell was summoned. In her
print frock, with her flaming hair tucked away under her
cap, she looked out of place in the exotic richness of Agatha's
bedroom. She suggested a marigold in an orchid house.
She came and stood at the bedside, looking at her employer
with eyes that were respectful but unembarrassed.

" Sit down, won't you ? " said Agatha, raising herself
upon one elbow and looking kindly at the girl.

Kell sat, with a trace of nervousness, hardly knowing
where to place her reddened hands.

" I wanted to talk," continued Agatha, " about this
marriage. Naturally it is rather a surprise to us. You must
forgive us if it is so."

" Of course, I see that, my lady," rejoined Kell. After
a pause she continued in the careful speech she used with
her employers, " I know he is above me in station. But I
think I can make him happy. He is so different from most
gentlemen."

" He is indeed ! " thought Agatha. Aloud she said :
" Have you thought—forgive me if I am impertinent—
have you thought at all about ways and means ? Do you
think you can afford to marry, in fact ? "

" Oh, yes," said Kell, looking surprised. " We were
going to begin buying our furniture at once."

" He has four hundred pounds a year, I believe," murmured Agatha.

" Plenty girls in my class marry on less, Lady Clewer.
I'd think very poorly of myself if I couldn't manage on

eight pounds a week. And we've got something saved for our furniture."

" But then the standard of living would be rather different. You couldn't live like cottagers, quite." Kell looked unconvinced. " Or would you ? "

" We thought so," the other girl admitted. " We don't want anything different. I'm not marrying him because I want anything different. I don't like his being in a different class to me. I'd rather he was the same. For us to try to live like gentlepeople would be silly. It wouldn't suit him nor me."

" Then what are your plans ? "

" There's a little cottage out Bramfield way, my lady, that would do for us very well. I like Bramfield, because I've a married cousin living near there. And he likes it because of his pictures. He often goes over there to draw out the scenery."

" Does he ? Do you like his pictures, Ke . . . I can't call you Kell if I'm to be your sister-in-law, can I ? May I call you Dolly ? It seems to be more sensible, doesn't it ? Tell me how you like his pictures."

" I don't know." Dolly looked confused. " I hardly understand such things. He seems quite set on it, as you might say."

" Do you think he'll go on painting when you are married ? "

" Why, yes ! What else would he do ? A man must have something."

" But you don't admire his work particularly ? "

Dolly flushed, feeling that her loyalty was in some sort attacked.

" I think he's very clever to draw out all those things," she said defensively. " And they're very like, I'm sure. I think the machinery in that picture of the traction engine has come out quite beautiful. But I don't understand such things. At school I was always bad at the drawing."

Agatha turned to another aspect of the case and asked :
" What are your immediate plans ? It will be very awkward
for you during the next few weeks, won't it ? Are you
finding it difficult ? "

" Well, they don't know in The Room yet," said Dolly.
" But I've nothing to be ashamed of when they do."

" No, indeed ! But I was wondering if it would be
easier for you to go away for a bit. Have you no friends
you could stay with until your marriage ? "

Dolly shook her head.

" There's only my aunt," she said. " And she won't be
too pleased. She doesn't hold with people marrying above
them."

" We'll think out a plan," said Agatha. " I'll get up now.
Could you send Pauline to me."

Dolly rose, her round face very pink.

" I have to thank you for your kindness to me," she said.
" I know it is difficult for you and all the family, and I shall
always be grateful to you, Lady Clewer, for treating me in
such a friendly way. I don't know whether you and
Sir John and old Lady Clewer won't think that I ought to
try and live like a lady when I'm married. But, to my way
of thinking, we'd look more foolish if we did that, and give
the family more to be ashamed of, than if we went on in
the station we are used to."

" But you see, Dolly, it won't be his station."

" I know, my lady. No more this isn't." Dolly was
becoming earnest and idiomatic. " James and me . . . we
are just suited to each other like. We'll be just a little sort
of class to ourselves, I should say."

" That will be it," said Agatha enlightened. " Well . . .
if you are both happy . . ."

Then, remembering John's instructions, she repeated his
warning as well as she could. Dolly listened with dignity.

" We don't want anything done for us," she said. " And

I can promise that we won't burden you. We wouldn't like to lose our independence, you see."

" Very well, as long as I've made it clear to you. . . ."

" It's quite clear, thank you, Lady Clewer. We'll remember it."

Dolly withdrew and Agatha embarked upon her toilet. Later in the morning she climbed the unaccustomed stairs to James's attic. The artist, his arm in a sling, sat before the portrait of " Jellybelly," which had remained on the easel since the day of the accident. Agatha turned her eyes away from it hastily, with that instinct of self-preservation which James's work usually evoked.

" I came up," she said, " to talk about you and Dolly."

" Well ? " he asked truculently.

" I think things will be rather difficult for Dolly, you know."

" You can make them difficult."

" I don't want to. Please believe that I don't want to. What I want to say is this. Wouldn't it relieve the situation a good deal if you both came with me up to town and stayed in an hotel somewhere until after the wedding? You'll have a lot of shopping to do and it will be easier all round. I've not proposed this to John yet, until I saw what you and Dolly think. But I believe he would think it a good plan if the marriage is really coming off soon."

" Thank you, Agatha. But I don't see, if you are nice to her, that she would have such a bad time here."

" But the other servants ! "

" What could they do to her? Dolly won't mind."

" Yes she will. Dear James, if you are going to marry her you must try to think of things from her point of view. Can't you see that ? "

" Have you spoken to Dolly ? "

" Yes. And I believe she would like the plan if I suggested it."

" Well," he said, " I'll agree all right, if you will be my
guest while we are in town, Agatha. Will you do that?
I've been yours quite long enough. It's time you were
mine."

" Well, James . . . I don't quite like . . ."

" You want to stop it? " he asked, looking at her keenly.

" What? The marriage? No I don't." She hesitated
a moment and then said: " I don't at all. I believe it
ought to be a great success."

" Agatha! Then you are really on our side? "

" Yes. I believe I am."

" Well, I wouldn't ever have guessed. Though I always
thought, you know, that you were a nice creature. Nicer
than anyone except Dolly."

He smiled at her, his plain face creased into an unaccustomed beam of delight.

" You are . . ." Words failed him. " I can't tell you
what I feel. But I'll never forget it. Nor will Dolly. It
makes it all so much easier. I used to think sometimes that
you weren't one really though you looked like one."

" Like what, James? "

" Oh . . . one of those women . . . like Mamma and
Lois and Cynthia . . . a lady, you know. Not like Dolly."

He fell silent, smiling delightedly at her. Then, suddenly
inspired, he jerked his thumb towards the easel.

" You have it."

She controlled her features and hoped that she had given
no hint of her dismay. But he was, fortunately, quite
convinced by her words of gratitude.

" Shall I bring it down to your room? " he asked.

She tried to imagine its stark contours in the luxury of
her bedchamber.

" Where on earth can I put it? " she asked herself, as she
stumbled down the garret stairs.

CHAPTER IV

THE BRAXHALL FRESCOES

I.

SIR THOMAS BRAGGE set his house upon a hill. It was built, regardless of expense, upon the most prominent site in all Berkshire. Its uncounted windows, flashing in the sun, were visible in every direction for many miles. Locally it was known as " Bragge's Barracks."

It marked, monumentally, the excessive prosperity of Sir Thomas during the war with Germany. His income had, in five too short years, increased tenfold, and his notion of a suitable house kept pace with it. He looked back now with contempt at the mere bungalow, the country cottage, which he had designed for himself in the spring of 1914, and was profoundly thankful that it had never been built. He could not have lived in it with dignity after he became a millionaire. When he thought of this escape it was to agree weightily with his mother-in-law's theory that this terrible war had been sent to us for our good.

Upon another point he frequently found matter for self-congratulation. His house, if built before the war, might have been commandeered for public purposes. He would have been obliged, perhaps, to offer it as a hospital, since even financial success has its drawbacks. Public opinion, which he never flouted, might have driven him to such a display of patriotism, but he would have detested the depreciation of his property. Lyndon, so he understood,

had suffered considerable damage. All the paint had been
kicked off the kitchen wainscot, and the carved banisters at
the head of the long gallery had been knocked to bits by
careless men bringing down a coffin. At least, he had heard
as much from Lady Bragge ; he himself had visited the
place but once during its transformation and had been
sadly scandalized at its altered appearance. It had scarcely
seemed to be the same house ; so much of its indefinable,
leisurely charm was gone with its decorative mistress.
Devoted wholly to practical and unlovely ends, it had taken
on a new aspect of bare austerity. He could not recognize
it as the shrine of ease whence he had plucked his Cynthia.

His mother-in-law, brisk and competent in her red
commandant's uniform, had been, of course, in her element.
He had no fault to find with her activities. But it had given
him a disagreeable shock to discover pretty little Mrs. Ervine,
dishevelled and slightly perspiring, in the scullery. She was,
he considered, a great deal too good looking and too gently
nurtured for that kind of heavy work. He was sorry for
Ervine, who would find his wife very much gone off when
he came home on leave. It had been a great relief to him
that his Cynthia had shown no aspirations towards the
canteen or the operating theatre, but was content to
organize Charity Matinées and make bandages twice a week
in the most beautiful of veils. As for young Lady Clewer,
he had nothing but applause for her promptitude in
absconding from Lyndon. She was most wise to hand over
the whole concern to his cousin Marian, for the duration
of the war. The mere surrender of her house testified
sufficiently to her public spirit, and it had been done with
consummate tact, for Marian was born to be a commandant.
And in London there had been plenty for Agatha to do.
She had presided over countless committees, her beautiful
eyes had wrought havoc for some months in the Intelligence
Department of the War Office, and she had even worked

in a canteen for a week or two. On the wings of Peace she had returned to Lyndon, and Sir Thomas could once more visit the place without shock to his sensibilities.

He could, with reason, call himself happy. The war, bereaving in some way the huge majority of his acquaintance, had brought nothing but blessings to him. His relations had all done their duty and were little the worse for it. John Clewer had contracted a strained heart, the result of gas poisoning, and his brother James had a permanently stiff leg, but that was really all. Not many families could be said to have escaped so lightly. The House of Bragge, unpolluted by the assaults of war, rose swiftly upon the conclusion of that Peace for which they had all worked so hard. It was the consecration and embodiment of the new order, and Sir Thomas loved every stone of it.

Braxhall, for so he had called it, stood at the head of a wide, well-wooded valley. Its gardens and pleasure-grounds extended down a steep hill for nearly half a mile, towards an excellent trout stream which wound through green fields. The house itself was finished with all the speed possible to a wealthy builder, but the setting, which had to be wrought out of the bare hillside, took some time in the making. Already, however, rustic bridges spanned the trout stream, rustic summer-houses dotted the bleakness of the slope, and geraniums flamed in stone vases along the numerous terraces. Wooden and iron pergolas marked the spots where Sir Thomas intended to have rose avenues ; a paved formal garden with a fountain and orange trees in green tubs had been sunk in a sheltered spot to the west of the house, while the hill was crowned with a wonderful sparkling array of glass-houses.

The interior was not completely arranged when the proprietors first came into residence. The principal suites of rooms had been furnished, but the chief glory of Braxhall, an enormous banqueting hall, was not, as yet, in use. This was to be the family dining-room ; upon a raised dais at the further end Sir Thomas and his lady intended to eat their lunches and their dinners.   Its unusual largeness gave them no qualms ; the pride of possession would enable them to hold their own against its proportions and the rich amplitude of its mural frescoes.   Sir Thomas calculated that in another six months his house would be in perfect running order. In three years he could begin to take a pride in his garden, which now demanded so much from the eye of faith.   In three years, therefore, he, who had already so far outspanned his goal, would have nothing left to wish for.   Nothing save, perhaps, a doctor who would keep off the topic of strokes.

With his lovely wife upon his arm he was inspecting his domain one fine morning, absorbing at every pore the concrete pleasures of ownership.   Cynthia was more languid in her appreciations, but she was probably enjoying herself or she would not have consented to come upon such a tour at all.   They paused before the level flats, newly sown, which were to become croquet lawns and tennis courts.

" Now, that's a good bit of work ! " exulted Sir Thomas.

" It's very slow, isn't it ? " observed his wife.

" Slow ! D'you call it slow ? What ! I'd like to see it done quicker.   I'd-like-to-see-it.   There's not a man in England who'd have got that job through so quickly.   But I'm not so bad at getting a thing done quickly when I want it.   I said to Harvey I wanted the best man I could get. He said : ' If you want the thing well done, Sir Thomas, Jacobs is your man.   He'll grow you a perfect lawn in half the time anybody else would, on this side the Atlantic,' he said.   ' Get him to do it and you'll see the grass grow.   Of course, he'll cost you a pretty penny, but I take it, Sir Thomas, that you won't mind that ? '   ' No,' I said, ' No ! You're right, Mr. Harvey.   I don't mind.   Get the thing done ! Get a good man and damn the expense.   But I must have something for my money. When I buy, I buy in the best market.' 'Well,' he said . . ."

" It looks very ugly now," interrupted Cynthia, who had heard this saga before.

"Well, I don't know," Sir Thomas argued. "It's a good bit of work, Cynthie. And a good bit of work is never ugly to my mind."

This æsthetic flight was lost on Cynthia. She sighed :
" Lyndon has spoilt me a little for lawns, I suppose."

Though revelling daily and hourly in the countless things which Sir Thomas provided for her, she was obliged occasionally to bait him a little with reminders of those possessions which no money can buy. Sir Thomas, remembering the Lyndon turf, the fruit of several centuries of patient husbandry, grew a shade more purple.

" Lawns aren't everything," he contested, a little sulkily. " If I'd wanted nothing but a lawn I'd have bought that place, Aldstone Priory. But you said you didn't like it. And you were quite right, I'm sure. By the time we'd put in central heating, and a few bathrooms, there wouldn't have been a decent room in the house."

" I know," said Cynthia placatingly. " Let's go and look at the peach house."

This was a line in which Lyndon could not compete. There were no glass-houses upon any private property in Great Britain which could compare with those of Braxhall. After an exhaustive tour, Sir Thomas suggested that it must be fully lunch-time, but was reminded that they could not eat until Lois and her mother had arrived.

" Well, I hope they'll come soon," he said. " I'm hungry."

They wandered round to the uppermost of the garden terraces, and looked down the valley. Upon the road, some three miles off, two cars were seen approaching. These, as they drew nearer, proved to be Braxhall belongings. The foremost, a pale blue limousine, was always sent to the station to meet visitors, while the other, if necessary, brought maids and luggage.

"That's them," observed Lady Bragge.

Sir Thomas cheered up.

"Just time for us to have a cocktail before lunch," he said. "It takes seven minutes to climb the road hill."

Cynthia nodded and they retired indoors for refreshment.

Ten minutes later the bustle of arrival filled the marble spaciousness of the entrance hall. Marian Clewer, active and handsome in her tussore silk dust-coat, paused in the great doorway, glancing about her with appreciation. She loved coming to see Cynthia and could never visit Braxhall without a sense that all her toil as a mother had not been wasted. Lois, who followed her, cast glances which were less complacent and more critical. With a thrill of inward repulsion she beheld Cynthia and Sir Thomas descending the shallow stairs side by side. They evoked in her mind a medley of exotic images: a magnolia and a peony . . . a satyr and a naiad . . . a silver moon and a rubicund sun. She could never see them together without an invasion of contrasting ideas.

They were very pleased to see Marian; her admiration for all their possessions endeared her to them. To Lois they were cordial, as befits kindred, but their geniality had a note of reserve in it. Despite their saving insensibility, they had perceived that Braxhall did not impress her as it should, and they distrusted her accordingly.

Marian kissed her younger daughter gravely and tenderly, and, in a lower voice than usual, asked dear Tom after his gout. Cynthia was immediately aware of something odd in her manner; a little of her customary elasticity was gone. There was a hint of forced cheerfulness, of inner trouble bravely endured.

"Something's upsetting Mother," she told Sir Thomas, when she had sent her guests upstairs. "Did you notice?"

"No! I noticed nothing. She seemed quite cheerful, I thought."

"Not a bit of it! That's her smiling-but-resigned face. I know it."

"I wonder!" exclaimed Sir Thomas in alarm. "I wonder if she got rid of those rubber shares when I told her to. I do hope . . ."

"Oh, I shouldn't think it's anything like that," said Cynthia decidedly. "I can't imagine Mother losing money!"

"Well, I'm sure I hope not," said Sir Thomas. "You must try and get it out of her."

"Oh, she'll cough it up fast enough. She's just longing to, I expect. But she wants to prepare us first by this graveside sort of cheerfulness. . . ."

"Well, pump her at the first opportunity."

When Marian and Lois reappeared they all took lunch in the panelled room used as a dining-room until the banquet hall should be ready.

"I'm dying to see the frescoes," exclaimed Lois as she helped herself to stuffed olives. "Are they very lovely, Cynthia?"

Cynthia was silent for a few seconds. Then she said: "Well . . . I wouldn't call them lovely myself. I think they are perfectly hideous."

Sir Thomas looked unhappy, and protested:

"Martineau saw the south wall when he was over here in the spring. And he said that they were the finest bit of work, of the kind, ever done in England."

"If only they stand the climate!" observed Lois. "Hubert says . . ."

"They'll stand it all right," pronounced Sir Thomas. "You must remember this new central dry-heating I've put in. It's guaranteed to remedy the defects of a damp climate. When you step into that hall, you step into the

Sunny South. It might be Italy. If no mural frescoes
ever stood the climate before, you've got to remember that
there's been no hall built exactly to suit them, like mine is.
Of course, it's cost me . . ."

" If it's never been done before, how do you know all
this ? " asked Cynthia derisively.

" Now, Cynthie ! You know that when I once tried to
explain the apparatus to you you went to sleep. You don't
want me to begin all over again ? "

" Mercy, no ! I only mean that you're trusting pretty
much to the shop, or wherever it is you got it from, and
they may be doing you."

" Oh, indeed ! They'd be sharp customers if they could
do that. No ! I've been into the thing, I tell you, and . . ."

" What is the subject ? " interrupted Marian.

" The Rape of the Sabines," replied her daughter.

" The . . . ? "

" The Rape of the Sabines."

" Oh, surely not ? " exclaimed Lois.

" You're making a mistake, Cynthie," said Sir Thomas.
" It's a Bacchanal. You've mixed it up with those tapestries we got."

" Oh, well," said Cynthia, " it's all the same thing really.
A lot of people prancing about with nothing on. I'm sure
I wouldn't know what it was meant for."

" I shouldn't have thought a classical subject would suit
James," said Lois. " What does he know about Bacchus ? "

" Well, I don't want to criticize," said Marian, who liked
nothing better. " And I do think it's very nice of you and
Tom, Cynthia dear, to give James this work. He must need
it with all those little children. But I can't help feeling
it's a pity, in your lovely dining-hall. I think you should
have got somebody really first class."

" But, Mother," protested Lois, " you don't understand.
It's not because they want to be nice to James that Tom

and Cynthia are having the frescoes. At least . . ."—
realizing the painful candour of her statement—" of course,
it's very nice for him. But, really and truly, Hubert says
there is no one to touch him in these large decorative
pieces. . . ."

"Well, I don't understand it," said Marian. "I don't
see what Hubert has to go upon. James never painted any
frescoes anywhere before that I've heard of. Sherry,
please ! "

"Ervine knows what he's talking about," asserted Sir
Thomas. "If he says James Clewer is the best man, I'm
content to take it that he is. Where I'm not qualified to
judge, I'm content to take the opinion of an expert."

"But Hubert used not to admire James's work," argued
Marian.

"James has improved a lot lately," explained Lois.
"Besides, all the canons of artistic taste have changed so
much lately. It's the war, you know," she added vaguely.
"Hubert says his experiences in the army have influenced
his ideas of art a lot. He says he feels he needs something
much more dynamic than he did before the war."

This sounded so impressive that everyone was silenced,
and Marian concurred gravely with :

"Of course, the war has changed us all very much."

The Bragges and their guests, munching their turbot,
reflected for a while upon the extent to which they had
been changed by the war. Marian at length observed that
even poor James was a good deal altered. Perhaps she
meant that he was more dynamic, but she said :

"He's improved a lot in looks. They made him hold
himself so much better in the army."

James had joined the army with characteristic suddenness,
while his relations were still very busy discussing some
light form of war work which he could do. No feat of the
imagination could transform him into a British officer,

and yet, what else could he be? John and Hubert were already in training camps, and these deliberations had been carried on mainly by the Ladies of Lyndon. It was in the summer of 1914, before the rush for munition-making, and there really seemed nothing for it but to put him into the Red Cross as an orderly. Marian thought that he could carry stretchers, but Lois, who had got a First Aid Certificate and knew all about such things, maintained that he could not.

Finally there came Dolly's letter to Agatha with the news that James had enlisted in the Wessex Fusiliers, along with several Kell cousins. While he was at the Front Dolly let her house and went to live with her aunt in Devonshire, so that Lyndon had seen very little of her. Lois caught sight of her, briefly, in London about eighteen months later. She was standing upon a pile of milk cans in Victoria Station, a child in her arms, waving good-bye to a trainful of shouting, cheering men. Lois learnt that James was in the train, returning after six days' leave. She realized that she had seen the trio entering the station some minutes before, and, though finding their appearance vaguely familiar, had failed to identify them. There were so many families who looked like that. It struck her that the singularity of these relations of hers lay in their absolute ordinariness, their embodiment of a type. James, in his great-coat and with his bulky kit on his back, was no longer conspicuously uncouth. He looked like every soldier who ever returned to battle, and Dolly, his wife, in her undemonstrative fortitude, was like all the women who saw their men go.

As she had nothing better to do, Lois took Dolly to a neighbouring tea-shop, where they ate tepid poached eggs and tried to be civil to each other. But they could not honestly feel that they had got very far. Young Henry, James's son, did not interest Lois. He was rather plebeian looking, with scanty ginger hair; much too like all soldiers' babies, she thought. There had been, subsequently, two others, a girl and a boy, also red-haired. Kell was evidently a dominant type.

When James was invalided out of the army with a permanently crippled leg, he returned with Dolly to their cottage in Oxfordshire, and began to paint harder than ever. Nobody paid much attention to him until the echoes of war had subsided a little. Then it appeared that he was being talked about. Hubert went to a small exhibition of his work in some obscure place or other, and came home much disturbed. Hubert and Lois began to speak a little carefully of James. Before long they had almost managed to forget that they had ever spoken otherwise.

Cynthia and Sir Thomas completed this renovation of the family attitude when they offered to James the work of decorating their banqueting hall. They did this upon Hubert's recommendation. Having approved of the initial design they had departed for a long tour in the Riviera, leaving the artist to perform the work. He had lodged, in the greatest luxury, in the furnished part of Braxhall during the whole period, waited upon by an army of servants, and with permission to get down any number of models, if he wanted them, and quarter them upon Sir Thomas as long as he pleased. Even a car had been left for him.

The work was finished and James gone before the owners returned from the Continent. It was to celebrate the opening of the hall for practical uses that Lois and Marian had been invited to Braxhall. They were the first of a family house-party collected for the occasion. A great luncheon, to which half the County had been invited, was to take place the following Thursday, when the hall was to be used for the first time and the frescoes generally exhibited. Reflecting upon this party, Marian asked anxiously whether James was to be present.

" No," said Cynthia. " He can't come, or won't come,

I don't know which, unless Dolly comes too. And Dolly can't come without the baby, for a very pressing reason."

Marian raised her eyebrows delicately.

" How like Dolly ! " commented Lois.

" I always did think her rather like a cow," said Cynthia.

" Still, you know," said the hospitable owner of Braxhall, " they could all come if they liked."

" Oh, no ! " said Cynthia distastefully. " They look so like a family party at the Zoo."

Lois agreed. It was more than possible that the guests on Thursday might find the frescoes a little hard to swallow. To meet the artist and family, as well, might amaze them beyond recovery. It was really better that James should lurk mysteriously in the background. Lois had already begun to talk a little romantically about him and to hint at a " Bohemian marriage." She did not state, in so many words, that Mrs. James Clewer had been a very capable housemaid, but people gathered that she had been beneath her husband in station. It was supposed that she might have been a model or a chorus girl. Lois did not enlarge upon Dolly's extreme respectability.

" Then who else is coming to stay here ? " inquired Marian.

" John and Agatha and Mrs. Cocks come to-night."

" And, by the way," put in Sir Thomas, " I've invited that cousin of the Cocks's, that doctor, what's his name ? ... The shell-shock man ... Blair ! I met him yesterday, coming out of the club, and told him about the frescoes. He seemed interested ; said he'd always been interested in James and his work. So I told him to come here, and he's coming to-morrow, Cynthie. That's all right, isn't it ? I told him that the longer he stops the better pleased we shall be. There's plenty of room here, luckily."

He paused, uneasily, for the three women had exchanged glances. They sat stubbornly silent, and he asked again :

" That's all right, isn't it ? A cousin of Agatha's, and a
good man at his job. Peterson was talking about him the
other day. He says that there isn't a man in Harley
Street . . ."

" Oh, yes, I daresay he's an excellent doctor," said
Cynthia coldly.

Marian irradiated discretion and changed the subject.
But it would have been obvious to the veriest dolt that she
had been touched in a tender spot. She began to inquire
after the garden with a slight accentuation of the gently
martyred air which she had displayed on entering the
house. She was, obviously, hiding a wounded heart. Sir
Thomas, baffled as only a man among discreet women can
be baffled, raised an eyebrow at his wife. But Cynthia
would not look at him. Inspired by his bad angel, he
followed up his first blunder by another and a worse.

" And how's John been keeping these days ? " he asked.
" Heart not giving him much trouble, I hope ? "

This was, it appeared, a perfectly disastrous inquiry.
Marian turned pale, Lois crimson, and even Cynthia left
off crumbling her bread and coloured a little.

" You ain't still anxious about it ? " demanded Sir Thomas.
" You should make him see a specialist, a really crack
man. . . ."

" He has seen a specialist," said Marian with reproving
dignity.

" Yes," persisted Sir Thomas. " But has he seen a good
one ? "

" Naturally."

" Because you ought to be careful what you are doing,
you know. Can't play fast and loose with that sort of thing.
I heard of a chap the other day, young Baines, son of my
friend Baines, up in Liverpool. He got gassed, just like
John, suffered with his heart, and what's more he died of
it. These poison cases are no joke, let me tell you."

Marian glanced appealingly at Cynthia as if demanding how much longer they were going to have to endure this sort of thing. Cynthia said :

" Hush, Tom. We all know that."

" Well, the Baines's didn't. I mean they didn't wake up to the seriousness of the thing until the poor chap collapsed. Of course, their doctor must have been grossly careless, but there it is. And you know, Marian, all these Talbots have rocky constitutions. . . ."

" Thank you," replied Marian, who had been sitting with compressed lips. " You need not instruct me as to John's health. I happen to have brought him up."

" If you've finished your dessert," said Cynthia, " perhaps you'd like to come down to the hall and look at the dadoes . . . I mean the frescoes. I'll have coffee brought there."

They passed through the entrance hall and proceeded down a corridor paved in black and white marble and panelled by long looking-glasses. Folding doors upon the right led into the hall, and opposite them hung a large portrait of Lady Bragge. It had been painted very recently by a fashionable artist who could be trusted to do credit to Cynthia's gown. She wore her pearls, with a voluminous wrap of rose-pink brocade, slipping off her milky shoulders, and she carried an ostrich fan.

As the guests passed through the doors into the hall, Sir Thomas dropped behind and whispered to his wife :

" What was the matter at lunch ? What did I say wrong, eh ? "

Cynthia shrugged her shoulders and replied coldly :

" I'm sure I don't know."

She walked into the hall and left him to his perplexities. They entered under a minstrels' gallery, hung with purple velvet, and passed solemnly over the polished floor into the centre of the chamber. A row of windows in the north wall gave a fine view of the Berkshire Downs. Upon the wall opposite the frescoes unfolded themselves in three tremendous panels, so complex, so strangely glowing, so crowded with swift life, as to smite the perceptions with a sense of absolute shock. Behind the dais at the further end, where the banqueting table was set, a fourth and still more violent panel suffered slightly from the oblique light, but became clearer as they approached the dais step.

They all looked at the paintings for a very short time, and then hastily removed their eyes and concentrated their attention upon the furniture and fittings of the room. Even Lois had not the courage to study the Bacchanal for long. There was something in the piece which abashed her profoundly, but whether it was the incongruity of these shameless gods of an older world in so modern a shrine as Braxhall she could not tell. Anyhow, she was not equal to looking at them under the pained eye of her mother, and she decided to come again when she could be by herself.

The furniture was scanty. Upon the dais stood the table, its sable surface still innocent of the goblets and trophies which Sir Thomas meant to put there. High carved chairs with cushioned seats stood round it. But the rest of the hall was splendidly bare. Electric candelabra hung at intervals from the richly moulded ceiling, and the windows were draped, like the gallery, in purple velvet, blazoned with armorial devices in gold thread. This gave the place something of the solemnity of a ritualistic church in Lent. A gilded grating, about a foot high, skirted the base of the walls round the entire room : this was part of Sir Thomas's dry-heating apparatus, whereby warm-air shafts were run up behind the walls on which the frescoes were painted.

" We mean to keep it empty, like this," explained Cynthia. " The table on the dais will seat as many as we shall want in any ordinary way. We can put up trestle tables in the rest of the hall on special occasions like Thursday. But generally we shall keep the floor clear for dancing."

"We've a first-rate Victrola up in the minstrels' gallery," added Sir Thomas.

Lois glanced up and saw the top of it just visible over the purple hangings. In the effort to stifle a sudden paroxysm of laughter, she moved to one of the long windows and looked out on Berkshire. Sir Thomas sighed, his eyes following her wistfully. He said with regret:

"I wanted stained glass, but Clewer wouldn't have it."

"We got a killing letter from Dolly when we were at Monte Carlo," said Cynthia. "She said she felt she ought to let us know that James was home again, because a man had come here to see about the windows. Whereupon James threw up the work and went home to Bramfield, saying he couldn't paint frescoes in rooms with stained-glass windows."

"I'd half a mind to tell him he needn't come back," observed Sir Thomas. "I wanted those windows. I'd an idea that I'd like a series, allegorical, you know, showing the advances science has made during the reign of Queen Victoria. Railroad, and telegraph, and photography, and so on. But, as he was obdurate, I had to give it up. I was determined to have the frescoes, so I had to let him have his way. Anyone can have stained glass."

"That wasn't the only thing he was tiresome about," said Cynthia. "He would put that wall into three panels when we wanted two."

"Yes, we wanted two, with a plain division in between for Cynthia's portrait to hang on—that picture that's hanging outside the door. I had it specially painted to hang in this hall. But no! He wouldn't hear of it! Said he wouldn't leave any space for the portrait anywhere."

"It really might have been his house from the way he talked," continued Cynthia. "He had the portrait moved out of the corridor while he was here, so that he shouldn't have to see it when he came in and out of the hall. He said something or other very violent about it . . . I forget what."

"Jealous! That's what it was," chuckled Sir Thomas. "All these artists, y'know! They all hate each other like poison."

"It's a great pity to have that lovely picture hanging outside in the dark corridor," said Marian regretfully. "But there isn't room left for it here that I can see, not in a good light. He's filled up every inch of space. But couldn't you bring it in and put it on an easel, just at the corner of the dais? I think pictures look rather nice on easels like that. You could drape it or ornament it in some way."

"Oh, no, Mother! That would be quite impossible," expostulated Lois. "It would be absolutely out of keeping with the frescoes and the whole hall. It would look very foolish."

"Well, perhaps . . ." said Marian. "But it seems a great pity. How stupid of James not to have left any room for it! That's just the reason why it's nice to employ relations, that you can ask them for those little accommodations which you wouldn't demand of strangers."

She glanced once more, disapprovingly, at the riotous walls, with revolt in her honest soul. She could not bear the frescoes; upon no panel could she rest her eyes without meeting something which made her feel uncomfortable. Nor was it the prevailing nudity which overset her, but a kind of elusive familiarity which pervaded all these fleeing nymphs and pursuing satyrs. They were very much more convincing than any Bacchantes she had ever encountered before and their orgy was therefore more embarrassing. They discomposed her as much as if they had been personal acquaintances.

Cynthia was faintly aware of this too, but it did not distress her. On the contrary she felt that the whole thing was rather daring, and, in her indolent way, she liked to be daring. She savoured in advance the faces of the County dames when asked to sit beneath these unhallowed walls. Though persistently disclaiming any interest in the paintings, she secretly found them diverting.

Sir Thomas was bewildered by a number of sensations, but clung with determination to the most gratifying. He had a unique dining-room. Already in his mind's eye he saw Braxhall and its frescoes as one of the glories of England, a Mecca for American tourists. Of course, he thought the paintings very indecent, but he understood that this did not signify if the subject were classical. He had been similarly scandalized by Botticelli's " Birth of Venus," when he first met it, and had lived to learn that there was nothing the matter with it. He was always seeing it in the most chaste interiors.

Lois was flustered. She contemplated these flaming manifestations of the mind of James, and admitted to herself, in a spasm of honesty, that she did not know what to make of them. She could not really tell whether they were good or bad until she had heard what Hubert had to say. Hubert had been away on a fishing holiday in Norway, and was not expected at Braxhall until the evening before the party.

The clock in the tower above the hall struck four and they were all amazed. Luncheon at Braxhall was always a lengthy meal, and to-day they had been late. In half an hour tea would be administered to them among the orchids in the drawing-room. For this occasion a change of dress was necessary and they all dispersed.

Later in the evening Sir Thomas sought his lady in her bower and testily began :

" Now perhaps you'll be good enough to tell me what

was the matter with your mother at lunch. You've been sitting with her long enough to find out, I should hope. Is there anything serious wrong with Clewer's heart?"

Cynthia, who was rubbing orange stick on her nails, replied: "Yes. A good deal is wrong according to Mother. She seems to be quite upset about it. He may die at any moment, or something like that. Anyhow the specialist took a very gloomy view of him. But mind you don't talk about it, for nobody is supposed to know."

"Good God!" exclaimed Sir Thomas in deep concern. "You don't say so! Is it his heart?"

"Yes, I think so. It leaks or does something. I've really forgotten what. But you'd better ask Mother, if you want to know. She's bursting with details. I never can remember that sort of thing."

"But can nothing be done?"

"Well, of course he ought to be taking great care of himself. Only she says he won't. Can you reach me those little curved scissors on the end of the dressing-table? Only you must be careful not to show you know about it when he comes. He hates any fuss. He only told Mother in the deepest secrecy because he wanted her to help him put his affairs in order."

"Dear! Dear!" murmured Sir Thomas, appalled by the practical bearings of this detail. "That sounds bad."

"I don't know if it's true, but Mother says that the specialist thinks he can't last more than a few months in any case. But she's apt to exaggerate. Of course, she went off and told everybody she could think of, by way of keeping it a secret. Lois and Hubert have heard all about it. But that's neither here nor there. John mustn't know that we know."

"Can't last more than a few months!" cried Sir Thomas. "Is that a certainty, Cynthie, or is it merely a scare? He looks ill, but not as ill as that. How much chance is there of his improving? Is it the effect of the gas poisoning?"

"I really don't know. You know what Mother is like; she's very mysterious and won't tell you anything until you've asked a lot of questions, and then she pours it all out. It always annoys me so much that I don't ask."

"Well! Well! What specialist did he see?"

Cynthia reflected and then said:

"Mother did tell me, but I've forgotten. She said he was a very good man."

"Perhaps it's just a scare," said Sir Thomas hopefully.

"It might be," replied his wife, without emotion. "You never know. But Mother seems to take it pretty seriously."

"You're a cold-blooded little woman, Cynthie! You don't seem a bit upset about it."

"I am very much upset. I think it's most harrowing and all that."

"Rough on his wife," he continued after a pause. "How worried . . ."

Cynthia laughed.

"She doesn't know anything about it, my dear Tom."

"She doesn't know?"

"No, indeed. And she mustn't be told, what's more. John is quite determined about it. You should hear Mother on the subject! He says that nothing will induce him to trade on his wife's pity."

"What the deuce does he mean by that?"

"How should I know? Only . . . if they don't get on well . . ."

"Oh! Don't they get on well?"

"Mother seems to think they don't. And, by the way, you have dropped a brick about asking that Mr. Blair down here."

"Blair? Oh, yes! Now what's the matter with him?"

"You're generally more up in the family gossip."

"Family gossip? What family gossip? Oh, there's nothing in that old tale about him and Agatha, surely?"

"I'm only going by what Mother says. I've not seen them together personally; at least, not for ages. So I can't pretend to have an opinion. But she got the wind up that time in the middle of the war when he was back in town after he'd had pneumonia or something. She says that he and Agatha were never to be seen apart, and people began to think there was too much of it altogether, considering John was away, don't you know."

"But nobody seriously suggested that there was anything in it, did they?"

"Don't ask me what people suggested. You know perfectly well what they'd be most likely to suggest. Anyhow, Mother was greatly relieved when he went off to the Balkans, and she says she's noticed that they seemed to be avoiding each other when he came back. She thinks it's a good thing and is very furious that he is coming down here."

"But . . . Cynthie . . . you don't think . . . ?"

"I'm sure I don't know. I'm not in their confidence."

"But they are bound to meet sometimes," he argued. "And I should have thought this was as safe a place as any, with your Mother and hers in charge, so to speak."

"Oh, I don't object to his coming. It's Mother who's afraid he'll break up the happy home. I'm sure I don't mind one way or the other. Though he'll be a boring guest. I never could see anything in him myself."

Sir Thomas thought it out and then said decisively: "She's got too much sense. She'll never compromise herself. Not she!"

"I've always thought her too good to be true," said Cynthia, "but I'm inclined to think she'll manage her affairs quietly."

"Still, I don't want any scandals, open or otherwise, in this house."

"You can't help it very well, now he's accepted your invitation. I expect it will be all right. I'm sure I hope so."

" I'm not surprised at him, not at all. Poor chap ! He isn't the first, and he won't be the last, not by a long chalk. But she's always been so uncommonly discreet. He'll be the first . . ."

He paused. Cynthia said nothing but looked disagreeable. " How do you know ? " she inquired at last.

" Oh, well, I should imagine so," he replied lamely.

2.

" My dear, what a place ! " commented Mrs. Cocks. " Did you ever see anything like it ? "

She turned from her sitting-room window to a renewed contemplation of the magnificence within.

" Yes," said Agatha. " It's rather like the home of a rich man on the films. There is the same prevalence of orchids and little statuettes."

" I never go to the horrid things, so the comparison doesn't strike me."

" You should see my lodging ! John and I have a bridal suite, the grandest you ever saw. All done in lavender silk with great bunches of lilac and lilies of the valley. The bed in my room is as large as Dolly's parlour at Bramfield. I'm sure it is. Louis Quatorze, so Cynthia tells me. They were spacious days. Four people could easily sleep in it without discommoding each other."

" They often did," said Mrs. Cocks in an interested voice. " This notion that even two are something of a crowd is quite a modern idea. I was reading the life of Mdme. de Montespan the other day and it struck me forcibly what much more sociable habits they had. You should read that book, Agatha ; it would amuse you. Tell me, have you pictures of highland cattle in your sitting-room ? "

" No. We have a Greuze and two Brangwyns. The highland cattle are only temporary. The furniture shop

supplies them with the suite and they are put up until
Sir Thomas has collected some genuine works of art to
replace them. Your rooms can't be quite finished yet."

"Oh, I see! Well, I'm glad they begin with creature
comforts. I can do very well with the cattle, and I appreciate all this luxury."

"Do you? It surfeits me. I shall return to Lyndon
singing ' Be it never so humble . . .' "

"Ah! You care very much for Lyndon, don't you? "
said Mrs. Cocks quickly.

Lately she had felt in need of reassurance concerning
her daughter's happiness. She liked to hear Agatha speak
of her possessions with an inflection of pride or joy. Agatha
nodded an assent and stared out of the window, her fingers
drumming restlessly on the sill. Mrs. Cocks remarked with
irritation that her hands were growing a little thin.

"Yes," agreed Agatha. "My wedding ring has had to
be made smaller."

After a pause she added :

"I do love Lyndon. Living in this house makes me
realize how much I love it. When I'm at Lyndon I have a
feeling sometimes that it doesn't matter what follies we
perpetrate because it will survive us. It was made by more
sensible people than we are. And sensible people will live
there again some day."

"Dolly and James, or their descendants, will live there
some day," said Mrs. Cocks significantly.

"Well, they are the most sensible people I know,"
returned Agatha. " By the way, I'm going over to see them
to-morrow.; I must say good-bye to them before I go to
Scotland. Will you come? "

"I positively must write letters the whole of to-morrow,"
said Mrs. Cocks, shaking her head. "Otherwise I should
love to see their household. I can't picture it at all."

"Oh, it's funny, but exactly what you would expect.

Dolly has a girl in to help her with the Monday washing, and does all the rest of the housework herself. And there is an army hut in the garden, with glass panels in the roof, which James uses as a studio. Dolly tells me she's only been inside it once in three months, and that was when she thought Henry had swallowed a button and wanted the doctor fetched in a hurry."

" But what does he do when he isn't painting ? "

" Oh, he digs in the garden in the evening, in his shirt-sleeves, and he gets a bath on Saturday night, so I understand. And on Sunday he puts on his best suit and takes Dolly to chapel."

" Aren't you touching it up a little, Agatha ? "

"Indeed I'm not. Come and see for yourself. And he never paints on Saturday afternoons, or Sundays, or bank holidays."

" Then the *ménage* is entirely run by Dolly ? "

" Absolutely. The house is Dolly's house. He has accepted her ideas of domesticity *en bloc*. I gather that the only thing they ever fell out over was a dispute about a hat. She wanted him to go to chapel in a bowler, like any other Christian, and he flatly refused. He said a bowler hurt his head. They became very acrimonious about it until Dolly realized that no bowler on earth would fit so large a skull. So she got him a Trilby hat, which perches very oddly on the top of his head, and all was peace."

" But one would have thought that his artistic temperament must have rebelled in some way against this life. It's so humdrum ! "

" It seems to suit him. They've got the usual little sitting-room with lace curtains, and an aspidistra and a horse-hair couch, and ' The Soul's Awakening,' and a plush tablecloth, and china children in gilt swings on the mantelpiece. I don't think he regards them as ornaments at all. He simply sees the whole as an expression of Dolly. And, as he's devoted to her, he doesn't object to it."

" I don't understand it."

" I do and I don't. I can see how harassed he'd have been with a wife who had any pretensions to taste; who went in for peasant pottery and Russian linen and expected him to react. But still, I get puzzled. I haven't looked properly at those frescoes in the hall yet, because Lois would keep talking about El Greco, and I had to attend to her. But when I think of them, and then think of James sitting in his parlour with such visions in his head, I just gasp ! He must be so absolutely independent of externals. Accidental surroundings, I mean, like wall-papers. But I suppose that his upbringing partially explains it. Lyndon was so uncongenial to him that the whole of his essential character was developed in spite of his education and not because of it. His abnormal contra-suggestibility is the result of his attempts to protect himself."

Mrs. Cocks recognized an exotic word and knew at once where it had come from. She looked at her daughter long and critically. In that lovely person and countenance she perceived sufficient cause for uneasiness. A shade less beautiful than formerly did Agatha appear. There was a certain sharpening of feature : the eyes were shadowed. Something of the bloom had gone. Agatha had never, at any time, advertised happiness in her carriage. But she had been serene and now was untranquil. Sombre sometimes, and then feverishly animated, she had lost her poise. And she was growing thin. To her mother's anxious heart these portents boded the premature decay of a youth which had bloomed too early.

" Malt and cod-liver oil," she muttered from the depths of her reflection.

Agatha laughed, divining the chain of thought which led to such a remark.

"What! In the middle of the summer? And at my age? "

" Your age ! It's nothing. You're a baby still. However,

I don't think this is a very healthy place, although it stands so high. It must be enervating or something, for nobody here looks well. John especially."

Agatha's face hardened.

"John is quite well, I think," she observed.

"Well, I'm glad you think so, for he doesn't look it. But they all seem to be out of sorts. Cynthia blooms, of course, but poor old Sir Thomas is dreadfully melancholy at times. He struck me as being in very low spirits indeed at lunch to-day. Did you notice those enormous sighs he kept heaving? I was quite sorry for him. And as for Lois, she looks terribly pinched and haggard."

"I don't think she has been very well just lately," observed Agatha with a sigh.

"Hasn't she? Well, and isn't that very unusual with her? And Marian is the worst of the lot! What on earth is the matter with her? Why does she persist in looking as if she were bearing up only for our sakes?"

"I don't know at all. I think she's annoyed about Gerald coming."

"Gerald? Gerald Blair? He's not coming here, surely?"

"Yes. He's coming this evening in time for dinner, I believe."

Mrs. Cocks could not conceal her dismay.

"What for?" she said.

"You'd better ask Sir Thomas. He asked him. To see the frescoes, I suppose. How long is it till tea? I think I'll explore these woods a little. I feel stifled in this house. . . ."

A few minutes later Mrs. Cocks watched her running down the terraces into the valley. She crossed the stream by a wooden footbridge and paused long upon it, regarding the slow, innocent flowing of the water. Then she wandered on and was lost among the trees, walking with the listless impatience of a mind in conflict.

Mrs. Cocks turned from the window and paced the room, possessed by many perfectly reasonable fears. Her anxiety was no longer to be stifled. She was convinced that she had already ignored these symptons of nervous upheaval longer than was safe. She could not continue to tell herself that all this was merely the result of the war, of four years' protracted strain. It might be true, but it was not to the point. As she watched that restless figure walking among the trees, she had realized fully that the issue now lay, not with causes, but with possible consequences.

Two days at Braxhall had been sufficient to show her that the young Clewers were at odds with one another and with life. It was obvious, moreover, that the trouble had been going on for some time and was working to a cumulative crisis. Agatha could scarcely speak to or of her husband save with a kind of suppressed exasperation, while John was uniformly morose. Under these conditions the advent of Gerald Blair must be regarded as an appalling catastrophe. Nothing could have been more unlucky.

Mrs. Cocks had stoutly refused to listen to those veiled fears which Marian would have imparted to her two years ago, before Gerald removed himself to the Balkans. As Agatha's mother she was bound to declare that there was nothing in it. But she knew in her heart that there was plenty of cause for alarm. No one could have been more deeply disturbed than she : no one had been more inclined to fear that these two were on the verge of loving each other again. She was forced, for her peace of mind, to look upon the affair as a proof of Agatha's levity rather than as a symbol of constancy. Ignoring the possible effects of her own strategical error in sending him down to Lyndon in the spring before the war, she told herself that Agatha, in her husband's absence, was finding entertainment in the revival of an old flame. Agatha was not, evidently,

framed by nature to be a grass widow, but she would settle
down when John came back.

John's demobilization, however, had worked no miracles.
And Mrs. Cocks was beginning to gauge, for the first time,
the strength of Gerald's " upsetting ideas." He had really
succeeded in imbuing Agatha, to a certain degree, with
views which, for want of a better word, she was forced to
call socialism. She had traced to his disturbing influence
a volcanic notion which had seized Agatha in the spring
of 1918. This had been the wish to do some very hard
work. Agatha, whose war activities had always been of the
lightest, insisted suddenly upon a twelve-hour day in a
canteen, a phase which had lasted nearly three weeks and
which had only ended with the inevitable physical collapse.

And now, as the mother paused, uncertain as to her
wisest course, but determined that someone must be spoken
to and something must be done, Marian Clewer knocked
at her door and invaded her with that air of forced cheerfulness which was beginning to exasperate everyone in the
house. Mrs. Cocks purposely ignored it, a fatal mistake,
for a very few sympathetic leads from her would have
drawn from Marian the whole tale of her anxiety about
John. And, as she herself said afterwards, of course, if she
had known that . . . !

" Well, Marian," she began brightly. " This is the first
time I've really seen you since we arrived. What a magnificent place it is ! "

Praise of Braxhall brought a real gleam of pleasure to
Marian's brow, as she seated herself a little heavily by the
window. She looked round her with contentment.

" It is a very lovely place, isn't it ? " she said. " It
makes me very happy, every time I come here, to see
Cynthia so comfortably settled. It's a wonderful thing,
Ellen, to feel that one's daughters are absolutely happy in
their marriages. Of course, it's given to few."

" It is," agreed Ellen, scenting an attack. " By the way, how is Lois ? I don't think she's looking quite up to the mark."

Marian beamed triumphantly as she acquainted Mrs. Cocks with the nature of Lois's indisposition.

" Of course, nobody knows of it yet," she said. " Lois and Hubert are quite delighted. And so am I. At our age there is a great satisfaction in being a grandmother, isn't there ? "

" Of course, you don't count James's children," parried Mrs. Cocks at once.

" Well, no. A stepson isn't quite the same thing. Besides . . . one's daughters . . ."

" If Cynthia ever has a family, there will be plenty of room for them in this house," observed Mrs. Cocks, who knew very well that Cynthia would have nothing of the kind.

Marian ignored this thrust and continued :

" I'm so especially glad for Lois because there is no doubt that she and Hubert do have their little differences."

" No doubt at all," said Mrs. Cocks promptly.

" Though, of course, they mean absolutely nothing. An ideally devoted couple ! Still you know that sort of thing, trivial things in themselves, of course . . . in time are apt to become serious. And children smooth them out so. They take a young couple out of themselves. I was very sorry that Lois didn't begin much sooner. I think it's the greatest pity . . . however . . ."

" When do you expect . . . ? " interrupted Mrs. Cocks.

" Next March."

" I'm very glad ; especially when you are all so pleased."

" I have, I suppose, a great deal to be thankful for. Though of course I have troubles. . . . Still it would be terrible to feel that either of my daughters was unhappily married. I can imagine nothing more frightful for any mother. Where is Agatha, did you say ? "

" Gone for a walk, I believe."

" She does not look well. I was quite shocked when I saw her ; really, I hardly like to say it, but she is losing her looks rather, poor girl."

" Oh, she needs a change. London gets stuffy. Scotland will set her up."

" Yes, yes ! It will be a good thing to get her right away up to Scotland. Ellen, I'm most distressed that Mr. Blair is coming here. Believe me, I knew nothing about the invitation until it was too late. I would certainly have stopped it if I could. But Tom, ignorant of the particular reasons against it, invited him without telling us."

" I don't think you need worry about that. I don't think I know of any particular reasons against it," replied Mrs. Cocks stiffly.

" Don't you really ? " asked Marian. " Personally—of course I'm given to plain speaking—personally I think it's the greatest pity Agatha should see much of him while she is in this unsettled state."

" I don't think you need trouble about Agatha. It is quite natural that she should be very much attached to Gerald, though I know I have never succeeded in explaining this to you. They are cousins and were brought up together. Practically brother and sister."

" But there was never anything more ? No engagement of any kind ? "

" There was certainly no serious engagement. There was the usual kind of boy and girl flirtation, perhaps. But you must know, with daughters of your own, how ephemeral such things are."

" I'm glad to say that I've had nothing of the kind to deal with in the case of my own daughters."

"Really?" said Mrs. Cocks. "Oh, well, perhaps not. No ! "

Her smile infuriated Marian, who added : " But then, they both have great natural discretion."

" So has Agatha," returned Mrs. Cocks hotly. " But with anyone so attractive there are bound to be these little episodes. One gets to take them for granted. After all, Marian, even if he is still rather obviously *épris*, he isn't the only one, is he ? "

" Perhaps not. But still I think it's a pity he should be coming here just when poor John . . ."

She checked herself, but Mrs. Cocks took her up :

" Poor John ! I don't understand this ' poor John ' attitude which you have all adopted. You seem determined to make a martyr of him : to suggest that Agatha doesn't treat him properly."

" Agatha makes no secret of the fact that she doesn't care a rap for him."

" Has she said so to you ? "

" No ! Of course not. But her manner to him . . ."

" She has never been demonstrative in public. I should be sorry if she was."

" But it isn't only in public."

" How do you know ? Don't you think that you are drawing upon your imagination ? "

" No, I'm not. She has been quite changed towards him ever since he was demobilized. She can hardly be called a wife at all."

And Marian supplied details which, if true, left little doubt as to the gravity of the young couple's estrangement.

" How do you know all this ? " demanded Mrs. Cocks. " You only can know from one source. John has obviously been complaining to you. If he does that, instead of managing his matrimonial affairs for himself, I can quite understand Agatha's feelings."

Marian began to be aware of her own rashness, for her statements had no positive foundation. They were based upon assumption only—inferences drawn from a few bitter remarks made by John when he was arranging with her for the disposi-

tion of his affairs. She began to think that she ought to go
and see Cynthia about the table decorations for Thursday.

" Then Agatha has said nothing to you ? " she parried
feebly, as she got to her feet.

" Agatha is too loyal," said Mrs. Cocks grimly. " She
would never complain of her husband."

Marian, having eased her bosom of some of her furniture,
departed. She left a sadly discomposed mother. Mrs. Cocks
was aghast, furious, and convinced that instant action was
imperative. All her vague anxiety had been turned into
indignation : she felt that John was unpardonable. Previously she had been inclined to pity him, though not very
much. So great was her estimation of Agatha's attractions
that she could not really think of him but as an uncommonly
lucky man—nearly as lucky as her own husband had been.
Still it must have been a little trying to return from the
Front to a lady in so irritable a temper. But this whining
to his stepmother put him out of court. No high-handed-
ness on Agatha's part could justify it. He must be made
to feel that wives are not kept thus.

Resolved to lose no time she set off at once in search of
him and had the good fortune to locate him alone in the
billiard room. Closing the door firmly behind her and
seating herself with decision, she opened fire :

" Now, John ! What's all this trouble between you and
Agatha ? "

" Why should you think that there is trouble between
us ? " inquired John.

He stood stolidly before her, so still and unblinking that
she began to wish he would fidget.

His question disconcerted her. She could not say :
" Because your stepmother said so," without betraying
Marian's confidence. She was too loyal to her own sex to
acquaint any man upon earth with the indiscretion of
another woman. She replied :

"Well, it's obvious."

"I suppose it is," he said slowly. "But Agatha has said nothing to you herself?"

"Nothing. I think she would think it disloyal."

She hoped this indirect shaft would go home. But John was reflecting deeply with bent brows. At last he said:

"Well, I haven't an idea what the trouble is. Agatha is the only person who does know, I should think."

His eyes were feverish and weary, and it struck her that he was a very bad colour. He certainly looked ill, but an aggrieved note in his voice hardened her heart against him. She saw quite clearly now that his calm assumption of possession must be shaken. He must be made to see that he stood in danger of losing Agatha altogether; and if the idea was unpleasant to him, it was no more than he deserved. Anger blinded her to the perils of the course she had chosen. She had really persuaded herself that a little jealousy would be very good for him—would wake him up to the fact that he had a wife worth fighting for.

"Well of course," she began, "though she's said nothing to me, I have formed my own opinions and I think I'd better tell you what they are. I feel that a great deal is at stake for you and Agatha just now; the whole happiness of your after lives perhaps. No! Don't interrupt me, but listen! You must put up with a little plain speaking, my dear boy. I think you and Agatha have got to the critical phase when—how shall I put it?—the . . . the honeymoon stage of married life is over. The only strange thing is that it should have lasted so long. Very few couples, I should imagine, preserve their first ardour for eight years. But you've been exceptionally lucky."

"I don't quite see what you are driving at. I haven't changed. I love her as much as ever I did."

"Quite so! And you think that is a sufficiently good

reason why she shouldn't change either. That is so like
a man! I believe you all regard a woman's passion as
something like electric light, to be switched on and off as
you want it. Don't you think that you've been taking her
a little too much for granted? Because nothing, let me
tell you, is more fatal where a woman of her temperament
is concerned. I know, because she is very like me. You
must never let her feel that you don't regard her as a prize
and a privilege. For goodness' sake, sit down! It bothers
me to see you standing like that."

He fetched a chair and carefully sat down opposite her.
She continued deliberately :

" I expect you know that you won her from another man."

" What's that ? "

" Oh, hasn't she told you ? Funny girl! It's quite true.
There was a schoolroom attachment which gave me a good
deal of uneasiness at one time. Of course, she forgot it all
very comfortably when she met you. But I mention it
now because I think you should realize, with a girl like
Agatha, that these old flames are always just a little
dangerous. Especially in a matrimonial cross-roads like
that which you are facing now. Unless you can manage
to keep your hold on her . . ."

" I like this! You talk as if marriage has no obligations,
Mrs. Cocks. I've been a perfectly good husband to Agatha,
and I'll thank her . . ."

" Technically, John, she'll always be a perfectly good
wife to you : you know that quite well. I'm not discussing
her principles. But the heart, you see, cannot be bound.
No person on earth can undertake to stay in love. If you
want her to do that you must rely upon yourself and not
upon the obligations of the marriage service. I'm saying
all this because, as he is unfortunately coming here . . ."

" He! Who ? "

John's face was grey.

" Gerald Blair. That's the man I'm talking about."

" Blair ! Blair ! What has he to do with all this ? "

" Nothing. Except that, as I say, you won her from him once. He is, I think, beginning to interest her slightly again. And I want to point out to you that it is probably your fault. You haven't been taking sufficient pains to interest her yourself. When you marry a woman like Agatha you must live up to her. My dear boy, don't go that colour ! There's nothing serious in this affair. D'you think I'd have spoken of it if there was ? To you, of all people ? No ! I only regard it as a symptom that she feels you have been taking her too much for granted."

" How long has this been going on ? " he said, staring at her sombrely.

" Oh, my good John ! Nothing has been ' going on.' "

" Blair ! " he said again. " Blair ! "

Mrs. Cocks began to wonder if this were not altogether too much of a good thing.

" You say they were engaged ? "

" Wanted to be engaged. It all blew over completely. Only lately . . ."

" No," he said, " not lately. Longer ago than lately. . . . I'm beginning to see it now. . . . Yes, of course. . . ."

" There I'm sure you are wrong. It's only since the war. . . ."

" No. It was before the war. There was that time he came down to Lyndon. I remember. . . ."

" You are making too much of it," began Mrs. Cocks anxiously. " There could have been nothing then, I'm certain."

" She had a photograph. . . ."

" What photograph ? "

" Of herself and Blair. In a tin locket. Taken at a fair or something, she said."

" Oh, that fair ! I remember ! But she was hardly out

of her cradle then. Only sixteen or thereabouts. I packed
her off to school."

"She kept the photograph."

"Sentimental creature!"

"She isn't sentimental. I'd think nothing of it if she
was."

Mrs. Cocks pulled herself together.

"All this is nonsense, John. There could have been
nothing that time before the war. She was on perfectly
good terms with you, wasn't she?"

"She seemed to be."

"If I'd thought you were going to take it this way I
would never have spoken. I thought you had more sense
of proportion."

"I've been blind! . . . Blair! And that's why, oh God
damn it all, that's why she's always sneering at me for being
too rich!"

"Too rich?" echoed Mrs. Cocks blankly.

"Yes, too rich. She's got very socialist lately, don't
you notice?"

"Well, she has said some very strange things. But I
thought it was this house which had got on her nerves.
I never could see that she objected specially to spending
money on herself."

"Nor I. But I couldn't remember where I'd heard
these views before. I've got it now."

"Yes, he has strange ideas. And she has always been
influenced by them to a certain extent. After he went to
the Balkans, that time when they had been seeing a good
deal of each other . . ."

"What time?"

"Oh, that time in the war, after he had had pneumonia.
You remember, surely?"

"I don't. I was at the Front, unfortunately."

In the ensuing pause Mrs. Cocks began to grow desperate.

" Well," said John, " when he went to the Balkans, what did she do ? "

-" Oh, nothing. Only worked in a canteen : but I felt he put her up to it. It's no use your looking like that, John. I merely wanted to show you the sort of thing that is liable to happen if you let Agatha get out of hand. If you insist upon taking it *au grand sérieux* you'll simply make trouble. And, above all, try to remember that nothing is more likely to exasperate her than the idea that she is being discussed and criticized. Family criticism is a deadly thing."

" I agree with you."

" Make love to her, as you used to do, and she'll forget all about him. In a year's time you will laugh at all this."

John did laugh, a little unpleasantly, and she began to feel that nothing she could say further would improve matters.

" That was tea, that gong," she observed. " Are you coming ? "

" No. I think I'll go fishing."

" John, you realize that if I thought there was the slightest danger of her caring seriously for Gerald I would never have spoken to you ? "

" Yes, I see that. I quite believe you think there's nothing in it. But it's opened my eyes to some things that have puzzled me. You can't live with a woman, and be fond of her, and not know when she's got something on her mind. It's my belief that she's loved that fellow all along. Except for a very short time when I swept her off her feet."

" I'm sure you are mistaken. And even if it were true, John, it's no use putting it into words like that. It's a great pity. She's married to you and must make the best of it."

" She is and she must."

He held the door open for her, and she gave up the attempt to reason with him. She was uneasy and almost sorry she had spoken. She had wished to bait him a little ;

to brace him up by suggesting that he had a rival. She had not supposed that he could be capable of any desperate jealousy; his self-confidence was too genuine for that. But she thought that a small attack upon his complacency would be good for him.· He must be made to realize his own extreme good fortune in being "most damned in a fair woman." For Mrs. Cocks held the views of a lady who is beautiful, gently nurtured, bred to claim homage as her due, heiress of all the achievements of civilization and profoundly ignorant of its basic brutalities.

A few phrases, caught as she crossed the ante-room, restored her belief in herself. Through the open door came the emphatic voice of Lois :

" . . . and if it's only half as pronounced as it was in London, two years ago, it's enough to kill poor John outright."

Lois and Cynthia fell suddenly silent at her entrance, and as she sipped her tea she felt that she had, on the whole, done very wisely. It was true that John had taken her words far more seriously than she had intended, but if the whole family were discussing the affair like this it was obvious that he must hear of it sooner or later, and she was glad that she had got in her say first. Braxhall, as she saw it, contained a good deal of inflammable material. She had little doubt of her daughter's ultimate discretion and had genuinely persuaded herself that the affair was, for Agatha, a mild sentimental adventure. But she was deeply alarmed at the possibilities of family gossip in such a house.

Reviewing her three young people, as she grasped them, she thought that they should not be hard to manage. Here was John, aggrieved and resentful, his petulance continually inflamed by the ardent sympathy of his stepmother. Agatha was obviously more than a little bored and ready to grasp at an occasion for emotional entertainment. Gerald, she supposed, was like nothing so much as a fluttering moth, drifting helplessly back to his candle, despite the counsels of prudence. Altogether the situation, spiced by the malice and inaccuracy of the other ladies, had the makings of a very fine explosion. There would certainly be wigs on the green if a woman of tact and determination had not, by heaven's grace, been upon the spot.

She was right, as far as she went, but she had the misfortune to gauge the emotions of her protagonists at far too low a point of intensity, misled by the understatements of modern speech. Disturbances which she beheld as embryonic had already reached the most sinister proportions; her trio were rushing together, doomed to inevitable impact. She knew nothing of the misgivings, the sense of inward betrayal, with which Gerald Blair had accepted Sir Thomas's invitation. She could not guess his resolution, faithfully kept since his return from the Balkans, to see his cousin no more; or how that resolve had been overthrown by a chance report that Lady Clewer was looking miserably ill and unhappy, an idea which gave him such anguish that he was constrained at last to end it by coming to see for himself.

Likewise she underrated the effect of her bracing counsels upon her son-in-law who was, at that moment, lashing the trout stream in a mood which rang all the changes upon despair and fury. Of the three, indeed, Agatha was the least discomposed and the least deserving of compassion. She was still able to disguise to herself the nature of her own feelings. For her the mere prospect of seeing her cousin again, after a long separation, had so much of pleasure in it that she was able to postpone the thought of ultimate issues. She knew that he had avoided her since his return to England; she believed that she knew why. She had applauded his wisdom and grieved over its cruelty. Now that he had inexplicably changed his mind she was able to stifle apprehension in her gladness that he had done so. She walked about the woods until she was tired and then returned to Braxhall. Finding that the hour was still early, she lay down with a book upon a sofa near the window. There, half hidden in a haze of cigarette smoke, she was found by her husband on his return to the house.

John, during the interval by the river, had become an angry man. In the first shocked perception of the truth he had been too much stunned for emotion. He had stated the facts with a sorrowful calm, seeing them too clearly to be resentful. But this spasm of insight was short-lived. An accurate realization of any truth is generally followed by a mood of bitter rebellion against it, and in such a mood he sought his wife. She roused herself to greet him with that conscientious friendliness of tone, that manufactured interest in his affairs, which so deeply exasperated him.

" Well, what have you been doing ? "

" Fishing."

" Did you catch anything ? "

" No."

" How tiresome for you," she murmured, and waited a moment.

As he did not seem to be inclined to talk she returned to her book. At the end of a couple of minutes, aware that he had not moved, she glanced up at him again. He was looking at her with some earnestness. She asked :

" Did you want anything ? "

" No."

" Is anything the matter ? "

" No."

" Sure it isn't the Scotch express ? "

She referred to a difference of opinion which had occupied them earlier in the day, concerning the time and route of their journey North. She felt that she had been obstinate and was sorry for it. Half consciously she gave him that swift, upward smile with which she had been wont to reduce him. It reached him now, in his trouble, like a mirage, a hint of unsubstantial bliss. He was consumed by his need of her, by the impossible hope that she would love him again and help him to escape from all this grief and fury, the uneasy, insecure present, and the implacable menace of the future. He fell on his knees at her side and would have taken her in his arms, but she recoiled.

" I only wanted to make it up," he pleaded almost humbly.

" I know. You have only one way of making up our disagreements and I find it monotonous."

The heavy fog of rancour, which had momentarily lifted, clouded his mind again. He turned from her and stood looking out of the window. It was as though he had met the full shock of his own doom for the first time—had received his first inkling of life's impermanence. A man of sufficient courage and small imagination, he had taken the doctors' verdict with equanimity. The thought of death was very disagreeable to him but it had no appalling significance. He had seen it often enough, aad had faced it continually, as a matter of course, for four years. He did not wish to leave a world which he found very pleasant, but he was protected by that providential egoism which shields most normal people. He had no real conception of the universe going on without him. His agony at the thought of relinquishing his wife had been tempered by his inability to imagine her continued existence after his own dissolution.

But now the merciful veil was torn from his understanding and he was learning the vanity of all property. A sense of possession had informed his entire attitude towards his surroundings; his love for Agatha was permeated by it. And this sense was outraged by the realities forced upon him. He grasped his limitations, knew that he would lie forgotten, senseless clay, while she, the living woman now before him, would pass into the possession of another man. It was one thing to know that she might marry again; it was another to imagine her married to

Blair. His spirit could not submit to such a possibility, and
yet he knew that he was helpless.

A car was climbing the long hill, and the sound of its
approach floated distinctly through the open window.
Agatha heard it and was transformed, glowing warmly, for
she knew that it brought her cousin. It was an instant's
self-betrayal, but it revealed her to John, who had turned
sharply and marked the fleeting radiance. He left her
immediately, unable to trust himself in speech.

She dressed for dinner hastily and went down to the
marble corridor leading to the hall. Gerald was there and
she watched him for a moment unperceived, as she stood
at the turn of the stairs. He looked very uneasy, as though
he had arrived by mistake into this sanctuary of the sleek,
the idle and the luxurious. His bearing was that of a
stranger in a strange land, and he was having a look at
Cynthia's portrait with a public gallery expression on his face.

She decided that she would take him with her to see
Dolly and James. He would like their household. It
would be nice to take someone there who found it as admirable as she did. In another second she would call to him,
and see him start, and turn and smile at her.

" Did you arrive in your evening clothes ? " she said.

He did not start as much as she had expected, having
braced himself for this encounter so tremendously that
nothing could quite take him by surprise. But he was a
little pallid as he came towards her.

" No," he said, " I didn't. But I changed in record
time. I thought it was later than it is."

They sat down together on a carved settle and plunged
into the instant, eager conversation of their youth. She
tried to describe to him the frescoes in the hall. The effort
overset them both and their mirth, floating upwards,
greeted the other inmates of Braxhall as they descended
the stairs in procession.

3.

She took him over to Bramfield the next day. Dolly heard the car turn into the lane and was at the gate to welcome them. She was not much changed since the days of her Clewer servitude. Her figure was broader, perhaps, but her hair still shone with its old flame and her freckled face was comelier than ever. Henry and little Agatha clung to her skirts, while in her arms she held Jimmy, her youngest.

"Well, Agatha," she cried, as she kissed her sister-in-law, "you are a stranger! I thought you were never coming to see us again. But you've been busy, I expect. Sonny! Kiss your Auntie, you bad boy! It's funny how he hates it: thinks he's too old. How do you do, Mr. Blair? I'm very pleased to see you. You will be staying at Braxhall, I suppose?"

"I was wondering if you'd remember me," said Gerald as he shook hands.

"I should think I did," Dolly assured him. "You came to that lecture Mr. Ervine didn't give, in the Lyndon Reading Room. I remember. Shake hands with Mr. Blair, children."

She took them up the garden path, pausing to allow them to admire the lilies and hollyhocks in the small beds.

"Yes," she agreed, "they are a sight. We got second prize at Bramfield show last year, in the cottage garden competition. I always said we might of got first, if James hadn't spent so much time on the vegetable marrows. He was quite gone on them, and couldn't attend to nothing else."

"And they didn't count?"

"Not as flowers, they didn't. They are vegetables, you see, Mr. Blair. We had one was the biggest in three parishes. I told James about a young fellow I knew that grew a prize marrow and carved a verse of a hymn on the rind. 'God

moves in a mysterious way,' it said. And when the marrow
grew, it grew. James would have it that he must put something on ours. So he drew out a picture; Jonah sitting
under a gourd, like in the Bible. But as the marrow got
bigger it went sort of crooked, and spoilt it. He was vexed
about it."

"How is he?" asked Agatha.

"Very well, thank you. Though his leg pains him now
and again. He's apt to get rheumatism into it. He's working now, so I won't call him, if you don't mind. But he'll
be in for tea and he'll be ever so glad you've come. If I'd
known, Agatha, I'd have made drop scones. And I'd have
put Sissy into that frock you sent her. I do think it's lovely.
I don't know wherever you got that nice embroidery. I
never saw anything like it before."

"I got it at the Russian shop in the Brompton Road."

"Oh, Russia! I expect they do lovely work there. But
tell me, do you think it's all true what it says in the papers
about these Russians?"

"It can't all be true," began Gerald at once.

"That's what I say. It sounds awful! James read me
a bit out of *John Bull* last Sunday that said there wasn't
a house left standing, not a man, woman nor child left
living, where the Red Armies had been. And then we read
some more in the *Daily Herald*, only this time it was about
the White Army. And James said: 'Well, but isn't that
the other side?' And I told him you can't believe everything you see in the papers."

"It's very difficult," agreed Agatha thoughtfully. "It's
broadminded of you, Dolly, to take *John Bull* and the *Daily
Herald*. We only take *The Times*."

"Well, we don't get time to read the paper every day.
But we do a bit on Sunday. Come into the parlour, won't
you? I do believe you've not been here, Agatha, since we
bought the gramophone."

" No, I haven't. Dolly, how exciting ! What did you do that for ? "

" James got it for my birthday. That is it."

" But it's a beauty ! These cabinet ones are so much the nicest."

" It's second-hand," said Dolly. " We couldn't have got such a good one new. But James got this off a friend that was short of money and wanted to get rid of it. It's as good as new."

Agatha felt vaguely surprised at the idea of James having a friend. But, when she thought it over, she could see no reason why he shouldn't.

" Those cheap ones," continued Dolly, " well, they wouldn't do at all. We didn't like all that sort of scraping they made ; you can't seem to hear the music. But this is just what we wanted. I'd play it to you now, only James isn't here. I expect he'll turn it on after tea."

" Oh, I do hope he will. What records have you got ? "

" Not many yet. We haven't had it so very long. We've got a lot out of the ' Messiah.' That's my favourite piece. I sung in it once in our chapel choir at home. It's grand ! But I expect you've heard it often. Then we've got a thing, I think it's called ' Chaconne,' that James likes. He heard it in Paris. And we have some comics for the children. And I got ' Take a Pair of Sparkling Eyes ' when I was over in Oxford once. I think it's a very pretty song, but James regularly has his knife into it and broke it by accident. At least, he said it was. Sissy, lovey, just look into the kitchen and see if the kettle's boiling ! "

Dolly spread an elaborately embroidered linen cloth, with a crochet border, over the plush table cover and fetched out the Spode tea-things which she had inherited from her grandmother. Sissy and Sonny were invested with bibs and mouthed their grace with some promptings.

" You'll have eggs with your teas," pursued the hostess,

" after this long drive ?   James always gets eggs when he's
been working all afternoon. Oh, yes, you must ! How many
would you like ? Mr. Blair could do with two, surely ? "

She was very much put out at their refusal, but relented
when they described to her the meal which they would
have to eat on returning to Braxhall.

" Not really ? " she exclaimed. " Then I don't wonder
you won't eat much tea. And I expect you ate enough
lunch to feed a poor family for a week, didn't you ?
But . . . ! D'you mean to say they eat all that ? "

" Eating's nothing," said Gerald. " You should see what
they drink ! "

" Oh, it is wasteful ! I do think it's shocking ! Now at
Lyndon sometimes I used to be surprised at all the food
that got eat up in the dining-room.   But that wasn't
nothing to this ; and it was before the war too.   But these
new gentlemen, like Sir Thomas, they don't seem to mind
what they do. I don't like all that waste. I wonder now
how much butcher's meat goes into the housekeeper's room ? "

Agatha was unable to enlighten her on this point and a
moment later she laughed at herself for the question.

" It was a silly thing to ask, for I don't believe, Agatha,
that you know that much about your own house."

Gerald was intrigued by the manner of the two women
towards each other. It was not quite what he had expected.
He had gathered that the family thought Agatha too
friendly with Dolly. But he had never been able to imagine
them on terms of perfect familiarity. He had always
pictured Agatha as the more assured of the two, smoothing,
in her tactful way, the small difficulties of intercourse. He
saw now, however, that Dolly dominated the alliance. He
perceived in her manner, moreover, a hint of mocking
tenderness, a very guarded gesture of compassion. It was
possible to believe that she pitied Agatha for some reason,
and it occurred to him that she would not readily sympathize

with purely imaginary ills. He wondered if Agatha had confided to her simple bosom some of the hidden disquiet of which he was now so poignantly aware. He hoped that this was so. She could not have a better confidante. Since he himself could not inquire into the trouble, since it would be dangerous for him to try, he was glad that she had Dolly. But he would have thought that the spectacle of so much conjugal serenity, such maternal complacence, must be torture to a woman like Agatha, tardily reaping the bitter fruits of her mistaken marriage. Her fortitude in enduring it indicated a generosity of temper which rejoiced his loving heart.

The voice of James could be heard halloing through the house for his tea. His wife called to him :

" It's here ! We've got company." To the guests she explained : " We generally get it in the kitchen when we are alone."

The master of the house joined them. He was paler and a good deal fatter than of old, and he walked with a decided limp. His large face creased into joyful smiles when he saw his sister-in-law, and he greeted her affectionately.

" You remember Mr. Blair, James ? " prompted Dolly.

" Of course I do. You are Agatha's friend, aren't you ? It's a long time since I've seen you, though. Where have you come from ? "

" I'm staying at Braxhall," said Gerald.

James looked very much surprised.

" What for ? " he demanded.

" He has come down for the fresco lunch," explained Agatha. " And I want to know why you aren't all coming. You certainly should, you know."

A peculiar expression eclipsed the candid sweetness of James's smile. For a second he looked positively venomous, Then he became merely sulky.

" I'm never going near that place again," he averred.

" But I thought the frescoes looked very nice," persisted Agatha.

He regarded her closely and in some astonishment.

" Have you seen them ? " he asked.

" Well, I've only had one little peep. I haven't looked at them properly yet."

" No ? " said James.

Then he turned to Gerald and demanded :

" You seen 'em ? "

" Not yet."

James assented as though he had been quite sure of the answer. Dolly, meanwhile, had been looking uneasy and now introduced a change of subject :

" They've been looking at the gramophone, but we haven't played it yet. Henry ! Don't get putting your fingers in the jam ! Now, if you do it again you'll get a good smack."

James's face cleared instantly.

" Oh, have you ? Wouldn't you like to hear it ? Shall I play it to you now ? "

He put on a record of Mdme. Clara Butt singing " I know that my Redeemer liveth," to which they all listened reverently while they ate their bread and radishes. Upon the faces of Dolly and James was written a complete, uncritical joy in their new possession. It was obvious that they loved an excuse for playing their gramophone.

" It's almost as good as real, isn't it ? " said Dolly.

Even Gerald, who hated gramophones, had to admit that this was the least offensive that he had ever heard.

" Now we'll have the ' Chaconne,' " breathed James.

He had stopped smiling and a slight quiver ran all through his large body. The others fell silent and in the hush of the small room Agatha felt an instant's pang of unreasoned fear of him. He fetched the record and put it into place with the soft, mysterious gestures of a priest at the altar.

Dolly and Agatha listened with the religious expression of women who are making a genuine effort of intelligence. Dolly plaited her cotton skirt into creased folds between a work-stained thumb and finger. Agatha sat very still. Everything in the little parlour was like a dream, unsubstantial as the thick yellow splashes of sunlight which dappled the geraniums in the window and fell in sleepy pools on the carpet. In the middle of its warm illusion the motionless solidity of James seemed to melt, his brooding impassivity to shiver and break, until the vibrant air was alive with his thoughts. As for Gerald, he was a thin flame burning somewhere in the shadows of the room.

When the concert was over James was instructed to take Mr. Blair out to the bench by the porch for a smoke. Dolly and Agatha retired upstairs to the privacy of the conjugal bedroom, where Jimmy got his tea and Agatha powdered her nose. The two women lingered some time, discussing the technical side of the child's arrival.

"I was laid up longer than the other two times," said Dolly. "I wasn't back to work not inside three weeks. I don't know what Auntie wouldn't have said to me. She's always on to me for turning into a lady. Mrs. Hickman, the woman that came in to do for me, was a low sort of person. The dirt! You'd be surprised; just in that little time! 'Well,' I said, when I came down, 'the first thing I do is to have a good clean round.' I was glad James was away at Braxhall most of the time doing those frescoes. It would have been very uncomfortable for him, not getting his meals nice like he's used to."

"Have you seen the frescoes, Dolly?"

"No, I haven't! Not yet! And between you and I, Agatha, I'm worried about them. He's been so funny. To begin with he was quite all right, just like he always is over his things, you know. Quite taken up with them. But then Sir Thomas kept writing and going on at him, saying they wanted stained-glass windows, and this and the other, and I don't know what all. Until he got quite disgusted. And I got afraid, really I did ! For you know he's dreadful when he does lose his temper, which isn't often, thank goodness ! "

" I rather gathered that the Bragges had been a little trying."

" That's right. And it isn't only this. That Cynthia, you know, well I suppose I shouldn't talk back at her as she's James's sister, but first and last she's been very nasty to us. Very nasty she's been, just in little ways. But she was never kind to James : he hasn't told me the half, I'm sure, but he remembers it all. He remembers too much, as I often tell him. Because most of it happened when they was only children, and I don't like holding things up against people. It's not Christian. Quiet now, Jimmy, you greedy boy ! You've had quite enough for one while."

" Let me have him for a bit."

Agatha took the child while Dolly buttoned up her frock and put a few pins into her hair. The room was very small and almost filled by the double bed and the baby's cradle squeezed against the wall. James's Sunday clothes, newly brushed, hung over the foot-rail of the bed, and Dolly now folded them neatly and put them away in the bottom drawer of a little wardrobe. Agatha tried to imagine herself and John submitting to the enforced propinquities of such a marriage chamber and felt dismayed at the idea. It showed her how slender was the bond between them. Their union would have been quite unendurable if they had been forced to live as Dolly and James lived, as the majority of the human race have to live, without the means for privacy.

Her mood of the moment was such that she was inclined to view her own advantages over Dolly in the light of a calamity. She envied a simplicity of existence which, at another time, might have struck her as wanting in refinement. Seeing all things from her cousin's standpoint, and exaggerating, if possible, his distrust of those civilized amenities which depend upon a large income, she found the Bramfield household an admirable institution. She saw in the undecorated austerity before her a symbol of that marriage which endures against accident, against shock and change, because illusion has no part in its foundation. Such a companionship she had once desired for herself : she believed that it would mitigate the unbearable solitude of her spirit. But she and John could never compass it. She had forfeited such hopes for ever and ever when she became his wife.

"Do you know that a million married people are now living apart ? " she asked Dolly suddenly.

"What's that ? "

"A million married people are at this moment living apart in England alone. And, dear knows how many more don't want to."

"Well, I never ! " Dolly was shocked. "Is that really true ? Isn't it awful ? The papers is full of these divorces nowadays."

"What's the cause of it all, do you think ? Why are there so many more unhappy marriages than there used to be ? "

"I don't think there are any more than there used to be, I don't. Only people won't put up with things, not like they used to. It's the same all round. Look at the way people used to have to work before there was any Unions. Twelve hours a day, even for little children ! It was awful ! Auntie used to tell me about when her mother was a young woman, away up in Leeds ; and you couldn't believe that such things could have happened. People must have taken things a sight more quietly than they do now."

"Then you think there were always unhappy marriages, but people didn't rebel against them."

"Yes, I think so. My mother! When I think of what she had to bear! No woman wouldn't stand it nowadays."

"But isn't it a good thing, don't you think? Why should people endure misery if they can escape from it? When a person rebels, it's progress really."

"Well, I don't know, Agatha. I see what you mean and I'm sure you are right in a way. Only I get thinking sometimes. . . . It seems a pity. . . . Sort of like this. The way we go on now, people act silly and then find out new ways so as not to suffer for it. They don't study not to be silly. That isn't going to make the world any better, not in the long run."

"But is anything likely to make the world better in the long run?"

"Godly living will," said Dolly firmly, "and nothing will do instead of that, not if it's ever so."

"Oh, Dolly! But what is godly living?"

"I should have thought you'd know that as well as I do. It's obeying what our conscience tells us."

"But if you've made a mistake so that you can't . . . you can't . . . if you have got yourself all into the wrong atmosphere. . . . What I mean is, you can't be godly or anything else genuine if you are absolutely out of harmony with your life. Listen! Suppose a woman was married to a man who wasn't unkind or unfaithful or anything, but she just found she didn't love him, and felt that her life with him was absolutely at variance with her conscience . . . and . . . and there was another man . . . whom she ought to have married, who had the same ideals, with whom she could lead a better life? Which do you think she ought to do, stay with her husband, or go to this other man?"

"I wouldn't like to say," said Dolly, looking embarrassed. "How d'you mean, lead a better life?"

"Well, if the other man had . . . say, a religion that she believed in and that her husband couldn't ever, ever understand. After all, it says in the Bible 'leave all and follow Me.' I don't want to be blasphemous, but couldn't it be a sort of . . . call ? "

"I don't know, I'm sure. I never heard of anyone getting a call that way, though I've heard plenty of people telling about their religious experiences."

"But it might be."

"Well, I suppose it might. Only it seems a funny idea. I think anybody'd have a hard job to persuade themselves that it was right. Why, supposing she had little children to care for ? "

"Oh . . . I mean a woman without children."

"Did you ? But then there'd be her husband. What would he do ? He'd have to get another woman to look after him most likely. And she wouldn't be his wife, not unless he had enough money to divorce the first one. And then they'd be living in sin."

"I . . . meant . . . fairly well off people, who could afford divorce."

"Oh, I see," cried Dolly enlightened. "You mean a lady, not any sort of woman ? "

"Y—yes. I suppose I do naturally think of a lady when I think of an imaginary case."

"Well, you see, I naturally don't."

"Is there so much difference ? " said Agatha wonderingly. "But if it was any woman, Dolly ? Would you condemn her if she left her husband and went to a man she loved better ? "

"I couldn't say unless I knew her. I would if I thought she was light. But it isn't only that kind that do such things."

Through the window the smell of lilies was blown in from the garden and the voices of Gerald and James murmured on in intermittent conversation. The noise of

THE BRAXHALL FRESCOES   215

the car in the lane reminded Agatha that she must get
home early. She began to tie her veils.

On the way home she said to Gerald :

" Dolly thinks that our much-vaunted civilization is too
much occupied with palliatives. She's very strong upon
the folly of substitutes for godly living, as she calls it. She
thinks we concern ourselves too much with averting the
consequences of our own acts instead of eradicating folly
and vice themselves."

" Dolly's views," said he, " are so sound that they are
apt to be a little obvious. What desperate remedy was she
referring to in particular ? "

" It was divorce," said Agatha, after a moment's pause.
" We were discussing unhappy marriages and whether there
were more now than formerly."

Gerald looked straight in front of him and said in a
detached, discursive tone :

" Nobody but the parties themselves can say what
constitutes a happy or an unhappy marriage. Evils which
to one section of society, or one generation, seem quite
unbearable are beside the point to another. I remember
seeing that so strongly once when I was reading some letters
written by an old boy in the seventeenth century (I rather
think it was Halifax) to his daughter. He was obviously
devoted to her ; and his advice about bearing ill-treatment
from a husband comes as something of a shock. I don't
think it referred to any special husband : I mean I don't
think she was even grown up at the time. It was just on
general principle. He counsels the child as to the best way
to endure brutality, drunkenness, and flagrant infidelity
as if they were inevitable, as they probably were in those
days. But he was a sane man, and very fond of the girl,
and one gets the impression that he quite expected her to
be happy and prosperous, as I've no doubt she was."

" It's very odd," said Agatha. " I suppose it all depends

upon what one expects to get. In a way marriages of convenience must be much more likely to be happy than marriages for love, because they are based on less extravagant expectations. Either way it's a toss up."

"It's ultimately based, I fancy, upon the question of common ideals; unity of outlook. Whether the pair concerned have the same conception of their environment, the same purpose in life. The usual considerations determining a love match don't necessarily ensure that, any more than would the business propositions behind a marriage of convenience. Look at our present host and hostess! They are, to me, as good an example of a happy marriage in one way as Dolly and James are in another. I can imagine either making another partner miserable. But together they are complete, and Braxhall is a wonderful expression of their joint outlook."

Agatha was silent, her mind busy with unspoken applications. She was dismayed by the unconcealed bitterness of his tone toward Braxhall for she felt that Lyndon fell under the same condemnation. The Bragges merely proclaimed blatantly an ideal of life which, in her own household, was discreetly and beautifully intimated. So, in the light of their earlier encounters, did she interpret all his scornful remarks. But she did him an injustice. He was long past criticizing anything that was hers.

He changed the subject, feeling, with an obscure sense of self-preservation, that matrimony, happy or otherwise, was no safe topic for himself and Agatha. He said that he was intrigued by James and the frescoes.

"I don't understand him. There must be something behind it which nobody can have understood. He spoke in such an odd way when I was sitting in the garden with him. I shall go and have a look at the things as soon as I get back."

"What did he say?"

"He seemed almost apologetic about them. And yet

defiant. He said that he considered they were as good work
as ever he'd done, and that Sir Thomas could always
whitewash the wall if he didn't like it, but that he, James,
wouldn't alter them for anybody."

" Of course, they are all rather . . . bacchanalian, but
I don't think the Bragges seem to mind."

The car swung into the long road leading up the Braxhall
valley. Beside them the stream wound through the fields, and
" Bragge's Barracks " frowned upon them from the heights.
Agatha realized with a pang that her afternoon of happiness
and freedom was nearly over ; she was returning to a prison,
and would soon be plunged afresh into that abyss of
irritation, suspicion, veiled criticism, secret conclaves,
tactful hints and plain speaking. The clarity of mood, the
singleness of mind, which she could only achieve in Gerald's
company must inevitably be shattered. She had looked
forward to taking him to Bramfield ; she knew that he
would like Dolly and James, and she revelled in the sense of
companionship, of comprehension, which had been theirs
since childhood. In her exaltation she could believe that
they were both entire strangers to Braxhall, travellers from
another world, gayer, simpler and more vital.

Anxious to prolong her reprieve, she suggested that they
should walk up through the gardens.

" We can cross by the footbridge," she said, " and send
the car up by the road. There is plenty of time. It's not
six yet."

He acquiesced and they stopped the car. A steep stile
took them into a square field peppered with mushrooms.
Gerald, the glare of the collector in his eye, immediately
began to pick these, swearing mildly at deceptive puff-balls.
She watched him, still possessed by the conviction, common
to all lovers, that she had discovered the secret of the
universe. Her amusement was tender and beguiling.

" You are one of those people who can't pass a mushroom.

I know! My mother is like that. She will walk ten miles carrying one."

" Still," he protested, " even one is nice in a stew. . . ."

" They will be excellent in our hash to-night, I've no doubt. What will you do with them? Which chef will you give them to? "

" It's sheer waste to leave them."

They crossed the little footbridge into the garden. Gerald held his hat full of mushrooms in both hands, very carefully, like a chalice. The silence and the sun absorbed and enfolded them; the extreme degree of isolation in which they walked was intensified by the fact that they were visible from every window on the south side of Braxhall. They ascended towards that observant, many-eyed façade as adventurers approach a hostile stronghold.

Slower and slower grew their pace as they mounted from terrace to terrace; longer each pause as they turned to look down the valley. Nothing stirred in the picture below them; not a cow or a sheep moved in the unbroken green of the fields and the heavy foliage on the opposite hillside was as massive, in the strong sunlight, as a tapestried picture.

" How warm and tame these woods look! " said Agatha suddenly. " You would never think that at night they are full of lost souls."

" Oh, those owls! Did you hear them? "

" They went on all night. They were worst about half-past two."

" I know."

Each had a vision of the other lying awake in those long haunted hours when the valley echoed to strange cries and a low mist from the stream lay over the fields. They resumed their climbing and did not pause again until they had reached the topmost terrace of all and stood close beneath the walls of Braxhall. Then Gerald spoke impulsively, in obedience to a decision which he had just reached :

" I suppose lunch to-morrow will be over by three o'clock ?
I must get away by the three-forty."

" Oh, Gerald ! You aren't going ? Not to-morrow ? "

" Yes." He spoke a little unsteadily this time and did
not look at her. " I think I ought to be getting back."

She stared at him, an icy terror spreading over her, so
that she shivered in spite of the strong sun.

" I really oughtn't to be away at all, just now," he added.
" But I wanted to see . . . to see those frescoes, you know."

He regarded his mushrooms unhappily. He had made
up his mind that another night of listening to the Braxhall
owls would be as much as he could bear. To himself he
repeated in mental reiteration :

" Too risky ! Altogether too risky ! "

They moved on into the house. When they reached the
marble corridor she had collected herself sufficiently to
remark : " Oh, yes. I suppose you oughtn't to leave your
work for long."

He nodded and began to mount the wide, shallow stairs.
She watched him until he had turned the corner. He was
still carrying his hat reverently, like a chalice.

4.

He was scarcely out of sight before Lois came hurriedly
through the folding doors of the banqueting hall. She
advanced in the greatest agitation, calling softly to her
sister-in-law. The pallor of her tear-stained cheeks roused
Agatha, for a moment, from the stupor of misery which
had overtaken her.

" What is it ? What is the matter ? " she cried.

Lois sank on to the bench beside her and began in a low
voice :

" Oh, Agatha ! It's so dreadful ! Listen ! Hubert is
come . . . and . . ."

She paused to give a loud sob.

" Dearest Lois ! Tell me what it is. What can have . . ."

" Can you come into the hall for a minute ? No, wait ! I'd better tell you first what has happened."

" Have you had bad news ? " asked Agatha, wondering if Hubert had been speculating.

" No ! No ! He came, and I took him to see the frescoes. Oh, dear ! Oh, Agatha, did you see anything wrong with them ? "

" My dear, I know absolutely nothing about pictures."

" But you don't need to, to see this. How can we have been so blind ? It's incredible ! I saw it directly he pointed it out to me. And you can't think how angry he is. He says I am absolutely incapable of looking observantly at anything. . . ."

" But what is it ? What is wrong with them ? "

" Oh, it's perfectly wicked of James. It really is. He's put in Tom and Cynthia."

" Put in ? "

" Into the fresco. They are quite unmistakable. Hubert says he doesn't know when he's seen anything more savage. He saw it the moment . . ."

" Oh, it can't be. I don't believe it. I saw the frescoes myself. Where are they ? "

" In the centre panel, over the dais. Don't you remember those people reclining at a sort of banquet . . . absolutely gorging. . . ."

Agatha reorganized her memory and recalled with a shock of alarm an incredibly aldermanic figure, which she had set down for Silenus, taking his ease, if she remembered correctly, in the arms of a slender, blonde hussy. . . . A horrible doubt was born in her mind.

" Let me look ! " she cried, and then asked : " Who is in the hall ? "

" Only Hubert. He's the only person that knows, so far,

except John. John saw it at once when we told him, and he just wants to murder James. And he said we'd better find you and consult what's best to be done. So we both went to look for you. I don't know where he's gone; up to your room, I expect. I . . . I don't think he knew you had gone out with Mr. Blair. But I happened to look out of the window and saw you coming up the hill. So I ran out to stop you."

" I see," said Agatha, too much preoccupied to notice that Lois was blushing " Let's go into the hall."

She followed Lois through the big doors. They discovered Hubert, in a transport of fury, pacing up and down and viewing the unspeakable paintings from every part of the room. Agatha looked at the panel over the dais and turned pale. It was quite undeniable that the central figures of the piece were more than reminiscent of Sir Thomas and Lady Bragge.

She looked for a long time in shocked silence and then said faintly :

" I suppose it's having no clothes on that makes one slow to recognize them."

" I suppose so," said Hubert grimly. " But I found no difficulty in seeing it the moment I came into the room."

" But then, you know, the first time I saw it they were both here, with their clothes and everything . . . it distracted one's attention a certain amount."

" I see it more strongly every minute," broke in Lois. " I've seen Cynthia look like that a dozen times, when she is a little anxious what Sir Thomas will say next. Late on in dinner, you know, when he's rather . . ."

" I'll go down to Bramfield to-morrow and kill James," said Hubert.

Agatha was looking intently at the piece and now asked :
" What are all those people doing on that li tle hill behind the group ? What are they building ? "

" A temple ? " suggested Hubert uncertainly.

" It's Braxhall," she vowed. " It's this house as you see it from the valley."

" Perhaps," he agreed. " But it doesn't signify. It isn't nearly so obvious as these people in the foreground. Among all these bosky hillocks and leafy groves it will pass unnoticed very probably. The other can't."

" I don't think there are any other portraits," said Lois, who had been looking anxiously at the other panels. " Not of people we know, anyhow. That's some comfort."

" I shall go round and kill him," repeated Hubert with gathering venom.

" I wish you would," muttered Lois.

" When you think it was on my recommendation . . . Of course, I ought to have known that he wasn't to be trusted. I knew he was getting riled with the way Sir Thomas went on, and I half suspected that he had some dirty trick up his sleeve. But I depended on Lois to let me know if anything was wrong. I ought to have known that she is about as much use as a sick headache. I ought to have known, after all these years. . . ."

" But Lois wasn't the only one," interrupted Agatha. " We've all been blind. Look at John ! And my mother, and Lady Clewer, and the Bragges themselves ! You are the first person to notice it, Hubert, as far as I know."

" Well, I can't understand it ! You simply can't have looked at the thing."

" No. I don't think we did. That's it. At least it is in my case. There is always something in James's work which makes me very reluctant to look at it. I couldn't say why."

" Of course," said Hubert bitterly, " anybody could be excused for not recognizing their own portraits; and I suppose that the rest of you were so steeped in the Bragge atmosphere, don't you know. . . ."

He broke off with a shrug. He could not forgive them for not having warned him. His taunt was directed at his wife but it stung Agatha intolerably. Convinced that her cousin was fleeing from Braxhall because he could endure it no longer, she resented any implication which would put her in such a galley. It was an insult to say that she was steeped in Bragge atmosphere. Confronted with this epitome of it, she found it all as detestable as anybody could. Neither James nor Gerald could hate it worse.

" But what about the party ? " Lois was saying. " That's what we wanted to consult you about. What are we to do ? Can it be put off ? What shall we say to the Bragges ? "

" Couldn't we persuade them to have lunch in the panelled room ? "

" It wouldn't hold half the people. Besides, the whole thing is got up especially to exhibit the frescoes."

" Well," said Agatha, thinking swiftly, " we must let things take their chance. I would suggest that we say nothing to anyone. Not till after the party. It can't be put off now."

" But supposing people see . . ." began Lois.

" Can't we trust that the majority of the guests will be as unobservant as we have been ? I don't see why not. They won't expect it, you know ; and most people don't see things they don't expect. And they will all be eating lovely food ; food good enough to absorb their attention completely. Besides, a lot of them will have their backs to that particular panel."

" I shall give myself away," said Lois. " I shall blush whenever I look at the thing."

" If ever I do anything for that fellow again," said Hubert, " I'll be boiled alive ! "

" And for relations too ! " cried Lois. " It's simply disgusting ! When we have all been so . . ."

She was disconcerted by something in the faces of the

other two, and did not attempt to specify what his family had always been to James. Instead she added :

" I'm sure we all recognize, now, that he is justified in his claims as an artist."

" I never heard him make any," murmured Agatha.

Hubert was studying the fresco again and now commented : " I always did think that Sir Thomas looked like a satyr. I remember it struck me the first time I saw them sitting together under a tree. A satyr and a nymph ! Oh, yes . . . but it wasn't Cynthia though, it was you, Agatha."

" Cynthia or me ! " thought Agatha. " It doesn't matter which. We are both the same type to James . . . and Gerald."

" But even if we get through this awful lunch safely," demanded Lois tearfully. ". . . What then ? "

" We'll have to see," said Hubert. " I think I agree with Agatha. Since we can't postpone the lunch we must go through with it, and in that case the fewer people who know the truth the better.. Your mother doesn't know, Lois ? "

" No. And what she'll say when she finds out, I don't know. She will make James sorry."

" What about your mother ? " went on Hubert, turning to Agatha. " Should we tell her ? Would she help us to carry things off ? "

" Heavens, no ! On no account ! She's the very last person to tell. Though she's generally so quick that I can't think why she needs telling. But she would be so frightfully amused—you must forgive me for saying so, Lois. It wouldn't be safe. She wouldn't be able to help telling people, or at least prompting them to guess."

" Oh well, then, in that case . . ."

" We must try to keep her very busy and animated all through lunch so that she simply doesn't look at the thing. . . ."

The dismayed trio stared at the thing and wondered how

anyone could possibly be prevented from looking. They started guiltily as John flung open the door at the end of the hall and slammed it behind him. He joined them without a glance at the frescoes and addressed himself to his wife.

" I didn't know you had gone for a walk. I was looking for you."

" I went over to Bramfield to see Dolly and James," she replied in some surprise.

His face, at the mention of James, grew a shade blacker.

" Oh, yes ? I thought I saw you walking across the valley field just now."

" We got out of the car by the footbridge and walked up the garden."

" I know. I saw you from the staircase window."

Hubert and Lois looked at each other, and Lois broke in :

" I found Agatha in the hall, John, and brought her in here. I didn't know you were still looking for her."

" I wasn't. I was coming down to fetch her when I met Sir Thomas, who began to talk about his peach house. I couldn't get away."

" About these frescoes . . ." began Hubert timidly.

" Eh ? The frescoes ? " asked John vaguely. Then he recollected himself and exclaimed : " Oh, damn the frescoes. Do what you like about it. They are no business of mine."

And he turned again upon his wife a regard which said that here was a business which touched him too nearly. Hubert seized Lois by the arm and almost ran her out of the hall.

" Well, but," she whispered as soon as the door had closed behind them, " Agatha shouldn't walk about in front of the windows with Mr. Blair just when poor John is so ill."

" She doesn't know he's ill," returned Hubert violently. " It's . . . it's unfair not to tell her. It's . . ."

"Hush! Somebody will hear. Wasn't it awful? I never saw anybody look so angry. His face was quite blue. It must be very bad for him."

" It's not our business," said Hubert firmly.

They stole away.

John, left alone with his wife, turned upon her furiously. " You went to see Dolly and James, did you? Well, you won't go again."

" John! What is the matter with you? You've no business to lose your temper like this. What do you mean? I shall certainly go if I please."

" I won't have it. I forbid you to go there again. You are not to see James any more, or his wife. You must drop them, see? It's the encouragement you give them that lets us in for this sort of thing."

He waved a hand at the frescoes.

" But I'm very fond of him," she protested vaguely, still at a loss.

" You are fonder than is prudent of several of your relations, aren't you? "

She started, stared, and grew very pale. He was, indeed, appalled at what he had said, and repented instantly. He had been stung beyond endurance by the sight of that slow, intimate ascent through the Braxhall gardens. He was determined to end, one way or the other, a situation which was becoming intolerable. The irrevocable words now lay between them like a flung gauntlet. Nothing could unsay them ; but Agatha, after a moment's consideration, made a visible attempt to ignore them.

" We'll discuss James later . . ." she said. " The business before us now is the frightful party to-morrow. . . ."

But he thought that he might as well go on as he had begun. " The party to-morrow won't concern us," he told her, " because we shall not be here."

" John? "

" We leave here first thing to-morrow morning."

Her eyes questioned him and he flung the reason at her.
" I won't have you driving about the country with that
. . . that fellow. You will leave Braxhall to-morrow and
I won't have you seeing him again."

" Do you mean Gerald Blair ? "

" I do."

She considered this for a moment and then asked :

" And what makes you take this line ? What cause have
I ever given you ? What have I done ? "

" You've lost your head over him. It's perfectly
obvious to anyone. And it's enough. I'm not taking any
risks."

She opened her lips for a denial which would not come.
Instead she cried out :

" Risks ! What risks ? Do you want to insult me ? "

" This sort of thing has got to stop," he said doggedly.

" What sort of thing ? "

" Your whole behaviour. I tell you I'm tired of it.
You treat me like a discarded lover."

" Do I ? Do I ? Well, so you are ! " she cried, her voice
rising.

Disgusted at her loss of self-command and the vulgarity
of such a scene, she added in a lower voice :

" You are. You've never been anything more. Never a
real husband. Not more than Tom is to Cynthia. Our
relationship may be legal, but it isn't marriage. Nothing
can make it that."

" Really ? And what is it then ? "

" It's been my fault," she conceded earnestly. " I ought
never to have married you. We have no ideals in common.
I've never been a real wife to you. Nothing more than a
mistress ; nothing more. . . ."

" It's a pity you feel like that," he said bitterly. " But
I'm afraid you'll have to put up with it."

Then he burst out again :

" Oh, hell, Agatha ! Can't you speak the truth ? Can't you think straight ? You married me and you've got tired of me. And you've invented all this humbug about common ideals to justify your infidelity. That's the long and short of it."

At the word infidelity she swung round, her conscious innocence flaming in her face.

" Never for a moment . . ." she began, and then broke off. " But it's horrible to have to make denials—to exculpate oneself ! If you can believe . . ."

Tears, the first he had ever seen her shed, choked her speech. Smarting under a sense of undeserved insult, she stood before him weeping silently. He beheld her beauty and her grief with a fierce throb of satisfaction. To make her suffer was at least a reassertion of power. He became dominant and calm.

" We go to-morrow," he repeated.

She answered, very low :

" We needn't . . . for the reason you mention. . . . He is going away immediately after lunch."

A spasm of anguish shook her and he heard himself saying coldly :

" Oh, I see. Is that why you are crying ? "

His heart had begun to do strange things and it occurred to him that this interview, if prolonged, might prove fatal to him. He had no wish to die at Braxhall. Glancing at her from the door, before he left her, he saw that she had not moved. She was still standing on the dais step, both hands pressed to her bosom, while the fresco panel flamed above her stricken head.

Gerald, upon reaching his room, had, in a thunderclap of energy, sat down and written the opening pages of a paper upon " The Experiments at Nancy " which had been

simmering in his brain for some time. He was wonderfully
relieved by his sudden decision to quit Braxhall upon the
morrow, and to see his cousin no more. Anguish it might
be, but it was at least a termination of the conflict. He
was able, for the first time in many weeks, to lose himself
in his work. He wrote, absorbed, for nearly an hour, and
then, pausing for an instant's relaxation, recalled idly the
mysterious utterances of James about the fresco. He
remembered that he had meant to visit the hall immediately
upon his return, and accordingly he set off, descending by
a small staircase, close to his room, which gave him access
to a door opening immediately on to the dais. He was,
therefore, precipitated within a few feet of Agatha before
either was aware of the other.

She was seated upon one of the chairs set round the dais.
Her elbows were on the table and her face in her hands.
Her whole attitude bespoke an abandonment of grief. She
had evidently failed to hear his approach over the thick
dais carpet.

He stood poised for flight. Prudence inwardly counselled
a prompt withdrawal; passion impelled him forward.
Lingering, he was lost, for she raised her head and saw him.
She betrayed no surprise, but fixed upon him a regard of
infinite sadness, and sat motionless in her chair, the slow
tears still rolling down her cheeks.

He was inured to women's tears; he had seen too many
of them. But all his experience had never shown him a
creature who could weep so beautifully. No sobs shook
her; she was composed, mistress of herself, save for these
silent, persistent signals of woe. He had, among his patients,
a reputation for complete immunity; no nervous collapse
could soften or alarm him in Harley Street. Had she
brought her tears there it is possible that he might have
checked the flood with a few bracing words and a glass of
water. But affection had undone him, as it has betrayed

better men, and, instead of resorting to professional advice, he was moved, he hardly knew how, to fling himself at her feet, to call her by every endearing name which occurred to him, and finally, with a sense of foundering rectitude, to clasp her to his heart and entreat her to tell him her trouble.

Of the subsequent conversation neither retained any very clear impression. It was an affair of mutual declarations, and in a very short time they arrived at the conclusion that a further separation would be impossible to them. They must defy all the forces which had divided them ten years earlier, and this must be done at once. Agatha's misery appeared to both of them as something no longer to be borne, and they believed that their immediate union would be almost certain to abate it.

"We must get married," Gerald stated. "We ought, of course, to have got married ten years ago. We'll go abroad somewhere until Clewer divorces you, and then we will be married."

"But do you think that will be right?" demanded Agatha hopefully.

He looked surprised, and a little put out.

"Right? What do you mean exactly? I think it's the wisest thing we can do under the circumstances. And anyhow we are going to do it."

"I mean, can you do it with an absolutely free conscience?"

"N—no, not exactly. I couldn't say that."

Agatha did not like this at all.

"You can't do what you think wrong," she said doubtfully.

"Oh, yes I can," he assured her.

"But it must be right," she argued. "We were meant for each other. It was my marriage that was wrong."

He agreed, but said that he would, he thought, condemn behaviour like theirs in anyone else. He reminded her, a little shamefacedly, that he had accepted John's hospitality and was returning it by stealing his wife. But she insisted that they were justified. He thought it rather tactless of her thus to harp upon the most painful element in their situation. He had overlooked, for a moment, a woman's capacity for sanctifying her passions by an ideal. She had succeeded in persuading herself that flight from her husband was the only remedy for an enormous wrong, the only means whereby she could release her better self for a life of austere endeavour. Her natural aptitude for symbolism had led her to perceive a deep significance in the events of the afternoon. The impression of the fresco was strong upon her, and she believed that in renouncing her married life, with all its luxuries, she was pledging herself to a very noble path. She could only repeat, rather resentfully :

" It seems right to me."

" Well, that's a good thing," remarked her lover.

He took a short turn down the hall and returned to the dais step, looking up at her.

" I don't want you to deceive yourself," he said anxiously. " I don't want you to be rushed into any course which you might afterwards regret. I should be a scoundrel if I took advantage of what appears to be a slight confusion in your mind. I wish I knew what to do ! "

" I thought we'd settled what to do."

" Yes, but I want you to be quite sure. Think it over ! Don't decide now. Tell me to-morrow. Remember I'm ready to take your word as final. I'll take you off at any moment if you like, or I'll go away and never see you again if you'd rather. But it must be either one way or the other. I'm not going on like this : it's unendurable. Think it over and tell me."

She realised that the abruptness of his speech was calculated. He was deliberately trying not to appeal to her emotions, but to summon to their aid those rational faculties still left to them. He tried to leave her without further speech, but she called him back.

"Gerald! Are you quite sure that you want me to come? You aren't being a good Samaritan, are you?"

"Want you? Of course I want you! I always have. But that isn't the point. I've done without you up till now, and I can doubtless go on doing without you, if I have to. But I won't stand seeing you unhappy like this. It's more than anyone could bear, loving you at I do."

"But you could get on without me if you had to?"

"Why . . . yes . . . I suppose so. . . ."

"Then I've no business to come. My justification . . ."

"Oh, Agatha dearest, can't you think straight? . . ."

At this point Mrs. Cocks burst in through the door at the end of the hall. She glanced at the cousins, her eyes sparkling with instant displeasure.

"Agatha!" she exclaimed. "Do you know that it is five minutes to eight? Are you never going to dress this evening? I've been waiting for you, upstairs, for at least three-quarters of an hour."

"Is it really so late, Mother?"

"Yes! Yes! Hurry, child! Hurry, Gerald!"

She swept them from the hall and carried her daughter upstairs. Dismissing the maid, she declared that she would supervise the hasty toilet herself.

"Pauline would be much quicker," maintained Agatha.

"Perhaps. But I want to do some plain speaking which can't be accomplished before Pauline. What were you and Gerald quarrelling about when I came in?"

"We weren't quarrelling," said Agatha after reflection.

"Weren't you. You looked as if you were; you were looking defensive and he reproachful. And, by the way, may I ask if you and he have been in that hall ever since you came in this afternoon ? "

" Oh, no ! I was there with Lois and Hubert. And then John. Gerald had only just come."

" Oh, really ? That's not as bad as I thought. Still you know Agatha, when I saw you coming up through the garden . . ."

" Good heavens ! " cried Agatha impatiently, " how many more ? Did everybody in the house see me coming up through the garden ? "

" I expect so. That's where you are so silly, dear."

" I never knew it was such a monstrous thing to do."

" Now you are being even sillier. Tell me, who else has seen you ? "

" Oh . . . Lois and Hubert . . . and John. . . ."

" John ! What did John say ? "

Agatha made no reply, but dabbed powder on to her nose with shaking fingers.

" You've put on too much," observed her mother critically, and she fetched a damp sponge and removed it all. " Now begin again. Tell me . . . is John annoyed? Have you quarrelled with him ? "

" He blames me," began Agatha, and stopped with a gasp.

" What for ? "

" For the same reason that Gerald blames me."

" Oh ! " Mrs. Cocks was at a loss. " But I thought you said you had not quarrelled with Gerald."

" Nor have I."

" But you have quarrelled with John ? "

" Yes. They both want to know if I can't think straight."

" What shoes will you wear ? Is John jealous ? "

Agatha was silent.

" It's only natural," continued her mother, as she folded up discarded garments. " You can't have it both ways.

I've never seen a more devoted husband. You wouldn't
like it if he got tired of you ? "

" I shouldn't mind."

" Well, of course, if that's your line, I don't blame him
if he does resent it a little. In fact, I think he'd be justified
in consoling himself elsewhere. Do consider the possible
consequences of such behaviour, child. With a man like
John you can't afford to run risks."

" Thank you, Mother, I'd rather not discuss it."

" Try to look at things a little more from his point of
view. What, after all, did he marry you for ? "

" Oh, please, Mother, would you mind going ? Will you
please leave me alone ? I want to be by myself. I . . . I
won't come down to dinner, I think."

" Good heavens ! Child ! Are you ill ? Don't go that
colour ! Sit down and let me get you some sal volatile."

" No. I'm all right. I'm perfectly all right. I only
want to be by myself."

" But if you are too ill to come down to dinner, you are
too ill to be left alone. I shall stay with you and make it
clear that you are really unwell. I'm not going to have
Marian saying that you are sulking after a scene with John.
Are you sure you can't come down ? It would look much
better if you could."

" Well, yes," said Agatha, whose colour was returning.
" I will come. Could you find my Spanish comb ? And
I'll have that black lace shawl. It's somewhere in the
wardrobe."

" You are still very white. I should put on just a very
little touch, if I were you. You don't want to go down
looking conspicuously pale. Of course, John is such a
paragon of a husband. . . ."

The gong, heralding another of the endless Braxhall
meals, reminded Mrs. Cocks of the need for haste. She
turned to the wardrobe without another word.

5.

Towards four o'clock upon the following afternoon Lois stood on the topmost garden terrace, watching a car which sped along the valley road. It contained the last of the guests who had lunched at Braxhall. She stood attentive until it had turned the corner and then heaved a great sigh of relief.

Hubert had been instructed to take Mrs. Cocks to some retired place and keep her there. He had evidently done his duty, for nothing had been seen of the pair of them for above an hour and a half. Lois thought he should be released and set off in search of him. She found them in the sunk garden : they were sitting upon a stone bench by the fountain, absorbed in animated conversation. Hubert, though sprightly, was, to the practised eye of his wife, at the point of exhaustion ; but his companion was enjoying herself vivaciously.

" The guests have all gone," said Lois, joining them.

" Gone ? No ! It must be very early ! " cried Mrs. Cocks. " Nearly four ? I couldn't have believed it ! I'm afraid I've been very uncivil ; I do hope Cynthia won't think so. I never meant to stay here so long. But your husband has been telling me such killing stories, Lois."

" Cynthia has gone up to rest, and Sir Thomas is having a cocktail somewhere. I heard him calling for it."

" But are they all gone ? How annoying ! There are several people I particularly wanted to talk to. Why were you so amusing, Mr. Ervine ? "

Hubert, who had been amusing because told to be so by Lois, said that he was very sorry for it.

" I wanted to find out how many people have noticed that the Bragges have set up a portrait gallery. Most original, I call it. I hear that you all discovered it yesterday, and I think it most unkind of you not to point it out to me."

" Dear lady," began Hubert, " we meant for the best."

" Oh, I know you did. And you were perfectly right. But you see I never noticed it until the middle of lunch. I pointed it out at once to Mr. Chaytor, who was sitting next to me. But he was very crushing. He merely said that he had already observed a resemblance, and changed the subject. I think he was rather scandalized. And the man on my other side was deaf. I was longing to find someone to laugh with about it. Do you really mean to say that the Bragges don't know ? "

" Not yet," sighed Lois. " But they'll have to be told, I suppose."

" James is really a wag. When will you tell them ? "

" Oh, Mrs. Cocks," interrupted Lois, " Agatha was looking for you everywhere. She wanted to see you before she went. She told me to tell you she'd left a note for you in your sitting-room on the mantelpiece."

" Went ? Went where ? "

" Away from here. Back to London, I suppose. She went by the three-forty."

" But they aren't going till Saturday. We all go up to Scotland together."

" Oh, John hasn't gone. Only Agatha. She went in a great hurry just after lunch. She didn't even have time to say good-bye to Cynthia. I met her on the stairs taking leave of Sir Thomas, and she told me she had to run because her car was round, and asked me to give you her message about the note."

" This is very strange ! " exclaimed Mrs. Cocks jumping up. " I can't understand this. I must find John."

She hurried off towards the house, and Lois sank upon the stone bench beside her husband and felt in his pocket for a cigarette. He lighted it for her, and another for himself, remarking as he threw away the match :

" I suppose we can now say ' Nunc Dimittis ' and what not."

" You did nobly, dear ! I felt that our only hope was to keep her away from people. When I glanced across the table and saw by her expression that she had seen, I thought all was lost. But your skill in keeping her in seclusion has saved the day. What did you tell her stories about ? "

" Oh, the Jews mostly. We began with the frescoes, of course, and I propounded my theory that art is in for a golden age because all the profiteers are going to patronize it. This, I say, is due to the prevalence of Semitism. Formerly the Jews pretended not to be Jews and spent their money on baronial halls and portraits of Norman ancestors. Nowadays, when the whole world is run by 'em, nobody's ashamed of being a Jew. They build their own houses, and don't waste money on second-hand stuff. They patronize contemporary art. From that we got on to swapping stories about our Jewish acquaintances."

" But Sir Thomas isn't a Jew."

" No. But he meekly follows the beaten track of the leading profiteers who mostly are. But tell me, how did this affair go as a whole ? What was the impression you got ? How many people would you say spotted it ? "

" Oh, a good many. But most of them were too well mannered to show it. They were too much shocked and embarrassed to be amused."

" Then on the whole it was better than it might have been ? "

" I don't know ! It was pretty grim. I hope I'll never have to live through such another day."

" So do I."

" In the beginning I thought it was going off better than I could possibly have supposed. I was astonished."

"I know. When the thing was so blazingly obvious to me, I could not see how they could miss it. And when we got to the joints without a hitch, I began to be positively elated."

"There is a good deal in what Agatha says. I think his work repels most people. They have a sort of instinct not to look at it and they don't."

"They certainly don't. The lady on my right put up her lorgnettes and had a very brief squint and then put them down with a click, and said : 'I hear Mr. James Clewer is a great Socialist.' I thought that this was a new phase in Brother James, and said I didn't know anything about his political opinions. And she said wasn't it true that he had married a working-class woman and lived like an artisan ? I said that I believed that it was. She said that was what she meant, and that she detested Socialists. I said I did too. Whereupon we talked Bolshevik atrocities, and I don't think James or the frescoes were mentioned again."

"One of my neighbours asked me if Mr. Blair was James," said Lois. "I said no, and asked him why he thought so. He said because he looked so miserable and out of it."

"Blair certainly looked sorry for himself. And so, by the way, did M. le Mari. But Agatha seems to thrive on it. I don't know when I've seen her looking more magnificent."

"Perhaps she enjoys keeping two men miserable. She was in splendid spirits—so very animated. She was laughing and talking away all through lunch. Generally she leaves that to other people."

"Well, to do her justice, I think she was making a genuine effort to keep the family flag flying. She was the greatest support to us. No one in her vicinity had eyes or ears for the frescoes."

"That is so," admitted Lois. "Yes, I really thought we

were safe until that awful moment when I caught sight
of Mrs. Cocks's face. It was lucky that we had short-
circuited her by putting her between the proper Mr. Chaytor
and the deaf Sir Nigel."

" I know. And almost immediately afterwards I became
aware that a horrid silence was stealing over the nearest of
the trestle tables. And there was Clewer, sitting perfectly
mum, and not attempting to keep up the conversation.
He was a broken reed ! "

" It's the first time I've ever known him fail in his social
duties."

" Yes. He's pretty cut up about Agatha, I really believe.
I suppose there was slaughter after we left them in the hall
last night."

" How long ago it seems ! "

" Yes, we've lived through a lifetime of care and anxiety
since, haven't we ? It was quite a game to watch it spreading. It would have been funny if it hadn't been so grim.
That look of incredulity dawning on one face after another !
Still we got off better than I expected."

" Oh, but Sir Thomas's speech was terrible ! I thought
it would be the last straw. The manners of the English
are incredible, as you say. One can't overstate their sense
of decency. They just all looked a little uncomfortable,
for the most part. Very few exceptions."

" And anyone would look uncomfortable at any of Sir
Thomas's speeches. His articulation was so uncommonly
thick that I began to think of strokes, didn't you ? "

" Oh, but when he proposed James's health . . . ! "

" Still he was so maudlin and incoherent by that time
that most people couldn't have heard much of it."

" Well, one or two who had behaved beautifully up
till then began to get a little hysterical. Is that Mother
calling ? "

Marian had come to the end of the terrace and was

hailing them. Her tones were significant and peremptory. When they joined her she inquired in lowered accents :

" Have you heard ? "

Lois nodded.

" It's wicked ! It's monstrous ! " broke out Lady Clewer. " Such a thing has never happened in the family before."

Lois and Hubert could well believe this.

" We shall never be able to hold up our heads again."

" Very few people know as yet," consoled Hubert. " And perhaps something can be done ? "

" I should hope that very few people did know ! May I ask how you did ? Who told you ? "

" As a matter of fact," hesitated Lois, " we knew yesterday ? "

" Yesterday ! " shrieked Marian. " You knew yesterday ? "

" Yes, but we thought it would be better not to distress you by speaking of it until after the lunch party. We discussed it with Agatha. . . ."

" You discussed it with Agatha." Marian was so much taken aback that she could only whisper. " How could you discuss it with Agatha ? "

" Well, we thought she would be a good person to talk it over with."

Marian stared at them with her mouth open. At last she managed to ask :

" Did you begin on it, or did she ? "

" We did. And she advised us to say nothing about it until after lunch to-day."

" I'll be bound she did. But I simply cannot understand such disloyalty in either of you. It was bare-faced connivance ! You should have come to me at once. And think of poor Tom and Cynthia having such a thing happen in their house ! It's disgraceful ! And now it's probably too late to do anything, though Mrs. Cocks is going off at once to see what she can do."

"Mrs. Cocks!" exclaimed the other two. And Lois added: "What can she do? Where is she going? Not to James, surely?"

"To James? Of course not. Why should she? Lois! Hubert! You don't mean to tell me that James has had any hand in this affair?"

Lois and Hubert looked at each other, and Hubert said cautiously:

"Please, Lady Clewer, what are you talking about?"

"Why . . . this step of Agatha's! Don't you know? She's gone away . . . run away . . . with her cousin. With Mr. Blair. She has left John."

It was now their turn to be speechless.

"She left a note, a wicked, cruel note, for John," went on Marian with rising indignation. "And one for her mother. Of all the horrible things. . . . But what were you saying about James?"

"That's nothing. Something quite different," said Hubert. "This frightful news . . . I can't believe it. It can't be true. There must be some mistake."

"I insist upon knowing at once," said Marian sharply. "Lois, I command you to tell me; what has James been doing?"

"Oh, Mother! That can wait! Are you sure that this about Agatha isn't all a frightful mistake? I knew they left by the same train; she made no secret of it. But that doesn't prove . . ."

"The note she left for John was perfectly unambiguous. He showed it to me."

Lois, to her extreme surprise, burst into tears. She was fatigued and bewildered. Hubert and Marian, remembering her condition, became alarmed and consoling, blaming each other for having subjected her to the shock. She sobbed noisily upon Hubert's shoulder for a few minutes, and then collected herself sufficiently to ask:

"What did John say?"

"He said nothing. He was so frightfully moved that he couldn't speak. He just handed me the note and walked out of the room. He'd written on the back of it, 'I shall make no attempt to follow her, I am going down to Lyndon to-night.' This was just after the last of the guests had gone."

Lois collapsed again.

"Oh . . . Oh . . ." she wailed. "Why must all this happen?"

"Lois, my darling, my precious, don't. You'll make yourself ill."

"Oh, Hubert! I can't bear it! After this awful day with James's horrible frescoes. . . ."

"James? Will you tell me what this business of James is, please? Hubert! You are evading me. I won't have it!"

"Oh, well, it's got to be," sighed Hubert, and told her.

Her incredulity protected her for some time. Even after they had revisited the hall and inspected the paintings she insisted that they must have been changed since she last saw them. She maintained that she could not have failed to recognize them. When, after long argument, the truth assailed her, she became too deeply shocked for any demonstrations. Lois and Hubert waited for a torrent of vituperation, but she said nothing. In silence she left the hall and stumbled down the marble corridor into the drawing-room. They followed her, literally clinging to each other in terror of what she would say when she once began. She had sunk on to a chesterfield, and Hubert, really alarmed by her grey colour, went in search of restoratives. She had barely reached the point of interjections and gasps when Mrs. Cocks, a Bradshaw in one hand and a fountain pen in the other, stormed into the room.

"There's this five-fifty-five," she began, and then ex-

claimed with some commiseration : " Good heavens,
Marian ! How ill you look ! "

" James . . . these frescoes . . . Tom . . . Cynthia,"
began Marian faintly.

" Oh, the frescoes ? Oh, yes ! I'm very sorry for you
all about that affair, indeed I am. But listen, Marian.
Can I speak to you privately for a moment ? "

" You needn't mind Hubert and Lois. They know all
about Agatha going, if that is what you want to talk about."

" Oh, indeed ? I'm very sorry for it. Of course,"
Mrs. Cocks turned to them, " I know you will be discreet.
It's very important that this affair should go no further.
I'm hoping to find Agatha in town this evening and to bring
her back with me. I beseech you, Marian, to say nothing of
it to anyone else. Is it necessary to tell the Bragges ? "

" They ought to know what has been going on in their
house," began Marian firmly.

She was beginning to feel a little better.

" At least say nothing till we have seen what can be
done," entreated Mrs. Cocks. " For John's sake, I should
have thought you'd wish to keep it quiet. Just listen ! If
I take this five-fifty-five, I get to London . . . let me see
. . . I've lost the place. It's quite tolerably early in the
evening, anyhow. I shall go straight to Harley Street, and
find out where he is staying. They know I'm his cousin, so
they'll probably give me his address if I'm a little pressing.
Then . . ."

" But I must go over to Bramfield immediately !
Immediately ! " cried Marian starting up. " I must make
James change that horrible thing. He must paint it out.
He must do a new one. I'll make him. It's disgraceful.
Hubert ! can you order a car for me at once ? . . ."

" Oh, Marian, do listen to me for a moment ! What do
the frescoes matter, after all, compared with this ? Could
you see John for me and find out if he . . ."

But Marian burst out afresh :

" Oh, why couldn't you have told me yesterday ? We could have hung a curtain over that back panel."

" Good God ! " cried Hubert in horror. " You couldn't have done that. It's the best panel of the lot. You can't hide away work like that. . . ."

" Don't speak in that cynical way, Hubert ! "

" I'm not being cynical, Lady Clewer. There are some things you can't do, and . . ."

" Can't I ? You wait and see what I can't do ! I tell you, if James won't alter that horrid thing I shall strongly advise Tom and Cynthia to distemper it over."

" Well then, I wash my hands of it," said Hubert furiously.

" It's a pity you ever had anything to do with it, Hubert. It was you persuaded them to have James. I was always against it."

" Oh, Mother, how could Hubert know . . . ? "

" Marian, I don't believe you want me to bring Agatha back. Can't you see that my business is urgent ? Urgent ! It can't wait ; I've no time to lose. You can distribute the blame about the frescoes at your leisure after I'm gone. You have no sense of proportion."

" I'm sorry for you, Ellen. I pity you deeply. I see that it must be a great shock to you . . . for you never would see. . . . Of course, it's less of a blow to the rest of us simply because we did recognize. . . . But what do you want me to do ? "

" I want you to speak to John and tell him I've gone after her. Tell him I'm convinced it's all nothing : all a mistake. Do try to persuade him to be a little kind, if . . . when I bring her back with me. However much he feels he has been in the right, do beg him to be generous ! I expect I shall take her back to South Kensington to-night, and to-morrow we will come back here."

"I will see him, Ellen, but I doubt if he will ever forgive her."

"But perhaps he may find that he has not so very much to forgive. Do entreat him to keep an open mind."

"Very well. But it's no use your bringing her back here to-morrow. He is going down to Lyndon to-night, and I shall probably go with him."

"Oh? Then we'll come to Lyndon."

"Oh!" cried Marian wringing her hands. "When I think of my poor Cynthia! So horribly insulted! Other people have scandals and divorces . . . but this! It's so unusual! Nobody . . . nobody ever had anything like this in their family. And Cynthia of all people! She deserves it so little. She has always been such a discreet child. Tom will be beside himself. Unless . . . unless I can make James alter the thing before they find out. Don't tell them, any of you! Do be careful what you say to them."

"I will say nothing! Nothing!" said Mrs. Cocks, perceiving her advantage, "if you will promise not to speak of this exploit of Agatha's until I have been to town. Please, Marian! Wait at least until to-morrow."

"If you like, Ellen. Though mind you, I don't expect you will be able to do much. But I must go to Bramfield and see James. Then I'll go to Lyndon. I needn't tell Tom and Cynthia I'm going via Bramfield. . . ."

"And I must pack if I'm to catch the five-fifty-five. . . ."

Both matrons hurried from the room, their excited voices dying away as they ascended the stairs. Hubert picked up the half-finished glass of brandy and water which he had fetched for Marian. He offered it to Lois and, when she resolutely refused it, drank it up himself.

"Do you think," Lois whispered, "that Agatha really has . . . ?"

"I'm afraid it looks hatefully like it," he said gloomily.

"It's a pity she didn't know how ill John really is."

"She ought to have been told."

"I don't believe she'd have gone if she knew, do you ? "

"Oh, she couldn't ! A woman would have to be an absolute devil to be as heartless as that. And she has a kindly nature, I think."

"Yes, she is kind." Lois was still too much shocked to be conventional. "Poor Agatha ! I'm very sorry for them all. Aren't you, Hubert ? "

Hubert was on the point of saying that he wasn't particularly sorry for Gerald Blair. But he had the wit to refrain, and remarked instead :

"Perhaps her mother will be able to bring her back. Look here, Lois ! If she's going to town to-night, and your mother and John are going to Lyndon, we shall be left alone with the Bragges. I bar that. I couldn't stand another meal in that hall. We'll go too."

"But, Hubert, where ? We can't go home to-night. They don't expect us for one thing."

"We'll stop somewhere in town to-night, and go home to-morrow. We'll get that five-fifty-five Mrs. Cocks goes by. Look sharp and see to our packing ! We've just time. I'll find Bragge and make our apologies."

"But it's so rude."

"We've done enough for 'em for one day. I'm going, anyhow. If you like to stay by yourself you can."

"We'll never have time."

"Yes we will if we are quick. Do run, Lois. Just get together our things for the night, and your woman can follow us with the rest of the luggage when she's packed it. I'll give you dinner in any pub you like and you can choose your show afterwards. I'll take you to hear Wagner if you want. Only do hurry ! "

Lois yielded and ran upstairs to harry her maid through a hasty packing. Hubert found Sir Thomas and manu-

factured a sufficiently credible excuse for their sudden
departure. In a very short time Braxhall was emptied of
its guests. The long table was removed from the dais in
the hall and replaced by a smaller one, suitable for two
diners. There, in spacious magnificence, Sir Thomas and
his lady devoured their evening meal, solemnly, slowly, and
for the most part in silence. Occasionally the owner of
Braxhall broke into a monologue.

" Odd thing they all had to hurry off like that. But
they were very sorry to go. They said so. Hard luck on
them, having to go. We shan't have any bridge to-night.
However ! I think they enjoyed themselves. I-think-they-
enjoyed-themselves. But we shan't have any bridge
to-night. No ! No bridge ! You and I will have to get
out the cribbage board, Cynthie."

Lady Bragge helped herself to iced asparagus.

" Went off very well indeed, the lunch did. Very well !
Quite a new thing in these parts, I should say. A unique
experience for everybody there. That's what it was. A
unique experience. I never heard before of an American
lunch in honour of a work of art. No more did anyone
else, I'll be bound. No ! Quite a new thing. Pity James
Clewer wasn't there. He'd have enjoyed it. I like to see
people enjoying themselves. But I proposed his health.
I didn't forget that. A good sort, James ! I like him.
I-like-him. Blood is thicker than water, when all's said and
done. I said so in my speech. A decent fellow. Weought-
toamadeimcome. . . ."

Tears stood in Sir Thomas's eyes as he repeatedly averred
how much he liked his brother-in-law.

Cynthia said nothing but went on eating her dinner.
Occasionally she stared idly about her, at her food, at her
husband, at the frescoes, with the same exquisite, enigmatic
contempt.

CHAPTER V

THE FOOLS' PROGRESS

I.

LOIS said :
"I hate to disturb you, dear, but isn't it time you went to dress ? "

"I expect so," said Hubert without moving.

"Very well, then. . . ."

He sniffed appreciatively the warmth of the peat fire and turned a gloomy eye upon the uninviting dusk beyond the window.

"I don't want to go," he said, not for the first time.

"I'm sorry if it bores you, but I really think you should."

Lois spoke with decision, looking a little like her mother. There was already a hint of the same massive contours about her jaw. He, for his peace of mind, did not observe it for he had risen to tap the barometer.

"I shouldn't wonder if there was a frost to-night," he protested.

"Take the foot-warmer and the fur rug," she advised.

Making a final effort against the benevolent pressure which was forcing him out of his house on so unpleasant an evening, he turned on her and said :

"Look here! I don't really see why I should go. They don't particularly expect me. It won't be in the least rude if I don't turn up. They don't want me. They are your friends, you know ; and if you don't go, I don't see why I should. And it's the kind of thing that bores me stiff."

248

"I'm sorry I can't come," she pleaded, "but I really oughtn't to, you know. It wouldn't be a suitable party for a young woman in my interesting condition."

"I wish you wouldn't use such vulgar expressions," he complained. "I can't think where you pick them up. 'Interesting condition' is very low."

"I got it out of Dickens: it's mid-Victorian. But I could say much worse. I could say 'in the family way.' 'A party in the family way.' . . ."

Hubert drew himself up into a mid-Victorian husband, and thundered:

"Be silent, ma'am, and don't pollute my house with such coarse expressions. . . ."

He was interrupted by the parlourmaid who came to carry out the tea. Hastily he left off being Mr. Caudle and picked up the *London Mercury*. Lois crossed to the window and drew the blue linen curtains, shutting out the chilly twilight. She could afford to make jokes about her condition since it scarcely troubled her at all. Though she was nearly seven months gone, her cheeks still bloomed and she moved buoyantly.

The clock struck, and Hubert remarked with relief:

"It's only six. I needn't dress yet."

"The car is ordered for a quarter to seven, and you'll take all of three-quarters of an hour."

"But that will get me up to town at seven-thirty, and I don't need to be there before nine, surely?"

"You'll want dinner first. Aren't you dining at Eaton Square? I told Mother you would be, when I rang her up this morning."

"Uncommonly officious of you, Lois! I never authorized you to say such a thing. I'd meant to dine here and go up afterwards, if I felt inclined, and if it wasn't too cold. But this absolutely pledges me. I suppose your mother is expecting me now?"

"I'm afraid so, dear."

"All the same, I don't see why I should have to go to the Martins' if I don't want to. What, exactly, do you expect me to do when I get there?"

"Oh, my dear Hubert! We've been into all this before."

"Yes, you've told me what I ought to do, but not how I'm to do it. I'm to lead the fellow round, I suppose, and introduce him to all the people you and your mother think he ought to know."

"That's the idea."

"And what earthly good do you think that's going to do him or them? Haven't you learnt by this time that it's quite impossible for the family to run him?"

"But, Hubert, this is the whole object of getting him and Dolly to come and live at Hampstead."

"I never could see any object in their living at Hampstead."

"Of course, Chelsea would have been better, but Dolly had all these ideas about the children getting good air. And there are artists at Hampstead. But the point of the whole thing is to get him into congenial society; to get him to meet more people and get known a little. I've been so pleased about his getting this invitation to the Martins'. It's just the sort of thing we want. He will meet exactly the right people."

"All right, let him meet them! What good do you think that will do? What sort of impression is James likely to make on the right people, or they on him? Can't you see that he would much sooner stay at home with his Dolly?"

"Dolly is invited too, to-night."

"Is she? Then I don't really think I need go. She'll look after him quite capably. I shan't go. I'll run up and dine with your mother and come back."

"Oh, Hubert, please! Remember James is my step-brother. . . ."

"Whom you've always understood. I know."

"Don't interrupt! Yes, I do understand him. I discovered him long before anyone else, now didn't I? Ages before you did. . . ."

"It's a pity you didn't discover him a little sooner over that Braxhall affair. . . ."

She put her hand over his mouth and stopped him. The smouldering bitterness in his heart was instantly quenched: he caught her fingers and kissed them.

"All right!" He sighed. "I'll do my best; I promise I will. I'll go. Only you see, I don't think it will do any good. I'm coming to the conclusion that our cue is to leave him absolutely alone. He's of age, and a married man, and what not, and I shouldn't wonder if he knows what he wants better than we do. Honestly, my dear, I think your mother is making a mistake in trying to turn him into a tame family genius at this time of day. But I'll do what I can."

"It's just that he needs to know a few more people and go about rather more," repeated Lois with conviction. "He's never been among really congenial people . . . creative artists. . . ."

Hubert was silent, since he disagreed with her. He sat by her side and absorbed regretfully the beauty and comfort of his home, still but half resigned to his enforced departure. They were in the living-room. There was nothing so Victorian as a drawing-room in Hubert's house; only a library, a hall dining-room, a music room, and a living-room, besides a billiard-room in the garden, and quite enough too, as Dolly had observed when she heard of it. The house, which was called Killigrew's Croft, suited Hubert and Lois very well. It was in Buckinghamshire, near Amersham, within easy reach of town, yet sufficiently out of it to pass as country. Outside it was rather ordinary, and suggested the placid comfort of a retired stockbroker. But the interior was very Georgian. The carpetless floors, the severe whitewashed walls, the Russian linen, the black

divans with their brilliant cushions, the John drawings and
the peat fires were all there. Hubert liked it immensely,
and felt that it was exactly right. So, had he been born a
generation earlier, would he have regarded a Morris paper
and Willow Pattern china. But he did not suppose that
his house was at all individual, having spent his life in
homes exactly like it. Lois, born in Manchester, and reared
at Lyndon, was still inclined to regard it as unique. She
thought it a great deal more tasteful than the home of her
girlhood, and often argued with Hubert about it. She
could not grasp his admiration for a house so unlike his own.

"Looking at this, one would never think you admired
Lyndon," she would say, comparing the yellow washed walls
of her living-room with the Chinese paper in Agatha's drawing-room, all strange birds and exotic vegetation. "It's so
crowded! Every sort of style, all mixed up. Think of
those lacquered cabinets and the Queen Anne Talbois
cheek by jowl in Agatha's bedroom."

"I never was in Agatha's bedroom," said Hubert wistfully. "What was it like?"

"Like nothing on earth. A wonderful Elizabethan bed,
all hung with old Italian tapestries. And, I think, an
Aubusson carpet. And a Louis Quinze dressing-table, and
a crystal jug and basin from somewhere in Hungary. And,
by way of pictures, a Gainsborough portrait, and a landscape, Cotman, I think, and ' The Rake's Progress ' in funny
little black frames all along the chimneypiece. And a good
deal of carved jade and ivory lying around. It was just
like all the other rooms in the house, only she had seized on
the very best things."

"I can't imagine it."

"Just a muddle! Not any clear expression of one kind
of culture. If all the things had been English, or all French,
or all Chinese!"

"But that's England, you know, Lois. Just that!

There's nothing in England so English as a house like Lyndon. A medley of races and civilizations and ideas, all chucked together anyhow, and yet . . . not chaos . . . but a whole . . . a living, individual whole."

" I didn't know you were so patriotic."

" No more did I. I've always considered myself rather cosmopolitan. But, when I think of Lyndon I feel sorry. Sorry all that should go. It's so absolutely ours, you know, and it's melting like snow in the sun. Now a room like this," he waved a hand round his living-room, " you might find in any capital in Europe at the present moment."

" Well, if you are so discontented with it, change it ! It's yours. You say you admire Lyndon, but you don't copy it, I notice."

" Copy Lyndon ? Oh, Lord ! Copy Lyndon ! My dear girl, I couldn't ! It can't be copied, that's just it. One man didn't make it ; it's been the work of generations. The smell of it ! That smell of stone passages and beer ! No one can build a new house and put a smell like that into it. Think of all the storms it has weathered ! It's survived the landscape gardening of the eighteenth century, and the flagrant bad taste of the Regency, and Victoria's upholstered mahogany, and the æsthetic monsoon of my childhood, Walter Crane and all that, yes, and the recent deluge of peasant handicrafts and chromatic barbarism. These impermanent things go over it in waves. Our house, for instance, is just part of a wave, and quite a nice wave too. But Lyndon is a rock. The whole effect remains essentially the same, though it emerges from each wave with a few more things scattered over it as relics of the epoch. Lovely things . . . the best that each particular tide has produced. . . . Pity it should go ! "

" Why do you talk of it going ? Nobody wants to burn it down."

" A house dies with its family. Lyndon has come to an end.

It's nothing better than a museum now. And a museum isn't a living thing; it's a mausoleum for bygone cultures."

" John may go back there in the spring, Mother says. So it won't have been empty for so very long. Six months can't turn it into a museum, surely?" she asked, with some derision.

" N—no," he replied uncertainly.

He had always thought of Lyndon as Agatha's house, rather than John's, and, to him, its history was ended upon the day when she fled to Corsica with her accursed cousin. But he knew better than to air this idea, especially when Lois was already a little irritated. It was, in truth, hard upon her to have to listen to these glorifications of Lyndon when she had spent so much of her rebellious youth in trying to escape from it.

Pondering upon these conversations, he sat beside her, holding her hand in somnolent content until the clock struck a quarter past six. Pressure was again exerted by his wife. " You positively must dress," she urged, and he capitulated.

Upon his way to town, however, his indignation boiled up again. It was bad enough that he should be forced to spend the evening with the Martins. He had begun to grow out of the atmosphere of guarded Bohemianism in which they moved, and expected to be bored. But it was monstrous that he should have to dine with his mother-in-law as well. He raged dimly against the conspiracy of women which netted him in. He had always hated Eaton Square, and just now he knew that there would be long, unsparing inquiries about Lois and her health. Besides, he might see John, and he hated meeting John. He knew that he ought to be sorry for the fellow; that his was the gesture of the Levite who passed by on the other side; but he could not help it. John was too unfortunate; it was impossible to forget that his wife had deserted him in a particularly heartless manner, and that he was dying by inches. It was really tactless of him, all things considered, to hang about London in this way. He should have buried himself and his sorrows in some decently distant place. He was not, it seemed, too ill to shoot in the country at week-ends. Hubert thought that he should stay there altogether.

He supposed that John was right, on the whole, not to plunge into the scandals of a divorce. It was decent of him, anyhow. But it made the affair so unofficial : so preposterously delicate. One never knew where one was. It was impossible to talk to anyone of the Clewer connection for five minutes without getting on dangerous ground. The thing had become a question of clan loyalty, and everybody in the family was expected to lie fluently in the cause. It was a silly fiction, this upholding of Agatha's respectability in the public eye, for the whole story was bound to come out sooner or later. She was showing no disposition to leave her cavalier, and her reputation could only be held together as long as she was content to lie concealed in Corsica. Hubert racked his brains to remember the details of the official explanation. Supposing Stella Martin were to ask him to-night how long Agatha would be abroad ! Should he say he didn't know ? Or was he supposed to know ? He ought to have asked Lois.

But he did not, willingly, discuss Agatha with his wife. Within the tribal group there was, of course, no charity for the lost mistress of Lyndon. It seemed to him sometimes that they were almost too hard on her. He knew that she had believed badly ; she could scarcely have behaved worse ; but he could never listen to the abuse which the other women poured out upon her without a pang, the stirrings of an emotion which was not condemnatory. He remembered how lovely, how unlucky, and how kind she had been. Yes, and still so young. He would much rather not think of her at all.

Instead he thought of James, aggrievedly. Why should he be burdened with James ? He did not mind having him as a brother-in-law, at a convenient distance. Sometimes he was rather proud of the connection. But taking him about was another matter. It made one so horribly conspicuous. Wrapped in these gloomy reflections he arrived in Eaton Square, and, as the car drew up, resolved that his boy should marry an orphan. He would do for his son what no one had done for him; he would see to it that the lad never met any young woman encumbered with surviving relations.

He was relieved not to find John among the chesterfields in the drawing-room. When last he had dined there he had sat for a quarter of an hour with John. Three times he had asked nervously whether there was anything in the evening paper. John had told him thrice, with a kind of abstracted patience, that rubber was still going down. That had been the whole of the conversation between them. To-night, however, Marian trailed in alone. She wore the kind of informal dinner gown which suggests a solitary meal. She had aged conspicuously during the past months; her elaborate brown hair was now flecked with grey and a settled melancholy made her face look heavier. But she was still a fine woman, with every appearance of vigour and health. Trouble had not bowed her white shoulders or dimmed her little blue eyes. She said that John had gone for a week to Sussex to stay with friends.

" I like him to get the change and the interest," she said, " though I feel he's hardly fit for it. He should really be nearer to good doctors. It would be very awkward if . . . if he was taken ill or anything when he was staying with people. But he won't give in, poor boy, or be treated like an invalid. It's pitiful ! Now tell me how Lois is."

Hubert immediately regretted John, whose presence would have protected him. He said :

" Lois is very well."

" Is she getting about a certain amount ? " asked Marian tenderly.

" Oh, yes. She seems to be very energetic and active. We go quite longish walks."

" She must be careful not to overdo it."

Marian sounded disapproving, but he rejoined brightly :
" She's taking every care of herself, I'm sure."

" It must be a very anxious time for you."

" Oh, no," he protested, " I'm not anxious. She seems so well."

But she was quite determined that he should be anxious, anxiety being, in her opinion, the only proper state of mind for him.

" If it wasn't for John," she said, " I could be with you a great deal more."

" Thank God for John," thought Hubert, " he has his uses."

" It would be a great relief to me if I could be with Lois and make quite sure . . ."

" Dinner is served, my lady."

" She'll begin again in the dining-room," thought Hubert as he armed her downstairs.

But he had forgotten the servants. She could not begin again while they were present. Indeed she ate most of her meal in silence, for she was so preoccupied with John's misfortunes, James's misdoings, and Lois's condition as to be really unable to talk of anything else. Hubert was permitted to enjoy the very good food in peace, and when, at length, they were left alone together, he short-circuited a return to Lois by plunging into the question of James.

" I understand," he said, " that I am, as it were, to chaperon him at this party ? "

" Oh, Hubert, if you would ! And if you'd give him a hint, just a little hint, now and then, how to behave, it would be so. kind. I'm so glad he's been asked ; this sort of thing is so good for him. I'm rather disappointed, you know, in the results of the Hampstead move. I had hoped for better things. It was such a piece of work to get them

to move at all. He was so stubborn; I don't think he'd
have given in if their landlord at Bramfield hadn't given
them notice. Then I talked to Dorothy, and got her to
see all the educational advantages of having the children
near London. Just imagine, she and James had contemplated sending them to the little village school near by!
I was horrified. I didn't like to say what I thought to
Dorothy, for of course she was at a National School herself,
but I spoke to James and asked him how he could think of
it. And he said she had been to the school one day to have
a look at it herself, and was quite satisfied with it. It was
a very small school, and he said "—Marian blushed at such
coarseness—" he said that she only saw one child that she
was at all doubtful about, and she caught it coming out
and had a look at its head, and was quite reassured."

" Not really ? " said Hubert with a grin.

"I don't see anything funny in it," said Marian. "I
feel it's all rather sad. What is to become of those poor
little children? Still, I persuaded Dorothy in the end.
I pointed out what a much better studio James could have,
which she appreciated. She admitted that it was always
rather difficult getting models, and so on, when they lived
so far out in the country. And, of course, when she saw
reason the battle was won. He always does what she wishes."

" But you aren't satisfied with the result ? "

" Well, you see, I wanted him to know more people.
You've no idea, Hubert, how curious people are about him.
People who've seen his pictures. I've been asked about
him so often by people who are anxious to meet him. But
I don't know. It seems hopeless! Living at Hampstead
hasn't done him a bit of good; it hasn't altered him in
the very least. As I say to people . . . that unfortunate
marriage! It will be a drag on him all his life. It makes
his house quite impossible. I took Mrs. Downsmith there
the other day to call, and really that girl has absolutely

no idea how to do things. Tea ! You should have seen it !
Shrimp paste in a pot, and we were offered eggs. And after
tea they played us tunes upon that awful gramophone.
I really didn't know which way to look, and I could see that
Mrs. Downsmith thought it all most extraordinary. Coming
home I said what I could about artists' households being
always rather Bohemian, and she said : ' Bohemian isn't
the word I'd have used somehow.' "

" No, it's the respectability which baffled her, I expect.
If James and his family lived in romantic squalor in a one-
room studio, they would be much more conventional."

" It's very sad. But I feel that if we could get him right
away . . . away from his wife. . . ."

" She's invited to-night."

" Oh, is she ? I am sorry. That is unfortunate ! It's
quite unnecessary that she should be asked to places with
him. That is a pity ! "

" But he won't go anywhere without her."

" Oh dear, how difficult it all is ! Of course, people
can't be expected to invite her to their houses. She oughtn't
to expect it. Can't she see what a drag she is on him ? "

" But she's quite respectable."

" Y—yes. But impossible socially. It would have been
better . . ."

Marian broke off and did not state what would have been
better. Hubert inferred that Dolly would have been less
of a drawback if she had come from a meaner stock or were
not properly married.

Coffee came in. Marian had instituted a small coffee-
making machine on a wheeled table and brewed the drink
herself before leaving the dining-room. Agatha had had
one at Lyndon, and there were coffee percolators now at
Braxhall and Killigrew's Croft. But Hubert thought it a
pity. They none of them did it properly ; even Lois fussed
over it. No woman could make coffee as the peccant

Agatha had made it, lazy and amused, with one eye on the bubbling percolator and all her attention for her guests. He could even remember tenderly the evening when, absorbed in somebody's witty conversation (it must surely have been his own) she had forgotten to fasten something or other and the whole thing had blown up, spattering half a dozen shirt fronts. Alas, poor Agatha! It was dreadful to think of her abdication; to imagine her drinking her coffee in some grubby Corsican inn, counting Lyndon well lost for love of the insignificant, the quite undeserving Blair. Hubert would not believe it.

A moment later he learnt that he need not believe it, for Agatha was no longer in Corsica.

"There is one thing," said Marian mysteriously as she poured two cupfuls of water into the percolator, "that I wish you'd tell Lois. That is, if you think that it won't upset her in any way."

"Yes?" he said, hurrying her past Lois.

"I couldn't tell her this morning on the telephone, because one never knows what the servants may not overhear. One has to speak so clearly; I've often been annoyed about it. But I've heard that Agatha and . . . and her cousin are back in town. I'm keeping it from John, of course."

"Oh, really?" murmured Hubert, feeling uncomfortable, but strangely excited.

"If it's true, it's most inconsiderate of them," pursued Marian weightily. "The least they could do was to keep away. But I met Lady Peel yesterday, and she told me that she had just been with Ellen, with Mrs. Cocks, I mean, and that she said that she was expecting Agatha home shortly. It was most awkward for me because I had just said she would be abroad some months longer. I thought Lady Peel looked a little queerly at me. It's a pity that Mrs. Cocks has not got a more reticent nature. I can never be quite sure how much she tells people."

" But perhaps Agatha is coming home alone," suggested Hubert.

" I'm afraid not. I mean I'm afraid they are both coming, and it's too much to hope that they are not coming together. I was determined to make sure, so I sent Miss Barrington, who is absolutely discreet, round to Harley Street this morning to ask when he was expected back. She saw a parlourmaid who said he was coming to-day or to-morrow, she believed, but that she didn't think he was coming there, and he wouldn't be seeing patients yet awhile, and she could forward letters but couldn't give an address. So it looks like it."

" Yes," he agreed. " It does look rather like it."

" Will you tell Lois, or shall I write a note to her ? "

" Oh, I'll tell her."

Hubert could not see why the tidings should disturb his wife to any great extent.

" Of course, it's hard on John," he added with some compunction.

" I shall keep it from him as long as possible. It's very upsetting for us all. I only hope Lois . . ."

" It's really time I got off," exclaimed Hubert, glancing at the clock. " I'd better get to this place punctually, hadn't I ? No knowing what James mightn't be up to if I left him to himself."

And he fled.

2.

On his way to Chelsea Hubert's brain was busy with this new development of affairs. Ought he to tell anybody who inquired to-night that Agatha was now back in London ? And what on earth was going to happen next ? Of one thing he was certain, knowing the family : there would be scenes and indignant letters and diplomatic discussions. What a confounded nuisance it all was.

Penetrating into the main reception room of Stella

Martin's house in Cheyne Walk, he peered nervously through the heavy fog of cigarette smoke in search of his inconvenient brother-in-law. The heat of the room made him feel rather giddy and he was deafened by the high, staccato symphony of cultured conversation. He could not see Dolly or James anywhere. Freaks he saw, of every sort and size ; freaks who would make even James look almost normal. He saw celebrities, and minor celebrities, and people who looked like celebrities but couldn't be, since he did not know them. At last he saw his hostess and made his way over to her.

Stella Martin was a lively, pretty woman with long earrings and a cigarette perennially falling out of the corner of her mouth. She had been a great friend of Hubert's in his salad days, but he had begun lately to find her rather boring. She had become Lois's appendage, and he still liked her well enough when she was not trying too desperately to avoid the commonplace. He often complained to Lois that the woman positively collected shady characters. Lois had disagreed with him and said that Stella surrounded herself with men of talent.

" But the ladies . . ." he had expostulated.

Lois admitted that the ladies were sometimes rather odd, but maintained that they were the kind of ladies who have had, throughout the ages, a particular attraction for men of talent. And anyhow it was very conventional of Hubert to object to them. Hubert, who had begun to discover that there is, nowadays, a certain distinction in conventionality, did not wilt under this taunt as much as she had hoped. He agreed.

" We have a pretty amusing crowd to-night," said Stella. " You know most of them, don't you ? I'm sorry Lois couldn't come, but I think she was very wise not to turn out this wicked night. It's much too cold. It was nice of you to come, Hubert."

" She was very sorry to have to give it up."

" She must come up and have tea with me one day when
I can have her all to myself. Mr. and Mrs. Clewer are here,
by the way ; I don't see them at the minute, but I know
I've shaken hands with them."

" Oh, they are here ? "

" Yes, or at least they were. You'll find them if you
look. And Lawrence Argony may drop in later on. It
will be a great feather in my cap if he does, for you know he
never will go to evening parties. Have you seen his portrait
of Garry Shandon ? I haven't, but, after all I've heard,
I'm longing to. Mick says Garry is rather vexed about it.
But I don't know what else he expected, do you ? "

She turned to other guests, and Hubert resumed his
search for Dolly and James. He came to the conclusion
that Stella's ladies were rather more respectable than usual.
Listening to their vehement conversation and watching
the bobbing of their bobbed heads, he decided that he was
in for an evening with London's women of talent. Though
he saw a few who might be said to have one foot in the
demi-monde, he was sure that they had got in to-night
upon some intellectual ticket. They must have written
an autobiography or a novel or something. Friends greeted
him and he found himself pouring forth, a little absently,
a small but regular stream of witty remarks. Half of his
mind was occupied with the thought of Lois and his nice
quiet house where he would rather have been. He was
immensely pleased to find that he could think of his home
with such a pang, and his impersonation of a man about
town at a party in Chelsea was spiced by the thought of
the domestic fellow that he really was. Then he caught
sight of Dolly, with James beside her, sitting on a distant
divan. Very mournful they looked, in this strange galley,
and their faces, when they perceived him, lit up with a
ludicrous relief. He crossed over to them and they made
room for him with alacrity.

"Oh, but I'm glad you've come," cried Dolly. "We were just wondering if it was too soon for us to go. It's so awkward us not knowing any of these people."

"Well, I can introduce you to any amount," said Hubert, mindful of his mission and trying not to look at James's dress-clothes. "That's a friend of mine over there. The man with the eyebrows. Binns, the architect. Shall I effect an introduction?"

"No, don't," said James. "I want to look at him. He's got a very nice head, especially at the back. I couldn't see it if I was talking to him."

"James says all the people here are out of drawing," said Dolly doubtfully.

"They are certainly a queer-looking lot," said Hubert, agreeably convinced that he looked quite normal himself.

"You may say so," she affirmed with more ease. "I never saw anything like them. I said to James when we first come in : 'Well, the Zoo isn't in it!' Not but what it isn't a very nice party," she added, remembering her manners. "I always tell James it's good for us to go into company once in a while. But we are still so upside down, getting into the new house ; it was quite a job getting here at all to-night."

"D'you think my clothes smell too much of camphor?" asked James. "Dolly was very worried about it."

"It's the first time he's had them on in years," she explained. "That's why they fit so sort of loose on the shoulders. In the army they made him hold himself so straight."

"And for the same reason they fit sort of tight in front," said James.

Hubert sniffed and said doubtfully :

"I smell something . . . but it isn't like camphor exactly."

"Oh, I expect that's Sanitas," explained James cheerfully. "I sprinkled on a little. I thought it would drown the camphor."

" Which was silly," commented Dolly. " If anybody has to smell of anything, camphor's better than Sanitas."

" And how is the new house getting on ? " asked Hubert.

" Oh, nicely, thank you. There's a studio for James that we've got ever so nice. Better than anything we've had before."

" It's quite a good house," said James. " And Dolly has made it look exactly like our last one, so there is nothing to worry about. I thought at first I shouldn't like it, but I do quite."

" There's a basement kitchen, though," said Dolly, " which is a nuisance. I don't like the children getting all their meals down there. I said to old Lady Clewer, ' Well, I don't think the kitchen's very nice.' And she said, ' Perhaps you won't be in it so much now.' But, as I say, wherever else should I be ? But, as we've a room on the ground-floor that we don't need, I'm having a nice little electric range put in there, and a sink, and I'll do most of my cooking there and we'll get our meals handy. It's nice and sunny. The garden at the back isn't up to much, but there's always the Heath for the children to play on. Sonny has fallen into that pond already, but that's only what's to be expected."

" We had to paper the whole house," said James. " Mamma wanted us to distemper it, but we don't like distemper."

" No," rejoined his wife. " Just like a prison or a hospital ! A nice bright paper is ever so much more cheerful. Eh, James ! There's Mr. Argony ! "

The big gun of Stella's party was making his way slowly through the room, growling replies to the greetings which washed round him like a tide.

" He does do it well," said James appreciatively. " Just like Sissy feeding chickens."

" Do you know him then ? " asked Hubert in surprise.

" Oh, yes," Dolly told him. " He often comes to tea

with us. He and James like to get a good talk. You know
what men are! Talk the hind leg off a donkey and then
have the face to bring it up against the women. They go
on about these pictures of theirs."

Lawrence had by now perceived them, and, shaking
himself free from his ardent acquaintances, he joined their
group. Hubert, who knew him slightly, offered his greetings. The great man stared at the trio, his heavy eyebrows
shot out in a frown of perplexity. He seemed to find them
unexpected. Having revolved them in his mind for a
second or two, he exploded:

" I have it! Brothers-in-law."

" Stepbrothers-in-law," corrected James. " His wife
is my stepmother's daughter."

" His wife is your stepmother's daughter?" repeated
Mr. Argony. " His . . . wife . . . is . . . your . . .
stepmother's . . . daughter? His Wife. . . . Oh, quite
so! Quite so! How are you, Mrs. Clewer? I'm glad I found
you here, James, for I came especially to find you. Someone
told me you'd be here. Can you come round to my place
to-morrow? I've got to talk to you about something."

" To-morrow is Sunday," calculated James. " I can't
come in the morning. . . ."

" Well, don't come in the morning. Come in the
afternoon."

" But I could come in the morning," went on James
laboriously, " if I went to chapel in the evening. Dolly,
shall we do that? "

" Oh, settle it between you," said Lawrence amicably.
" Any time will suit me. I shall be in all day."

" When are you coming to tea with us again?" asked
Dolly. " You haven't been, not for a long while."

" Oh, I'll come soon," he assured her, and was taken away
by his hostess.

Hubert was able to put the question which had been

burning within him ever since he became aware of an intimacy between Lawrence Argony and the Clewers.

" I suppose you've heard of this portrait of Garry Shandon ? " he said. " Nobody's seen it yet, of course, but . . ."

" I have," said James.

" You have ? "

" Yes," said James, adding kindly, " it's very good."

Hubert gave it up and resolved to tell Lois that never again would he undertake the social pilotage of James. It was absurd ! It was like a minnow trying to steer a whale. He was relieved when he saw Stella descending upon them with a black and white striped lady in tow.

" You three have monopolized this divan long enough," she declared. " I must break you up. Hubert, this is Mrs. Taylor, who wants to know if it's true that you and Lois have been to Madeira, and if it's nice there. Mr. Clewer, there are some people in the next room who are dying to meet you. . . ."

She carried off poor James who, in his dismay, was almost clinging to his wife.

Hubert, marooned upon the divan with the lady who wanted to know about Madeira, found it very difficult to keep his attention fixed. Fortunately she did not require much to set her going. He bent upon her an interested eye, and occupied his mind with the idea of James and Lawrence Argony. If only he could manage to convince Lois that this friendship was of his making, how pleased she would be ! But he could not claim to have had any hand in it ; James had brought it off without the help of his relations. Still this was, surely, the sort of thing she wanted. She would be glad when she heard of it.

" In those days," said a voice at his side, " my state of mind was one of wonder without curiosity."

" How very uncomfortable ! " he murmured, noting that

he was no longer listening to Mrs. Taylor but to a good-looking elderly man with grey whiskers. Stella must have substituted this new one at some moment when he was not attending.

" Curiosity," said the stranger, " is necessary before any great work of art can be produced. I trust you agree with me ? "

" Quite ! " concurred Hubert. " Exactly ! "

His mind reverted to a picture of Dolly blowing the children's noses, and spreading their jam for them, while James and Argony growled technicalities at each other across the kitchen tablecloth. Or did they have tea in the parlour on these occasions ? Perhaps Argony got an egg, being a fellow-worker.

" But don't you think," said the lady with the Spanish comb (at what point had they absorbed her into the group ?), " don't you think that the individual must realize himself before he can create ? "

" He must, indeed," said the grey whiskers. " There must be no repressions, no inhibitions. . . ."

They seemed to be so beautifully occupied with each other that Hubert thought he could slip away unnoticed. He became aware that Dolly was beckoning to him across the room. She was standing half hidden by a curtain drawn across the door of a small conservatory, and she struck him as being a trifle flushed and in some distress. When he had joined her, her agitation was manifest.

" I want to go home," she said wrathfully. " I want to get away from here. Let's find James and be off."

" Come and sit in here," said Hubert soothingly. " Come and rest a little and let me try and get you an ice or some coffee."

He moved to take her into the conservatory but she drew back quickly.

"No," she said. "I can't go back in there. He's inside still."

" Who is ? "

" That young fellow." A fleeting smile crossed her troubled face.

" Fact is, we'd better move away. He can't get out very well till we've gone."

" But what has he done ? "

" Well . . . that's asking ! Though it isn't so much what he's done as what he said. He ought to be ashamed of himself, and so I told him."

" Oh, do please tell me what he said," cried Hubert, edging round the curtain to get a look at the young fellow. " I'm dying to know."

" Oh, I couldn't ! Not to anyone ! Excepting only James. But this is a shocking place ! It is really. I want to get out of it quick. The sights I saw when I was sitting in that conservatory ! I never did."

" But it can't have been anything so very bad. . . ."

" Oh, I don't know. I thought when I first come in : Well, they look a godless lot ! And I thought right."

Surveying her comely face and sturdy, supple figure, sharply outlined against the black curtain, Hubert felt a kind of sympathy for the unknown culprit. There was something very attractive about her—primitive but compelling. And it must have been uncommonly difficult to find anything to talk to her about.

" How did you get there ? " he asked.

" Oh, Mrs. Martin introduced him and took James away. Do let's find James ! I can't think where he can be. I haven't seen him this half-hour."

" Perhaps he's in the other room."

They set off in search and Dolly, perceiving Mr. Argony in the middle of a group, ran up to him crying :

" Oh, Mr. Argony ! You haven't seen James anywhere, I suppose ? "

The people who were being fortunate enough to engage

Mr. Argony's attention were deeply outraged and looked the intruder up and down with amazement. She was so provincial, in her ready-made tea frock; so plainly not of their world. Lawrence, however, beamed and reflected:

" James, when last I saw him, was sitting with a lady in a small recess on the stairs. A remarkably beautiful lady, as far as I remember. He is probably there still. You'd better look after him, Mrs. Clewer."

Profoundly disturbed, she returned to Hubert and whispered : " He's sitting on the stairs with a beautiful lady ! Isn't that a funny thing for him to do ? I've never known him do it before. Whatever can have come over him ? "

" Perhaps it's this godless house," suggested Hubert maliciously.

" It might be. You never know," she said mournfully. " It's what I said—this is a dreadful place. He's usually as quiet . . . But with all these hussies . . . ! "

She glared at the nearest, but he reassured her.

" That one is all right. All that powder is only camouflage. She writes history books, and is a notable matron. She has five perfectly good children at home."

Dolly sniffed. In order to pacify her he suggested : " Shall I go and inspect James and his lady ? Then I can report on the state of affairs."

" He never sat on stairs before."

" I rather thought Argony said a recess on the stairs. That is better than actual stairs, don't you think ? More dignified ? "

" I don't think that's any better, I don't."

" Oh, yes it is. They are probably sitting on two chairs. . . ."

" It might be a sofa. There was a sofa in that conservatory. . . ."

" Well, I'll go and have a look."

He made his way out on to the landing where some intelligent person had turned off most of the lights. Upon each stair he fell over a couple of fellow-guests, and his passage through the obscurity was marked by a continual stream of apologies. He became aware that Stella's party was not entirely confined to the middle-aged. The younger generation was there all right, but it had not favoured the strong illumination of the rooms above. Reaching a view of the recess he perceived that Argony had been perfectly right. Even in that dim light he could identify one of its occupants as James; the large face looming over the crumpled shirt front could belong to no one else. The other, a mysterious feminine presence, was half concealed behind a curtain, but, despite the dark and a distance of several yards, Hubert got the impression that she was a lovely creature. Their attitude was intimate and absorbed —their conversation eager. Hubert hovered uncertainly, a thousand new-born surmises seething in his brain, and then approached them.

A better view of the lady gave him pause, and he jerked backward, speechless, wondering if he could run away. There was no time, however, for she had turned, recognized him, and half risen. He pulled himself together and advanced to greet her, wondering if sisters-in-law are not, on the whole, the most trying sort of relation.

" I heard you were expected back to-day or to-morrow," he said. " But I didn't think I'd see you here."

" I came hoping to find my mother," she explained. " I went round to South Kensington, but she was out and the maid rather thought she would be here. So, as I know Mrs. Martin fairly well, I came straight on. But I hear she hasn't come. She must have gone somewhere else ! "

" I haven't seen her," said Hubert. " Then you got back to England . . . ? "

" This morning."

" They had an awful crossing," appended James. " She says Blair boasted all the way across France that he was never sick, and then he was much sicker than she was."

"Oh, yes . . ." said Hubert uneasily.

Agatha slipped a hand through James's arm.

"Is Dolly here ? " she asked.

"Oh, yes ! I'll go and find her and tell her you are here," he said joyously. "She will be pleased."

"Tell her that I'm going in two minutes, but I'd love to see her first," Agatha called after him.

Hubert was left alone with her in the recess. Instinctively he drew the curtain further across, shielding her from the observation of passers on the stairs. She laughed a little as she saw his gesture and sank on to her corner of the sofa, motioning him to sit by her side. Her composure relieved him. He had thought distractedly that he would not know what to say to her : he now remembered her facility for silence. He need say nothing at all if he so preferred it. He felt stealing over him that potent serenity which he had almost forgotten, and which was part of the charm she exerted. He told himself that she was beyond criticism ; beyond it, at least, when one was with her. In retrospect, when one had forgotten a little what she was really like, it might be possible to condemn her. It seemed to him as though this alcove was too small a place in which to cabin all her marvellous beauty. She was fairer than ever before.

Presently it occurred to her to ask :

"How's Lois ? "

"Lois is very well," he told her, with a certain hesitation.

"She's not here to-night ? "

"No. She's down at Killigrew's Croft."

"I'm sorry to have missed her."

He said nothing, and in the pause which followed she pondered upon the hint of reserve with which he had spoken of his wife. Did that mean that Lois was, inevitably, one of the people who must be relinquished ? It could only mean that if she wished it herself. Hubert was not

the man to coerce his wife in such a matter. But of course
it did! She sighed, for she had been fond of Lois. Still
. . . she had come back to face the music. . . .

Clamour without told them of the approach of Dolly
and James who, in their rash descent, had fallen foul of the
stair haunters. James was heard to ask indignantly :

"Why are all the lights turned off? It's impossible to
see. Oh! Here's the switch."

Light flooded the landing and staircase. Dolly stood,
doubtfully, in the entrance to the alcove, looking at Agatha
with a face in which perplexity and compassion were
mingled.

"Well, Agatha," she murmured, "if this isn't a
surprise!"

"Dear Dolly!" cried Agatha a little breathlessly, "aren't
you glad to see me?"

"Of course I'm glad," said Dolly, embracing her with
gravity. "But I must say . . ."

She paused, plainly at a loss, and James put in :

"Come upstairs and find some place where we can sit
and have a good talk. It's so dark here."

"I'd rather stay here if you don't mind," said Agatha.
"There are so many people that I know upstairs, and I'm
so tired. I don't feel up to meeting them all. And, Hubert,
I'd give anything for a drink."

"I'll get you a cocktail or something. Dolly, what can
I get for you?"

"Oh, I wouldn't say no to an ice, if you could find one.
You go too, James, and get us something to eat. I'm quite
hungry, now you come to mention it."

Hubert and James departed and found the illuminated
staircase perfectly clear. Faint rustlings and whisperings
from the darkness of an upper flight told them whither the
youthful horde had migrated. When they returned with
plates and glasses, the two women were seated close together

upon the alcove sofa, talking with animation. Hubert
heard Dolly say:

"Well, if, as you say, they are wearing them longer in
Paris, I suppose they'll be getting longer over here soon.
I must say I'm not sorry. These short skirts don't suit
anybody like me that's got thick legs."

They all sat down in the very constricted space and ate
their provisions. James observed genially:

"How the Clewer family do collect into lumps! I've
noticed we always do it. Draw the curtain further across,
Dolly, so that nobody can notice that we are all relations.
Then Mrs. Martin won't think she ought to come and break
us up."

On the landing outside hung a picture which had struck
Hubert's attention earlier in the evening. To him it
suggested brawn in an advanced stage of decomposition.
But to two guests who were coming upstairs it had, apparently, other significances. The party in the alcove
overheard the following conversation.

"Fine thing that!"

"Very fine! Lowe!"

A third was evidently being summoned upstairs.

"Come and look at this."

"Quite good, yes," said Lowe, after a pause for observation.

"A good bit of colour that, when you see it in the right
light," pursued the first speaker, coming down to particulars. "Decent colours!"

"Very fine thing . . . uncompromising sincerity. . . ."

"Yes . . . rather nice colours. Let me see . . ." Lowe
hesitated, ". . . it's a lobster, isn't it?"

". . . Er, no. . . . A Madonna and Child, I believe.
But of course that's immaterial!"

"Oh, quite! That doesn't signify. Nice colours!"

"Yes. Good colour. . . ."

They drifted on.

Hubert and Agatha heard a strange sound which neither of them had heard before in their lives. Dolly was, possibly, more used to it. James was laughing loudly.

3.

Agatha made no long stay at Mrs. Martin's party but returned early to the small hotel where she and Gerald were staying. She found him at the writing-table in their room, deeply absorbed in a publication terrifically entitled *Brain*, upon which he was making notes. The set of his mouth and the nervous, unconscious tapping of his foot as he read told her that he was working hard. Without an interruption or a greeting she composed herself in an arm-chair upon the hearth, to wait until he had done. To her surprise a small fire was burning smokily in the grate.

He, jerking himself with an evident effort to a recollection of her presence, inquired abstractedly whether she had seen her mother. She told him of her fruitless quest, and said that she would go round to South Kensington the first thing in the morning.

"Did she leave a message for you ? " he asked, frowning.

"No, nothing ! But Meadowes seemed to know I was expected back, so she must have got the letter I sent her. No note or anything came for me here, I suppose ? ' '

"Not that I know of."

"She might have written," muttered Agatha.

"Was it a nice party you went to ? "

"Quite nice."

"You didn't stay very late."

"Not very late. Have you been working all the evening ? "

He did not answer and she saw that his attention was returning to *Brain*. Leaning back in her chair she abandoned herself to the melancholy of undisguised fatigue until he said, without looking up from his page :

"You'd better get to bed. Don't wait for me. I shall be some time yet."

"I think I'll wait," she said. "I want to talk to you when you've quite finished."

The silver travelling clock, one of Agatha's wedding presents, ticked on the mantelpiece; it looked out of place among Gerald's pipes and tins of tobacco. The sounds of London outside died away into post-midnight silence. Still his pen scratched and the pages rustled. The fire sank together and she tried with a poker to stir it into a remnant of heat. She was exhausted by her long journey, for French second-class railway carriages were still a new experience to her and the crossing had been a nightmare. The disappointment of missing her mother had been the final blow. This chilling silence staggered her; she had been quite unprepared for it. She had expected stormy re-criminations and reproaches, together with the blessed assurance that she had an unfailing partisan. Now everything was uncertain, and she dreaded the interview before her.

Too tired to think, she smoked several cigarettes and fell into a sort of chilly doze. Her childish mind, straying unhappily through the void like a lost bird, circled inevitably towards the thought of Lyndon. It was an ark, a shelter of comfort and solace. She could sit dreaming of her lost home by the hour, supporting herself by recollections of its enduring beauty. It gave her escape from sordid discomfort and fretful anxiety. In this bleak London winter she thought of warm sun, and the lawn and cedar tree, and the smell of cut grass. But often, when she had found the Mediterranean too hot and glaring, she had remembered the cold, wet winds of early spring, and daffodils, and rooks blown among the elms by the home farm.

At last Gerald shut up his book, and came across and knelt beside her, spreading cold hands towards the sinking fire.

"I'm afraid there's no more coal," she said. "Are you cold? I'm glad you had it lighted."

"Oh, I'm quite warm. I thought you'd be cold when you came in. It's a bitter night."

"You aren't warm," she told him, chafing his fingers gently. "You are cold and tired. Would some Oxo warm you up?"

"Well, it would be rather nice."

She hunted in the tray of her box and produced a small spirit lamp, a cup, a saucepan, and a tin of Oxo cubes. She rather enjoyed making Oxo, for it was a new accomplishment. Life in small Corsican inns without a maid had taught her several strange things, and it was still a novelty to minister to the needs of another person.

Gerald regarded his mistress with a faintly puzzled amusement, as she busied herself boiling the water. She was not unaware of this, and the beginnings of resentment stirred in her tired spirit. Keenly sympathetic though he might be in life's more urgent stresses, he was a little obtuse in small things. He could not realize how excessive was the degree of adaptability demanded by her existence with him. According to his ideas they had lived in no small luxury. He had always taken her to far more comfortable inns than he would have selected for himself, so anxious was he to make things easy for her.

"I saw Dolly and James," she said.

"Oh, did you? What were they like?"

"As nice as ever. They were at the party. So was Hubert."

"Oh! You saw him?"

"Yes. He was . . . just flustered."

"But you didn't see your mother?"

"No. That was what I was wanting to talk to you about. It struck me on the way home that it was just as well I didn't see her, for I've never really settled what to say to her. I've always rather counted on her taking the initiative. But, supposing she doesn't, what line am I to take ? "

" Well, Agatha, say exactly what you like. I mean your relations with your mother are entirely your affair. I'll back you up in whatever you say, of course. That water's boiling!"

She began to stir the Oxo.

" Well, then, I'll ask her if she has any idea what John is going to do, and why he doesn't seem to be taking any steps to divorce me. And if she doesn't know, I'll try to get her to see Lady Clewer and find out. I may say that we're going to be married the moment I'm free, mayn't I ? "

" Of course."

" I want to get her to see how much better it would be to end the anomalous position we are in now, at the cost of an open scandal if need be."

" Yes."

The pair paused, while Gerald sipped the Oxo, sitting at her feet. At last he said :

" Agatha, my dear, would you care to go to America ? To New York ? "

" I ! Why ? Are you thinking of going there ? "

" Yes. I've been offered work there. I found the letter waiting for me in Harley Street when I went round there this afternoon. My friend Green, who used to work with me, is running a new sort of clinic and wants me to help him."

He plunged into a long and highly technical description of the kind of clinic it was. At last she said wonderingly :

" Then it would be the kind of work you like ? "

" Oh, yes. Quite interesting, I think. Of course, the salary is very small, but it would be enough, with what I've got, to keep us in tolerable comfort, I imagine. But I'd only accept it if you cared to go too."

" Is it a permanent thing ? Does it mean spending the rest of our lives there ? "

" Well, yes. It pretty well amounts to that. It will

mean several years there anyhow. I thought it mightn't
be a bad thing, if you approved, that is to say. We could
get right away."

" But your practice here ? "

He gave her a swift, surprised look, and said nothing for
a few seconds. Then he replied indifferently :

" It isn't the sort of thing I really hanker after. I get
too many of the idle rich, and their ailments are so much
alike that it becomes monotonous. The proletariat offer a
much more varied field."

" But my mother . . . everyone . . . said that you were
getting on so brilliantly well here."

" I had a sort of vogue with your mother's friends. That
is because just after the war nervous breakdowns became a
fashionable complaint. Soon they'll take to something
else, and where should I be ? "

" I was reading in the paper about the slump in Harley
Street and how all the specialists are doing so badly."

" Bound to happen with the wealth of the country
changing hands so rapidly. The people who used to be ill
can't afford it now. And the New Rich haven't learnt to
be ill yet. They still regard ill-health as a misfortune,
probably, and not as an absorbing way of spending money.
It will right itself in time."

" Then you would really like to go to America ? "

" I should quite. It depends entirely upon your decision."

She felt at the moment that New York was the last place
in the world she would wish to live in. But she replied :

" I don't mind particularly where I live. Really I don't.
I'll go quite happily anywhere that you have to go."

" Right ! I'm glad you're so decided. I thought you
might rather hate the idea."

" Did you indeed ? You were right ! " was Agatha's
inward comment.

Why on earth should it be New York ? Almost any other

place would have been better. She had always disliked
the idea of it, a great, noisy, new city, perpetually in a
hurry. If it had to be the States, why couldn't it have been
Virginia, or California, or somewhere in the South? She
was all for warmth at the moment.

Gerald was saying:

" Then I'll find out the particulars of the thing and
close with Green if it's all satisfactory. The only drawback
is that he wants me rather soon; almost at once, in fact.
I'm afraid I shall have to be off in six weeks at the outside.
That would give me time to dispose of my affairs here.
You could, of course, come over later, if you didn't want
to leave England so soon. Or you could wait here until the
divorce proceedings were through, and then come out. In
that case we could be married as soon as you arrived, but it
would mean a longish separation."

" Does Dr. Green know of your . . . position? I mean
would it make any difference to his offer that we shall
probably be in the divorce courts? "

He shook his head.

" No, I don't think so. I'm almost sure it wouldn't.
But I must find all that out. In fact I expect I'll have to
explain the circumstances to him."

" I think I could be ready to leave England in about six
weeks. It's really quite a long time. I'd rather not stay
here and be divorced all by myself."

" Just as you like. Only I must go then if I'm going at
all. He wants my help in getting the thing started. Otherwise, of course, I wouldn't contemplate leaving you."

" No. We'll consider it to-morrow when I have seen
my mother. We shall know better what to do then. I
can't think why John hasn't divorced me. I made sure he
would be very prompt about it. And he should have no
difficulties at all; his case is perfectly clear."

" Well, you must talk to your mother about it."

Silence again overtook them, this time prolonged and mournful. The hour was late and the fire quite out, but neither made a move to leave the cold hearth. Their brief, bleak colloquy had given them too much to think about, and they crouched over the ashes, pondering. Gerald was asking himself, with that wearing, secret uneasiness which now so frequently assailed him, whether she would be happy in this new life. He was beginning to feel that this beloved, yet incongruously magnificent creature, whom he had so unexpectedly acquired, was a charge—an obligation. Beholding her at Lyndon, he had raged against the opulence of her setting; but a mere removal had not satisfied him. He now felt that he must himself provide some sort of background for her; she was more inseparable from backgrounds than he had thought. He had already half forgotten that tide of indignant pity which had driven him to snatch her from Braxhall. Though obstinately counting himself a happy man he would sometimes pause and gasp in amazement at what he had done.

Still he loved her intensely, and sustained himself with an impassioned belief in her fortitude. Not many women would take the prospect of exile in an alien, uncongenial country as she had taken it. But he did not tell her this, which was a pity, for she wanted to hear it. She was discovering that he took her virtues for granted and she was not sure whether she liked it. But he would have thought it rather insulting to tell her how noble she was, so he said nothing.

"That's not an alarum clock going off upstairs?" she cried. "It must be late! I can't bear to think of people getting up already; I need to recruit a lot of energy before I can even think of a new day."

It was indeed late in the following morning when she finally dragged herself from her bed and set out on her anxious pilgrimage to South Kensington. Upon the road she rehearsed all that she must say and it seemed to her that she was quite ready for the encounter. She would point out that she intended to go to America with Gerald, and that, in this case, divorce would be the simplest remedy. She must display no regret, no penitence, and no exaltation. Emotion of any sort would put her at a disadvantage. Calm common sense was the only platform on which to meet her mother.

As she stood on the doorstep she felt that she was very calm and sensible indeed. But she no sooner caught sight of her parent, waiting at the head of the stairs, than a part of her defences began to slip from her. She had been a fool to think herself ready, when her mother would, in every one of life's emergencies, be always so infinitely more prepared.

"Well, Agatha . . . what kind of a crossing ? I was afraid it would be rough. So sorry to have missed you last night."

Meadowes faded away down the hall as Mrs. Cocks kissed her daughter. They went into the drawing-room and sat down on a sofa by the fire. The hearth was dominated by a large wooden frame on which was stretched squared canvas, half worked into a thick woolly rug. Mrs. Cocks displayed it jubilantly.

"It's perfectly fascinating," she said. "You do it with this little needle, threading it through and through . . . so ! Of course the designs you get in the shop are hideous, but you can do your own. I was in the British Museum the other day, looking at their carpets, and I've got several new ideas. I've made two already. One I gave to Lady Peel. The other was the first I made ; it isn't very interesting. I put it in that peculiarly draughty place on the landing by the bathroom. It's just the right size. You must come up and see it after lunch."

Agatha admired the rug and wondered if her mother was being unexpectedly subtle or more superficial than usual. She had looked for censure on the very doorstep.

Was all this talk of rugs merely meant to disconcert her—
to put her to the necessity of opening the difficult question
herself ? Or was her mother really indifferent and in-
curious ? She sat for some time listening to inconsequent
gossip, until she could bear it no more.

" Mother," she began, " I rather wanted to discuss some
of my private affairs with you."

Her mother's reply enlightened her not a little, revealing,
as it did, a carefully rehearsed attitude.

" Of course, that is as you please. But unless your plans
are of a kind that I can countenance and approve of, the
less you tell me the better. As my daughter I don't want
to lose you, so I'd really rather not hear anything that
might make things difficult between us. Remember,
Agatha, at present I know nothing of what you have been
doing lately, except that you have been abroad for a time."

Agatha recognized this line of argument, for she had
heard it before. Mrs. Cocks had always been a little
inconsistent in her ethical conventions. The line she drew,
where the social irregularities of her friends was concerned,
had strange curves in it. Agatha often thought that she
strained at gnats and swallowed camels. She would exclude
one from her house, in rigid disapprobation, and welcome
another, equally culpable, with warm cordiality. " Of
course I know nothing of all that," was her plea on these
occasions, " and I don't see that it's my business to know."
A policy of invincible ignorance. She was now evidently
prepared to maintain, in the face of an outraged world,
that she knew nothing of her daughter's misdoings.

Both women were silent for a few minutes and then
Mrs. Cocks said carelessly :

" I've had a fire lighted in your room, as you will be
wanting to unpack this afternoon, I expect. When are
your things coming round ? You haven't got a maid with
you, I suppose ? You'd better let my woman do it for you."

" But you weren't expecting me to stay here, Mother ? "

" Why not ?   I thought you might like to be here for a week or two."

" I don't think I can leave Gerald, thank you. We are staying at the Talisman Hotel, you know."

Mrs. Cocks flushed with irritation. It was really very tiresome of Agatha to ignore her plea for reticence.

" I don't know that I particularly want to hear about that," she said with cold distaste. " But since you insist upon talking in this way, may I ask how long you intend to continue thus ? "

" Until we can get married. I want John to divorce me. I can't think why he doesn't. Mother ! I know you think it all very wrong, but . . ."

" You can hardly expect me to approve," broke in Mrs. Cocks, impulsively forgetting her rôle of cool incuriosity. " You've dragged my pride in the dust. I can't possibly hold my own with Marian Clewer now, and you've no idea how odious she's been. I'm quite defenceless. When she brags of her daughters, what am I to say of mine ? "

" I'm very sorry, Mother."

" I can't understand it," continued Mrs. Cocks bitterly. " I cannot understand it. I couldn't have believed you capable of such folly. To risk your position and reputation like this ! Because, even nowadays, you would be considered *déclassée* by most nice people, if it became generally talked about. Fortunately, hardly anyone does know, outside the family. I think a lot of people guess that you are not on very good terms with John, but nothing worse than that. If you will come to me now, you are likely to get out of it all a great deal better than you deserve."

" But, Mother, I want John to divorce me, and then people must . . ."

" John is not going to divorce you. And very rightly. He cares for the scandal if you don't, and he isn't going to have his name dragged into publicity like this. And allow me to tell you that you will live to thank Heaven that he had such good sense and moderation."

" But unless he divorces me, I can't marry Gerald."

" I cannot see why you should be so anxious to rush into a second marriage when you did so badly over your first."

" But he has to go to America in six weeks and I want to marry him and go too."

"America ! In six weeks ? My dear child, the quickest divorce that ever was heard of would hardly enable you to remarry in time for that. But what on earth do you want to go to America for ? "

" I don't want to go there particularly. But Gerald has to go, and I naturally want to go with him. He's got work there."

" Oh, well, of course, if you insist upon living with him, emigration will be his only chance of supporting himself— and you. You've probably ruined his career here. Yes ! Since he has had the misfortune to love you, my child, he'd better try the States."

" Do you really think that ? " murmured Agatha turning pale.

"Of course I do. It's obvious to anyone. His practice here will fall to pieces as soon as ever this scandal comes out. Bound to ! His best type of patients are exactly the sort of people who would have nothing further to do with him. People that one knows. But tell me . . . is this work in America well paid ? "

" Not very, I believe."

" And have you considered how you will like straitened circumstances in . . . in . . . wherever it is. . . ."

" New York."

" New York ? Oh, it's quite impossible ! My dear Agatha, you've never been there. I have, so I know what I'm talking about. You wouldn't stand a week of it. It's

the most entertaining place—for the very rich. But only
for the very rich. Unbearable otherwise. You surely
can't contemplate such a thing? You don't know what
you are doing."

" Well . . . you see . . . I love him."

" Love him ! But eight years ago you loved John."

" I was mistaken. I didn't."

" How do you know that this is not a mistake ? "

" I always loved Gerald. But I didn't always know it."

" Then you did very wrong to marry John, that's all I
can say,"

" I know."

" I can't understand it. But then I never could understand these things. I can't understand how you, of all
people, could be so ill-bred."

" Do you think it is ill-bred ? "

" Yes, I do. It's very vulgar. But it's the same everywhere, nowadays. In all the books one reads, on the stage,
all over the place. All these violent passions ! It's the war,
I suppose. But that sort of thing has always rather disgusted
me. I daresay I'm out of date, but it revolts me."

Agatha reflected mournfully upon her recent sentimental
journey. It seemed, at that particular moment, to have
been all customs houses and rough crossings. She could
not remember any violent passions anywhere.

" I don't think you are quite fair," she said defensively.
" I don't think Gerald and I are very passionate people,
whatever else we might be accused of."

" But if you haven't even the very inadequate excuse of
passion, why in Heaven's name have you misconducted
yourselves in so frightful a manner ? Do explain yourself,
Agatha ! You told me just now, with some fervour, that
you love him."

" So I do ! So I do ! "

" Very well, then. What, exactly, do you mean by that ? "

"Oh, don't you know what I mean?"

"I can't say that I do."

"Well . . ." began Agatha laboriously, feeling how hopeless was her task, "he's the only person in the world that I've ever wanted to . . . to make happy . . . to give to . . . to make sacrifices. . . ."

"I see!" said Mrs. Cocks drily. "And what sacrifices have you made for him so far? Apart, I mean, from the loss of principle, position and reputation, which was, after all, mutual."

Agatha considered, with a shock of dismay. The past months, reviewed in the light of her mother's derisive irony, did not seem to be very full of sacrifices, as far as she was concerned. She had in no way requited his unremitting vigilance for her happiness. So far, he had been the victim of their escapade. "No," she said candidly. "I've not done much for him as yet. But I'm going to."

"No you won't. You never will. Don't deceive yourself, Agatha. You aren't that type of woman, though you may occasionally wish you were. You are the sort of woman who takes, who accepts sacrifice; the prize and privilege of successful men, not the helpmate of the failures. You were expensive to produce and you are even more expensive to . . . to keep. Don't wince like that! It's a very useful type, and stimulates nine-tenths of the culture and civilization in the world. But you are frightfully mistaken if you think you can change your nature. You have never, in all your life, put up with anything you disliked, or done anything you didn't want to. You can't begin now."

"I'm not so very old."

"Too old to change your character. And anyhow it's unfair to experiment on poor Gerald. If you think you can go with him to America and be a good wife to him in poverty and discomfort, you'll make the mistake of your life. You haven't the strength of character. You'll bring misery and disillusion on him. Have you thought of the consequences, supposing you couldn't stand it ? "

" Other women . . ."

" Other women are trained in harder schools. Just consider for a moment the sort of middle age you are storing up for yourselves."

Agatha had a moment's horrible vision of herself growing old, an inefficient, fretful figure, clouding his life with her querulous demands and eclipsed beauty. Had she that generous love which survives the hard middle years? Hastily banishing the nightmare, she said with decision :

" There will be hard times, of course. But we shall get along as other people do."

" Don't make the mistake of supposing that you have a noble character because you would like to have one. It's rank folly."

" But I've burnt my boats. I'm his, now. I must go where he goes. People may not know it yet, but that doesn't alter the essential fact. It's true that I'm taking great risks. But I must. I can't leave him, Mother, whatever you say."

" You must leave him for a little time, at any rate. I'd hoped to persuade you of that without being forced to tell you something which I really have no business to speak of, since I promised not to. But you compel me."

" Oh, no, don't, if you oughtn't ! " cried Agatha shrinking back.

" I'm afraid I must, for nothing else will make you see reason. Besides, it's something which you have every right to know, and which you ought to have been told long ago. In fact I spoke pretty plainly to Marian about it. I said that she had absolutely no right to keep it from us. It . . . it explains why John is not getting a divorce. I went to see Marian soon after you left Braxhall, to talk things over, you understand, and find out what John meant to do.

And after a good many preliminaries I began to gather how ill he really is."

"Ill! Is he ill?"

"Very ill, dear. He has been for some months past. He was when you were at Braxhall. I got it out of Marian that he'd seen a specialist just before that time. It was that old heart trouble, you know."

"But I knew he'd seen a specialist. He saw Sir Newman Crawley. But he was quite reassuring."

"I'm afraid he wasn't. You were most unjustifiably kept in the dark. His verdict was very grave."

"Grave! . . . What did he say?"

"This is bound to be rather a shock to you, dear. He ... he practically told John that he was . . . dying. He gave very little hope of his recovery. . . ."

"Mother! Oh, Mother! No!"

"He said that it would probably be quick," said Mrs. Cocks, looking into the fire. "A few months, he said. . . ."

"But he said all this before we went to Braxhall? Before we went?"

"Yes. Of course he should have told you."

"Before we went. . . ."

"I consider that you should have been told at once. I suppose he wanted to spare you, poor boy, as nothing could be done. Still, I might have been told. But he only confided in Marian, who of course told Lois, and Hubert, and Cynthia, and Sir Thomas, and Dolly, and James for all I know, but elected to keep it secret from the people most concerned. But had you absolutely no idea of it?"

"What?"

"Don't gape like that! I don't believe you've heard a word I've been saying."

"I'm sorry. But what have I done! Oh, what have I done! I might have known."

"Of course, if you'd known, this . . . regrettable precipitancy . . ."

"Oh, hardly that ! We'd been in love for ten years."

"And did quite well without each other. It's a pity you couldn't keep it up a little longer."

"Oh, Mother, don't ! Don't be so cruel. Anyhow, it's not that I'm thinking of. But I've been so unkind to him. Oh, perhaps it's not true ! "

"I'm afraid it is, dear."

Mrs. Cocks put a few stitches into her rug. Agatha was walking distractedly about the room, delving into the past.

"Poor John ! Oh, I ought to have known ! But why ? Why didn't he tell me ? I don't blame him, though. I know quite well why he didn't. I was abominable to him and let him see I didn't love him. Oh, but of course I wouldn't have left him if I'd known. At least, not like that. But then, what would I have been worth even if I had stayed, if it was only for that ? I don't wonder he didn't tell me. He would have, if I'd treated him better."

"I don't know that it makes so very much difference to John," said Mrs. Cocks dispassionately. "The injury which you've inflicted upon him would be the same, whether he were well or ill. I don't expect he feels it any more bitterly on that score."

"I'm not thinking of that so much as the hateful way I baited him before I left him."

"And I'm not really thinking of John at all. And it's rather sentimental in you, Agatha, to do so at this late hour. If you were going to consider his feelings you should have done so sooner. No ! I'm thinking of the perfectly unnecessary way in which you have compromised yourself."

"I don't see what else could have happened really," said Agatha dejectedly, as she sat down again. "Once it was a declared thing between me and Gerald, I suppose I must have gone to him. Only it would never have come to such a point, that time at Braxhall, if I'd known about John. How horrible it all is! However, it's done now and can't be undone. I must try to think what is best to do next."

"Quite so. And you have to remember that your reputation is still undamaged. The family will remain silent for John's sake."

"But that can't last for long."

"I hope you'll see the sense, now, of coming to me here, at least until . . ."

"But, my dear Mother, what's the use of that? If I go to New York in six weeks' time with Gerald, what's the use? . . ."

"I think you must wait here quietly until you can join him to be married."

"Oh, no! We couldn't be separated like that."

"I think you owe it to John. I really do." Mrs. Cocks was playing her last card and her face bore traces of anxiety. "So far you haven't brought public disgrace on him. And that is what he minds, you know quite well it is. If you leave Gerald now and live here with me for a month or two you will save your husband's name from dishonour. I think you've no right to refuse that to a dying man."

"I must see what Gerald thinks," said Agatha uncertainly. "He will know what is right. He has a finer conscience than I have."

"Has he, indeed?" said Mrs. Cocks.

"I can see your point of view. I'll put it to him."

"I'm sure he'll think as I do. Let him go out to New York, and you can follow him when you are free. After a decent interval. Surely it would be better, from all points of view? We might both go out; it would look more respectable. And then you could marry him out there. I know it sounds callous to talk about the future in this cold-blooded way, but one must look ahead."

"It . . . it would be bound to be fairly soon, wouldn't it?"

"Oh, yes, quite. I gather there is, practically speaking, no doubt about that."

Mrs. Cocks longed to add : "You needn't be afraid your husband will not die," but she checked herself in time and continued relentlessly :

"For one thing, if it's all decently and respectably done, and you don't compromise yourselves by rushing off together before you can be properly married, it will be so much easier for you to return to England eventually. Supposing Gerald changed his mind about his work and wanted to come back and take up his London practice ? You would infinitely prefer that in your heart of hearts, wouldn't you ? You don't surely want to spend the rest of your life in New York ? "

Agatha shivered.

"Why invite a scandal when you can avoid it ? I should have thought your affection for Gerald would have made you consider his position and career a little more."

"You see," exclaimed Agatha, "I rather think it is on my account that he has accepted this work in New York. I think he thought, poor dear, that it would be easier for me. And if that is so, I don't think I ought to let him go without me."

"Well, at least, come here until you go. Don't go on blatantly living with him as long as you are in London. I really think you should have more consideration for all our feelings than to do that. Besides, the Talisman is such a respectable place ! It's where all the head-mistresses go when they come up to attend conferences. I shouldn't wonder if you got turned out when the managment discover who you are. And they are bound to do that before long. How shall you like that ? "

"Oh, it is difficult ! I'll go off now and consult him," conceded Agatha.

"Stay to lunch first. There is plenty of time."

Mrs. Cocks was unwilling to let Agatha go until she had forced her to a decision.

" But I said I'd be back for lunch. He will wait for me."

" Ring him up and tell him you are staying here."

" I could do that."

Agatha went to the telephone. As she waited for Gerald, she said reflectively :

" It wouldn't be a long separation. Only six weeks."

" What, child ? " Mrs. Cocks looked up from her rug.

" Oh ! Oh, no ! Not long. The most married people are sometimes parted for as long as that."

Agatha addressed herself to the telephone :

" Oh, Gerald, is that you ? I'm speaking from South Kensington. I'm stopping to lunch, so don't wait for me. . . . Oh, not badly. . . . I'll tell you when I get back. . . . I don't quite know. . . . If I'm not back by tea-time, ring me up, will you ? Good-bye, then."

She hung up the receiver, and found that her mother was looking her over with approving eyes.

" You're in very good looks, my dear. You've quite got back your colour. I don't know when I've seen you look better. Corsica has evidently built you up. Come down to lunch."

The two women strolled downstairs. Agatha stifled a small pang of compunction at the thought of poor Gerald lunching in the hotel all by himself. As a matter of fact he had taken the opportunity to escape from the menu cards and the sweet-peas and maidenhair fern and all the flummery which so exasperated him at an hotel meal. He had sought an eating-house near Guy's, a haunt of his bachelor days, where he was almost sure of picking up a friend to share his chops and beer.

4.

Hubert, borne as far as Cowper in his passion for the eighteenth century, had re-read the *Winter Morning's Walk*. He became enchanted with it and insisted upon reading extracts to Lois in spite of her visible absorption in a volume of Marcel Proust. The next day was bitterly cold and he was very anxious that they should set forth upon a Winter Morning's Walk of their own, but she would not be persuaded. In the afternoon, therefore, feeling every inch a country gentleman, he set off by himself. He strode through several farmyards and looked severely at some pigs. He thrashed with his stick at such poor weeds as the season had spared. His hope was that if he crossed a sufficient number of fields, and climbed a few score stiles, he might, permeated by the beauties of the wintry landscape, achieve that mood of philosophic reverie which gives distinction to the poets of Cowper's age. If fields and hedges failed to produce the right effect he might try a country churchyard.

He had observed that the fellows usually begin by cataloguing the scenery, and he obediently scrutinized the view, moving the eye, as the poet directs, " from joy to joy." But, gaze as he would, he remained cold. Emphatically that, for a bleak, black wind swept from the steely sky and whistled over the stubble, nearly flaying him. His nose turned blue and his eyes began to water; it was the kind of day when no clothes seem thick enough.

" It needs a frost, I suppose," he reflected, " and snow, and icicles hanging from the old barn roof, and what not. Something more like a Christmas card."

He thought sadly of Madeira, where they had intended to spend the winter, and, as a fresh gale came down the hill, he wondered if Madeira would really be warm enough. The shortening afternoon gave him a good excuse for turning homewards.

Having reached his garden, however, he perceived Lois at the window of the living-room, and immediately underwent a recrudescence of the country gentleman. She beckoned to him but he ignored her and began a solemn tour of the estate, minutely examining each much-pruned rose-bush in the bed under the window. He hoped that he did not look too cold and miserable. Lois opened the long window and called to him to come in, but he hardly heard her in the frenzy of excitement with which he stooped over an extremely small bush. Then he straightened himself.

"Lois!" he called. "Just come and look here!"

"What at?" she called back, shivering in the window. "Do come in out of the cold. I've had a letter. . . ."

"I do believe . . ." he said, in deep concern, ". . . I'm very much afraid it's the blight!"

"The what?"

"The blight! . . . Er . . . rose blight."

"Is there such a thing?"

"Of course there is."

She came out and joined him.

"I don't see anything wrong," she said.

"I don't like that funny reddish colour at the end of that twig," he commented anxiously.

"Aren't they always like that at this time of year? And anyhow you can't do anything about it, even if it is. You don't know what to do."

Hubert looked pained at such an accusation. He said, with becoming gravity:

"I'll have to consult with Saunders."

"Now do come in. I've something I want to talk to you about. . . ."

He followed her into the genial warmth of the living-room and just managed to suppress a sigh of ecstasy as the window closed behind them.

"I had a nice bracing walk," he told her. "Pity you wouldn't come. Those pigs at the old farm are very fine. I had a look at them."

But she was so intent upon a communication which she wished to make that she had no time to be a country gentleman's wife. She did not even notice that he was aggrieved about it.

"It's the most extraordinary thing," she said, "and you will have to speak to James. He pays too little consideration, really, to poor Mother's feelings, and it's disgusting after all she's done for him."

"How often have I told you," said Hubert furiously, his grievance taking shape, "how often have I told you that I will not speak to James about things? Why should I? He's more trouble than he's worth. If anything is to be done with him one of you women had better talk to his precious Dolly. That's the only way to deal with him."

"Dolly is as bad as he is. She's worse. They are both disgusting, but he has some excuse. He's always been eccentric, and anyhow, men have different standards. But Dolly shouldn't countenance it. At least, one expects people of her class to value respectability. One would think she would be more particular."

"What have they been doing now? I thought Dolly was too respectable, if anything. That was your mother's view when last we discussed her."

"Mother writes that she really can't go there any longer. She can't countenance the way they receive Agatha. She says that Agatha is up at Hampstead so often that one can never be really quite sure of not meeting her."

"But Lois . . . I told you that at the Martins' party the other week we all . . ."

"That's different. That's in public. Of course, in a private family affair like this, one has to behave civilly in front of people. Dolly and James did quite right: I was glad to hear that they had that much *savoir-faire*. But it's quite a different thing asking her to their house."

"It's rather funny, when you think how very lately it was Agatha we all blamed for receiving them. But really, my dear, I think it's entirely their business who they ask to their house."

"Have their family no claims? When you think of what we have all done for them! Where would they be if it wasn't for us? You'd think James would have more feeling of loyalty to his brother. You'd think a respectable creature like Dolly would draw the line somewhere."

"I daresay she does."

"I tell you she doesn't. If, knowing the facts, she can go on asking Agatha to her house, it shows that she doesn't."

"I don't see that follows," argued Hubert. "It merely shows that she wouldn't draw the line where you do. Her conventions are not the same as yours."

The word convention drew her fire, as he knew it would. She plunged after it, off the main track of her indignation.

"Conventions? Who is talking of conventions? I don't consider myself a very conventional person. . . ."

"Don't you?"

"No, I don't. As people go I should say I was very tolerably broadminded. Anyhow, I'm much less conventional than you are."

"Very possibly," agreed Hubert in an irritating voice.

"So you can't talk."

Hubert said nothing, but picked up the evening paper and settled himself in a comfortable chair by the fire. Lois, finding herself in a cul-de-sac, made one of those unexpectedly swift returns to the main issue which so often surprised him:

"Anyhow this question of James and Dolly has nothing to do with convention."

"I should have thought it had."

"It's . . . it's simply a matter of decent feeling."

"Same thing . . ." Hubert was heard to mumble.

"It's not. It isn't at all the same thing."

"I think it is."

"I say it isn't."

"What attitude," demanded Hubert, after a pause, "should decent feeling have prompted Dolly to adopt towards her sinning sister?"

"Don't be flippant, Hubert! I feel very strongly about this."

"I observe that you do. But I'm not joking, Lois. I want to know. How should Dolly behave to Agatha?"

"She should make it quite clear . . . as soon as she has the opportunity to do it privately, I mean . . . she should make it obvious that she disapproves of her."

"But, I just put it to you, supposing she doesn't disapprove?"

"Well, then, she should."

"Why?"

"Oh, Hubert! How can you ask? And she pretends to be religious!"

"But her kindness to Agatha may be on religious grounds, you know. Eating with publicans and sinners, even with scribes and pharisees, has been sanctioned by an unimpeachable precedent."

"Yes, perhaps. But it isn't only religion. It's the flagrant disregard of all social . . ."

Since convention was the only word which suggested itself to her, Lois left this sentence unfinished and went on to the third item in her charge.

"They ought to remember what they owe to the family."

"But what do they owe?"

"What does anyone owe? If I had treated you as Agatha treated John, would you like to see your relations welcoming me with open arms?"

Hubert was struck by this.

"No, I can't say I should," he said thoughtfully. "A little hurt, I should be."

"And for Dolly and James especially, when you think of everything that has been done for them. Mother, and

John, and you and the Bragges. If you think how we've
all helped in James's career! You don't remember, because
you didn't know us then, but I do, how Mother worried
herself getting him good lessons and sending him to Paris
and all. It's really rather wonderful when you think she
isn't his real mother. And she had to stand no end of
criticism from his own relations for not sending him away
to school; that old Major Talbot and Mrs. Gordon Clewer
—all quite odious about it, and insinuating all sorts of things.
They none of them could see that she was keeping him at
home because she thought he would develop better there,
and that a boy of his temperameht couldn't be treated like
the average. And then think how John let him go on living
at Lyndon, just letting him paint and go his own way
without a word of criticism! Not many young artists have
such obliging brothers. And then his marriage! I don't
see how he could possibly have married if the family hadn't
been so nice about it. He never considered, I suppose,
when he was allowed to marry with so little trouble, what
a blow it was to all of us. We all had to make sacrifices.
And then think of the trouble you took to get him work!
And Cynthia and Tom and the way he treated them. And
the whole business of the Hampstead move. Mother was up
there every day for a week, seeing about it. And you taking
such trouble to introduce him to people; turning out on cold
nights to take him to evening parties which bored you frightfully. Oh, I know it's a privilege to have him in the family,
but it's a great burden too! And he's not a scrap grateful!"

Hubert meditated on this catalogue in some awe and said:

"He certainly has a good deal to thank us all for. But
do I understand that your mother actually met Agatha at
Hampstead?"

"Yes. She went up to see Dolly about a servant or
something. And James calmly took her into the sitting-
room, where she found Agatha helping Dolly to make

herself a blouse, if you please ! You'd have thought they'd have the sense, under the circumstances, to show Mother into another room. It was most awkward."

" And what happened ? "

" I'll read you what Mother writes."

Lois picked up a letter and read :

" Though I was very much taken aback, I was not, on the whole, sorry to have an opportunity of expressing my feelings. I was a little afraid lest my manner at Mrs. Townshend's might have been misunderstood. . . ."

" You see, explained Lois, " they had met before. Mrs. Cocks, since she got Agatha to go back to her, has taken her about a good deal. She wants to whitewash her as much as possible, I suppose. And Mother met them at an "At Home" and had to be civil, or people would have thought it odd." She resumed her reading :

" I said nothing. I just said : ' Oh, Dorothy, if you'll excuse me, I'll come another time. Or perhaps, if Lady Clewer is not going to be here for long, I could wait in the studio until she is gone.' Just like that, taking no direct notice of her at all. James, as you may imagine, failed to grasp my meaning, and said : ' Why do you call her Lady Clewer ? ' But I think his wife understood. I went and sat in the studio. Would you believe me, I was there for twenty minutes before Dorothy came in. Even then she did not apologize. I said very little ; I told her that I could not visit at Hampstead while such disagreeable things are likely to happen. She tried to excuse herself, of course, by saying that they had not expected me. But, as I said, that only makes it worse. It's admitting that they do these things behind my back."

" She just ignored her," said Hubert thoughtfully. " If it had been you, Lois, what would you have done ? Would you have done the same ? "

" I think so. If I had had the presence of mind. But I'd have got flustered ; Mother is always so sure of herself."

" But I don't understand. I don't quite get your point of view. I've known you receive people who, to put it baldly, were no better than Agatha, and who had fewer claims on your affection. And, after all, the scandal has never been public and she's living quietly with her mother now."

" Yes, but it's the family side of it. . . ."

" You mean that you are ready to accord a toleration outside the family which you withhold inside it ? "

" Of course, I might have known that you would take Agatha's part," cried Lois angrily. " All men do, it seems."

" Oh, good heavens ! " groaned Hubert. " Why can't you keep to the point, Lois ? These digressions make all our discussions so lengthy."

" That's exactly like you ! When I bring up an argument you can't answer, you always call it a digression. You know quite well that you can't be unbiassed about Agatha. You can't deny it."

" I don't deny it. But I deny that it has anything to do with the point. I want to extract from you some explanation of your most unreasonable definition . . ."

" Very well, then, if you admit that you are biassed where she is concerned, it seems to me that your whole position is unsound. . . ."

" Your most unreasonable definition of toleration as . . ."

" Hubert ! I wish you'd listen to me and not try to interrupt so constantly. It's very bad manners, and we'd get on so much better if you ever listened."

" On the contrary, you interrupted me. But we'll let that pass. I'll listen in silence until you've quite finished, if you will try to abstain from hurling unanswerable but perfectly irrelevant truths at me and asking me to deny them. It gives you a specious air of victory, but it doesn't in the least disprove my point, you know."

" I'm glad you admit that they are truths. Since you admit that, where Agatha is concerned, you are not qualified to hold an opinion . . ."

" I've admitted no such thing ! "

" Hubert ! You are perfectly impossible ! If you won't let me speak, I won't try."

And Lois bent to poke the fire with hands that shook with wrath.

" Since you must drag personalities into this discussion," went on Hubert, more gently, " I'd like to say this. It doesn't seem to me that you can be very friendly with a person, fond of them and accepting kindness from them, and then suddenly chuck them. Agatha has been very kind to us both, Lois, and we have been fond of her. It seems to me to give her a claim on us. And I expect Dolly feels that way too. She owes a lot to Agatha. You don't mean to tell me that you can, at a moment's notice, forget the friend-ship of years? It's so unlike your usual generosity of temper."

She said nothing, but kept her face averted. He was suddenly aware that she was on the point of tears, and he instantly grew remorseful. The quarrel became insignifi-cant, and he asked himself angrily why she should not be unreasonable if she wished. He cursed himself for having lost his temper and was glad when tea appeared, since it would give him an opportunity of ministering to her.

" Wouldn't you like to have it on the sofa? " he suggested. " Let me pour out."

She refused coldly and they began the meal in an uncom-fortable silence. She was wondering whether any man ever ends any argument with his wife without suggesting a cup of tea or a lie down. She wondered this because it simply did not occur to her that husbands have more forcible weapons at their command. The occasion of James and the window, the only occasion in her life when she had not been treated like a lady, had faded from her mind. It did not lead her to speculate why it was that Hubert never boxed her ears when she annoyed him.

He was seeking for a topic which might mollify her. At last he inquired equably if her mother's letter had any news of John.

" Gone down to shoot at Lyndon," said Lois shortly.

" Has he got friends with him ? "

" I believe so."

" I shouldn't have thought it was very good for him, should you ? "

" No."

" But I suppose it's a change for him."

" I suppose so."

" Damned uphill work ! " he protested inwardly.

Her humours, however, were seldom long-lived. She was not a sulky woman. When, after tea, he came to light her cigarette for her, she unbent and retained him with a caress.

" I hate quarrelling," she murmured.

" So do I."

" What do we do it for, then ? "

" I shouldn't think we are worse than anyone else."

" We quarrel about such silly things. James ! "

" Not James particularly. It might have been the new tennis courts or a railway time-table. It was merely a little ebullition of the sex discord."

" No, it's generally James. At Lyndon it was the same ; he was at the bottom of every family row I can ever remember. He's so different from us ! Like a cuckoo in a sparrow's nest."

" I was thinking the other day . . . you know, I shouldn't be in the least surprised if he set a fashion. A cult of domesticity. I expect all talented young men in the next generation will marry housemaids and wheel their children out in perambulators on Sunday afternoons, and talk in words of one syllable. It's always the accidental, the chance result of education and surroundings, which makes an impression on the second-rate mind. They'll copy his work, of course, but that's nothing to the way they'll copy his personal eccentricities."

"Hampstead and Chelsea will look very odd when they are full of people modelled upon James. Dull too!"

The telephone bell rang and Lois went to answer it:

"Hello! Hello! Yes, it's me! Lois speaking! Oh, yes, I'll tell him."

She turned to Hubert.

"It's Mother. She wants to speak to you."

Hubert took the receiver from her.

"Yes! . . . Yes? Oh! Oh, yes, what is it? . . . Oh! . . . Oh, I'm very sorry! Where did you say? Oh, yes, I'll tell her. Yes, I'll be careful."

He put his hand over the mouthpiece and turned to her. "She wants me to break to you that John died at Lyndon this afternoon," he said in an aggrieved voice. "I can't see why she couldn't tell you herself. Shall I offer to go up? She was speaking from Eaton Square. They'd 'phoned from Lyndon."

"Yes, you'd better."

He turned to the telephone again.

"Oh, I've told Lois, Lady Clewer. Yes, she's quite all right. I don't think you need worry about her. Shall I come up? I can come at once. Are you alone? . . . Oh! . . . Well, ring us up if there is anything that we can do, or if you want me for anything. . . . Oh! . . . Yes, I will if you like. But I really think there is no need to worry."

He put up the receiver and rejoined his wife by the fire. "The Bragges are with her," he said. "And she says I must on no account leave you. I'm to ring her up last thing to-night and reassure her about you. She seems dreadfully afraid that you'll be very much upset."

Lois was looking as if she could have wished herself a little more upset. She said gravely:

"Poor John. It's very sad."

Hubert agreed that it was.

" I wonder if he was shooting this morning. This cold day. . . ."

Hubert nodded.

" Poor Mother! She was as fond of him, you know, as if he had been her own son. It will be very hard for her."

The tears which she could not shed for John rose into her eyes as she thought of her mother's distress.

" I'll go up to-morrow," she said, " and help her about getting her things. I'll need clothes myself."

Her mind was occupied with the subject for some moments, and then she said lamely :

" Of course, expecting it as we have been for the last few months, it's less of a shock. . . ."

It was as though she were excusing herself for not feeling more.

" It's a queer thing," said Hubert, " to think of James at the head of the family. I wonder if he'll live at Lyndon ! "

Lois looked really shocked.

" Oh, Hubert ! Isn't it awful ! But it must be faced, I suppose."

" There are bound to be great changes."

" I wonder what Agatha will do now, Hubert."

" Do ? Why she'll marry Blair of course."

" I'm not quite sure," said Lois thoughtfully. " I think her mother is working against it, you know. I think, now she has got hold of Agatha, she will throw all her influence to delay the marriage in the hope that it won't come off."

" I should have thought that it was quite inevitable."

" Well, you know, Agatha's position is quite assured. She isn't publicly compromised ; she won't have to marry him. She's young and beautiful and well off. Her jointure must be ample. Mrs. Cocks might well think she could do better for herself than marry Mr. Blair."

" Mrs. Cocks might, but I doubt if Agatha would. I

won't believe it. I can't believe she'd chuck Blair now.
I think you do her an injustice, Lois."

"Well . . . we'll see."

"But could you forgive her if she turned him down ? "

"No. I don't think I could."

"She'd brand herself as a light woman," he said gravely.

Lois blushed at so outspoken a definition, and said
quickly : "I don't want to be unjust to her. It all depends,
I think, upon the influence of Mrs. Cocks. I don't want to
be hard on Agatha, really I don't. But I feel she has every
virtue except character. She has no real principles, only
nice manners. When you first get to know her you think
that such charm and kindness must have something funda-
mentally fine at the bottom of it. But you gradually grow
impatient with her and you end by thinking that all her
goods are in the shop window. But I'm sorry I spoke in
that petty way of her before tea."

"Oh, that's nothing. I'm sure I was most insufferable."

"We must try not to quarrel when we have a family to
educate."

"Indeed we must ! If I forget myself you will have to
say : ' Hubert ! And before the children too ! ' "

Lois laughed and they drew in closer to their bright fire.
The bitter gale outside moaned among the larches, but
they did not hear it, so entranced were they with their own
living future. The storm swept the wintry land and sang
a dirge in the void chimneys of Lyndon, swaying the
tapestries in that room where John lay, so soon forgotten,
in the chilly magnificence of a bed which had once belonged
to Agatha.

5.

Mrs. Cocks watched her daughter tear up her fourth
attempt at a letter, and refrained from suggesting that
there was a block of scribbling paper in the writing-table

drawer. It was certainly a waste of good note-paper, but it would not do to interfere at this point. Agatha took a fresh sheet, wrote some kind of invocation at the top, and paused despairingly.

Mrs. Cocks bent over her rug to hide a smile. She suspected that this letter was to Gerald, and, if it was difficult to write, so much the better. The more often Agatha tore up her beginnings, the more likely was she to say the very things which it was most desirable that she should say.

"My dear!" declaimed the mother to herself, recounting the history of this crisis to an imaginary familiar, "I did nothing. Absolutely nothing! I said nothing. I just sat still and let it work. And at the last moment, without a word from me, she came to her senses. I never felt more strongly how wise it is not to interfere in other people's affairs. As one grows older one learns the folly of it."

It struck her that Agatha's mourning was really a little too much modified, even for these days of flighty widowhood. As soon as the crucial point of Gerald Blair was settled she must have a campaign with clothes and insist upon their being blacker. But not just yet. Essentials must be fought out first.

"There is nothing like Providence," she reflected. "When you think of the risks the child has run, she is really likely to come out of them very well."

Agatha was reading Gerald's letter over again. He wrote:

"DEAREST LOVE,

This is an impossible situation to comment on, isn't it? I shall never, for the rest of my life, escape from remorse when I think of poor Clewer, and I expect you feel pretty much the same. I'm desperately sorry about it, and I don't wonder if his relations feel inclined to shower all sorts of curses on our heads.

But now about us, since it's no use maundering over follies which can't be remedied. Dearest, I can't help being very glad that we can get things put straight before I sail, though it sounds brutal to say so. I'm arranging about a special licence immediately and would like to see you as soon as possible, for we shall have a good deal to talk over and settle. When can you see me? I'm not supposing that you can possibly manage to sail as soon as I do, since it's such short notice, so I'm taking no steps about fixing up your passage until I hear from you. Is that right? I have in fact made up my mind to do without you for some months longer, but you must try to come over as soon as ever you can, for you've no idea how much I miss you all the time.

I'm getting intensely keen on the job, you'll be glad to hear; the more I learn of it the more I like it, which is uncommon luck.

Ever yours,
G."

It was such a confident letter. Not even " Shall I see about a special licence? " but " I am arranging about a special licence immediately." Its confidence appalled her. She felt totally unable to tell him that she was unsure in her own mind; that she doubted her power to be happy in New York or to make him so. She took a fresh sheet and wrote:

" MY DEAR LOVE,

I'm glad you've been so prompt about all arrangements. Come and see me early to-morrow. I rather think I could manage to be ready to sail when you do, if it's possible to book my passage as late as this. I cannot endure a further separation if it can be avoided. But we will discuss that when you come.

Always your loving
AGATHA."

She then reverted to an earlier page, on which she had written " Dearest Gerald," and added :

" I'm afraid you'll think I'm failing you horribly, but I really think it would be a pity for us to get married in such a hurry. We must allow a decent interval to elapse. My leaving you and coming here was a concession to the proprieties, and having gone that far, we might as well do the thing thoroughly. Couldn't you go out for a year or eighteen months, and then, if you liked the work, I could join you and we could be married ? Or you could come back if you had decided against remaining in New York. I don't want to make you feel I'm backing out, my dear, but I think it's rather a pity to let ourselves be rushed in any way. There is no need. We have behaved badly about John and I feel that it would be bad taste, under the circumstances, to force things blatantly upon the world by getting married the moment I am free.

I can see you any time. I go out in the afternoons occasionally for a short walk, but otherwise I'm pretty sure to be in, as I'm not, naturally, going about very much just now. I do want to preserve decorum, as far as possible, in this very difficult position.

Ever yours most affectionately,
AGATHA.

(Don't be angry with me for feeling all this, Gerald dear.)"

These letters she placed side by side and looked from one to the other helplessly. Then she rewrote the second, leaving out the words " There is no need," for she blushed when she thought of Gerald reading them. But still, she could not decide which to send. The second letter, even when amended, was a contemptible production ; she knew what Gerald would think of it. But she considered that it would be even more cowardly to send the first unless she was sure that she could live up to it. She would be jeopardizing his happiness in order to sustain her own self-esteem.

Glancing furtively at her mother she blessed the rugs which were apparently so all-absorbing. Advice and interference at this moment would be the last straw. But her perplexities had evidently passed unnoticed. She sat weighing one letter against the other until the maid came in with the afternoon post. There was a note directed to her in Dolly's neat board-school hand :

"MY DEAR AGATHA,

Can you come up some time, quite soon, please, and see James and I ? We are very much upset about something, and would like your advice. We would come to you only James is working very hard all day now and in the evening it's difficult for us both to get away as the girl goes out. So we hope you won't mind us asking you to come, dear Agatha, and that you are feeling alright and not too much worried by the Trouble in the Family. With very much love from us both, yours affectly,

DOLLY AND JAMES CLEWER."

Agatha determined to go up to Hampstead that very afternoon. Also she would postpone her decision about these letters she had written until after her visit. It struck her that her point of view depended enormously upon domicile, and a few hours in another *milieu* might throw fresh light on the situation. She reacted to life so differently in different places, and the most decisive step of her career had been taken because she had been at Bramfield and at Braxhall upon the same day.

She put the two letters into two envelopes and tucked them away into her handbag. She would post one when she got back from Hampstead. Then she said to her mother :

"I'm just off to see Dolly and James."

"Oh?" said Mrs. Cocks doubtfully. "All the way to Hampstead? How will you go?"

She had reason to suspect the influence of Dolly and James.

"I can go by Tube."

"I don't know that I quite like that. After all, child, you are, in the eyes of the world, a very recent widow. It isn't quite the thing to go rushing round London in Tubes like this."

"It's very unlikely I'll meet anyone we know. I'll keep down my veil. I'm afraid I must go."

"Very well," sighed Mrs. Cocks, who was afraid to draw the rope too tight. "But I think you ought to be back for tea. It isn't really decent that you should be going out at all, except for a little exercise in the gardens. Of course it's dull, but one must observe some forms. Why don't you occupy your mind with some solid reading? When your father died, I remember, I read all through Prescott's *Conquest of Mexico* during the first few weeks of mourning. Of course it's a little heavy. But why don't you read Mdme. de Sévigné? She's very amusing. I'll look her out for you."

"I'll try to be back for tea," conceded Agatha, and escaped.

An unpleasant wind, icy and dusty, blew in her face as she picked her way up the hill from the Tube station. It was an unbecoming day and she felt blue and pinched; she had a suspicion that she looked old. Hampstead, usually so pleasing a place, seemed to her dirty, noisy, and incredibly cold. She tried to sustain herself with memories of the warmth of Corsica; of long days by the sea, watching its blue glint through the arbutus trees. But then, the South could be squalid too. Remembering the smell in the inns and the flies on the ceilings, she thought that it could be worse. On the whole squalor in warm countries was more intolerable than squalor in cold. New York, so she understood, was given to extremes of climate; torrid in summer, frigid in winter, it was probably squalid all the time.

Turning a corner by South Kensington Station she had caught a glimpse of herself in a long glass by a shop door. She had seen a pallid, disgusted-looking lady, well over thirty, whom she had scarcely recognized. She had never known that it was possible to look so commonplace, and the idea nauseated her. She tried to believe that Venus herself would appear insignificant in such unkind weather, and then remembered a young woman of about her own age who had passed her a moment later and whose beauty was preserved by a closed car and Russian sables.

When she had entered upon the silent residential quarter in which Dolly and James were established she unfastened her handbag and drew forth the first letter that she had written to Gerald. She glanced through its honest, loving sentences, and then tore it up into very small fragments. These she scattered to the implacable wind to be blown for ever about the Heath from the grey ruffled pond to Parliament Hill.

Then she mounted James's doorstep and rang the bell. The girl admitted her and said that Lady Clewer had just run round to the grocer's, but Sir James was in his studio. James at the same moment appeared at the end of the passage and greeted her joyfully.

"Dolly's out," he said, "but she'll be in in a minute. Come into the studio where it's warm. We have a fire there."

He led her down the hall where Clewer mackintoshes hung in symmetrical rows, through a covered passage, into the large comfortable studio which had been built out into the yard behind. She paused on the threshold with a cry of surprise, for against the wall, in a good light, there leaned that portrait of James's mother which had once hung in Eaton Square.

" How did that get here ? " she said.

" Mamma made me bring it back after the . . . the funeral," he explained. " I'm very glad to have it. It's good, don't you think ? "

" I've always thought it good."

He looked at it attentively and then pronounced :

" Too many of them altogether."

" What ? Portraits ? "

" No. Lady Clewers. There's this one, and there's Mamma, and there's you, and now there's poor Dolly, who detests it. That's too many."

" There certainly does seem to be rather a crowd of us."

" It's a good thing you won't be one for much longer. I suppose you will be getting married soon ? "

" Well . . . yes . . . sometime, I suppose."

" It will be nice for you to be an honest woman again," said James kindly.

Agatha agreed that it would be nice, recognizing some conjecture of Dolly's in this artless repetition.

" You'll find you are much happier altogether when you have got out of the family," he assured her. " Did Dolly tell you how worried we are ? "

" No. She only said something. . . ."

" There she is back ! I heard someone at the back door. I'll just call to her that you are here."

He leant out of a window which gave him a view of the tradesmen's entrance and shouted :

" Dolly ! Dollee ! Agatha's here ! Oh, it isn't Dolly, it's a man. What is it ? Oh, the Gas ! Oh, yes, can't you come again when my wife is in ? I don't know where it is, do you ? Very well, then, I'll let you in. Can you show me how to do it or do you do it yourself ? You'd much better wait till my wife comes in. Yes, I'm Sir James Clewer all right. Oh, Dolly ! There you are ! Agatha and the Gas are here."

Dolly dealt with the Gas and came up into the studio. She wore a new black dress of far more lugubrious appearance than Agatha's grey furs and looked unexpectedly bereaved. She kissed Agatha with a perplexed mournfulness and dragged a chair up to the fire for her.

"How nice of you to come so quick," she said. "Has James been telling you? What do you think?"

"I haven't told her yet," said James, fetching chairs for himself and Dolly. "It's Mamma's newest idea, Agatha."

"It isn't as if it wasn't bad enough us coming into a title we never wanted," began Dolly wearily. "We don't like being Sir James and Lady Clewer all of a sudden. It isn't what I expected when I married James. It doesn't suit our style of living. But what must be, must, and since it's the will of God I suppose we oughtn't to complain."

"I don't suppose it's the will of God at all," interposed James. "Why should it be? Why should He want to make me a baronet, I should like to know?"

"If He hadn't, He wouldn't of let your poor brother die," explained Dolly severely. "But what I mean to say is this. We don't want to let it upset us more than we can help, do we?"

"You see," continued James, "Mamma came up here yesterday and wanted to know when we were going to move into Lyndon."

"You could have knocked me down with a feather," said Dolly. "Just when I'd got that range put into the back parlour and the whole house papered. I didn't want overmuch to come here: I didn't think it near so healthy for the children. But since we are here I'd sooner stay. There's no question but it's better for James and his painting."

"Yes, this house suits us," said James. "We've got everything here how we like it. Do you think it's fair to make us live at Lyndon, Agatha? She says that it's my duty now to keep up my position."

"And the worst of it is, there's a lot in it," said Dolly sadly. "I sometimes think that he ought to go. There ought to be some of the family live at the House. I quite see that."

"What I feel," said the hopeful James, "is that it's so much more your house than ours, Agatha. It's just the place for you, and you and Blair would do much better there than we would. Now you are going to be married, couldn't you go and live there and be the family for us? You like Lyndon, don't you? Better than any other place? I know you do. Then do please go!"

"Oh, dear James, it's quite impossible. . . ."

"Wouldn't Blair like it?"

"He's going to America in a fortnight," she said quickly.

"What? For ever and ever?"

"For some time, I'm afraid."

"But aren't you going too?"

"N—not yet. . . ."

"But you will eventually, I suppose. Oh, dear! Then that puts an end to my best plan," said James dolefully.

Dolly was almost tearful.

"Oh, Agatha, I am sorry! We shall miss you ever so! I don't really know however we'll get on without you, so kind as you've been. But you must write to us a lot."

Agatha felt too jaded and dejected to tell them that she had practically decided not to go. It would have needed so much explanation. They had supported and encouraged her in every vicissitude, so far, believing that she was bound to Gerald as they were bound to each other. This deliberate desertion they would never understand. She could picture quite clearly Dolly's look of startled disapprobation and James's compassionate gravity. She wondered why she knew so well how James would look. Hadn't he, once

before, looked on her with pity and proffered advice which
she had not taken ?   Her mind swung back to her wedding
day and she remembered that he had said :

"Don't go if you don't want to. . . . They are very
silly, you know, but you shouldn't pay any attention to
them.   I don't. . . ."

Bending her head towards the fire, so that they might
not see her twisting face, she said to James and his wife :

"No, I'm afraid you must count me out as far as a tenant
for Lyndon goes.   But really, I don't see why you should
worry.   I shouldn't let them make you go if you don't want
to.   You've always been the most sensible person I know,
James, about refusing to let other people interfere with you.
You've never allowed them, so far, to distract you from
anything you want to do, or confuse your ideas as to the
essential things for your own happiness.   Why should you
allow it now ?   I certainly wouldn't go and live at Lyndon
if I were you.   It would upset your life horribly.   Oh,
you've done so well up till now !   Don't let them persuade
you against your will !   You mustn't go."

"I don't want to," he said.   "But Dolly thinks . . ."

"Goodness knows I don't want to neither," broke in
Dolly.   "But there ought to be the family living in a place
like that.   James has got a duty towards it.   He's a rich
man now and, of course, he'll find it much harder to know
how to act right.   It says in the Bible that it's easier for a
camel to go through the eye of a needle . . ."

"That isn't as bad as it sounds," interrupted James in
an instructive voice.   "Miss Barrington explained it to
Cynthia and me once.   And she said that the eye of a needle
was really a gate in the walls of Jerusalem. . . ."

"If the Lord had meant that He'd of said so," replied
Dolly with conviction.   "Anyhow the meaning's plain.
It's much more difficult for James to go to heaven now
than it used to be, so we've got to be more careful how we

behave. We are the Family now. We don't want to be,
but we are. And we've got this house; we don't want it
but we've got it. It's the state of life to which we have
been called."

"Well, I'm not going," announced James, who had
evidently made up his mind. "Nobody can be called to
two states at once and I shall stay here and paint. You can
go if you'd like, Dolly; I won't interfere with what you
think is right."

"James Clewer! What a shocking thing to say! We
can't be parted, and you didn't ought to speak of it, not
even in fun."

"I'm not in fun."

He rose and crossed to the wall where his mother's picture
stood. After looking at it for a few seconds he said again:

"I'm not in fun. You ought to know that. You know,
you both know, how I hated that place! Even after you
came, Agatha, it was never the sort of place I like, though
it was better. Things were quite different for me when
once I got away from it. It may be very beautiful, and so
on, but it isn't my sort of house and never will be, not if
I'm the Family fifty times over. I won't have my children
living there. I've got away and got my own place for them,
and if we went back they'd never have a free moment.
We've got a duty to them. I'm sorry, Dolly; I know I
generally do what you want, but this time I'm not going to."

Dolly, after the shortest of pauses, signified a tranquil
acquiescence in a decision which she saw to be irrevocable.
She turned to Agatha and asked:

"And what do you think we should do with the house,
then?"

"What about your stepmother, James?" asked Agatha.
"She's the person who has always run it really. Would she
like to go on there?"

"We hadn't thought of her," said James.

" After all," pursued Agatha, " she's lived there a great number of years. And done it very well. Couldn't you ask her to stay on for a bit ? Later you might feel differently about going back yourselves."

" That would be almost as bad as letting it," objected Dolly. " I mean, I'm sure she's a kind woman and very good to the poor and all, but I don't like her way of doing things. She doesn't do them quite like the lady of such a house ought to do. She isn't like you, Agatha, for instance."

" Dolly, I think you are much too feudal. You want to put the clock back. You want to revive a state of things which is past and gone for ever. What did I do for Lyndon when I had it ? I enjoyed it very much ; it suited me to live in it, but I did nothing for it and in the end I disgraced it. I know I belong by race to the ' Bless the Squire and His Relations ' galley, but it's out of date, all that sort of thing. I never made the smallest attempt to uphold it. It's she, with all her modern activities, and her dairies, and her laundries, and village institutes, who is ready to shoulder responsibility. I know she domineers, but think how she works ! Think of all the dull hard work she's done since she came to Lyndon ! She's what is called middle class, but she's ready to take on all the unpaid public work, she and her like. Lyndon's hers. I belong to a class which is of no account now."

" They do say that these people, what made their money in trade, are getting into all the old houses nowadays," agreed Dolly.

" If we went to live there ourselves, you know, Dolly, we couldn't push her out of it. She's dug herself in all right," said James, " and how should we like that ? "

" Well, we needn't decide all in a minute," concluded Dolly. " Let's think it over. I daresay you are right, Agatha. I wish you didn't have to go to America all of a sudden. I'd been counting on you to set us right in quite a lot of things. We'll often need someone to advise us now. Oh, dear!"

She sighed lengthily. Agatha had never seen her so unsure of herself.

"What date are you sailing?" asked James suddenly. "Couldn't we all come and see you off?"

"I don't quite know," replied Agatha. "It's such very short notice."

"Why aren't you going when he is?"

"Well, my passage isn't booked for one thing. . . ."

"Oh, I see!" he exclaimed enlightened. "You wouldn't have gone if John hadn't died."

"Hush, James!" admonished Dolly.

"But I don't see why," he complained. "If she could go to Corsica, why not to America?"

"There are plenty of reasons," said Dolly tactfully, "which might not occur to a gentleman. But I do wish you could go same time he does, Agatha. It will be a job for you to go alone. I should hate it if James was to go and leave me to get there by myself."

Agatha had a vision of the courageous Dolly and her children, harassed but indomitable, loaded with strange luggage and armed with third-class tickets, setting forth to the ends of the earth in pursuit of James. She jumped up and began to pull her furs round her.

"You'll stay to tea, won't you?" exclaimed Dolly. "If you'll excuse me while I get it. I sent the girl out with the children when I came in."

"No, do you know I don't think I can. I said to my mother that I'd be in for tea."

Agatha's heart was as bleak as the skies outside and she wanted to escape from Dolly and James, and their insufferable security in each other. Some of her misery was written in her face, for James said quickly :

"I'll walk with you down to the station."

Dolly stood on the doorstep and watched them to the corner of the street. The wind, swirling in bitter gusts, blew her bright hair round her face and fluttered her black skirts, revealing the serviceable green petticoat beneath. When the strange couple, James broad and shambling, Agatha slim and elegant, had disappeared, she sighed and turned into the house to get James his tea.

"Aren't your feet very cold?" asked James, seizing Agatha's arm and piloting her down the hill. "You ought to wear woollen stockings like Dolly does."

Agatha did not reply : she was much embarrassed by the long veil which hung from her little hat. It blew all ways at once, and wound itself round James's neck, and round every lamp-post that they passed. They came to a pillar-box and she reflected that, with the fountain pen in her bag, she could have addressed her letter. She would have posted it if she had been alone : but such a deed could scarcely be perpetrated on the arm of the upright James.

At the station he took her ticket while she tucked her loosened hair under her hat and redraped her veil becomingly. He put her into the lift and stepped back, waiting to see the last of her. He gave her a painstaking, reassuring smile ; a mute kindness spoke in it, and she had a sudden desire to run back to him and lay all her case before him.

The impulse came too late. She had barely sketched a movement forward when the iron gates clanged between them and she was plunged into the abyss.

THE END

was born on 23 April 1896 in Hyde Park Gate, Kensington. Her father was a barrister and she was the eldest of four children. She was educated at Cheltenham Ladies' College and Somerville College, Oxford where she read Modern History. Her first published work was *A Century of Revolution* (1922), a textbook on modern European history. Her first novel was *The Ladies of Lyndon* (1923), preceding by only a year her major popular and critical success, *The Constant Nymph,* the novel which made her famous.

In 1925 she married David Davies, a barrister who became a Q.C., a County Court Judge and was knighted in 1953. They lived in Kensington (apart from wartime evacuation to St Ives in Cornwall) and they had one son and two daughters. Five plays by Margaret Kennedy were produced on the London stage, of which *The Constant Nymph,* written with Basil Dean and starring Edna Best, Noel Coward and John Gielgud, won great acclaim, as did *Escape Me Never* with Elizabeth Bergner. Both plays were successfully filmed. Fourteen more novels were published between 1927 and 1964, with a twelve-year gap between 1938 and 1950 when Margaret Kennedy was chiefly engaged in film work. Her first two novels after the war, *The Feast* (1950) and *Lucy Carmichael* (1951), were highly praised by British and American critics; the next, *Troy Chimneys* (1953), was awarded the James Tait Black memorial prize. Her short biography of Jane Austen was published in 1950 and she wrote another critical work, *The Outlaws on Parnassus* (1958), a study of the art of fiction.

After her husband's death in 1964 Margaret Kennedy moved to Woodstock, Oxfordshire where she lived until her death on 31 July 1967. Of her novels, Virago publish *The Ladies of Lyndon* and *Together and Apart* (1936).